Safe
in
Crab Apple Creek

DR. KARMLE L. CONRAD

Safe in Crab Apple Creek
By
Dr. Karmle L. Conrad

Visit our website **at** www.StillwaterPress.com for more information.
First Stillwater River Publications Edition
Library of Congress Control Number: 2015956410
ISBN-10: 0-692-56699-6
ISBN-13: 978-069256699-2

1 2 3 4 5 6 7 8 9 10
Written by Dr. Karmle L. Conrad
Cover Art and Interior Map by Jay Mooers, **www.edenparktales.com**
Cover design by Dr. Karmle L. Conrad
Published by Stillwater River Publications, Pawtucket, RI, USA.

DEDICATION

"For all the Dreamers - Always believe."

~Karmle L. Conrad

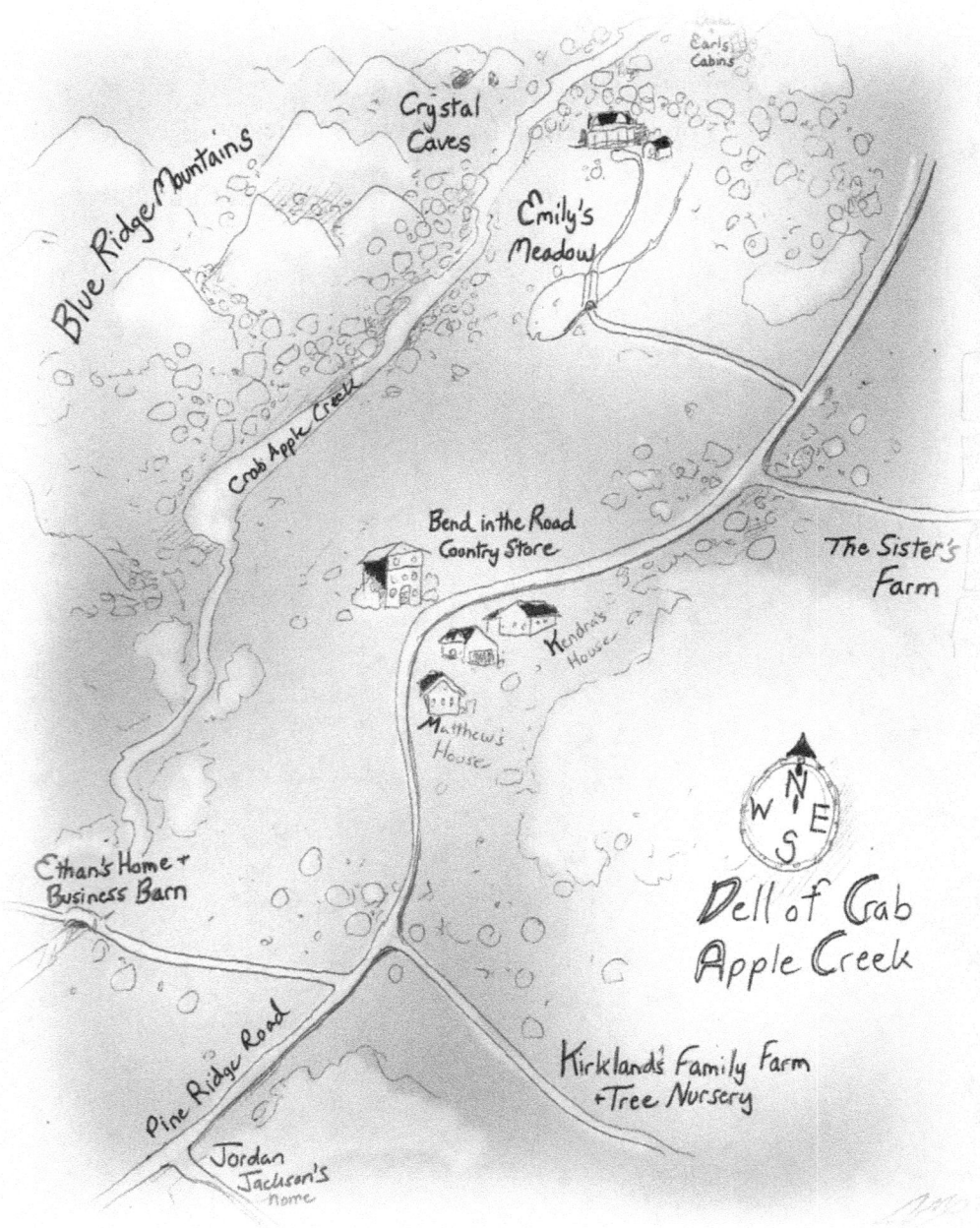

Blue Ridge Mountains

Crystal Caves

Earl's Cabins

Emily's Meadow

Crab Apple Creek

Bend in the Road Country Store

The Sister's Farm

Kendra's House

Matthew's House

Ethan's Home + Business Barn

N
W E
S

Dell of Crab Apple Creek

Pine Ridge Road

Kirkland's Family Farm + Tree Nursery

Jordan Jackson's Home

Map by Jay Mooers - www.edenparktales.com

CHAPTER 1

Everything was in place. Finally. Every little teeny-weeny, tiny, miniscule thing was in place. It had taken a long nine months of keen observation, planning, and cunning to get to this day. But today, the bruised and battered Barbara Ann Gordon would finally fade away forever and Emily Gail Henshaw would burst forth upon the world. Free. Powerful. In charge of her life. No more violence and hatred from her husband. No more living nightmares.

The nightmare began a little over a year ago when Barbara met Nick at a cookout at her friend Melanie's house. Barbara had agreed to come as long as Melanie wouldn't try to find her a date. Melanie was always trying to fix up her friends with potential husbands.

Melanie was convinced that every woman wanted to be married but Barbara was thirty-two years old and hadn't really thought about marriage much. It was not on the top twenty list of things she planned to accomplish in her life. If it came her way, so be it. If not, no big deal.

Nicholas Wade Gordon was definitely easy on the eyes - an eight out of ten on the Eye Candy Scale. He had dark hair with a slight wave, dark eyes, and a ready smile. He was about six feet tall, had a nice ass, and great body which was tanned to perfection as far as Barbara could tell. In his navy khakis and tan Polo shirt a little chest hair was visible at the neckline. He paid attention to whomever he was with - a great listener who leaned in when you explained something or told a story. With an air of confidence, he knew how to charm and make anyone feel important. Little did Barbara know that what she was witnessing was one of the world's greatest con men at work.

Melanie brought Nick over to meet Barbara.

1

Melanie smiled. "Barbara Jones, I would like you to meet Nick Gordon. He's a friend of a friend."

Barbara replied, "Nice to meet you." *And your body! Great eye candy!*

Nick took Barbara's outstretched hand in both of his, looked into her eyes and smiled, "Nice to meet you, too. May I get you a drink or something?"

"Yes…ah…a glass of white wine would be fine." Barbara could barely think let alone speak. Nick was gorgeous.

Nick walked over to the bar. Melanie looked at Barbara and smiled.

"What are you smiling at?" Barbara questioned.

Melanie replied with that 'you're hooked' look, "You. You like what you're seeing. I know that look. You're already thinking about long nights of slow sex with this guy."

Barbara sighed. "A girl can dream can't she?"

The next day, Nick called Barbara and suggested they meet for dinner. She agreed, and they found themselves settled by seven o'clock at a small table in a very exclusive restaurant. Gracious and kind, he ordered for both of them. At the end of the date he suggested they go to his place for a drink. Barbara agreed and followed Nick to his house in Mountain View Estates, located in the town of Mountain View just west of Portsmouth, New Hampshire. His home was situated on two acres of land, was large and was beautiful. Upon entering, he instructed Barbara to remove her shoes, leave her coat and purse by the door, and then follow him into the living room. The place had to be worth at least a million and a half, she thought. The decorations were perfect and everything was in its place.

As Barbara sat down on the couch, she grabbed a pillow to make herself comfortable and Nick immediately took it from her and set it back in its place. Barbara apologized for moving it. "Oh Nick, I'm sorry about the pillow. My error."

He replied, "No problem. It's just that everything has its place here and I like to see things just so."

Barbara thought it was a bit odd, but shrugged it off. Maybe he was nervous about having a woman in his house. The place felt definitely masculine with gold, navy blue, dark green and black colors and accents. The furniture was made from dark-stained wood and the couch was black leather.

Nick brought her a brandy.

Barbara replied, "Oh thank you, but I don't really drink - only a little wine once in a great while."

Nick shook his head and said, "But I took the trouble of opening a new bottle for you."

"Thanks anyway, but I don't drink. Maybe you should have asked first, then you could have saved it for another time." Barbara responded.

Nick raised his voice. "Don't tell me how to entertain. I know what I am doing!"

Barbara stood and walked to the front door, gathered her things and said goodbye as she walked out, "Maybe you should learn to be more gracious and not yell at your guests."

With that, she left, and Nick was furious. No one walked away from him. He would get even with her. He would apologize with flowers and nice notes then get her back here.

He would be kind and sweet, then he would take what was his. After all, he spent money on her and she owed him. He would seduce her then show her who was boss. All in good time, he reminded himself. Slow down. Save the anger for later. He needed a wife so the feds would stop looking at him. He knew they were watching him. He knew they suspected him of money laundering. But with a new wife, maybe they would leave him alone. He would apologize all over the place. He would get her back.

The next day, Barbara was shocked to receive a large bouquet of flowers from Nick along with an apology. He had sent them to her at work even though she didn't remember telling him where she worked. But she must have, or maybe Melanie had. They were lovely. A few minutes later, her office phone rang. It was Nick.

"I would like to apologize for last night. I was out of line and rude. I hope you got the flowers I sent."

Barbara replied. "Yes. I did. Thank you. They're lovely. It was thoughtful of you to send them."

Nick asked, "Would you please have dinner with me Friday night? That's just two days away. I would really appreciate the chance to apologize in person. You name the place and time."

Barbara said she'd need some time to think and would call him back. Nick agreed.

Barbara took a break and tuned into her Guides. She got the message that she would have to decide this on her own, knowing that everything happens for a reason.

Barbara was a psychic medium and had been since birth. She was secretive about her Gift.

Only a few others knew she even had the Gift.

She called Nick back and agreed to meet Friday night.

From that Friday on, things happened fast. He paid great attention to her, and was always kind, courteous and willing to listen. By the end of the third week, they agreed to spend a weekend away. They met at a quiet resort in the Green Mountains. Nick had her just where he wanted her.

After settling in he approached her with a smile and stood very close. He said, "I'm so happy we are here. Being next to you makes me want you... right now... right here."

He ran his hand up her arm and brushed her breast. Barbara shivered. She replied, "What makes you think I'm easy?"

Nick just looked at her as he stroked her cheek, "I don't think you're easy, just easy to be with. Your pulse has quickened and your breathing is rather fast. How about this?"

He leaned into her and kissed her as he ran his hand up her thigh and then brushed her breast again. She opened her mouth to receive his tongue as she ran her hand down his back, grabbing his ass and pulling it into her. She was demanding.

Nick put his hand up her shirt and grabbed her breast, stoking her nipple through her lacy cover. She grabbed his crotch and squeezed. Nick groaned. They both pulled back. Nick took her shirt off, then her bra and took her breast into his mouth, sucking and teasing her nipple with his tongue.

Barbara groaned and arched forward, pushing his head into her breast with one hand and squeezing his dick with the other. Nick lowered her to the floor, as he ripped their clothes off. He stood over her with his hard dick throbbing in anticipation of her touch. He would make sure she sucked him, too, before the day was done.

He crouched over her, running his hand over her mound. He slid his fingers into her. She was hot and wet. Barbara groaned as he stroked her. As she looked at him, he bent down and placed his tongue on her, teasing her. She pushed his head into her and told him..."Lick me hard and make me cum."

Nick smiled. He had her where he wanted her.

"Fair is fair," he said as he moved up her and knelt over her face. He took his dick and pushed it against her mouth. Barbara was surprised, then she smiled. Nick thought she'd be angry and upset. Instead, she began to lick and squeeze his hard shaft. He almost lost it. He was about to lose control when he caught himself. He never lost control. Never. That's how you got humiliated. He pulled out of her mouth, moved down and rammed his dick into her wet cunt. He was in charge now. He would decide if and when he would allow her to cum. She fooled him. She came almost immediately and pushed hard against him, grabbing his ass and forcing him further into her. She came so hard he lost control and climaxed with her. He rammed harder until he was spent. Then he collapsed against her.

After a few minutes, he pulled out and rolled away. She sighed and said, "That was great fun. You're pretty good at the sex thing."

He was furious but he knew he couldn't show it. He said instead, "You're not bad yourself. A little schooling from me and you'll be perfect."

Barbara parried with, "Really? You think you have a thing or two to show me?"

Nick smiled slowly. "Of course. We could spend a lot of time sharing secrets."

Barbara laughed, "Of course we could. Now, I need a shower and some food. Sex always makes me hungry. How about you? Hungry?"

Nick tried to pull Barbara close, but she rolled away and was off to the bathroom before he could grab her and show her he was boss. So he replied, "Sure. You fix us something to eat and maybe we'll exchange a few more ideas."

Barbara just laughed. "Me cook? No way. I order out."

Nick was slowly getting angrier and angrier. He was in charge, damn it. Order out? He didn't want anyone no one to know they were there. Or maybe, he would let her think she was in charge for now then slowly show her he was the boss. *Keep your anger to yourself, Nick old boy. Wait until you marry her. Then you will be totally in charge... of everything.* After all, he who was in charge never lost. Cool down. Patience. Just wait.

With a cruel grin, he called out to her, "What do you want? Chinese? Pizza? Burgers?"

She replied, "How about Chinese... crab Rangoon and sesame chicken? Thanks."

He called in their order and then began to make plans for his next move. He wanted them married no later than six weeks from today. Married? No way. He would just make it look like a real ceremony. He had contacts who owed him favors.

The weekend was full of hot sex, food and fun. Barbara liked the idea of seeing Nick, although there was something about him that bothered her. He was quick to get pissed off but then he quickly calmed down. Maybe he was just worried that she didn't like him. She had a feeling in her gut that there was more to this guy than he was willing to admit.

Nick told Barbara that he was in the import-export business dealing with antiques. He found things for private clients and arranged for them to be delivered. He was paid well for his services. Barbara told Nick she worked for an insurance company, handling their health care clients. She told him she wanted to finish her master's degree this fall.

Over the next few weeks, Nick relentlessly pursued Barbara, sending her cards and flowers, taking her out, and buying her intimate gifts. Barbara liked the attention as she had been alone most of her life. She didn't believe in the legal marriage ceremony but was kind of partial to having a companion one day. Maybe this was the guy. He was a good lover, but not great. Guess you couldn't really have your heart's desire all the time. Maybe this was all she was going to get. Most of the time, they had a good time although there were times when Barbara saw a flicker of possessiveness and control in Nick. He always picked the restaurants and places they went. He had a certain way he liked things in his home that really bothered her. Maybe after they spent some more time together, he would relax. About five weeks after they met, Barbara decided she was OK with having Nick as her boyfriend. They were walking along a secluded stretch of beach. He had a little something in mind to pay her back for the way she treated him the first time they had sex. He said he loved her all the time and she felt the same way about him. When she finally told him how she felt, he was thrilled. He grabbed her and kissed her hard and said he had been waiting for what seemed like forever for her to say that to him.

"I thought I was the only one who felt like that. I fell in love with you the minute I saw you at that party. You are so beautiful and sexy. I couldn't wait to touch you and make love with you. This is great! How about we celebrate tonight? I'll arrange everything and we can have a private celebration at my place. Just you and me and I'll show you just how great a lover I am. You're making me hard just thinking about you. Mmmm... nice and hard."

He pushed her against a rock and ran his hand up her shirt to grab her breast. He took her hand and put it on his dick and told her to squeeze. He pulled her shirt up over her head and sucked her breast while he took off his pants. He told Barbara to kneel down and as she did he pushed his dick onto her mouth. She pulled back and looked at Nick. She wasn't sure about rough sex and surprises and decided she'd be the submissive only this one time. Barbara looked at Nick and said, "How do you want it? Just tell me and I'll do whatever you say."

She was playing him. Nick thought she was for real.

He said, "Strip down naked, and undress me slowly while you lick me."

Barbara said, "But what if someone sees us?"

He replied, "Then they'll get a good show watching me control you."

She just nodded and lowered her head toward his cock, and smiled to herself. She could play along. She grabbed his dick and licked him hard and fast. He almost lost it. Damn. The bitch had to be controlled. He pushed her away, turned her around and tried to fuck her from behind. She moved away and said, "No! Not from the back ever. Other things are OK though."

He was pissed. He just smiled, took her hand and told her to make herself cum while he watched. She lay back on her clothes and put on a great show. He really thought she had cum. He lowered himself onto her and pushed her legs apart as her rammed into her.

She was ready. She continued to play along. She controlled him without his even realizing it. She positioned herself so that he rubbed against her mound every time he pushed into her. She came in an explosion, wrapped her legs around his ass and pulled him into her. She pushed up hard against him and pulled him deeper into her at the same time.

She made him cum. He rammed her hard again and again and she screamed in ecstasy.

He had lost control again, but this time it was OK. He needed her to think she controlled him. He was going to tell her they were going to be married next weekend. He needed her to be in an accepting mood.

After their beach sex, they walked back to their cars. Barbara was getting into her car when Nick stopped her and said, "Barbara, I just want you to know how special you are to me. No one has ever made me feel the way you do. I wouldn't do anything to hurt you or our relationship. I love you very much."

Barbara was thrilled. "I love you, too, Nick. See you tomorrow afternoon at your place?"

Nick agreed. "Yes. Bring your overnight bag."

Barbara left. She was thinking Nick was going to ask her to marry him. She was excited and called her friend Melanie.

"Melanie, ya got a couple of minutes? I'd like to stop by."

Melanie answered with an excited, "Yes. Does this have to do with Nick?"

Barbara laughed. "I'll see you in a few minutes."

When Barbara arrived Melanie was waiting outside.

"Well, did he ask?"

"Not yet, but I think he's going to ask tomorrow afternoon when I meet him at his house. I think I'm going to say yes, but I'm a little bothered about his anger issues. He gets angry so quickly. It's almost like a Dr. Jekyll and Mr. Hyde thing. And, he is so possessive about his place and how everything needs to be so exact. Only the way he says. it, it's kind of scary. Maybe he's been alone too long."

Melanie replied, "I think that's it. He hasn't had a serious relationship as long as I've known him and that's about five years. Maybe he just wants you to be so impressed with his house that you'll think he's a regular guy; not gay or something. Has he done anything to hurt you?"

"No! Just the opposite. He is kind and giving. He usually picks the restaurants we go to and a couple of times he chose my meal for me. I had to tell him not to do that as I had my own likes and dislikes. He was pissed the first time. The second time it happened, he apologized, saying he just wanted me to enjoy the evening without having to make a bunch of decisions. I was OK with that."

Melanie thought for a moment then said, "Maybe he's just worried that you won't like him. That's obviously not the problem now. You're gonna have to call me as soon as you can after he asks. Well, after the sex and all."

Barbara laughed, "Yeah, well, that doesn't seem to be a problem with him. He gets hard at the mere thought of sex. He's OK as a lover, but nothing great. But, I guess I'll just have to train him without him even knowing he's being handled... so to speak!"

They laughed for quite a while. Melanie and Barbara knew that if a woman wanted to be pleased with her sex partner's performance, the woman had to train her lover without him knowing it or he would get pissed off. Only once in a lifetime did a woman find a man who knew how to please a woman. A true romantic accepted that the woman's needs came first, and then learned together.

Barbara left with the promise to call as soon as she could get free. Barbara was a true romantic if truth be told. All her life she had dreamed of finding that one true love that would cherish her, accept her for who she was, and love her and encourage her to become more than she could even imagine. She knew Nick was not that man but he had a lot of what she was looking for. And, she did love him despite all his weird, quirky ways. She liked the way he paid attention to her every need. She liked the flowers, phone calls and gifts he gave her. She liked knowing he was there when she needed him... even for just the little things.

She would say yes, if he asked tomorrow. She was ready to settle down. No kids though.

Barbara had brothers and sisters and had watched her parents struggle with money trying to give them all that they needed. She did not have the energy for children. She loved her nieces and nephews for all the world. Yet she just didn't think she had the deep commitment that went with parenting. The love, yes. The rest, no. So she decided a long time ago not to have children. She told no one. She would not be telling Nick as he had already mentioned that he was not interested in having children either. He had not asked her about her thoughts anyway, she just knew she felt the same way. No problem. One less thing to discuss.

Nick had been raised in a troubled family. His father had been an alcoholic and abusive and his mother worked two jobs just to put food on the table. Nick was the oldest of seven and was expected to raise his siblings. No one had asked him if he wanted to; he was forced to. When his father was home, he was either sleeping it off or getting drunk. And when he drank, he was violent. All the kids knew when he was about to start hitting them so they would run away. Nick would gather them up and get them out of the house. He took them anywhere he could. The grocery store and the mall were the usual places. He would take the babies to the neighbors and keep the older ones with him.

After about an hour or two, he would return to find his father passed out. Then Nick would bring his brothers and sisters back home. His mother was often the target of his father's abuse. Nick didn't know why she didn't just leave. She was such a wimp. Didn't she care about her kids? So what if she was working all the time. They would all be better off without his dad around.

Nick left home when he was seventeen, as soon as his youngest brother could take care of himself. Nick never finished high school. He went from one job to the next, always looking for a fast way to make big money. He was street smart. He knew he was good looking and made sure he kept his body in great shape. He got a job in a gym so he could work out for free. He charmed the ladies and was quickly promoted to assistant manager.

By the time he turned twenty one, he had taken over as manager of the gym. He kept to himself and kept all his money hidden at home. He had also established himself with a wealthy client and began running errands for him. This paid well. For every errand he ran, delivering or picking up packages in art galleries, upscale hotels, and the like, he was paid anywhere from $100 to $1,000. He never reported this money and had it in a safe in his little run-down apartment.

By the time Nick met Barbara some ten years later, he had gone from being the gym manager to running his own import/export business. At least that's what most people thought. However, the client Nick had been running errands for while at the gym turned out to be a bit on the shady side. He liked Nick and brought him along as a partner. Nick was finally given his own territory and set up his own business. And it paid well. Nick had built his home on two acres of land in a posh new development within four years of leaving the gym. No neighbors nearby. He had set the house well back from the road. It had three entrances off two roads so no one would be suspicious about the comings and goings of different vehicles throughout the late night hours.

Nick kept to himself. He had learned that being charming and attentive made women happy. He had his favorite escorts but none of them were ever brought to his house. He would meet them at hotels, use them, pay them well, then walk away.

Barbara was different. He needed her to please his boss.

Their wedding was a small event that had only a few people in attendance. It was performed by a Justice of the Peace Nick had arranged. The dinner that followed seemed to be a happy affair. Barbara had asked her friend Melanie to participate as her witness. They had selected a simple white dress for the ceremony.

After dinner, congratulations and farewells were exchanged then Nick and Barbara made their way back to Nick's house. Barbara had moved in a few days earlier though she had put most of her things into storage and had not told Nick. She had a 'feeling' she would need everything again. Barbara had learned to listen to those gut instincts a long time ago.

Nick and Barbara settled into their life together and right away Barbara began to notice a few strange things about Nick. He wanted to know what she was doing ALL the time, but she blew him off. She worked, went to class then came home. Nick called her all day long and Barbara had to tell him to stop as her boss warned her about the extreme number of personal calls she was receiving on her cell phone. Barbara told Nick she was going to be fired if he didn't stop calling her so much, so, he stopped. Nick then added a GPS app to her phone to keep track of her.

The marriage began to fail almost from the start. Nick was paranoid about everything Barbara did. He berated her if she forgot something at the store. He constantly put her down about her college degree telling her she must have paid someone to get it.

And as violent people will often do, he escalated the violence by withholding sex from her as a form of punishment. She didn't care about the no-sex thing because it was the violent rapes that terrified her. Nick would grab her by the throat, pull her hair then throw her on the ground, stand over her demanding she strip and then he would force her to take him into her mouth until he came, all the while yielding a knife in her face. He even cut her a few times, just enough to draw a little blood and make sure she knew he was in control. He cut her in places no one would see. He never pleased her. It was all about him. When he was done with her, he would laugh then go out for the night taking as many whores as he wanted. He never used condoms. God only knew what diseases he was passing around.

Barbara was terrorized.

She began to plan her escape after a local law officer stopped her in the parking lot of her workplace, and asked her to accompany him to the police department. They had a few questions for her about Nick. 'They' were the FBI.

Barbara had no idea what she was about to learn about Nick. After a week of meetings with the FBI, the U. S. Marshal Service, and Interpol, Barbara began to learn a new type of terror - she was afraid for her life. The FBI said they would protect her and she agreed to enter a witness protection program with the U.S. Marshal Service. The roller coaster of extreme fear had just left the station and she was in the front seat.

Barbara soon learned from the agencies that Nick was part of a worldwide money laundering group. The group was known for its terrorist-type attacks and the ruthless way it ran its business. They were also involved in drug trafficking, human trafficking and gunrunning. This group had been named the 'New Russian Mob' because of Yuri Strovonovich. He was perceived to be the new Worldwide Mob Kingpin. Yuri had managers all around the globe ready to do his bidding.

CHAPTER 2

Finally, Emily was free. She woke up on this, the last Friday she would be Barbara Ann Gordon, as usual. Nick was getting dressed for his day of golf and whores. Emily had known about the 'Friday whores' for about six months now although Nick had no idea she knew. He would go play golf and then spend a few hours with a whore of his choice, returning home around 10 p.m. He had been doing this Friday thing ever since he 'retired.' He didn't work a regular job. He was into laundering money, drug trafficking, and other illegal money-making enterprises. Emily suspected the drugs, but she had no idea about the other specific activities Nick was involved in. She just knew his money was not earned in the usual, accepted way. The feds had no charges against Barbara. They knew she was not involved in the illegal activities.

In the preparations for her new life, she had been assigned an attorney to legally change her name. The cause being, 'violent abuse and possible death at the hands of her husband.' She had been informed by the FBI that the marriage ceremony had been a hoax. She was not really married. It was just one more thing to deal with, although it was a good thing. It was the deceit and lies that would take her a while to grieve through.

Everything had to be done very carefully and secretively so her fake husband would not find out.

On the days she had to meet with the witness protection team, she did the 'work-day' thing but never actually went to work. She called in sick on those days. She spent that time with the team preparing for her new life. She had told the FBI that she suspected her husband was involved in drug trafficking and other illegal activities. The U.S. Marshal's office and the FBI agreed

11

to place Barbara in the Witness Protection Program based on an ongoing investigation involving Nick and his dangerous associates.

So, this Friday, she once again prepared for work. Truth was she had resigned. She had been out of work the whole week. But she kept 'preparing for work' every day this week just like she always had. She left at the same time every day and returned from work at the same time every day. During these days, she was finalizing her plans.

And, now, Friday was finally here. Nick always left at 7:45 a.m. for his golf day. Barbara always left at 8:00 a.m. for work. She knew he waited around the corner to watch her leave. So she followed the same routine on this, the last Friday of her old life. She circled back, watched him leave his hiding spot and followed him about five miles to make sure he was not coming back. She knew he wouldn't keep looking for her. He called her at her lunch time and on her way home from work every day, so, she knew he would be calling at 12 noon. She wouldn't be answering.

Today, that phone would be smashed to bits and left in the kitchen trash.

Barbara returned home to pack the very few things she would take with her. She did not want anything from this house and this life to remind her of the violence, threats, abuse and rape she had endured as Nick's 'wife.' She was due in the Judge's Chambers at eleven with her team and the U. S. marshal assigned to her case. After changing clothes, smashing the cell phone and throwing it away, she took one last look around the prison that had been her home for the last year and walked out the door, got into her car and left, never to return. Never.

She became Emily Gail Henshaw at 11:08 a.m., putting Barbara Ann Gordon "to rest" once and for all. She was seen by the judge in her chambers, as had been pre-arranged, and granted a permanent restraining order against Nicholas Wade Gordon. Once all the paperwork was in order, she left the courthouse.

Emily's next stop was the bank where she and Nick had joint savings and checking accounts. She withdrew seven thousand dollars, left one cent, and removed her name from the account. She removed the whole forty thousand dollars from the savings account and closed it. The night before she had secretly closed the two credit card accounts that had her and Nick's name on them, telling the clerk that the cards had been stolen. No, she did not want new ones. She told the credit card company that the accounts would be paid in full. Thanks anyway.

The day before, the U. S. marshal's office had arranged for Nick's Swiss bank account to be seized and had placed half of the monies in an account for Emily Gail Henshaw. It was the sum of forty million dollars. Emily was set for a long time. She would be securing her own Swiss bank account on behalf of the marshal's on Monday, in New York City, on the way to her new life.

She now had forty-seven thousand dollars in her pocket to begin her new life. She left the bank with only one more stop to make. She bought herself a new car with the help of her new identity team. She arrived at the BMW dealer to pick up her new car at approximately 12:46 p.m. Thirty minutes later, at 1:16 p.m., Emily Gail Henshaw left her old life in the dust and set off for her new life in the Appalachian Mountains of North Carolina.

She could now eat anything she wanted, buy anything she wanted and DO anything she wanted. She was free!

And Emily could now use her Gift as a psychic medium out in the open. No more hiding. She would tell everyone who wanted to listen. She had never told Nick about this Gift as she had a feeling from the first time she met him that he should never know about it. So, with the protection of her guardians, guides, angels and fairies, she had kept her secret all this time.

She could now do her readings out in the open, tell anyone she wanted to that she was a psychic medium and have readings in her home. She would choose friends that had Gifts just like her and enjoy them.

She headed south on Route 95 toward Boston with the goal of eventually reaching New York City. It was just past noon and with traffic she should arrive in Manhattan around 8 p.m. No big hurry. Emily liked to drive and she was having fun in her new car.

Emily began thinking about how far she had come from the little farm in Vermont, just outside of Stowe. She had been a farm girl in all its elements - milking cows, gathering eggs, and tending to the truck garden the family had every summer. She had sold veggies, eggs, and flowers from their farm stand ever since she was a little girl. At first she worked alongside her mother, then, as she grew older, all by herself. Her parents were killed in a truck accident when she was twenty-one, away at college. She came home to settle the estate. She gave the farm to her cousin and his family. Her parents had been shrewd with their money and the investments had left Emily well taken care of. She finished college, found a job in New Hampshire and moved there when she was twenty-two. She changed jobs three times. She became certified as a health insurance specialist and her last job was with a private insurance company in Portsmouth. Emily had finished her master's degree in Alternative Health Care just a few months earlier.

As she looked around her, she realized she was already in Rhode Island and two hours had gone by. She laughed as she realized her Guides had helped her drive along, keeping her safe. She remembered the tunnel in Boston and the approaching signs about Providence. She made a pit stop and was back on the road in short time.

She was in Connecticut in just a little over an hour. The scenery along the lower part of Route 95 in Rhode Island and the beginning of Connecticut was all countryside. If you've ever driven the Connecticut part of Route 95, you know there's always construction going on somewhere. Always. Emily was ready for the delays as she had checked the possible highway slowdowns on the computer in her car. This car rocked!

She had gone to a class on how to use her BMW, 'Beemer.' Good thing. There were so many gadgets and things to know just to be able to drive the thing. The more the merrier. Emily decided to stop in Central Connecticut to stretch and have something to eat. She chose the town of West Haven. It was just a few minutes off the main road, near the ocean.

Emily got off at exit 42, turning onto Route 162, Sawmill Road. She followed the beach signs for about two miles, stopping for take-out along the way. She turned right onto Captain Thomas Boulevard, pulling into the Bradley Point Park public lot. She found a spot close to the water. She had always loved the ocean. There was something about it that drew her to it. The quiet power. The immensity. The life it held. The whales and dolphins were incredible to watch as they migrated north with their babies. Emily had been on a few whale watches and had fallen in love with these creatures on the very first watch she had been on.

She sat in her car, eating her fish and chips. As soon as she finished, she got out and bundled up for a long walk along the beach. Even though it was April, the ocean air was still a bit chilly. The warm summer air was on its way though. You could feel it.

She followed the walkway that ran parallel to Long Island Sound.

After a while, Emily stopped and sat on a bench. She was feeling a bit sad, thinking about the last year. She wondered how she could have been so naïve. She was a pretty good judge of character. She watched people a lot, enjoying them and learning which ones to stay clear of. The FBI had said Nick was one of the smartest con men they had ever encountered. He had fooled most people. They offered to get her counseling as soon as she was settled in Crab Apple Creek. She decided to accept their offer and knew there would be more moments of sorrow from the past year of her life. She asked her Angels to keep holding her and protecting her, thanking them for their love and protection so far.

Emily shivered and noticed that the sun had shifted, moving closer to the western sky, closer to sundown. She briskly walked back to her car as a chilly breeze had begun to blow. It must be about five o'clock she thought. She watched the birds and other people on the beach, saying hello as she passed them. They, too, seemed to be thinking about other things.

She brushed the sand from her feet, put her sneakers back on, settled into the car and returned to the highway. West Haven had been a good idea. A beautiful ocean town, friendly folks, good food and just what her Spirit needed. She was refreshed and ready to get to Manhattan for the weekend, tie up some loose ends, and enjoy being in New York City.

Emily arrived in Manhattan around 8:30 p.m. She was staying at the Four Seasons. After checking-in, she called room service for a light supper and showered while she waited. Her food arrived with the champagne she had ordered - Taittinger, her favorite. Yes, she deserved it. She had gotten away. She was celebrating Emily. She had survived a horrible year of terror. She would celebrate every day of her life. And to begin, she had ordered appetizers and champagne. Her favorite meal!

She fell asleep and slept the night through. This was the first time in a long time that she slept without the fear of being raped in the night. She awoke to a sunny April day around half past seven. She dressed and headed downstairs for breakfast. - she was a starvin' Marvin.

Shortly after she sat down, Matthews, the U.S. marshal assigned to her, joined her. He was dressed casually and they had arranged to meet as if they were old friends. He planned to stay close to Emily all the way to Crab Apple Creek. And then there, a new agent would take over her protection detail. Emily would have protection for a long, long time.

"So, how'd you like West Haven?" Matthews asked as he settled across from her.

"It's a very pretty little town. How'd you like it? Ever been there before?" Emily responded. "I see you are true to your word that I would not be aware of your presence - that you, my Team, are giving me my space. Glad to know you guys are around though. This whole thing really gives me the creeps."

Matthews continued, "I told you we would keep you up-to-date with everything. Nick is in a maximum security federal prison without bail. He is in isolation. No visitors, no mail, only his lawyers, and they are being watched. Two lawyers have been arrested on a number of charges who were connected with Nick. They are in the same boat as he is. He had to hire lawyers he doesn't really know, although we are checking on their backgrounds as well."

"I know there must be a huge web of people and places involved from what you have told me, especially around the drugs and money laundering. It probably goes around the world a few times. And, I know, you have made sure my new home is a safe place. It's just going to take a long while before I feel anything close to safe again. I have decided to accept the counseling you offered. Just let me know who to contact once I arrive in Crab Apple Creek. And, thanks."

"Just doin' my job, Ma'am," Matthews said with a smile. "So, what have you decided to do today?"

"I thought I'd take a Circle Island Cruise and wander around Central Park as long as you are with me. Wouldn't want to do that alone. Then, I have an appointment with the salon here for a make-over at 3 p.m."

"Sounds like a good plan. Let's eat breakfast and then get going. I'll just take a few minutes to update my partners."

Matthews left the dining room and returned just a few minutes later. Breakfast arrived and they chatted about normal stuff like traveling, the weather, and New York City.

The Circle Island Cruise was fun and interesting and offered much historical info. The boat was full and everyone seemed to enjoy the morning.

Emily and Matthews walked through a good portion of Central Park, stopping at Belvedere Castle, reading the historic markers and watching the street performers. Matthews asked if she would like a carriage ride. Emily accepted. She was having fun for the first time in a long time. She kept looking over her shoulder though, thinking that maybe one of Nick's contacts would be looking for her. Matthews took note of this and said nothing.

Emily liked the carriage ride. The driver was a hoot, teasing them about their accents and, because they weren't from the city, he shared little factoids about the park with them. The ride lasted about an hour and when it was over, they grabbed a slice and soda from a nearby pizza place.

Heading back to the Four Seasons, Emily thanked Matthews for the carriage ride.

"I love horses and buggies and that ride was really awesome. The driver was hilarious. I hope to have my own stable on the mountain soon. Horses are wonderful creatures and riding is a great way to get away and think. Maybe you can put me in touch with someone about that," Emily said.

Matthew replied, "You are very welcome. And, yes, I think I have a few connections with horse people. I noticed you kept looking around, checking to see if anyone was watching you. I know just saying you're safe isn't enough and this is going to take some time. You are doing a great job having just escaped twenty-four hours ago."

Emily looked down at her feet. She was close to tears. She shook herself and offered, "I appreciate your efforts and kind words. I'm just so scared. Nick must have connections everywhere. I know you are all doing your best and I really do appreciate it. My feelings are just so raw right now. I do need time to adjust. I also have a massage and acupuncture session scheduled for this evening to help keep me balanced. You probably already know that. I'm trying to take just little baby steps, one at a time right now."

"And you are doing a great job with those baby steps. As a matter of fact, your massage therapist works with us. She will take good care of you."

"Do you guys know everyone?" Emily laughed, a bit relived.

Matthews touched her shoulder and walked her inside. "Yes, as a matter of fact we do!" He said with a smile. "Now, off you go for your make-over. Enjoy."

Emily entered the salon, spoke with the receptionist and was escorted to a changing room. She emerged in a robe and slippers and her make-over began.

After her new hair style had been agreed upon, the pampering started in earnest. She was offered a foot massage and facial as well. She accepted. First was her facial, then her new hair style was created, and finally her foot massage. She was so relaxed she didn't think she could move. And she was hungry again. She ordered to-go and went to her room. She looked at herself in the full-length mirror and marveled at her new self.

Her hair had been long and bland. Now it was colored, highlighted and cut to just below the shoulders. It looked fabulous.

Emily ate her yummy food, took a quick shower and got ready for her evening of acupuncture and massage. She had chosen a hot stone massage with light muscle release.

Emily emerged around ten o'clock feeling like melted chocolate - relaxed, balanced and ravenous. And what was with the hungries today, she wondered. It was as if she couldn't eat enough. She realized that her meals and food had been planned for her for the last year and she hadn't really liked what she was given to eat. It was no wonder that she had lost over twenty-five pounds and her friends were asking if she was feeling OK. She did look a bit unhealthy at this weight. She would take care of that this weekend by eating what she wanted. Not all fun food, but a lot of it!

Another thing to work on - her eating habits. She would take the time to stock the food she liked in her cupboards and fridge and would eat regularly. Yes, her Spirit was hurting and so was her body. As a matter of fact, her whole mind, body and soul needed healing.

And that's what all the pampering was about today - taking care of Emily. And that's why she had chosen the mountains of North Carolina to live in. She resonated with the land and the mountains. She liked the ocean, too, and would travel there if she felt the need. But, it was the land, Mother Earth, where she felt the strongest connection. Her favorite pair of shoes were none - she liked feeling the earth beneath her feet. Being in New York was fun for a few days, but, honestly, she couldn't wait to get to her mountains. The Blue Ridge Mountains were calling loud and clear.

Sunday dawned clear and sunny again. She and Matthews took the Statue of Liberty tour. That afternoon, they found themselves in Chinatown eating dim sum. Emily told Matthews that she wanted to stay in for the evening. She was going to soak in the Jacuzzi, have dinner in the restaurant and then chill out for the rest of the night.

Matthews reminded her about their 10 a.m. appointment with the Swiss bank on Monday. She confirmed that she would meet him in the lobby at 9:30 in the morning.

Emily went to her room, changed into her swimsuit and was in the Jacuzzi fifteen minutes later. She loved the hot tub and stayed in until she began turning into a prune.

She returned to her room, changed and had dinner in one of the restaurants in the hotel. She was in bed by nine o'clock and fell asleep almost immediately. She slept deeply all night not even remembering her dreams.

CHAPTER 3

A gent Matthews and his team spent the night going over the details of the arrest of Nicholas Wade Gordon.

It had taken five long years of investigating, watching and planning to get this guy. He had come to the Marshal's and FBI's attention after he quit the gym. His bank account was bigger than his paycheck and the guy he was delivering packages for was known for his drug cartel connections, among other things. Yuri Strovonovich was well known to Interpol and was being watched by numerous federal and international agencies. He moved money around the world like peas on a plate. He was very careful about whom he brought onboard and Nick was just the kind of scumbag Yuri liked to play with.

Yuri had Nick checked out and knew he was an angry young man. He learned he came from an abusive childhood where he had no control over his own life. He was now a man who desperately needed to be in control of everything. Yuri began using Nick as a delivery boy, feeding his ego and power-lust with cash and empty promises. Nick believed every word. When Yuri suggested he leave the gym and join his business, Nick jumped at the chance. Yuri had him right where he wanted him.

Yuri began using Nick as his New England manager. Nick was in charge of collecting cash from drug dealers and hiding it. Yuri set Nick up with his own import-export business as a cover. Nick was taught a few things about antiques and priceless works of art so he sounded like he knew what he was talking about should anyone happen to ask.

His storefront had enough antiques to pass as a real business and was called "Bits & Pieces of New England." Nick had customers on a daily basis.

Sometimes he even sold a few things. The store was only open Thursdays and Saturdays as Nick explained he was out scouting for antiques and arranging for deliveries of new products and shipping for clients on all the other days of the week.

It sounded legitimate to most, but the feds knew better. They had been investigating Nick and his shop since the day it opened. Yuri was not happy about this. He suggested Nick get married to make it look like he was more of a regular guy. Yuri was so greedy, he would demand some of the strangest stuff from Nick. Once, he had Nick travel to Europe to a 'fake' funeral just to get the feds to stop following Yuri… or so Yuri thought. Yuri really was not a smart guy. But when Yuri 'suggested' something, you made it happen. So, an angry and violent Nick started looking for a woman he could manipulate and control to make Yuri happy. He needed someone who was plain, educated, had an honest kind of job and would believe every word he said. He would do anything Yuri asked because in the end, Nick planned to remove Yuri from the top job and make it his own.

Yuri was dark, evil and demonic in all ways. He walked in the world of the dark shadows. He was possessed by greed and the need to be in control of everything. Yuri was just a pawn, just like the way Yuri used Nick. Yuri Strovonovich thought he was in charge of the world. He thought he had it all. Truth be told, neither Yuri nor all the agencies investigating him had any idea who was really in charge and their ultimate goal… control of all the cosmos.

Yuri had been a small time drug dealer and money launderer for many years. Early in his career, he was approached by a nameless man through one of his trafficking connections and offered the chance to control all the drug deals and trafficking around the globe for an obscene amount of money. The only thing Yuri had to do in exchange was supply this connection and his peers with as many people as they asked for… to work in the business. Yuri greedily agreed! He began recruiting people to work for him that very day.

Odd thing was, every few months, a few of his workers would disappear. When he asked his connection what had happened, the nameless man said it was no concern of Yuri's and to find immediate replacements. Yuri did and kept doing so. Hundreds of his workers disappeared. Yuri assumed they had been murdered. Yes, they had disappeared, but not like Yuri thought.

The nameless connection was an extra-terrestrial being who walked with the Dark Force. He was a member of the Consortium of Nebulae, known throughout all existence as The CON. The CON was the purest form of Evil – The Dark Side. The CON had entities on planets across the universes, working at bringing other life forms into the Dark Life Force. Yuri had been an easy target for The CON. He was possessed by his lust for greed and power.

Yuri's obsession for control is what made him powerful. He would do anything to be in control and made sure his minions knew this. He really thought he was the top dog. He had no idea he was being manipulated by The CON.

The CON had been around since before time began. There was a battle going on between The Con and The NOVAE. The CON was Dark. The NOVAE was Light. The NOVAE worked hard to squash The CON. The battle raging on Mother Earth had been long and intense. The CON chose those souls who were selfish, cruel and hateful. Yuri was the perfect match. The CON found Yuri. Yuri found Nick. And, now, Nick had to find a 'wife.'

And Nick did just that. He had made connections with a few of his client's realtors, offering his assistance to new home and business owners looking for classic antique furniture and accessories. That is how he had met Melanie Phillips. He poured on enough charm to become accepted as part of her social circle, and that resulted in an invitation to a networking cookout at Melanie's house.

The day of the cookout dawned clear and warm. Nick was in a good mood as he had contacted Yuri a couple of days earlier informing him of his plan to attend the cookout and 'find' a wife. He had already met some of the people attending and had a couple of targets in mind. Yuri was pleased. And if Yuri was pleased, Nick was happy.

Nick made it a point of arriving about thirty minutes after the start time written on the invitation.

He didn't want to appear too eager. He had planned well. When he arrived, the party was well under way. He found Melanie and gave her the gift he had bought. A bottle of red wine in a wicker basket.

Melanie thanked him and suggested he get a drink and mingle. Nick did just that, all the while surveying the ladies in the crowd. He saw some he knew, nodded his head, waved then smiled. Then he began scanning the group for women he didn't know and watching them to see if they had husbands or boyfriends. He found three women that looked like they were alone. He began to walk over to one of them when he saw a man approaching him.

The man stopped next to Nick and said, "How's it going Nick? Looks like a great turnout today."

Nick had no idea who the guy was but he wasn't about to look like a dumbass, so he replied, "I'm doing well. It does, indeed, look like a great day. Is your better half with you?"

The man with no name replied with a laugh, "No better half today. I'm on my own. You alone? 'Cause that woman over there has looked your way a few times. She's hot. Look at that tight ass and those huge tits. Nice specimen, wouldn't you say?"

The guy was crass but it was true. Nick could see himself fucking her hard, controlling her, and this made him smile. He turned to thank the no-named man for pointing her out but the man disappeared. Nick looked all around but could not find him. Oh well, he shrugged, no great loss.

He spent the next hour watching her as she talked and laughed with her friends. She was beautiful. He found himself imagining how he was going to control her into marrying him to make Yuri happy and get him off his back. He leaned against a tree with a drink in his hand and began to fantasize. He would win her over with his great looks and charm. He would send her flowers and take her to dinner. He would finally get her hot for sex and then he would ram into her no matter what she said or did. He would own her and she would be grateful. She would beg for more and he would control the where and when of sex. After all, the man was the smarter and stronger one and the woman was there for his pleasure and to do as he demanded.

He was smiling outright when Melanie found him. She called his name and startled him back into the here and now.

"Hey Nick, what'cha thinkin'? Must be something good."

Nick coughed a bit and responded with, "The thoughts of what makes a happy couple. Melanie who is that woman over there? The one with the great body and gorgeous smile?"

"That's my friend Barbara. Would you like to meet her?" Melanie offered.

Nick stood up straight and motioned for Melanie to lead the way. "Of course I would. She's not married or anything, is she?"

Melanie looked over her shoulder at Nick with a sly smile on her face, "No. Interested?"

Nick heartily responded, "Yes… lead on if you would please."

Nick followed Melanie across the lawn to where Barbara was chatting with a few friends.

Melanie smiled at Barbara. "Barbara, I would like you to meet Nick Gordon. He's a friend of a friend."

Barbara offered her hand, "Nice to meet you." *And your body! Great eye candy!*

Nick took Barbara's hand in both of his, looked into her eyes and in a very deep, sexy voice said, "Nice to meet you, too. May I get you a drink or something?"

Barbara could barely think let alone speak. "Yes, uh, a glass of white wine would be good." Nick was gorgeous.

Nick looked over his shoulder while waiting for his drinks. He saw the look on Barbara and Melanie's faces. He knew he had made a great first impression. All those long hard hours at the gym were finally paying off. Now to keep pouring on the charm just enough to get a first date. Then, he would have her right where he wanted her. She would do as the wife for him. Yuri would definitely approve. He would have to get a picture with his cell without her knowing and send it to Yuri for his approval soon. He took the drinks back to her - his was only water. He never mixed pleasure with work, especially when money was involved. After all, this was just a bit of business to secure his place with Yuri. Nothing more.

Although sex on demand was definitely a big benefit this time. He would have sex whenever he wanted it. She would be his wife, his to do with as he ordered. He would make it seem like she was in charge when he would always be. He had to be. No one told Nick Gordon what to do.

He handed Barbara her wine and suggested they sit in the shade and get to know one another. She agreed.

For the next hour Barbara and Nick chatted about their jobs, their mutual friends and the things they liked and didn't like. Nick was a great listener, always deferring to Barbara and her thoughts and ideas. By the time the food was ready, they had found out that they knew the same friends and were both hard workers. Nick learned that Barbara was finishing her master's degree in Alternative Health Care and pretended that it was a great thing to do. Secretly, he hated Barbara for being smarter than him. No problem. He would make sure she had a job that used that degree to bring lots of money into the house making it look like he was successful.

They joined the rest of the group and the evening turned out well. He excused himself after dinner to check with Melanie to see if she needed help with anything. It was an excuse to get away so he could take that picture he needed. He did speak with her and then found a spot where he could take a few pictures without anyone noticing him. He got what he needed and sent them to Yuri. The response was immediate. Yuri would investigate Barbara and then get back to Nick.

The evening was winding down when Nick offered to drive Barbara home.

Barbara laughed and said, "Nick, I have my own car. But thanks anyway. The idea was sweet."

Nick apologized. "Of course you do. It was nice meeting you. Maybe we can get together for dinner or something soon. What do you say?"

Barbara thought for a moment. "OK. That sounds OK. Here's my cell number. Please call after five as I work and personal calls are frowned upon."

He took the note and agreed.

He didn't need her cell number. Yuri would get all the necessary information on her. Nick would have her address, employer, her phone numbers, birthday, everything, if Yuri approved. Yuri always knew everything about anyone his people came into contact with. That's how he stayed number one.

The next day Nick called Barbara and suggested they meet for dinner. She agreed and by seven they were settled at a small table in a very exclusive restaurant. He was both gracious and kind. He ordered for them both. At the end of the date, he offered for them to go to his place for a night cap. Barbara agreed and followed Nick to his house.

Nick brought her a brandy.

Barbara replied, "Oh thank you, but I don't really drink. Only a little white wine once in a while."

Nick shook his head and said, "But I took the trouble of opening a new bottle for you."

Barbara responded with, "Thanks anyway, but I don't drink. Maybe you should have asked first, and then you could have saved it for another time."

Nick raised his voice, "Don't tell me how to entertain. I know what I am doing."

Barbara stood and walked to the front door, gathered her things and said as she walked out, "Maybe you should learn to be more gracious and not yell at your guests."

With that, she left. Nick was furious. No one walked away from him. He would get even with her. He would apologize with flowers and nice notes then get her back here. No one told Nick Gordon what to do. After she left he was so enraged he threw a kitchen chair through the window. He had a couple of shots of whiskey and began to plan the downfall of Barbara Jones.

He received a text from Yuri just then. She was the one. Make it happen he said.

So, Nick sat back and began to plan how he would possess and trick Barbara into marrying him.

He began by sending flowers and an apology to her workplace. Yuri had supplied him with a ton of personal information on Barbara. When she called him, he asked if he could take her to dinner on Friday so he could begin to apologize for his bad behavior.

She said she needed some time to think about it, then got back to him and agreed.

From that Friday night on, Nick pushed hard to win her over. Sex was the next move.

So, he arranged for a weekend away after they had been dating for three weeks. Once settled in, he put the sex plan in motion. He would control every aspect of sex with her. She went along with everything he did to her. He almost lost it when he was in her mouth. That made him angry. He was in charge. So, he rammed into her and made her beg him to make her cum. She came right away and grabbed him, forcing him into her and he lost it. He rammed hard again and again. She needed to know who was in charge.

Afterward, he poured on the charm, complimenting her on how great a lover she was.

Over the next few weeks he wined and dined Barbara. Sex was a given. He continued to let her think she was the motivator.

Yuri was watching everything.

Nick finally proposed a couple of weeks later. Barbara took a little time to think about it then said 'Yes."

The wedding was a small affair with only a few friends and a dinner to follow. Then Nick changed and took total control over Barbara's life.

CHAPTER 4

Nick thought everything was going well right from the wedding on. He controlled everything Barbara did. He paid her back for the sex stuff by taking her whenever he wanted to prove he was in charge. He began slowly but escalated quickly to raping her as a form of control. He did this at night when she was asleep so she wouldn't have a chance to fight back, and she would as she awoke to a living nightmare.

Nick really thought everything was great. Barbara was terrified of him so he assumed she was under his control. The downfall of Nicholas Gordon began when Barbara was approached by a local law officer in the parking lot of her job one afternoon after lunch.

As Barbara answered questions about Nick, she realized he was a very dangerous man.

She told them everything she knew about him, including how he always had loads of money. She assumed he was dealing drugs or something. When the agents told her about his involvement with the New Russian Mafia, she became quiet and pale. She needed a few minutes to breathe and think. The agents were gentle with her and kept telling her they knew she was not involved in any way. Then they told her she would be under constant watch from this meeting forward.

Nick thought she was at work since he had checked her GPS right after lunch and it showed she was in the building. He never bothered to check it again until later in the day when she was supposed to be getting home. The agents knew this and had reset his GPS, making him think she was in the office. A specialized communications team kept resetting the GPS signal every time Barbara was some place different. This kept things quiet.

Nick was in his antique store planning a trip to Europe. He was supposed to be buying items to bring back to sell. He was really meeting with Yuri to begin the next phase of his job – human trafficking. Yuri had a vast network set up across Russia and the Eastern Bloc countries. He lured eighteen to twenty-one year-old girls with promises of living in America and going to college in exchange for childcare duties.

He carefully researched the applicants and chose only those who came from poverty stricken families. Once in place, they were used as prostitutes. Their families would not have the means to rescue the girls once he had them in his control even if they were able to get a letter mailed.

Yuri also operated a 'Mail Order Bride' scam. The women and men who answered these ads were sold into prostitution as soon as they 'married' their chosen partner. They paid huge amounts of money to be 'married' only to then be used as sex slaves. And this scheme didn't play out just in the U.S. Yuri had connections all over the globe. And, he was into child porn as well as buying and selling children to the highest bidder. He kidnapped most children and lured runaways with promises of food and shelter.

Nick was just about to board his flight to London on Friday when he was approached by three men in suits. He thought they might be Yuri's thugs making sure he got on his plane as ordered. Nick was dumbfounded when they quietly showed him their FBI badges and told him to walk with them without making a scene. He was strong-armed on both sides, so he had no choice. Nick was pissed and scared. He didn't know what was happening. He was read his rights as they walked down the hall, then they turned into a security area and disappeared through a door. They took him to a waiting black SUV where they handcuffed his hands and feet. His luggage was already in the SUV along with his briefcase.

Agent Rick Fielding, from the FBI, explained to Nick he was under arrest for money laundering, drug trafficking, tax evasion and acts of terrorism against the United States of America. Agent Fielding strongly suggested to Nick that he remain silent as every word he said would be used against him in the courts, both U.S. and international.

Nick was taken to a federal processing site where he was stripped, searched naked and then clothed in prison garb and placed in an interrogation room. He had bruises on his face and hands when the U.S. marshals and FBI agents came into the room to begin questioning him. He looked like Hell.

Nick couldn't believe what was happening to him. He was extremely careful with everything. He was the only one who knew what he did. Only Yuri had some idea of how Nick collected the drug money. Nick had his own 'business' going as well. He dealt with stolen goods, selling them to the highest bidder. And, these were high-end stolen goods. He was trying to control his panic when the agents walked in.

Agent Fielding began with, "Nicholas Gordon... Nick, do you have any idea why you are here? Are you aware of the charges against you?"

Nick replied, 'What the fuck is going on? I am a law abiding citizen and this is how I get treated? I want my lawyers. Now!

Agent Fielding countered with, "No problem. Please get Mr. Gordon's attorney's contact information and place a call, informing him that we have arrested Nicholas Gordon on all charges listed and that he can see his client in two hours at this address. Please take all precautions when processing Mr. Gordon's attorney. We wouldn't want anything to happen to him, now would we? Do you have anything else to say Mr. Gordon?"

Nick snarled back at Agent Fielding with a look that could kill, "No fucking way."

Agent Fielding stated, "Mr. Gordon, you will remain in this room until your attorney arrives in two or more hours. In the meantime, there will be three agents with you at all times."

Agent Fielding and the others left the room as three new big, strong-looking agents entered the room. It was a long three hours as it turned out. No one touched Nick. He was handcuffed to the table which was secured to the floor.

Nick kept going over the last few weeks in his mind. He just couldn't figure out how anyone knew what he was up to. His bitch Barbara was too stupid to know anything. Anyway, he had her under complete control. She was scared shitless of him, did everything he demanded, and followed the rules to the letter. Even so, he raped her repeatedly after drugging her dinner so she couldn't fight back. He beat her as well, rarely leaving marks anyone could see. When he did leave a mark, she stayed home, calling in sick. He refused to let her go to an emergency room for treatment, knowing she would report the abuse. If he beat her badly, he had a doctor on call that he 'owned' who would come over and fix her up. Bitch. Cunt. But she was a good fuck. He had been right about that. And, they did present themselves well in the community. Yuri was happy with the way things were going.

"Oh my God!" Nick shouted. He realized Yuri was going to have him killed when he found out he had been arrested. "Oh fuck!"

Nick broke out in a sweat as real panic began to set in. He felt liked a caged animal. Nick knew that Yuri had connections in every law enforcement agency on the planet. He knew Yuri's moles disappeared after being arrested. The kill always came from inside. It was never publicized. Yuri would let it slip that so-and-so had met an untimely death. This was one of Yuri's ways of keeping his slaves under control.

Nick sat there for what seemed like forever before Agent Fielding returned.

Agent Fielding stated, "Mr. Gordon, your two attorneys have been arrested on outstanding warrants. You will need to contact someone else. In the event that that you do not have anyone else to contact the court will appoint you an attorney. What is your choice?"

Nick paled and began to tremble. His attorneys arrested? Holy shit! Now what? He couldn't call his contacts and definitely not Yuri. What was he going to do? If he used a court appointed attorney, he could not tell him anything! He would be sent to prison where he would be killed or he would receive the death penalty for those bogus terrorism charges. He was a dead man either way. He was so scared, he pissed himself.

The agents looked at each other and knew Nick was in trouble. It was now well past midnight. Agent Fielding decided to put Nick in a holding cell until morning.

Again, Agent Fielding asked Nick for an answer.

Nick replied, "Get me an attorney."

Agent Fielding added, "We are going to put you in a solitary holding cell until an attorney can be arranged for you in the morning. These agents will take you there now."

Nick was put in shackles and walked what seemed to be a great distance that included two elevator rides to get to the holding cell. He was locked inside.

Nick yelled, "Hey, I need some clean clothes and a shower and some food!"

One of the agents answered back, "Tomorrow."

Nick began to yell and scream. There wasn't any furniture to kick, only a urinal. He was terrified. He wondered how long he would stay alive.

Agent Fielding met with his team and their supervisor to go over the information they had collected since Nicholas Wade Gordon had been apprehended. His two attorneys had been arrested for extortion, racketeering and fraud against the court among other things. They would not be tasting freedom ever again.

CHAPTER 5

Emily awoke on Monday morning, showered, packed, and had her breakfast sent to her room. As soon as she finished she went down to the lobby to meet Agent Matthews. She was already checked out and they set off for their appointment with the Swiss Banc. The meeting took about an hour.

As they left through a secure door that led out to the parking garage, Emily turned to Agent Matthews.

"Thanks so much for the weekend. It was fun and relaxing. I know you guys will be following me all the way to my new home in Crab Apple Creek. Will I see you again?"

Agent Matthews answered, "Most likely as I need to introduce you to our team on the mountain. I know you said you wanted to take your time driving up alone, so go ahead. We will always be close by - closer than you think. If you need me, just talk. Your vehicle is wired for sound. There is an open mic on the steering wheel. I'll be right there. No one is looking for you yet so you can drive alone for now. That will change soon enough."

Emily smiled. "Always on the ball. I will be driving for quite a while today as I want to get out of the city and get a lot of ground covered before I stop for the night. I will let you all know when I am getting ready for that since I know you will tell me what hotel is ready. I would really like a Jacuzzi available."

Agent Matthews laughed. "Of course. All the amenities. If you have a moment of panic, just push the little blue button on your key chain. We will all come running, no matter what. Even if you are not sure if anything is wrong, just push the button. It's our job to make sure you stay safe. Now, off you go.

I know you need a few minutes to set your GPS, so we have a car right next to yours to follow you out. Just wave when you are ready. If you need a break for a restroom or food, just tell me. We'll get in front of you and show you where to stop. Always look for the whale tail sticker in the back window on the driver's side with the letters CAC-100 on it. That's us."

Emily replied with, "Roger, 10-4." They both laughed and walked to Emily's car. As soon as she was settled she signaled with a wave and both cars left the garage. Emily followed her GPS instructions and was on the highway in about thirty minutes, heading west on Route I-78 into New Jersey. She was on her way to her new home in Crab Apple Creek, North Carolina.

Crab Apple Creek is located in the Blue Ridge Mountain Range of the Appalachian Mountains. The Appalachians are the oldest mountain range in the United States. It spans most of the eastern United States from Georgia right up through New England into Canada.

Crab Apple Creek was a little hamlet that was settled on a creek of the same name. The creek flowed into the Pine Ridge River, through the town of Pine Ridge, into the Watauga River along its winding pathway to the Atlantic Ocean in Charleston. Crab Apple Creek was northwest of Boone, North Carolina, almost into Tennessee. It had been a mere spot on the map for about two hundred years now. First settled by the Catawba and Cherokee Nations, it was then populated by settlers from Scotland and Ireland who named it Crab Apple Creek for the numerous Crab Apple trees found all over the mountains.

Emily had done a little bit of research about the area. She looked forward to spending time getting to know the area from the locals. She enjoyed hearing the stories her elders had shared with her as a young girl. She knew more stories awaited her in her new home.

As Emily settled back for the long drive, she began to look around. She was still on I-78, but had left New Jersey and was in Pennsylvania. She had just passed through Allentown and was headed to Harrisburg. She'd been driving about two hours and was ready for a short break. As is usual, it had taken extra time to get out of New York and New Jersey. There was road work being done and that slowed traffic, as well as an occasional accident and broken down vehicle.

She spoke to Agent Matthews and told him she would be stopping at the next rest area about ten minutes down the road.

Agent Matthews joined her as she got out of her Beemer. Emily stretched and headed toward the building. She needed to use the facilities. Afterwards, she joined some of the other agents who were all dressed to look like tourists. She knew there were others in a number of vehicles just outside. It was past one o'clock and she was hungry.

Emily motioned to Agent Matthews that she was going to get some lunch. He and U. S. Marshal Carla Sanchez joined her.

As they sat down at a table away from most of the other people, Emily asked if they had seen the waterfalls a few miles back.

Sanchez answered, "Yes. They were beautiful. I'm glad Matthews is driving so I get to look at the scenery when I'm not on my computer."

Emily continued, "I would like to go to Hershey, Chocolate Town and the amusement park. Is that OK with you?"

Agent Matthews replied, "Sure. It's about an hour down the highway, just before Harrisburg. Let's take in the sites and then stay the night just south of there.I'll arrange for a place to stay. Stay with Sanchez while I take care of the details. I'll be back in a few minutes."

Sanchez commented, "I've been to Hershey before. I'll show you around if you'd like."

Emily smiled. "Thanks. I would like that very much. I haven't done any traveling or vacationing in quite awhile. This should be fun."

Emily and Special Marshal Sanchez finished their lunch just as Agent Matthews returned.

Agent Matthews informed them that everything was all set. Hershey was about an hour and a-half away and the road was clear of traffic problems. The park closed at ten o'clock so they would have all the time they needed to see the sights. The hotel was about thirty minutes away. Agent Matthews had informed the area bureau and U.S. marshals of their new plans and everything was set into motion. There would be marshals at the park as well as at the hotel. There would be a lot of agents and U.S. marshals around Emily for many years to come.

They got back on the road and arrived in Hershey around three. They had been given a secure place to park and walked right in through the VIP entrance. As soon as they got out of their cars, new agents were waiting at the door. Emily was assigned three bodyguards, a woman and two men all dressed as tourists with shoulder holsters and ankle holsters. Their weapons were all hidden, of course.

Emily chose to go through the chocolate factory first. She liked to see how things were made. At the end of the tour, they ended up in the chocolate gift shop. Every candy product Hershey currently made was for sale along with other stuff such as mugs, clothes, and toys. Emily chose three miniature mugs with candy logos on them and, chocolate of course. Next they went to the amusement park.

Sanchez asked, "Do you like roller coaster rides?"

Emily shook her head and laughed. "NO! No way! You guys want to take a ride, go ahead. I'll stay here with my group. I'll stick to the slower rides."

Her group laughed with her. They all agreed roller coasters were not their thing.

Agent Matthews had just joined them and added, "I'd like to keep my lunch in place if you don't mind." Everyone laughed. Agent Matthews was watching Emily and noticed, for the first time since she had left New Hampshire, she looked a bit less terrified. She was still cautious and looking over her shoulder once in a while, but she was now enjoying the moment.

They spent the next three hours enjoying the park. Emily chose a ride on the carousel and her bodyguards joined her. No problem with this ride. They walked, talked and rode the rides, looked at the exhibits, and ate park food until about eight. Then Emily asked to go to the hotel.

Emily said with a smile, "Hey guys. I want to call it quits. I'm tired. Can we go home now?"

Her bodyguards softly laughed. "Of course. Let's go."

The agents and marshals had communication devices with open mics so as the group headed for the VIP entrance the cars were ready and running.

Agent Matthews asked Emily if she wanted him to drive for her. She agreed and slid into the passenger seat of her new car.

Agent Matthews teased her with, "So, now I get to drive your Beemer. This is great. How fast does this thing go anyway?"

Emily answered, "You ought to know. You were following me the whole way here."

Agent Matthews laughed then followed the caravan into motion.

As they merged onto I-78, Agent Matthews asked Emily how she was doing.

Emily was quiet for a moment then said, "I'm tired, so tired. I feel like I've been running forever with no end in sight. The park was fun. I haven't been away for over three years I think. It had been a couple of years since my last vacation with my girlfriends, and then I met Nick. And we all know how that time was spent. I guess I needed the park today just to prove I could do something on my own. I did have fun. The carousel was a blast. I think my bodyguards were OK with the rides I chose. I do not like fast motions except in airplanes. Before you say they do whatever it takes, it doesn't mean they have to like it. I am not a prima donna. I do care about the people you have assigned to me. I mean the agency has assigned to me. Oh boy, I think I'll stop talking while I'm ahead. I'll just close my eyes for a few minutes, OK?"

Agent Matthews answered, "OK. Just close them until we get to the hotel. I'll order a snack for you and you can sleep as long as you want."

He looked over at her and she was already asleep. He smiled. How could you not feel something for her with all the nightmarish shit she'd been living with for the past year. He knew agents weren't supposed to get emotionally involved with their clients, but, God, he and the teams were only human. They had discussed Emily's situation every hour since she became Emily. If you didn't develop feelings for her then you must be a machine. They all cared about her and would do anything to protect her. On that note, Matthews made a call to the Harrisburg contact to make sure everything was in place.

An alert had been sent out… DO NOT STOP. KEEP DRIVING UNTIL FURTHER NOTICE. It seemed there was a security scare at the hotel they were supposed to stay in and the U.S. Marshal Service decided not to take any chances. The problem was with a client that turned out to be a drug dealer. He started shooting in the parking garage because his connection had stiffed him on his money. Then he started shooting in the hotel hallway that connected to the garage. Security called the police and they arrived with the SWAT team ten minutes later. The hotel was now surrounded. The drug dealer was known to the feds because of his connection to Yuri Strovonovich.

They drove another two hours and finally arrived at the Fairfield Inn & Suites outside of Winchester, Virginia. The caravan was instructed to drive around to a secure entrance.

Emily awoke when the car was stopped.

As she looked around she asked with a puzzled look on her face, "Where are we? This doesn't look like the Sheraton to me."

Agent Matthews hesitantly answered, "We were ordered to drive another two hours. There was a security problem at the Harrisburg hotel."

"What do you mean by a security problem? I don't like the tone of your voice or the look on your face."

Matthews sat up straighter and in an authoritative voice answered, "A drug dealer went nuts when his connection didn't want to pay him. He began shooting up the place. SWAT surrounded the hotel. We were told to drive on."

Emily paled and began to tremble. "It was someone Nick knows, wasn't it?"

Matthews answered. "No. It was someone who works for his boss. Nick hasn't had the chance to talk to anyone about you. He was arrested and is in jail as we speak. He was apprehended Friday night. He didn't even know you had left. He never went home from his golf game. He went to the airport as ordered by his boss and was arrested before he could get on a plane to London. No one knows you're missing yet. We've been monitoring all communications. So, this thing in Harrisburg is not connected to you. It just happened at the same time."

Emily looked Agent Matthews straight in the face. "Nothing is a coincidence. All things happen just as they are supposed to. Not only do I believe this, I live by it."

She was visibly shaking now. Her teeth had begun to chatter. She was in shock. Everything had finally hit her at once. Matthews got her out of the car after signaling a distress code to the team. Sanchez was there with a wheelchair. She told Emily to sit. Emily fell into the chair. She didn't know what was happening to her. She couldn't focus.

Sanchez tried to give her a pill. "Take this. It will calm you down."

Emily refused. "I have my own herbs in my bag. Just get my little blue bag and some water for me. Please."

One of the members of the team got her bag and gave it to her. Emily took out two bottles of herbs and swallowed a capsule from each. She tried to do some relaxation breathing but still couldn't believe what was happening to her. By this time they had arrived at her suite. Matthews helped her sit on the couch. Sanchez sat next to her.

Sanchez told Emily, "I am staying here with you tonight. We have agents in each room next to us and in the three rooms across the hall. Matthews is directly across the hall from us. We have open mics so everyone will be able to hear us. Someone will be awake in each room all night, including me. Let's get you into your jammies and into bed."

Emily did just that. After getting into bed she realized she was hungry. She seemed to have some of her color back. She asked if they could get something to eat. She and Sanchez decided on what to order and the call was placed. The food arrived twenty minutes later.

Sanchez watched Emily while they were waiting for the meal. She noticed Emily was sitting up with her hands together in front of her, then she placed her hands on her lap and began to breathe softly and rhythmically while chanting. Emily seemed to change right before Sanchez's eyes. Her color returned, and her body visibly softened and relaxed. When the food arrived, Emily stopped chanting, opened her eyes and smiled.

"I am starving," she pronounced and with a smile she got up, got the food Sanchez had placed on the table, and began to eat.

Sanchez just stood there staring at her. "What did you just do? Whatever it was worked. You're a different person. You're relaxed. Your color is back. What was that thing you did?"

Emily kept eating and smiled, shaking her head up and down. "Yup. I am better, more grounded and balanced. That thing I did is called Reiki. It is an ancient practice of channeling positive energy to help restore balance to one's mind, body and soul. I am a Reiki Master. If you ever want to try it, let me know. I am still really shook up about that Harrisburg thing. I know those guys are everywhere. But since Matthews told me that Nick was in custody and hadn't been able to contact anyone, that kinda helps. I'm sure his attorneys have gotten the news back to whomever, but at least no one knows who I am or where I am and I look very different than I did just a few days ago. And, since I have a different name and all, even if they try to find me, it's gonna take a while since Barbara Gordon no longer exists. I hope. That is what I keep telling myself."

Emily had also cried out for help and protection from her Guides and Guardians on the Other Side as soon as she heard about the drug dealer in

Harrisburg. She knew she was being very well protected. So, she was going to keep focusing on that thought from now on. Baby steps. She needed to remember to just keep taking baby steps into her new life.

"What was that stuff you took? Those capsule things? It didn't look like any prescription I'm familiar with."

"Those were herbs. Herbal remedies. I prefer herbs over pharmaceuticals for everything. They are clean, natural and organic. The body processes them very quickly, uses what is needs, then gets rid of the rest easily. No build up in the tissues 'cause they are water based unlike a lot of pharmaceuticals that are oil based and build up in the fatty tissues of the body. Excess can and does cause imbalance which has been known to lead to chronic disease. Take birth control and hormone replacement pills, for example. They are oil based and the excess is not excreted through your urine. It is stored in the fatty tissue of your breast and uterine tissue. This has been a confirmed connection to breast cancer and uterine cancer. Oh, sorry for the lecture. Once I get started I need to be reminded to stop. Guess I'm feeling better, huh?"

Sanchez just stood there shaking her head back and forth. "Really? I never knew that. Not surprised though. It's all about the money with those huge corporations. Now eat. I'll join you." Sanchez knew everyone had heard Emily. Sanchez got a text from Matthews. She replied that Emily looked much better and seemed to be handling the current mess well. Soon after they ate, Emily lay down and was asleep right away.

Sanchez and Matthews met in Emily's living room and discussed a new strategy. It was well past eleven as they began to plan the next leg of the journey to Crab Apple Creek. Matthews explained the new orders he had just received. "I have been instructed to change all the vehicles. They all need North Carolina license plates. Residential. And the SUV's need to be regular colors with the bullet proof exteriors. HQ says this is going to take twenty-four hours to complete. We should have them by midnight tomorrow. They want us to travel through the night tomorrow night. We should be able to get to Crab Apple Creek within six to seven hours, including a couple of stops and all."

Sanchez agreed with Matthews. "My orders concur. Emily needs a day of rest so today that's what we'll do. Hang out at the pool, Jacuzzi, eat, and maybe shop nearby. OK with you if we walk outside a bit? Just next door if she wants to?"

Matthews. "Not sure. I'll run it by both HQ's and let you know what they say. Have you eaten yet?"

"Yes, with Emily. I didn't want her to feel weird eating by herself. I know you heard the conversation but you should have seen her when she was done with that Reiki thing. She was totally relaxed. Looked great. I think I'll try it one of these days."

Matthews replied, "I was surprised by how calm she sounded. Good. Maybe this Reiki thing is something the agencies should look into. If it worked for her, it could help with other clients and our own people. Not sure what to think. Oh well, now, about the shifts. What have you heard from the marshals?"

Sanchez explained the new orders. "I am to stay until six a.m. Then, a replacement by the name of Bourne is coming in for the remainder of the trip. The marshals don't want to have the same people in place. Might look weird. All the marshals are being replaced tonight. What about you guys?"

"Same here except for me. The agency wants Emily to continue to feel comfortable so they are keeping me but changing everyone else. That knock on the door is my cue to meet with the new guys and explain the plan. I'll be back when I'm done. Don't let anyone in here no matter what. I have my own key card."

"Yes sir. See you then."

Matthews left and Sanchez checked on Emily. She was sound asleep and looking quite peaceful. Good. She had a tough next few days ahead of her.

Matthews brought the new team members up-to-date then went back to Emily's room. He let himself in and found Sanchez facing him with her hand on her weapon.

"Just wanted to be ready."

"Good. Just got an update on Gordon. He's been interrogated, sent to a maximum security federal prison, and placed in solitary confinement to make sure no one kills him before we can get what we need from him. I'm not optimistic about that though. That Yuri guy has connections inside the agencies. Seems his attorneys were arrested when they arrived on outstanding warrants. Gordon was assigned a court appointed lawyer. We are trying to find out if any information was leaked about Emily. The agencies are checking on that on a global scale. Thanks for your service here. Greatly appreciated."

"You're welcome as usual."

Matthews left and Sanchez sat next to Emily's bedroom door for the remainder of the night. At six a.m. she was notified that her replacement had arrived. Sanchez knew Bourne and when she knocked on the door, she let her in.

Sanchez briefed Bourne on Emily's case, then woke Emily up.

Sanchez, "Sorry to wake you, but I need you to meet my replacement. Come on out when you're done in the bathroom."

Emily yawned and stretched. "OK."

Emily walked into the living room as Sanchez finished speaking with Bourne.

Sanchez introduced Emily to U.S. Marshal Mary Bourne.

Emily replied, "Nice to meet you. Why are you being replaced Sanchez?"

"Agency policy. Take care Emily. I wish you all the best."

"Thanks Sanchez… for taking such good care of me. I greatly appreciate it even if it is your job."

Sanchez smiled then left the suite. Bourne turned to Emily. "Emily, I know this changing of the guards can be a bit awkward. I'm here for the remainder of the drive to your new home. If you want to you can go back to sleep. I have been asked to inform you that we will be here until about midnight as our vehicles are being switched out. You can sleep late, hit the pool and hot tub, watch movies… whatever you want to do. Not a good idea to leave the hotel though. Just want to be extra careful. Agent Matthews will be here any time you want him. Just say the word."

Emily questioned Matthews. "What's goin' on? Why are the agents and marshals and cars being changed? Is something wrong?"

Matthews looked Emily in the eyes and said, "We are under orders to change everything just in case anyone has gotten word that you are gone. The new cars will look like ordinary cars everyone owns, the difference being they are being fitted with bulletproof exteriors and high tech stuff. The license plates are North Carolina registrations. The more ordinary they look, the less likely anyone will be looking for them. That's why it's taking so long to get them here. We have been ordered to travel at night as much as possible. We have about six to seven hours to go to get there. You want to get some more sleep?"

Emily just stared at Matthews. "Uh. No. What I'd really like is a big breakfast and a dip in the hot tub. Then maybe a nap or something. Any chance I could get a massage?"

Matthews answered, "Yes to everything. Bourne, why don't you order breakfast from room service for Emily and you and I'll arrange for the hot tub and massage. I believe we have agents for those things here on site."

Emily smiled at Matthews. "Of course you do."

Breakfast was ordered and delivered. Meanwhile, Matthews was in touch with HQ. They had been notified that an email had been received by one of their confidential informants that Yuri was pissed because he had just found out that Nick had been arrested and detained by the feds. Yuri was beyond angry. He had already killed five people. He was on a rampage.

The CON was watching everything. They were deciding if they needed to remove Yuri from the planet. They did not want any trouble with him. The high counsel was about to convene to discuss the matter at hand.

The Continuum of The Goddess Novae, known as The NOVAE, was aware of the energy shift on the Earth plane as well. They had sent protectors to surround Emily and all those working to keep her safe, both humans and

ETs. The NOVAE was the White Light, the good guys. They tried to keep positive balance throughout all existence. Emily was important to them because she was one of them. She had been on the Earth plane many times before throughout the existence of humankind. This time, Emily was the connection between Mother Earth and the NOVAE. Emily was a High Priestess of The NOVAE. She did not know this yet. She needed to be in a place of quiet and solitude, away from the cities and craziness that was modern day mankind. She was headed to the right place. Her one-hundred eighty acres in the Blue Ridge was exactly the perfect place for visits from the NOVAE. Her property was surrounded by National Park acreage. No one was around for miles. The comings and goings of The NOVAE and their ETs would not be noticed.

Right now, Emily was headed for the hot tub. A few of the team members would join her so she wouldn't look out of place as the pool area didn't open until nine a.m. and it was just about seven.

Emily sighed as she slipped in the bubbling, warm water of the tub. "Ahhhhh. This is exactly what I need. I love these things. I'm gonna have one set into the deck in my new place, surrounded by movable walls so I can enjoy it year-round."

The others agreed and conversation swirled around the joys of a hot tub, good drinks, good food and great friends.

Some of the group got out of the tub and jumped into the pool.

"Holy shit! It's a little bit cold in here after the hot tub. It's supposed to be good for you."

Another member chimed in, "I kinda like the difference. It shocks you awake."

Groans were heard all around and the pool crew soon returned to the hot tub. Emily was sitting on the side to cool down a bit. Someone came in with juice for everyone and they all took a moment to drink.

Emily returned to the tub with a laugh, "Just a few minutes more or I'm gonna turn into a prune forever. Thanks for hangin' out with me."

"No problem. This is one of the benefits of our job."

"I always like to start my day with a swim and a dip in the hot tub."

"No complaints from me."

Emily got out, wrapped herself in a towel, slipped back into her sandals and they all headed back to her suite.

"By all. See ya' later. Thanks."

"Yes, Ma'am. Just doin' our job."

Emily let herself in and found Bourne and Matthews standing near the door with their weapons visible.

Emily commented, "Nice to see you're ready to take out the bad guys."

Matthews commented, "Always ready. Just got word you were here when you walked in. The pool is just down the hall so no time really to notify us of your movements. I'll tidy that up right now."

Matthews got on his two-way and gave instructions that whenever Emily was going to change rooms, all agents and marshals would be notified with confirmation before she began to walk. All confirmed.

Matthews said to Bourne, "From this point on she NEVER leaves your sight. Got it?"

"Yes, sir, those are my orders."

Emily informed them that she was going into her room to change into her comfy clothes and take a nap. Bourne replied, "Good. As soon as you are dressed, please open the door so I can see you."

Emily, "OK." She went in, closed the door and less than two minutes later, the door opened and she smiled at them.

"All set. OK if I take a nap now guys?" She flopped onto the bed and was asleep before they could answer her.

Matthews offered, "Guess she's really wiped out from this whole ordeal. I would be. Stay close, even in the room with her. If anyone needs to get into the room, you will be notified first. Do not let hotel employees in. They are being kept off this floor for security reasons. Until we know if Yuri has put a contract out on her, we are going to treat this as a hostile protection detail."

Bourne replied, "I got the same information as you. Done. You are in charge of this detail. I will follow your instructions to the 'T.'"

Matthews nodded his head, "I know you are excellent at your job, that's why I requested you for this detail. Don't let Emily down."

Bourne said with determination in her voice, "I plan on doing my best by her. Thanks."

With that, Matthews left. Emily fell into a very deep sleep. And she dreamed.

She was floating, kind of flying along above the Earth. She was headed to the Blue Ridge. She hadn't planned this. It was just taking place. She began to descend and found herself in the Applewood Grove close to where her new home would be built. As she got her bearings, she felt as if she had been here many times before. A déjà vu feeling. It all looked and felt familiar.

As she began walking around the grove, the shimmering air began to take shape. Her friends had arrived. Some would call them extraterrestrials – ET's. Some would be fanciful enough to refer to them as shape shifters. They were all these and more. Whatever the planet they were on called for, they became that entity. Emily waited for all of them to complete their shape shifting. There were about eight all told. They greeted each other and walked to the rock formation they had created when the Earth was first used by humans. The

Applewood grove had been planted to conceal the circle. It was a circle within a circle with a flat stone on a raised boulder platform in the center. The circle stones looked like chairs. This is where they gathered, in the inner circle. They all sat down except for one of the beings. She went to the stone altar. She gathered fruits and flowers from the air and laid them on the altar. She gathered crystals and feathers from the air and laid them on the altar. She gathered earth and water from the air in small earthen vessels and laid them on the altar. Then she raised her arms, chanting a mantra of thanksgiving and called the fire to come to the altar. It came and burned, hovering just about the stone. She called for the air. It came in a soft swirl that encircled them all. The air and the water joined forces and set a mist above the grove to protect all that were there. Even the animals of the forest stopped to watch.

The high priestess finished her chant and began to speak to all.

"I have called you all here to give instruction for the healing of Mother Earth. We also need to discuss how we are going to win the battle with the CON. The White Light will prevail."

She continued, "Emily, you have done well, my sister. Your most recent suffering has paved the way for a most extraordinary event. You will continue to settle in this area, bringing forth your gifts and sharing and teaching the peoples of Mother Earth about the realm of the White Light. You will assist those that are awakening to their own gifts and offer healing to all. Your new home will be a central gathering place. Many will be called to find you so you can share the healing messages. They will come from all over the universes. Your time to be safe and happy has arrived. No matter what the CON may throw at us, we will shield and protect you. Blessed be."

Emily stood up, bowed then approached the altar. "Thank you my Sister. I have felt the preparations in my soul for a while now. Once I am settled and my home is built, I will be ready to embrace all whom you send my way. That is my calling." Emily returned to her chair.

Another rose. He was known as The Bear.

"My sister known as Emily, those of the forest, animal, mineral and plant, will assist you in everything. Just call upon us and we shall come."

The Bear sat down. Another rose. She was known as The Dancing Wind.

"Emily, the air will take care of you in all ways. We will be still. We will be strong. We will work with the water to hide you in the fog and mists. We will sweeten the night with music. Call upon us. We are here for you."

The Dancing Wind sat down.

Others rose. They were known as the Protectors.

One spoke. "Emily. We are here to protect you. You have already felt our presence these past few earth days. Just call out to us and we will wrap you in protection. You, and all those you need protected. Blessed Be."

They say down.

The High Priestess spoke about the ongoing battle between good and evil. The CON had to be dealt with rather severely as the Dark Energy had begun to get out of control. The High Priestess informed all that the High Counsel had a plan well under way to stop The CON from further damaging this planet. They would all be given information as needed.

There was silence in the Applewood Grove for a very long time. Then, the fairies, wood nymphs and little Earth protective entities began to sing and dance with joy. They knew that their beloved Mother Earth was going to be cared for by The NOVAE. They were happy. Their song sounded like a babbling brook as well it should. They were seen as colored flashes of light in the air as they flitted about and danced. Their laughter mimicked the sound of bells.

The High Priestess arose and called the gathering together once more.

"We have shared our information and plans have been solidified according to The NOVAE. It is time for us to leave and for Emily to awaken and remember everything.

"Let us leave this sacred circle and ascend once again. Emily, we will be close by at all times. Just send the thought and we will take care of you and yours. Blessed Be in the Light and Love of the Continuum of The NOVAE."

The High Priestess began to shape shift into little particles of sparkling light, gold, silver and blue. As she ascended, the others transmuted and ascended as well.

Emily began to wake up back in her hotel in Winchester, Virginia. She stretched and yawned. She was surprised to see that six hours had passed while she slept. She was smiling.

Bourne watched her as she woke. "Hi there. Must have been one hell of a great dream. You're smiling from ear to ear. Wanna share?"

Emily sleepily replied, "Ah. Nah. Just need the bathroom and some food. Whatever I was dreaming has made me hungry as a bear."

She was back a few minutes later. "How about a turkey club, no tomato, too slimy, toasted white bread, fries and a Sierra Mist and a class of ice?

"OK. I'll order for both of us," Bourne agreed.

After the order was placed, Emily showered, dressed and was back in the living room just as the food arrived. It was delivered by Matthews.

"New job, Matthews?" Emily and Bourne chimed together, then laughed as Matthews went about elaborately setting up their supper.

"How was your nap?" Matthews inquired.

"Just what I needed. Ready for some food and that massage."

"Just say when, and the therapist will be here to set up and take care of you"

"Great. How about around eight o'clock? I want a dip in the hot tub first. Is that OK?"

"Yes. They have a private tub for you to use."

"Oooh. Guess I should feel special."

Bourne saluted Emily, "Only the best for you!"

With that, the three of them sat down to supper. Matthews had ordered his and had it delivered with the rest. The chatter soon ended up around vacations... the best and worst and where would they like to go next. They laughed, groaned and teased each other while they ate. Matthews' phone beeped.

He stepped away to speak. When he returned he updated them with the latest information.

"Our vehicles are being delivered around ten p.m. The team and tech crews will take care of them. We are planning on leaving around eleven. Please make sure you are packed and ready to go. Let Bourne know what kind of munchies you want and we'll have your Beemer stocked and ready. Bourne will be riding with you or driving if you want. It's up to you."

Emily thought for a moment. "I think I'd like Bourne to drive to Boone. Then I'll take over so I can at least begin to get the lay of the land. Can we drive around Boone later today so I can find things before you all leave?"

"Emily," Matthews said quietly and calmly. "We are never going to leave you. We will always be close by... forever. We are going straight to your rented house in Crab Apple Creek from here, with a pit stop or two. We need to check in with the local team. Then, the team will change again. Once you have met everyone, you can sit down and make a list of the stuff you will need after you check everything that has been delivered. Remember how I told you we would outfit the house with everything you could possibly want and need? Well, we did. As far as groceries go, there is a general store called *The Bend in The Road Country Store* just three houses away. There you will find just about everything you could ever need. And yes, the organic and natural foods are plentiful. The two men that own it love that stuff. And, if they don't have it, they can order it for you. Or, you can order it online and have it delivered. The bureau would like you to lay low for a while and stay safe. ...at least until we have a hold on Yuri and his contacts."

Emily looked a little worried. She took a breath, remembering the dream vision, shook herself and said, "OK. Whatever you say. You guys know what you're doing. Here is a little list of munchies for the ride. I'll be ready at eleven. Thanks."

Matthews put his hand on her should and gave it a squeeze. "You're going to be OK. You're strong, intelligent and better than the bad guys. Now, go jump into the hot tub, enjoy your massage and I'll see you around eleven. Bourne, thanks."

Matthews left and Emily changed into one of her three new swimsuits. At least the shopping in NYC had been fun. So many new clothes, new styles, bright colors and soft jewel tones. She smiled as she looked at some of them. It was nice finally having the things one should have. Good food you like, clothes you like and, of course, the Beemer. *Woo hoo!*

Emily and Bourne went off to the hot tub in the VIP suite. Cold drinks and appetizers awaited them. After a long slow simmer in the tub, Emily realized she was hungry again. She invited Bourne to help herself and the two of them chatted while they devoured the basket of food and cold juices, water and mini-sodas.

While Emily was getting her massage, Matthews was receiving an update on Nick and Yuri and the drug dealer incident in Harrisburg.

It seems all three were connected, but the Harrisburg incident was not part of Yuri's plan - the drug dealer had acted on his own. Kill if need be, however, he wasn't supposed to get caught red handed. The SWAT team had surrounded the ground floor and the garage of the hotel as the place was being evacuated. The other floors were on lockdown. A special forces team had entered the ground floor and was just entering the connecting garage hallway when the drug dealer literally ran into them. He was immediately stunned and held on the ground with all weapons trained on him. He began to scream about killing all of them. He tried to get loose, but another round from the stun gun ended that struggle. His hands and feet were cuffed and he was carried to a waiting cargo van where he was secured to the walls. This guy was not going anywhere. Matthews and the rest of the team just shook their heads.

"Ya gotta wonder if this guy was on something. Must have been."

"Strovonovich is going to go ape shit when he hears about this one. Do we have anyone close to him?"

"We always have CI's in the area, but Strovonovich has closed himself off from almost everyone. There has been a little chatter but not much. The bureaus are all over this guy. This is a global thing now."

Matthews added, "Yes it is. That's why we have to be very careful with this operation. We must look like just regular people traveling around at night. We will all leave a minute after each other. You all have your driving strategies in place. Let's go over them one more time. We have seven vehicles. Mine will always be behind Emily. You other five have specific speeds to travel at, when to pass or hang back. Confirmed?"

They all answered, "Confirmed."

"Interpol will have two more vehicles with us. One leaving right before us and the other leaving right after out last vehicle. Emily and Bourne will be the third vehicle to leave. Interpol's drivers and cars are arriving now. They will be escorted up here by Special Agent Michaelson. Go get them now."

"Yes sir. I'll wait for your approval after I send the photos."

"Go. As for the rest of you, Emily is in her suite with the massage therapist. She will be ready by ten. Make sure you are as well. And, be ready to leave when the order is given. How are the vehicles, Gates? Are they ready for us?"

Gates replied, "Yes sir. They are cleared for our use."

"It's nine-thirty. Please make all last minute checks now and report back to me. Go through those vehicles with a fine toothed comb. Make sure the advanced first aid units are full and ready to use. Make sure your phones and radios are fully charged before we leave. And one last thing. If ANY-THING happens while we are driving, put plan SURVIVE into motion. Do not hesitate. Keep your mics open at all times. Understood?"

They all responded, "Affirmative."

"Let's get it done. I expect constant check-ins from this point forward."

The team began the last minute checks. Emily had just finished her massage and was relaxing. Bourne reported this to Matthews.

"Emily, the teams are in place. Time to get ready."

Emily dressed and set her things by the door. Bourne informed Matthews that she was ready. Matthews let himself in and looked around.

"Bourne, do a sweep. Emily, you OK? Ready to get to your new home?"

Emily, "Yes, I'm ready and OK. I'm a little apprehensive about this last drive. But, the farther away from New Hampshire we get, the better I feel. I'm ready to go."

Matthews motioned for her to follow him. As they left the room, three team members surrounded them and walked them to the garage.

Matthews spoke into his radio, "We are leaving now. Everyone get in place. Lead car signal when you're ready, then all vehicles radio me."

Bourne and Emily got into the Beemer, the rest of the team was already in position. The car had been stocked with a cooler in the back seat.

Bourne radioed Matthews. "Ready to go."

The lead car radioed Matthews. The rest of the team signaled as well. The lead car left the garage and all followed. They were on the highway and traveling toward North Carolina. Within five minutes of leaving, Emily looked around and said, "There's more traffic than I thought there would be."

Bourne replied, "Mostly truckers. It's better to drive at night. There's no road work and less traffic problems. I've been informed that we are clear all the way to Boone. Let me know if you need to make a pit stop."

Emily smiled, "That's a 10-4 good buddy"

Bourne laughed. "That's how it works out here on the long, lonely highways."

Matthews was listening and laughed. He was, again, amazed that Emily could find a moment of laughter in any of this. Most clients were eager to take something to keep them calm for a long time. Emily had refused medication. She said she had all the help she needed with her herbs. Must be true. She sure didn't look like someone who was afraid for her life.

Matthews asked for a check from the team. All was good. The next four hours went by quickly. Emily asked for a pit stop just outside of Glendale Springs. As soon as she got out of the car three team members surrounded her making it look like a group hug.

Emily, "*Awww.* I didn't know you cared. Let's walk over to the building while we chat. I really need to go."

The others laughed and joked right up to the door of the bathroom. Two women team members went inside with Emily. They both looked around and signaled all was clear.

Matthews met Emily and the crew as they left the building. "Everything OK, Emily?"

"Yes Matthews. We all feel better now. I'm going to take over driving from here on out."

"OK then. We're ready to roll."

CHAPTER 6

With less than an hour to go before their arrival, Emily began to get excited about her new home. It had all happened so fast she didn't have time to process much of it. But when she saw the mileage sign for Boone, the realization that she was starting her new life, free and clear of pain, almost made her cry.

Bourne was watching her. "It's finally sinking in, isn't it Emily? You really are free to do whatever you want. Rather unsettling, isn't it?"

Emily agreed. "Bourne, I'm sure you've helped do this relocation thing a few times. It's obviously my first. Yeah, just actually realizing I am going to have the home I've always dreamed of with the people I choose. It's very powerful and humbling stuff."

Bourne offered, "Just keep taking those baby steps Matthews told you about. Everything will fall into place just fine."

Emily kept looking straight ahead. "I will. Now, I just want to get there. Good thing this is on cruise control or we'd probably be doin' about ninety right now."

Matthews chimed in, "Good thing alright. Just a few more miles Emily. I programmed your GPS as you can see. It should show about forty-eight miles to go. We should be arriving in Boone in about thirty minutes. Follow your GPS south of Boone, then we'll go north on US-321 into Boone, then west-northwest to Crab Apple Creek. Remember, it's a remote little dell, dirt roads and all. The main road is paved. Everything else is dirt and gravel. Your new Jeep should be in your driveway when we arrive. Fully loaded of course."

Emily smiled and looked at Bourne as she answered Matthews, "You guys thought of everything. Is the Jeep dark blue like my Beemer? Wait, don't answer that. Of course it is. Hope you all are enjoying this conversation. I'm watching for the US-321 sign and the way home."

Bourne chatted with Matthews and the team for a bit. The signs for US-221 and US-321 began to show up.

They soon turned onto US-321 and were in Boone a short time later. It was a small town but seemed to have everything one would need, including Appalachian State University. Emily thought she might like to look into the place once she got her bearings. Never know what and who you might meet.

Emily drove through Boone and west, northwest on US-321. Her GPS instructed her to take a right onto North Carolina state road #1233. This was a two lane road in a remote area. Soon, she saw a small wooden sign for Crab Apple Creek pointing to the left. She turned left and a bit later she was in front of *The Bend in The Road Country Store*. It was only about five a.m. and there was a light on in the store and smoke rising from the chimney.

She had been instructed to stop in front of the store. She did. She got out and looked around. This was her new home. Small. Quaint. Quiet. There were a few houses across the road from the store and a single pump gas pump just to the right or east of the store. 'Unleaded Only' was the sign above the pump. This place looked as if it hadn't moved into the Twentieth Century let alone the Twenty-First. It looked like something from the Eighteen Hundreds.

The houses were small, only about three of them. One had a realtor's sign in front of it. The realtor's little home was white with black shutters. The other houses were dark red with beige shutters, and sage green with black shutters. All quiet colors. Some had their lights on already. As Emily looked back at the store, two men came out and greeted her.

The taller one said, "Good morning. You must be Emily Henshaw. Kendra told us to keep an eye out for you. She's the real estate person around here. She will be here in a few minutes. Come on in and have some coffee - pot's always on. My name's Michael and this here's my partner in crime, Ted."

Ted added, "Pleased to meet you. Why don't y'all come on in and have some breakfast. We got lots of stuff ready for you."

Emily smiled, and shook their hands, "Why thank you. This is very nice of you to do this for us. Come on guys, let's get some coffee."

Emily looked up at the store. They got the name right, that was for sure. The store really did sit on a bend in the road. The sign was made of wood and had been painted to look old and weathered. The store was set a ways back from the road, so you could park in the front between the Store and a raised flower bed that sat next to the road. It was quite wide and tall. It looked to go back a ways as well. It had windows everywhere that had the grids so they all looked like little picture frames. They were all lit up, looking as if they were inviting you to come take a peek inside. It had a porch that ran full length across the front of the building with stairs in front and on both ends. The store was painted dark red with white trim and black shutters all around it. The porch trim was all curly cues and twists. It was painted dark red and dark green with the pillars painted white. The store was two stories high with what looked like a tall attic on top. It had a rooster weather vane on the very highest peak. The vane was moving in the early morning breeze looking like it was trying to find someone up on the mountains.

There were signs on the front wall of the store that read, "King's Flour Available Here" with a picture of a sack of flour on the front. There were other signs like the one for eggs…"Fresh Local Organic Eggs." The gas pump had its own sign at the end of the porch showing the price. Today, a gallon would cost $3.46. There were barrels set off to the side, probably for veggies and fruit when the weather warmed. Right now, they had kindling and firewood in them. There were rocking chairs all about making the porch look comfy and welcoming.

Emily sighed. She walked up the stairs and into the store. It was just the same as the outside, warm and welcoming with a potbellied stove in the middle that had a fire going that seemed to warm the whole store. There were rockers near the stove, too, inviting you to sit and warm yourself. The floors were made of skinny wooden boards. They looked old and well-worn and creaked when you walked on them. There were shelves and countertops with everything you could need and then some. Food, clothes, paper goods, dry goods, medicines and herbal remedies, craft supplies, hunting supplies and more. There were two steps just after the stove that took you up to another level. "Oh my God!" Emily laughed out loud. There was a place to connect to the internet with Wi-Fi. Old and new combined. An old oak pedestal country table with eight wooden chairs was set up for you to use. It looked like an old country kitchen. There was a coffee pot, muffins and fruit off to the side with a sign that stated, "Help Yourself. Donations Appreciated."

This store was awesome. Across from the Wi-Fi area was a full deli counter that even had bagels and a variety of cream cheeses. Emily was going to like living here. She noticed a lot of organic and natural brand names around the store. This was going to be a great fit.

The team had settled around the store with coffee and breakfast. Ted asked her what she wanted.

"I'd really like a hot chocolate if you have it and maybe a poppy seed bagel toasted with real butter and cream cheese. I love those things."

"Sure. Coming right up. How do you want the bagel toasted?"

"Kinda dark brown please. And, easy on the cream cheese. I don't need a whole tub on there. Thanks."

Ted nodded at Emily and began to prepare her food. This was the first time since Friday that she felt like she could begin to relax. The team was relaxing, or at least it looked like it. Matthews was chatting with Bourne and another agent named Charles. They were laughing and carrying on a bit. She guessed this was a secure place.

Ted gave Emily her breakfast and she joined Matthews and the crew at the oak table. Extra chairs had been brought out for them.

Matthews looked at Emily and said, "This stuff is really good. Fresh coffee and fresh food. Some of it is homemade from what I hear."

Emily bit into her bagel closed her eyes and just smiled. After a minute she said, "Heaven. Just heaven. A girl could get used to this real fast."

A few minutes later the bells on the door jangled as a woman walked in. Michael and Ted greeted her. Matthews got up and walked over to her, introducing himself.

"Hi Kendra. I'm Special Agent Noel Matthews with the U.S. Marshal's Office."

Kendra shook hands with Matthews. "Good morning Agent Matthews. Nice to see everyone made it safe and sound. All the things you requested are in place. Let me know when you're ready and we can walk over to the house. The blue prints of the land are on the table there and the name of the construction crew you asked for. May I meet Emily now?"

"Sure. Come with me." Matthews and Kendra walked up the steps to the oak table. "Emily, I'd like you to meet Kendra MacDonald, the realtor who has been handling your property. Kendra, this is Emily Henshaw."

Emily rose and shook hands with Kendra. "Nice to meet you. Have a seat and some coffee while I finish my breakfast. These bagels are divine!"

Kendra laughed and patted her tummy. "Don't I know it. Nice to finally meet you, too. Ted, how about the same thing for me that Emily has? That looks scrumptious."

Ted nodded and got busy preparing Kendra's breakfast.

As Kendra and Emily looked at each other, they nodded and smiled a little smile of acknowledgement. They already knew each other.

They chatted as if they had just met. Matthews and the others offered ideas about the land and the house design for Emily. Emily listened and thanked them. She already knew exactly what she wanted.

Michael and Ted joined the group and began to fill them in on the local lore and the people that lived on the mountain.

Michael began the storytelling. "The official name of this mountain is Soaring Eagle Mountain. It was named, as far as we can tell, by the native peoples, the Catawba Nation, that lived here long before the Europeans came over. The Catawba have handed down stories from their ancestors about seeing lights in the sky. They assumed this was the Great Spirit sending the most sa-cred creature to communicate with them, the eagle. The eagle spirit was seen as the most sacred creature next to the Great Spirit as it could soar the closet and deliver messages to and from the Great Spirit. The Catawba and the Cher-okee inhabited this same area of the Appalachians. They were at war with each other. Messy stuff. When the Scots started to settle the area, they gave the mountain a more colorful and telling name - Moonshine Mountain - for obvi-ous reasons as they started the moonshine tradition as soon as they settled here. You'll hear the locals refer to the land as 'Shine' Mountain. It may be illegal, but there are a few old time moonshiners still working their trade. You'll get to know a couple of them 'cause they live on your land. Up to you if you want to chase them out."

Emily quickly replied, "Nope. They can stay there. No problem with me."

Michael continued. "Good. They'll appreciate that. They've been a bit feisty since they heard you had 'bought' the land. They'll turn out to be good friends to have, I reckon. They're located on a cold water creek up in the back of your land almost on the National Forest border. You may not see them, but you'll know they're around as soon as they hear that you're gonna leave them alone. Don't be surprised if you find a jug of shine on your back step."

Emily laughed. "Not sure what I'd do with it. I will try it just once so I can say I did. But, I'll probably keep it for company and cooking. Probably make a good sauce or two."

The group laughed with her.

Michael continued. "There are a number of Catawba descendants in the area, too. Some of the land you're getting is sacred to them. There is a burial place back there. Their chief asked if he could meet with you before you decide where to build. I could set up a meeting if you like. The same for the Cherokee tribe."

Emily nodded in agreement. "Give me a couple of days to get settled, then we can set up a meeting. I don't want to harm anything sacred."

Michael nodded. "So, that brings us to the two women that have an herbal farm here. Lots of herbs for sale... and then some. They'll find you no doubt. They're a couple of years older than you I reckon. You ought a' get along just fine."

Emily kept smiling. "I'm going to like these ladies. I use a great deal of herbs in my healing practice. I'm sure we will get along fine. I gotta tell ya though, I sure do like what I've seen and heard so far. And we've been here less than an hour."

Ted added, "This is a special place. Not a lot of people, but the people here are forgiving and welcoming. They let you know we're here and they let you have your space. Quite a bit of gossip goes on, but that's normal in these mountains. And, good, too, in case something happens and you need some help."

"That's going to be such a nice change from where I used to live. People there were a bit distant until they got to know you. Then, they warmed up but only a little."

Bourne concurred. "Same where I lived except they only liked you if you believed in what they believed in. That's why I relocated to D.C. A much better group of people."

Ted nodded. "Yup. Every place has its own flavor of people. These here mountain people are from hardy stock that had to settle the land with their own hands. Traditions from hundreds of years ago are still in place. You'll be experiencing some of those traditions soon like planting, quilting, summer, then harvest. Stuff like that."

Emily set back in her chair and stretched. "Can't wait. Bring it all on."

Matthews looked around. Everyone had finished their breakfast. "Team, it's time for the next phase. Thank you to those of you who are departing. Your service has been greatly appreciated. For those of you that have been assigned here, please check in with Kendra for your house assignment. Emily, let's you and I walk over to your temporary new home. Kendra, the key please?"

Kendra gave Matthews the key and told him which house it was. The departing team members said their good-byes and the others met with Kendra. Matthews and Emily started to leave the store.

Emily said, "Bourne, I see you're leaving. Thanks for everything. Be safe."

Bourne replied, "You're welcome Emily. You keep safe, too. Enjoy your new life."

Matthews led Emily down the front steps and crossed the road.

"The sage green one is yours for now. It has two bedrooms. I figured you could use one for a home office for all the building stuff. Here's the key. Shall we?" Matthews motioned for her to go first. She walked the few steps to the little house.

Truth be told, it wasn't that little. It had a cute front porch with a rocking chair and cracker barrel on it. There was a pot of pansies on the barrel. It was still cold in the mountains in April. Pansies loved the cold so they would be happy on Emily's little porch.

Emily walked up onto the porch and unlocked the front door. She took a breath and said a quiet 'thank you' to her Guides. She opened the door and walked inside.

There was a flash of light as she walked in. Her Guardian Angels were here. She smiled, thanked them all in a second, then they were gone. Matthews followed her inside.

Matthews asked, "So what do ya' think?"

Emily replied, "I like it. It has lots of warm, positive vibes. A good place to be."

"Charles is bringing your car and will unload it for you. Let's go in the kitchen and talk."

They sat at the round maple kitchen table. Matthews had a lot of stuff to go over and there were papers on the table.

"Emily, first of all, welcome to your new home. This house will be your home until your new home is built. I will introduce you to your bodyguards later. Right now, let's go over the necessary stuff. Here are the details for your new bank accounts. They're active and ready to go. We will be monitoring them only for outside inquiries - buy whatever you want. There is a separate construction account as you are aware. It is solely for the purpose of building your home, barn, stables, and whatever else you want, maybe even a garden or two. You put five million in it. Use it to pay the construction crew and all that as well as all supplies and furniture, appliances, and more. Anything connected with building and furnishing a new home including that hot tub."

Emily smiled.

Matthews continued. "We will be monitoring all bad guy activity and get you the information you need to be aware of. As of right now, Nick is in a federal prison awaiting his first hearing. He will be held there indefinitely. He has a court appointed attorney whose every move is being monitored. He can't take a breath without someone knowing about it. His money has been seized and taken into custody as well as all the properties he owns. The mob boss is being watched, too, and let's just say he's not a happy camper. He has no idea what has happened to you. We haven't heard that he is even looking for you. You are well protected. Any time you think something is wrong, all you have to do to is hit your panic button. We'll be right here. Any questions so far?"

Emily shook her head no. Matthews continued, "Let's take a look at the construction info. Your crew chief is Ethan Sutherland. His work is detailed, well done, and he listens to his clients' ideas and works well with them. He has solid, good client reviews and has been cleared to work for you. He is available as soon as you want to meet him. He will hand pick his crew to match the details of your preferred architectural style."

Emily replied as she yawned, "I have a very specific style in mind. How about we meet tomorrow? I would like to get some sleep now. It has been an exhausting five days."

Matthews apologized. "I'm sorry. Listen to me going a mile a minute. Of course you need some sleep and time to be by yourself. If you give me a grocery list, I'll take care of it. OK if I just come in and put things away?"

"Yes. And thanks. I'm headed off to bed." With that, she left the kitchen and headed for her bedroom.

Matthews took care of the groceries, and then left Emily alone for the first time since they had left New York two days earlier. The houses on either side of her had guards in them. Emily would be briefed when she felt better rested. Matthews was on her right, to the east. An agent named Henry George was on her left, to the west. George was one of the new replacements. He had grown up in the area and was ready to settle down for a while. He was to be a permanent body guard for Emily.

Emily slept until late afternoon. While she slept, the team changed and the new members settled into their homes. Assignments were in place. Emily's new life had finally started.

When she awoke, the realization that she was in her new home began to sink in. She smiled, stretched and looked around. The room was cozy. It had what looked like a handmade quilt on the bed, a small rocking chair, a dresser with a mirror above it, the usual bedside table with lamp and a braided rug on the hardwood floor. The closet door was ajar, just like she had left it. No one to run around after her telling her what she did wrong. She just might leave some clothes on the floor, too.

When Emily finally got up, she headed for the bathroom then the kitchen looking for something to eat. She discovered her cupboards were full and there was more food here than what she had put on the list for Matthews. It all looked yummy. The fridge was the same. Full. She decided to make breakfast. Everything smelled great as she sat down to eat. The eggs were the organic ones from the store. The bacon looked like it had been hand sliced and was thicker than the packaged stuff, probably cured at a local farm. The bread was a country potato loaf. Emily used to make homemade bread. Maybe she would try her hand at it again soon. She cleaned up and began to explore the house and all the stuff that was inside it.

After about an hour, her cell phone rang. She jumped then remembered it was a new one and Nick had no way of knowing anything about her. He was in prison.

So, she answered it. "Hello?"

Matthews was calling. "Hi. I see you're awake. Lights are on. Did you sleep well?"

"Yes. Thanks for asking. The phone startled me. I think I'll change the ring tone right away. That will help me know he doesn't know about me."

"I'm sorry. There are going to be things that take you back to that horrible time. The counseling I spoke about should help with the flashbacks. Have you eaten?"

"Yes. Thanks for stocking the kitchen. You put lots more stuff in here than I had asked for. I guess I'll have to get used to that, too, being able to have anything I want. The counseling will be a good thing. Just leave me the number and I'll call soon."

"OK. How about we visit your land tomorrow? We could ask the construction project manager to join us if you want to."

"I want to go there alone for the first time. Just point me in the right direction and I'll find it. If you have to go with me, I'd appreciate you leaving me there after we get there. It's something I need to do by myself."

"Sorry Emily, we do need to stay with you. We'll give you some space though. How about at two, tomorrow afternoon?"

"That sounds good. See you then. Bye."

Emily hung up. Matthews just shook his head. She was standing on her own two feet. She was taking charge. Good progress. He filed his report and then settled down in his place, right next to Emily's. There would always be an agent or marshal awake 24/7. No one would take a break when it came to keeping Emily Gail Henshaw safe.

As night fell, Emily could hear the sound of the birds settling in for the night. There was a light breeze blowing and it carried the sound of the creek with it, soft and gentle. Lights had come on in the other little houses along the country road and you could see and smell the wood smoke rising from their chimneys. As she watched out her window, Emily saw a couple walk over to the country store, hand-in-hand. This brought a bit of longing. She thought about what it would be like to have a partner, a soul-mate. She shook herself, sighed and got up from the window seat. Time to stop daydreaming and get busy with her new laptop and printer. She would sign on to the Internet for the first time as Emily Gail Henshaw of Crab Apple Creek, North Carolina. She liked the sound of that. It made her smile. Emily Gail Henshaw of Crab Apple Creek, North Carolina. Yes, indeed. It sounded just perfect for her. And this little dell was just perfect, too.

CHAPTER 7

Daylight brought bright sunlight with it. It was cold, though. Only 41 degrees. She remembered she was in the mountains after all. Emily bundled up in warm, fuzzy sweatpants, a long sleeved flannel shirt, and a new fuzzy robe. She wore thick soft socks and her new LL Bean lamb's wool slippers over them. She was comfy. It was time for hot chocolate.

It was very quiet here. As she looked out the kitchen window, she saw that there was a light on in Agent Matthews' kitchen. The store was dark although there were lights glowing on the second floor. She figured it must be the guys getting ready for the day. Emily wondered what time it was as the sun was just beginning to send beams of light through the trees. She was surprised to see it was only a bit past six. She was usually up already. Oh yea... a new life.

She sat with her hot chocolate and let her mind wander. A lot had happened since Friday. It was now Wednesday morning. It seemed as if it had happened in a flash and then, at the same time, it seemed to have taken a long time for those five days to go by. She began to feel her old self already, in control of her destiny, and in control of her mind, body, and soul again. A sigh quietly left her. She began to think about her new home. She knew exactly what she wanted - a Cape Cod style house with an old country farm atmosphere that included wooden floors, lots of windows, dormers. It would be log cabin-looking on the sides and back, and clapboard on the front. It would need a huge Victorian farmer's porch to encircle the entire building. The porch would have a variety of rocking chairs and porch swings hanging from the ceiling and a few cracker barrels just because they were wicked cool. It would have numerous electrical outlets set into the walls with round floor lights against the support posts that would throw light up the posts making them look like they were glowing at night. These would not be bright, as she wanted all her lights to be soft and warm and welcoming. Her home was going to have those windows with the grilles between the panes. It made washing them easier. It was to have three working floors and a walk-in attic with cupboards and shelves for storage. There would be gathering rooms on the ground floor near her office and a huge country kitchen. A great room would be in the front with two fireplaces. One fireplace would be on the outside wall and another would be in the middle of the house to be used for heat.

Emily was working on tapping into the geothermal energy in the mountain. There were hot springs on the property so she knew there would be a source of geothermal heating for her home. She would not have solar panels as she didn't want to attract attention to her home. There would be no wind turbines either - not until she knew she was safe. She smiled as she kept adding details. She would have the place 'wired for sound' all high tech with Wi-Fi just like *The Bend in The Road Country Store*. She laughed out loud. Boy, did that store have the right name. Someone had a sense of humor. It really was set back from the bend in the old country road.

She must have let her mind really wander because she found herself startled by an unfamiliar noise. She got up to check it out and realized her back was a bit stiff. A glance at the clock told her it was almost eight. Holy cow! She had been sitting there for over an hour and then some. She went to the front door, looked out and saw that a delivery truck was in front of the store unloading supplies. That must have been the noise. It looked to be a general food delivery company. And, yes, one of the agents, dressed like a local, was chatting with the driver as he worked offering a hand. Emily suddenly realized she was ravenous. She went about making herself an omelet, bacon, home fries and toast. She called Matthews and invited him over for breakfast. He accepted and showed up at her door a few minutes later.

Emily heard the knock and hollered out, "Come on in Matthews. The door is open and breakfast is ready."

"Mornin' Emily. You really should look out the window before you open the door."

"Oh, I never thought of that. Thanks. Is there a camera or something I could use instead of looking out the window? When you think about it, whoever it is would know I was here when they saw me looking out through the window."

"That's a great idea. I'll take care of it right now." Matthews got on his phone and got the whole camera thing started.

"Whoa. You work fast!"

"It's a great idea and so simple. Now, how about that breakfast? Smells delicious!"

"Have a seat. Here we go. Dig in." With that, they ate and talked about the dell.

Matthews told her about the small town of Pine Ridge. It was located about twenty miles down the road off the Pine Ridge River. It was about as old as Crab Apple Creek. The locals went there for the things they couldn't get at the country store.

He told her about some of the more colorful mountain people such as the sisters who ran an herbal farm. They were known to have all kinds of herbs. It was a very small operation, just for themselves. Legend said that there were still moonshiners in the area. Although the DEA had tried to find them, they had stopped as no matter where or how they searched, they could not be found. So, Matthews told her, as far as the feds were concerned, they didn't exist. There was a rather large working farm with animals, fruits and veggies and a tree nursery that sold to area merchants and the local folks. This was the Kirkland Farm. The family had been among the first to settle the mountain around three hundred years ago.

Matthews continued, "If you want to know anything about the mountain and its people, then you should go visit the Kirklands. They're really nice folks. They have a hundred plus acres just down the road away from the Pine Ridge road. Should take you about ten minutes to get there. You can buy their local organic foods and eggs, butter and milk from the farm stand any day of the week. I visited the place last fall when we began scouting for your relocation. They really know what they're doing. In the fall, they offer hay rides, pumpkin picking and horse drawn sleigh rides in the winter. This place is truly a time gone by. It's set back about a hundred and fifty years. Hard working dedicated people who take care of their own and anyone who happens to come their way. I'm gonna like living here myself."

Emily looked surprised. "You're going to live here? Because of me? What about your own family? Won't they miss you?"

Matthews rushed to say, "Emily, I'm a single man without any connections. My parents passed on a few years ago. My brothers and sisters live in other states. I take vacations like anyone else. I'm OK with this. I asked for it to be honest with you. I like these mountains and the energy here. I have vacationed in the area a number of times and always promised myself that I would settle here one day. That day came a lot sooner than I expected. I love my job and stay focused no matter what. Now, don't go blaming yourself for my relocation. As a matter of fact, I will be thanking you from time to time. So, are we settled on this point?"

Emily shook her head yes and smiled. "Glad to accommodate you then."

"So, what are your plans for today?"

"I thought I'd get settled in around the house then venture out in the Jeep. Kinda take it for a spin. Are we meeting the building guy today?"

"Yes, at 2 p.m., here. We are going to go up to your land after we look at the aerial photos and geological surveys. You have hot springs on your land so using their source for geothermal heat is a go. I think I told you about this already, didn't I?"

"Yes, just a little bit though. I want to know all about the details regarding the land and my home. I want to honor Mother Earth, and balance the use with giving back. It's a harmony, um.., a balance thing."

"Understood. That's why we hired this specific building crew. They're very aware and knowledgeable about all this stuff. The Soaring Mountain Builders is a company owned by Ethan Sutherland. He's a twelfth generation builder. His family has been in the building and construction trades since they settled here in the early seventeen hundreds, almost as long as the Kirklands. I think there's an ongoing tongue-in-cheek battle about whose family has been here the longest. It's kind of fun to listen to I suppose. You'll find out soon enough. The Kirkland's tree nursery supplies Ethan's projects with all the plant stuff they require. Anyway, write a list of questions for Ethan for this afternoon. If you don't need me for anything else, I'll get going. Work stuff. As promised, I'll keep you up-to-date on any news. For now, nothing has changed."

Emily walked Matthews to the door. "Thanks for the visit and all the info. I'll see you this afternoon. It IS ok for me to go driving around, isn't it? Maybe to Pine Ridge?"

"Yup. Just know our people will be following you in cars and on foot. They'll let you know who they are before you leave. See ya' this afternoon."

With that, Matthews left. Emily showered, dressed and stepped out of her house to be met by two men. They introduced themselves as her bodyguards, showed her their credentials and the special badge that had been designed just for her safety. She looked over towards Matthews' house and saw him on the porch nodding his head that all was OK. She saluted, then got into her new Jeep and set out for the town of Pine Ridge.

The road to Pine Ridge was a winding road, pretty much following the Crab Apple Creek to where it met the Pine Ridge River just at the edge of town. The mountains looked beautiful all lit up by the sun and the trees were moving gently in a slight breeze. It looked like some of the trees were putting on growth getting ready to set the first buds of spring. Emily saw rabbits, turkeys and pheasants wandering along the roadside as she drove. She was traveling a bit slowly as she wanted to take care not to hit these critters and she didn't know the road either, so she figured she had better be careful these first few times around the area. As she slowed for a sharp turn, she looked out over the mountains through a gap in the trees. They really did look blue - the name Blue Ridge was for real. And, there was a haze of sorts that hung over the tops that had a bluish tint, although it was really fog. She had never doubted the name, but it was cool to see it for herself.

Emily liked what she saw as she entered the town of Pine Ridge. It was old and new altogether. There were old houses on each side of the road. As she got further into town, she noticed some of the older houses had been turned into businesses. They still held the charm of a neighborhood, yet had added to the business end of things. A couple were bed & breakfasts places, and others were offices and retail shops. Side streets intersected the main road with mostly private homes along their winding way. There was a sign for a farm stand pointing to the left and a state sign showing the way to the Blue Ridge Parkway. An old fashioned looking gas station called Tom's Service Station was on the corner of Main and Maple Streets. It promoted full service amenities. It had those old signs advertising Quaker State Motor Oil and Penn-zoil on the front of the store along with a sign inviting you to get your State Inspection sticker every morning between 9 a.m. and 12 noon. There were the usual grocery store, hardware store and the Hanson's Drug store, owned by the Hanson family for over one hundred and fifty years. You could see the soda fountain through the front window. A block down Main Street was a bank next to the county Sheriff's office. As Emily drove toward the end of Main Street, she saw the Pine Ridge Feed and Grain store. There were several pick-up trucks parked in front. Their sign offered everything from feed and grain to clothes, farm machines and Wi-Fi. Emily headed back down Main Street and saw a sign for a doctor's office. She turned onto Pine Street. The next thing she saw was a small wooden sign in front of an old country home. The sign read *Doctor's Offices, part of Appalachian Regional Health Care Systems.* It looked old, but further inspection showed it was modern. There was a driveway that went to the back of the house and a few parking spaces. She drove a short distance more and found herself in the country again so she turned back around and found Main Street again.

Emily drove back up Main Street the way she had come. Down the road back towards Crab Apple Creek she saw a side road and decided to turn and go exploring. There were no houses as far as you could see. As she came around a bend in the road she found herself looking at the most beautiful house she'd ever seen. It was huge, made of wood and stone, had two floors, a full porch surrounding the place and at least three fireplace chimneys noticeable from the road. It was probably set about a half mile off the road on a small rise surrounded by trees. In the summer, you probably couldn't see the house when all the trees were full. As she got closer to the driveway, she saw a small sign that read, THE SOARING MOUNTAIN BUILDERS. The sign looked to have been carved by hand. It was beautiful. As she continued to stare at the house, a black pick-up truck came up behind her. She hadn't noticed. She was startled when she heard the horn honking behind her. She looked in her review mirror and saw the most gorgeous man she had ever seen in the driver's seat. She was stunned by his good looks and by the look on his face. He seemed to be a bit annoyed. He honked again before she realized she was blocking the driveway. She waved her hand as she moved away. He waved back with a dazzling smile as he turned into the drive and disappeared around a bend in the road.

Emily had to pull over. She was breathing fast and she was flushed. She needed a moment to compose herself. She had just had a moment of déjà vu. She could have sworn she had met this man before. But she knew she had never met him. She had never been in this part of the world before. Not in this lifetime. She didn't know how long she sat there, lost in thought, until there was a tap on her window. She was startled back into reality as she looked out the window and saw that gorgeous man that had been in the pick-up truck staring at her. She rolled the window down as he asked her if she was alright.

Emily blushed as she replied, "Oh, yes. I was just out driving around. I guess I went too far from town. I was just trying to get a feel for the place."

Ethan smiled. "So, you're new around here. Where are you staying?"

"In Crab Apple Creek for now."

"Good. Just a word of advice. You might want to stick to the more traveled roads. Some of the mountain folks don't take too kindly to strangers. Especially those driving around in fancy Jeeps like yours. They might think you're the feds trying to find their stills and stashes. Safer to stay close to the main roads if you get my drift."

Emily smiled back at Ethan. "Got it. Thanks for the tip. I guess I'll consult my maps the next time I feel like exploring the mountain. Take care." She had to take a big breathe just to steady herself.

With that she drove on until she found a place to turn around. That guy was waiting for her as she drove past. She smiled and waved before she disappeared around the curve. Oh my God he was gorgeous! Ruggedly handsome, his hair was long and pulled back into a pony tail. Not really long just about to his shoulders. It was light brown with a bit of a wave that you could see even with it being pulled back. His face looked tanned even though it was still cold outside. She guessed he must work outside year round. He looked to be about six foot two with strong broad shoulders, a lean middle, tiny ass and long legs that ended in work boots that had seen a few seasons or so. She bet those legs were scrumptious looking and even better to be wrapped around. He had on a work jacket that was opened to show a flannel work shirt that hung loose. She could just imagine how he looked under that shirt. She sure would like to get a chance to see for herself. She could just imagine him touching her and bring her to a full and luscious orgasm.

That thought brought her out of her daydream. She suddenly realized she was stopped at the end of the road. She must have pulled over while she was daydreaming. She laughed, than thanked her Guides for keeping her safe. She hadn't thought about sex for a very long while. She was thrilled that that part of her was still alive and well. Whew!

As she got her bearings, she realized she was starving. She decided to go back to Pine Ridge.

Just a bit down Main Street she found a local diner. She thought the place looked like something she would enjoy. She walked in and was greeted by the waitress. "Take any seat you want and I'll be with you in a minute."

Emily loved this place. It took you back a good seventy or eighty years or so.

Everything looked authentic. The booths had red leather seats and the chrome edged counter was ringed by round red swivel stools. The jukebox was in the corner and the soda fountain had real soda handles. The cash register had to be a good hundred years old.

The floor was made of thin planks of wood that looked worn in the path between the door and the register. The menu on the wall behind the counter boasted of the Blue Plate Special for the day... "meatloaf, mashed potatoes, homemade gravy and green beans all for $8.95." The prices were contemporary, the place was not. There were full picture windows along the front so you could see who was passing by and vice versa. Lots of waving and saying "Hey" going on. Everyone seemed to know everyone.

Emily chose a stool at the counter and was met by the waitress with a coffee pot. "Oh thanks. No coffee for me. But I would like a Sierra Mist or something like that if you have it."

The name badge on the waitress' uniform read 'Nancy.' "We have 7-Up if that's OK."

"Sure is, and thanks so much."

"No problem. Here's the menu. Let me know when you're ready to order. You're new around here, aren't ya?"

"Yes."

"Well, welcome to Pine Ridge and the Blue Ridge Mountains. Best place on God's green Earth with the friendliest people you'll ever meet."

"Thanks. I appreciate the welcome. Hope to be a regular as time moves on."

"You're always welcome at Hank's Diner," Nancy said as she set Emily's drink in front of her.

Emily smiled at her. "I'll have the tuna on white toast with American cheese and fries please. Could you make the fries a bit crispy? I love 'em that way."

"Sure darlin', no problem. Be ready in a few."

Emily looked around at the people as she sipped her 7-Up. They looked like regular working folks. A few teenagers were in a booth, laughing and teasing each other. The diner was busy. Emily looked at the clock hanging over the counter and saw that it was about noon. Not bad for all the sightseeing she had done. Then there was that man. A true ten on the eye candy chart, not like Nick had been. She could tell this guy was a hard working dude. He had the build of an outdoorsy type, and tools in the back of his truck.

She guessed he worked for the building company. Probably as a carpenter or something.

She wondered if he would be on the building crew for her home. Now, that would be a bonus by all means.

While Emily ate her lunch and watched the world of Pine Ridge go by, Ethan sat at his kitchen table and wondered who in the world that gorgeous sexy goddess was. He began thinking about what it would feel like to possess those luscious red lips, to run his hands over those perfect, round breasts and feel her body heat mixed with his. He was hard in no time. H was a healthy man. He had been in complete control of his emotions for over three years now, ever since his fiancée dumped him at their wedding rehearsal. She had walked in, informed him that she no longer loved him, announced the wedding and everything was off, then walked out as if it were just another day. He was in shock as were his friends. He had not trusted another woman since. His heart was shut down as far as he was concerned to the world of loving another woman. Not gonna happen to him.. no way! So, what in hell was going on with him? He was dreaming about making wild crazy love with a woman he had spent about thirty seconds talking to. This was not going to happen again. He stood up and began pacing around his big kitchen. He kept telling himself to stop thinking about her. She was just someone who was lost on the road. She was beautiful. He could get lost in her eyes. No. He had to stop thinking about that.

God, he had to go do something to take his mind off her. He decided to go outdoors and chop some firewood, not that he needed any. It was just a great release when your mind was messing with you or you were pissed off angry. He was angry with himself for even thinking about getting involved with someone. He had promised himself no other woman would ever hurt him the way his ex had. He was in control. Oh yeah, fat chance. He began swinging the ax and spent the better part of an hour releasing his frustrations at the way his mind and body were sabotaging him.

Ethan finally stopped chopping firewood and sat on a stump. He was hot and sweaty. He had taken off his jacket a long time ago. He found himself remembering that horrible day more than three years ago. He had arrived at the church in Boone about twenty minutes before the wedding rehearsal was to begin. He and his groomsmen were standing around talking with the brides-maids about the dinner party that was to follow. His fiancée had planned a fancy thing. Ethan liked simple and elegant, not big and showy. But he loved his wife-to-be so he gave in to her demands. They had all entered the church and were standing at the altar waiting for her when she arrived in jeans and a sweater. She proceeded to strut up to the altar area and announce that she didn't love Ethan anymore and was leaving. The wedding was off. She had cleared her things out of his place that afternoon and was moving far away. She left. Everyone was in shock. Ethan hadn't even had time to say anything before she was gone. There was silence all around. The minister was the first to speak suggesting they all go home and he would speak privately with Ethan. They all left and Ethan sat down. The minister tried to be comforting but Ethan was in such shock he didn't really hear him. His best friend took him home and stayed with him through the night. Ethan finally began to talk the next morning and it wasn't pretty. He hollered, went outside and threw logs as far as he could. He used words he didn't even know he knew existed. Then he cried. His heart was beaten and broken. He told his friend to go away. He kept to himself for the better part of two weeks, and didn't work. He handed the business over to his brother Ian and stayed away from everyone.

When Ethan did finally come out of hiding, he went about the business of building as if nothing had happened. He owned the company and he needed to be in control. He needed to be in control of his life, every aspect of it, from now on. No woman would ever hurt him like that again.

So, what was going on with him? He couldn't stop thinking about that woman in the Jeep. Fat chance he would ever meet her again. So, he figured all this crazy thinking would fade in a day or two. He'd be fine. Just keep busy and get good and worn out so he would be able to sleep at night. That sounded like a good plan. Only thing was he had a meeting with the U.S. marshals in Crab Apple Creek to discuss building a new home for some client of theirs. Good. That would keep him real busy, drawing up plans, calculating costs and materials, working with his brother, Ian, their architect on the design and de-tails. He looked at his watch and realized he only had about thirty minutes before the meeting. He ran through the shower, dressed, and was out the door in twenty minutes heading to Crab Apple Creek.

Emily had finished her lunch and was on her way to the hardware store to get a few things she needed. She left Pine Ridge around one and was back in Crab Apple Creek before two. She went about unpacking more of her stuff until she heard a knock on her front door. She looked out the window and saw Matthews. She let him in. No sooner had she closed the door when there was another knock. She looked out the window and saw the guy she had met on the road to Pine Ridge just standing there, looking hot. Oh, no, she realized, this was the builder guy, Ethan Sutherland. The owner of the building company that was going to build her new home. She took a breath and opened the door.

Ethan just stared at her. It was her. The woman on the road. He couldn't speak.

Emily offered, "Hello. You must be the builder from The Soaring Mountain Builders company. I am Emily Henshaw. Please come in."

Emily kept smiling as Ethan came into the house. He hadn't said a word yet. He was dumbstruck.

Matthews stepped forward extending his hand towards Ethan. "Hi Ethan. Nice to see you again. Hope everyone is well."

Ethan looked at Matthews and shook his hand as he stuttered, "Uh, Hi Matthews. Everyone is fine. Uh, nice to see you again as well."

Emily thought she was going to faint. Oh my God! This was the hunk she had met on the road. No way this was a coincidence. Those didn't happen. Everything happened for a reason. She had to take a deep breath before she spoke. Her insides were on a roller coaster ride.

"Ethan, come on in. We're set up at the kitchen table. May I get you something to drink? Coffee? Tea? Juice?"

Ethan followed her into the kitchen with Matthews. "Uh, yeah, some juice would be great. Anything you have."

"Matthews, you want anything?"

"Nope, I'm all set here." He hadn't missed the looks between the two of them.

As they settled around the table, Matthews took the lead. "Ethan, you're already familiar with this operation as you were briefed two weeks ago. Nothing has changed. This is a relocation project. Emily is in need of a new home and has her own ideas as to how that home will be built. You have been given the blueprints for the security requirements and have the plans in place. We are here this afternoon to begin the design details of Emily's home and to walk the land, choosing a place for the build. Let's get started.

Ethan put himself into work mode and they spent the next two hours looking at the aerial photos and geological maps, trying to find a place to build. It had to be close enough to the hot springs so pipes could be run underground for heating the home and water. It needed to be in a place that could have an access road built without disturbing the protected plants and habitat of the local animals.

With all that in mind, they set out in Emily's Jeep to survey the land. The sun would not be going down for another couple of hours so they thought they could get a head start on foot.

As they drove away from the dell towards the fire access road to the mountain, Ethan told them about the local folks. "There isn't any other home or building in this area away from The Creek. That's what the locals call Crab

Apple Creek. You are the only one who will have a place up here. I know you have a hundred and eighty acres abutting the national forest. That part of the forest is off limits to people. It is a wildlife sanctuary and refuge. Only the National Parks Department forestry wardens are permitted there and they go only if ordered to. You shouldn't be bothered by anyone except locals who live on your land. They are from a time long gone by and those of us in the area leave them alone. They come down to the store for supplies. To be honest with you, these guys are moonshiners. They're not a big operation by any means - mostly for the locals. I hear you told the marshals to tell them they were welcome to stay as they are. They sure will appreciate that. They live in the northeast corner of your property. That's what that blue mark on your map is. I suspect you will not be building close to them as there are no thermal springs near them anyway. You will probably find a jar of shine on your back steps once in a while. They are harmless and very appreciative of your decision to let them remain on the land. As far as they're concerned, they own the land they use because their families have been here since before time began."

Matthews laughed. "Emily, even the marshals don't know where they're located. They know how to stay hidden. It's been the guys at the store who have been the messengers between us and those two characters. The feds have decided not to find them as their operation is very small and involves only the locals."

Emily laughed as she said, "Great. Nice to know I will be accepted around here by the real locals."

They had turned onto the fire access road and stopped about a half mile into the forest.

Matthews spoke quietly, "This is the beginning of your land. Welcome home Emily."

She stood there and cried softly. She felt a piece of the past year finally beginning to slip away. It was quiet here. You could feel the wind in the trees and hear the soft sounds the animals made as they wandered about. Ethan looked at her and all he wanted to do was hold her and comfort her and let her know she was safe. Matthews put a hand on her shoulder and let her have this moment.

Emily took a deep breath. "Sorry guys. It's just been a hellish year and it finally feels like I just might be safe again. OK. Ready to walk. Shall we? Lead the way Ethan."

Ethan began walking the trail. He was torn. He wanted to destroy the person who was responsible for the terror he had seen in her eyes that made her cry. And, then, he just wanted to take her in his arms, comfort her and tell her he would protect her and that no one would ever bother her again. What a fine mess his emotions were in. He stopped after about ten minutes.

"This is one place where the hot springs come to the surface. As you can see, this is a large spring that is used by the locals from time-to-time. As we keep walking, I'll show you the spot where three more springs surface and where I think you may want to consider building. The site would be two miles off road from the access road. However, the way we are walking it, it is about a mile from here. About a fifteen minute walk. We'll look at the map when we get there. There are two other sites you may want to look at, too. But that will have to be tomorrow as they are farther in. Let's go."

They walked another fifteen minutes down a trail that had been recently thinned. Ethan stopped on a small rise that faced west. It was in a natural clearing. They had passed the three springs that Ethan had mentioned.

Matthews looked around. He liked what he saw as far as security was concerned. The forest surrounding the clearing was dense. There were openings in the forest where animal trails could be seen. They were narrow so not to be a worry at this time.

Emily looked around. She liked the clearing but the energy was off here. Something was not in balance. She spent a few minutes walking the perimeter and then came back to the top of the rise.

"This is beautiful. No doubt. But the energy is off balance. Not the place for me. How about we come again tomorrow morning to look at the other sites you mentioned Ethan? I'd like to see them as soon as possible please."

Matthews and Ethan nodded their heads.

"OK. How about an early start. Say around eight?" Matthews and Ethan agreed with Emily's suggestion.

"OK then. Let's walk back down to the Jeep."

They talked about the need for security and only one access road and driveway. Emily said she wanted her home to face west-southwest on the side of the mountain. She did not want to be on the top of anything. - too open to everyone. She treasured her privacy and needed to know she would be able to see who came and went. All agreed. They then discussed the forest itself.

Ethan began. "These mountains have been here since the separation of Pangea. They are the oldest formations on the North American continent. They look small compared to the Rockies because they have been eroded by climate and weather for millions of years more than the Rockies. They tell a magnificent story of the geological formation of the planet. Those hot springs are really release vents for active volcanoes. We do have an occasional earthquake around here. No more than a two or three on the Richter Scale. Once, I think they had a four something about twenty years ago but it was deep in the Earth and did little damage if any. Mostly shaking and such. Once in a while, when a natural landslide or land shift occurs, the most amazing crystals and gems are brought to the surface. I have a collection of my own as do a lot of the folks in the area. Those moonshiners have a quartz crystal that probably weighs about a hundred pounds. They won't let anyone touch it and only a chosen few have ever seen it. It's amazing with many points and colors. Yes, they let me look at it recently. They might let you look at it, Emily, since you're letting them stay put. It's worth asking about. Anyway, we get about three to four feet of snow a year. It stays in the mid-30's during the winter and summer temps are around the low 70's. There is the occasional snowstorm or blizzard. It just happens. And, there are some loud and crazy thunderstorms during the warm weather days. I wouldn't be surprised if they start to pop up soon since we are at the edge of winter and the beginning of the spring. Any questions so far?"

Emily stopped walking. "Wow. You are full of information. Matthews, did you know he knew all this stuff? I won't need the internet at this rate. I'll just call Ethan if I need to know something," she teased with a giggle in her voice.

Matthews laughed outright. "She's got ya there, Ethan. Emily, this guy holds a Ph.D. in geology and has been involved in several archeological projects in the surrounding area. Don't let that outdoorsman façade fool you. He is amazing when it comes to his mountain. His family has been here longer than records show. You tell her Ethan."

Ethan looked sheepishly at Emily and said in an apologetic manner, "Matthews is right. I wasn't trying to hide anything. Since we're at the Jeep, why don't I save the family history lesson for another time, maybe over dinner and a fire at my place sometime soon? You let me know. Time to get going as the sun is about to drop below the trees and you are not familiar with this road. If you'd like, I'll drive us back to your place so you can get an idea of how to maneuver this road."

Emily agreed and they all piled into the Jeep and drove down the dirt access road to the main road. By the time they reached the main road, the sun had truly set and the night was upon them. It was really dark. The only light came from the headlights. The moon hadn't risen yet but a few stars could be seen through the treetops.

Matthews offered, "How would you two like to join me at the country store for supper? I hear they have an amazing menu."

Both agreed. They parked at Emily's house and walked over to the store and settled in for an evening of good food and easy talk with all who came by. Michael and Ted joined them at the big country table. They took their orders, served them then sat and ate and chatted with them between customers.

Michael asked, "I see you went up the mountain. Did you find a spot you like yet?"

Emily replied, "No. We only had time to look at one site. More tomorrow. Ethan, do you know where the sacred native sites are? I don't want to choose a site then find out it's a sacred one."

"Yes, I know where they are located. No problem there. Once you choose your site, I'll set up that meeting with the chiefs of both tribes."

"Good. Thanks. Guys, you have outdone yourselves. This food is great. I may not have to cook at all with you two so close by."

Ted smiled. "We love to cook especially for people who appreciate good food and our efforts. Seconds anyone?"

All shook their heads no and sighed.

Ethan set back in his chair and stated, "Every time I eat here, you guys corrupt me more with your special sauces and good home cookin'. I think I'll have some water and just enjoy the company. Here comes Miss Cora. Now she's a character. Not surprised at her showing up so soon. She keeps her finger on the pulse of everything that goes on in The Creek. Hey Miss Cora… what's new?"

The men stood as she came in.

Cora marched over to the table. She looked to be in her late sixties or early seventies but she moved like she was a young woman. She poked a finger at Michael and stated, "So. We have a new one and you haven't bothered to tell me about it. What good are you?"

Michael smiled and said, "Now Miss Cora, if I told you everything I know you wouldn't have anything to find out and you'd be pissed-off bored."

"Michael, you're a real wise-ass. Didn't your Mama teach ya to respect your elders? I'm sure she did. You just chose not to listen. Ted, how do ya put up with this wiseass anyway?"

Ted laughed. "Miss Cora, I guess it's true what they say about true love…being blind to all the bad stuff."

"I guess so." Cora looked right at Emily. "So, who are you and why are you settlin' here? Aren't there better places for you to live in?"

Emily fired right back, "Sure. But this is where I want to be so I am gonna' build here and stay here. Got a problem with that? If ya do, Miss Cora, we can settle that right here and now."

Cora chuckled. "Yup. A right feisty one we got here. Seems to me ya can hold your own against me and that's saying somethin'. Well, better to have ya as a friend than an enemy. Welcome to The Creek. What's yur name?"

"Emily. Nice to meet you and thanks for the welcome. I'm not here to make any noise. Just want to settle in and be at peace. That OK with you?"

"Yup. Right fine with me. Now boys, did y'all see those crazy lights in the night sky a few days back? And don't try to tell me they was from airplanes and all. I know crazy lights when I see them. I've seen them all my life and know what I've seen to be UFOs. Well, did anyone see them or talk to y'all about them?"

Ted looked around at the others before he spoke. "Yes, Miss Cora, we all saw the lights, except Emily and Matthews. They weren't here yet."

"I know that. What do ya take me for… dumb? Well, where do ya think they were headed? I'm thinking the Applewood Grove. Seems they're always headed that way. They seem to stop right over the grove."

Ethan agreed. "Yup. I think that's where they were headed, too. I've been in the grove at night when those lights come over and I run like hell to get outta' there. Not sure what they are. Don't really want to find out alone, either."

Ted added, "The weird thing is whatever it is doesn't make any sound. It's absolutely quiet. Not a sound heard when they are here. Not the night animals or anything. They seem to hover for a few minutes, then move away in a flash. Gone. Not like any airplane or jet or whatever I've ever seen. And I should know, being a pilot and all."

Cora added, "That's what I'm sayin'. This time the lights were blue and purple and yellow like a fog movin' in. Then, a beam comes down to the grove for a minute and then just disappears. Strangest thing. I bet those natives know about them. They been here longer than any of us. Maybe I'll get over to the chief's house and talk with him. He probably has a better explanation than the local sheriff does. Those Catawba and Cherokee may have fought hard in the past but now they seem to be real peaceable with each other. I'll just amble over that way in a few days and see what I can find out."

Ethan shook his head at Miss Cora. "That sounds like a good idea. Would you please let me know what they have to say? Would be real interesting to us all."

"Alright Ethan. For you, I'll share the info. Time to be movin' on."

With that, Miss Cora Cartwright left leaving no doubt about how she felt about outsiders.

Michael, Ted and Ethan sat down shaking their heads.

Michael was the first to speak. "Whew! You sure made a good impression on Miss Cora. She's about as tough as they get around here and she likes you. Or as close to liking anyone as she can be. She must have been impressed with the way you stood up to her. She usually drives people away with her harsh talk. Good for you, Emily. You just passed the first test of acceptance around here. Looks like you'll do just fine in The Creek."

Emily looked at them all. "So, what's this about UFOs?"

Matthews was the first to speak up. "This place has a long history of reporting UFO sightings. The feds take no official stand. That's all I can say."

They all looked at Matthews with that 'We know you have more to say' look on their faces. They waited. And waited. And waited.

Finally, Matthews spoke. "If you'd like to have a friendly chat about local lore and legends then I'll add my own personal two cents worth. Other than that, I have nothing official to say."

Emily popped back with, "We get it."

Ethan stood to leave.

"Time to get along home. This has been a real treat. See y'all tomorrow. Emily, may I walk you to your door?

Michael and Ted exchanged looks and Matthews said his good byes.

"Why, yes. Thanks Ethan. See you tomorrow Matthews."

As they stepped out into the night, the clear, crisp cold hit them. Emily shivered.

"I know it's cold in these mountains, but to feel it after the warm cozy store is a bit of a wake-up call. Good thing my house is just a few steps away."

Ethan hooked arms as they walked across the road to her front door. Emily felt very warm and a bit giddy. It had been a long time since someone had touched her in a nice way. Ethan's hand covered hers as they reached for the doorknob at the same time.

Electricity shot through them. They looked at each other then quickly away. Ethan cleared his throat and Emily took a step back.

The just stared at each other for what seemed a long time. As Ethan moved closer to her Emily leaned into him. She could feel Ethan's breath on her face as his hand went around her back to steady her. She hoped he would kiss her. The thought of that strong mouth on hers was almost more than she could bear.

Ethan was fighting with himself. She felt so soft and warm through her coat. He wondered what she would feel like without any clothes. He wanted to take her mouth and crush it with his. He bent to kiss her and caught himself. He moved back a step and took a deep breath.

Emily did the same. "Well, I, ah, guess I should, ah, say goodnight now."

Ethan looked at her. She was blushing and breathing fast. "I guess so unless there's some details you have questions about." He couldn't believe he was suggesting they go inside together. He sure as hell didn't want to get involved again. No way.

Emily stuttered, "Ah, no, I mean, no thank you Ethan. It's late and I'm tired. I'll see you at eight tomorrow morning. And, uh, thanks for walking me home. It was very gallant of you."

She smiled as she let herself in and closed the door. She stood against the door for a moment. She was sure she was going to melt right then and there. She was wet! He was gorgeous, strong, and handsome. He had a rugged look about him and smelled of fresh cut wood. His hand was strong and gentle at the same time. How she'd love to feel that hand on her wet self. And, she was sure he had a hard-on. Oh fuck! What the hell was happening to her? She hadn't even been in her new home for more than a day or so and she was going nuts over one of the locals. And she would have to be around this guy for the rest of her life, especially since he was building her new place. She purposely moved away from the door, took off her coat and boots and went to the kitchen for something to do. She decided on some chamomile tea. Fat chance she would get to sleep but she had to try. Anyway, fantasizing about sex with Ethan would be considered a great pastime.

Ethan took off for his truck. He stopped in the middle of the road trying to remember where he had left it. He wasn't sure what was happening to him. He was always in control of everything. He looked around and saw his truck on the side of the store. As he got in and started it up, he had to sit for a moment and rethink what had just happened. There definitely was something between him and Emily. Any fool could see that. And when their hands had touched... Jesus! He could have sworn there was a lightning bolt between them. Sure felt like it. He had a hard-on before he even knew what was happening. He wanted to kiss her, to possess her mouth and touch her everywhere. Jesus fucking Christ he didn't need this. He had wrapped his heart up so tight years ago he was sure nothing would get to him. And now Emily. He was getting really hot. He rolled down all the windows even though it was cold outside and drove off towards Pine Ridge and his home. He had to think things through. Come up with some way to be all business around her. Stay professional and cordial. He'd think of something by tomorrow morning when they went back up the mountain to find that site for her new home. Jesus! This was gonna be a long project. She was building the house, stables and more. Probably gonna take at least a good year to get everything finished. Ethan looked out the front window and realized he was in his driveway in front of the garage. How had he got all the way home without remembering the drive?

CHAPTER 8

While Ethan and Emily were fighting fate, Matthews was on a conference video call with the bureau, the marshals and Interpol. Seems Emily's disappearance had finally been noticed by Yuri. He was beyond pissed. His pawn Nick was in federal lock-up, Nick's supposed wife Barbara couldn't be found anywhere and believe you me, he had enough contacts to find her, even if she were in a morgue in pieces.

The bureau and marshals had decided to step up the security on Emily. They were about to inform Matthews and the team of the new information.

Bureau Chief Johnson, U. S. Marshals, D.C., started with, "Matthews, you and the combined team are to be commended for your work thus far. Great job by all, especially you, their lead. Now, we have assigned three military type special ops agents to the mountain. They will be joining Ethan Sutherland's building crew for the duration starting tonight. They will report directly to you, Matthews, in about five minutes. Bring them in on this call. There are two men and a woman. Excellent in all areas of special ops including recovery efforts. Not that we are planning on anything like that. They will live in Crab Apple Creek and Pine Ridge. Ethan Sutherland is a retired special ops soldier. He has worked with us before. He is not being given ANY information about the operation this time except we want him to hire these three and have them work on Emily's project and one other in the area just the other side of Pine Ridge. Two of them will be on Emily's project at all times. They are master carpenters and the woman is an accomplished architect with a specialty in the field of alternative energy use… thermal springs. Fits right in with the building plans. The security plans should have been received by Ethan and you, Matthews. Confirm."

71

Matthews replied, "Confirmed. And that knock on my door is probably the new team members. Excuse me for a moment."

Matthews looked out the window and saw three people holding the specially designed badge for this project. He let them in and motioned them to the kitchen table.

"Here they are, Sir. Positive ID received. Welcome to the team, Anderson, Mellow and Murphy."

Chief Johnson continued, "Welcome aboard. Good to see you made it there. Report to Matthews about the equipment we have shipped to Sutherland. Please report to his place at zero five hundred and check the equipment. Report to Matthews. He will contact me. Let me know if any of the team need anything. Vehicles will be delivered tonight by twenty-two hundred hours. Five special mountain terrain vehicles, two sedans and two pick-up trucks with all the bells and whistles. Make sure you go over these vehicles in detail Mellow. I want a good report."

Mellow replied "Yes, Sir. As ordered Sir."

Chief Johnson introduced Interpol's connection for the Russian project. "Everyone, this is Sam Brown."

"Good evening everyone. Here I am known as Petr... that's Peter... Baronowski. I speak fluent Russian as I was raised in St. Petersburg. On to the business at hand. We have been following Yuri for a number of years. We have much information on him, but are unable to gather solid proof of his involvement in numerous murders, drug and money laundering, human trafficking and other dealings. Currently, he is on a rampage as his number one New England boy, Nick Gordon, has been caught red-handed and is in federal custody in solitary protection. His attorneys that were furnished by Yuri were arrested on outstanding warrants too numerous to go into and his Court appointed attorney is in protective custody as well. We don't want any of Yuri's contacts to get to him. The guy doesn't know what hit him. Anyway, we are pressuring Nick for information. He is not cooperating. He thinks he's a tough guy. His arraignment date is next Friday, in ten days. We are trying to arrange for the Judge to do the arraignment in his cell. High security issues at hand.

"All agencies have been monitoring all channels of communication since Barbara went missing. No one seems to have a clue as to what is happening. Yuri has people all around the globe looking for her. He sent a couple of men to the house in New Hampshire, but when they got within a few miles of the place, they turned around and left. Seems there were lots of unmarked cars sitting along the road. They got spooked. We followed them and watched when they reported to their contact. He promptly killed them and left them in an off-the-road run down area. The assassin has been taken into custody and is being questioned. Not very cooperative either. I'll turn this back over to Chief Johnson now."

"Thanks Sam. As for the incident in Pennsylvania... that was just pure dumb luck for us. Terrifying for Emily, I'm sure. We've been after that guy for about a year now. Got him and his drug dealing group on solid evidence. No connection to Barbara's disappearance whatsoever. A team was in place to apprehend the guy when you all radioed in about staying there.

"So, that brings us to today. We have added the special ops team as a precautionary measure. Just want to be sure Emily is safe. We've added new teams in strategic places around the globe in an attempt to apprehend Yuri as soon as possible. Please keep yourselves on high alert. Matthews, you have the newly added orders in place. Let me know if you need anything else. Yuri has people in Charleston, South Carolina and in Raleigh, North Carolina. We have them under surveillance 24/7 and will let you know if they do anything out of the usual.

"And, one more thing. We are aware of the moonshiners on the mountain. They are not a problem with any of the agencies around the globe. Yuri likes to involve the locals so stay tuned-in if anyone seems to be talking about them more than usual or if you see new faces in The Creek, as they call it. The store owners are sharp guys and full of information. Keep on good terms with them. Any questions?"

Matthews answered, "No Sir. We understand. Thanks for the conference. I will keep you updated as requested. Good night."

With that, everyone signed off. Matthews turned to the three new team members.

"Welcome aboard Anderson, Mello and Murphy. Your vehicles are outside as reported and ready for your inspection. Please be as quiet as possible. We don't want to bother the locals. Report to Ethan's place as ordered. Glad to have you aboard. We are planning an 8 a.m. gathering here, then a trek up the mountain so Emily can find the site for her home. The people here are laid back, intelligent and very hospitable. The country store across the road has great prepared food and a wide supply of groceries and other stuff. Mello, you will be living in Pine Ridge, about twenty miles down the road. You can stay here tonight and move into your place tomorrow. Anderson, you are on overnight security watch. Report to the house to my left. You'll find an agent there who will get you caught up on details. Murphy, you are off duty tonight. You will be replacing Anderson tomorrow after you report to Ethan's place. Any questions?"

All answered at the same time. "No sir."

"Then, off the two of you go. Mello, take the empty room down the hall. If you're hungry, there's food in the fridge and cupboards."

Mello laughed. "Thanks Sir. We ate about two hours back. I'll go get settled for the night"

Anderson and Murphy left as Mello went to his room.

Matthews worked for a while completing his logbook notes online, looked over at Emily's house and saw a light on in the bedroom. She must be exhausted after the trip up the mountain. He smiled as he remembered seeing her and Ethan at her front door. You never knew when chemistry would strike, he thought.

All the while Yuri was beyond furious. Why couldn't anyone find that cunt Barbara? No one disappeared off the face of the Earth. Well, that wasn't quite true. He had had several workers disappear over the years and he still didn't know what had happened to them. He suspected that the man with the black hat had something to do with it. That guy was scary beyond imagination. Yuri prided himself on not being afraid of anyone or anything. But that guy with the black hat was one to be careful of. That guy scared Yuri. He would just appear out of nowhere. Then, when he was done telling Yuri what to do, he would just disappear. Yuri would turn away from him then turn back and the guy was gone! Nowhere to be seen. Nowhere for the man to go. No buildings. He insisted on meeting Yuri in a huge open field in the middle of nowhere, miles from town. He would disappear into thin air. Gone. Scary.

Yuri was in his penthouse in Moscow. He was alone as he worked at his new plan for dealing with Nick and finding Barbara. She had to be killed. Nick had to be punished then killed. He was a weasel and would tell the feds anything they wanted to know just to save his own skin. Yuri needed to get to him before that happened. He had contacts in all the prisons around the world. Only problem was, The United States had incredible security and it was hard to buy someone to do the killing. He usually used another inmate already sentenced to life. Problem was, the feds could impose the death penalty on anyone involved in killing a federal prisoner in a global case. Nick was such a prisoner. Yuri had to be very careful with the disposing of Nicholas Gordon.

Yuri threw a chair against the grandfather clock in the hall. He was beyond pissed as hell. He threw back another shot of scotch. He'd been downing shots all afternoon and it was well past midnight now. He was on his second bottle of Dewar's. How dare that bitch try to ruin his drug business? She had to be found and dealt with immediately. He would tell whoever found her that they could do anything they wanted to her before they killed her. Have fun. Fuck her all they want. Do whatever. Just be sure she was dead when they finished with her. Then, he would have that person killed as well. No reason to leave a mess behind. He always cleaned up after himself but rarely did the actual killing. No one was more important in the world than Yuri Strovonovich. He set back on his oversized black leather sofa to think about how to kill Nick Gordon and passed out before he could even begin.

While Yuri slept, he dreamed one of the most horrific dreams he had ever had. It all started with dark shadows appearing in his penthouse. They just appeared while he was working at his computer. No sound. Just these dark shadows moving across the room towards him. He tried to call out to them and found he had no voice. He tried to stand up but found he could not move. He could barely breathe. The room became dark as the blinds were closed and the lights were turned off. Only the glow emanating from the shadows illuminated the space.

Then he was floating away from the room and out into the night sky. He was terrified. He had no control. The dark shadows were all around him as he lost consciousness. When he came to, he was in the middle of the empty field where he had ordered so many of the murders to take place. There were dead bodies all around him. Some were mutilated into pieces. Some were rotting. He was laid down in the center of all of this on a stone slab. He felt as if he were about to become an offering to some demonic entity.

The dark shadows began to take shape. They were dark gray, almost black in color although the color kept changing as if they were made of vapor. They had huge black and red squares where eyes would be and a long black slit across the front of the face. No hair or ears and a body with long tentacle-like arms and legs with fingers at the end. They didn't look like any fingers Yuri had ever seen. They were more like claws with openings on the end that could suck stuff in. They surrounded him. He looked through them to see the pieces of human body parts come alive. They were bleeding bright red and the faces were screaming. The legs and hands were moving by themselves. There must have been millions of pieces moving all around. Yuri was terrified.

The leader of the monsters, that's all Yuri could think they were, came to his side and began to rip his clothes off until he was naked. He tried screaming but still didn't have a voice. He tried to get up but was paralyzed. He could see and hear and feel everything. Other creatures came forward and started to touch him. They took hold of his penis and made him have an erection. He watched in disbelief as they placed another human like creature over him and pushed it onto his penis. They then made him orgasm several times while the human like creature was on him. He couldn't think. He kept trying to scream and move but couldn't.

They kept making him cum although he couldn't feel it. They finished making him ejaculate and finally removed the human-like creature from his penis. He couldn't even think at this point. He was in pain beyond description. He was numb with terror.

Then, the man with the black hat appeared and all the vapor monsters moved away from him. The man with the hat removed his hat and Yuri saw he was a monster, too. Yuri just stared in horror.

Yuri heard the words but could not see a mouth move, "You have greatly disappointed us. You have allowed many to be caught by the law people. You call them the police. This is the first punishment you will experience. Do not let anyone else get caught by your law people. We are watching you.

You have promised your life to us. We will take what is ours if you do not give us what is due. You are but a small piece of the whole. You will be terminated and replaced by someone else. Our goal must be attained."

With that, Yuri passed out. When he woke up he found himself on his black leather sofa. He was immediately terrified. He then talked himself into believing it was all a horrible nightmare until he tried to get up. His penis was on fire. His throat and gut felt like he had been badly beaten and kicked. He couldn't even move without screaming in pain. The truth slowly hit him. It had all been real. Oh my fucking God. What kind of shit was he involved in? Monsters did not exist. He was convinced of this. But what the fuck was going on? Had he been drugged and kidnapped to believe they were real? No way.

He was in charge of his life. No one else was more powerful than him. But there was some bad shit going on. He finally got up and found some pain drugs. He took them after he threw up. He got into a hot shower hoping it would ease some of the pain. It didn't. He lay down on his bed and passed out from the terror and the drugs. He slept for almost twelve hours. He did not dream.

The CON were furious with him. They had decided to take him and brutalize him because they could. They would do whatever it took to keep the humans in line. The CON had no limits to the torture they would use to work toward their ultimate goal of complete domination of all existence.

This form of brutalization was mild compared to others they used. They hoped the human Yuri would do what he was told from now on. If not, they would dispose of him and find someone else to do their evil work.

Nick, on the other hand, was having a living nightmare of his own. Even though he was in solitary he was scared stiff that Yuri would have him killed. His new attorneys would not listen to him. He kept telling them he had no idea what was going on. He was just an antiques dealer trying to do his job. The attorneys informed him that he had been trafficking in stolen goods and the feds had a lot of evidence against him. He should just cut a deal and he might get life without parole. The feds knew he was connected to this Yuri Strovonovich guy. Yuri was as bad as anyone could be. If Nick decided not to cooperate, the feds were going for the death penalty on terrorism charges which, his attorneys assured Nick they had plenty of evidence for and would get a conviction against him.

Nick didn't know how they could have any evidence against him. He always destroyed the paperwork and his bank accounts were handled by Yuri under other company names and places. And right now, he had other things to worry about. Nick tried hard not to fall asleep. The last time he woke up in the dark with something climbing all over him. When he got the light on he discovered a huge snake ready to bite. He screamed and the snake just disappeared. It just evaporated before his eyes. He didn't know what was happening to him. He looked everywhere and the snake was not to be found.

He finally fell back to sleep only to be awakened by a feeling like he couldn't breathe. He felt hands around his neck. He tried to fight the assailant off but he passed out before he could do anything. When he came back to consciousness, coughing and gasping for air, he was alone.

This was too much. Nick knew he would be harassed in prison but he hadn't thought he'd be attacked so much right away. He was convinced Yuri had hired assassins to kill him. Nick would probably be surprised and terrified to learn that Yuri had no idea where he was. Nick's new life of terror was just beginning. The CON was responsible for Nick's nightmarish episodes. Before it was all over, Nick was going to wish it had been just Yuri ordering the attacks.

CHAPTER 9

Ethan was up as dawn broke above the tree tops. It was cold and clear. He started the coffee, timing it to be ready after a quick shower. He had finally fallen asleep after midnight. He just couldn't stop thinking about Emily. Around three he woke up dreaming of sliding hard and hot into her wet and soft place and then he came. He was surprised. He hadn't had a wet dream that he remembered in a long time. Emily was going to be a problem. A sweet, sexy hot problem he thought as he dressed. His coffee in one hand, he began to make breakfast. He decided on a hearty one and was cleaning up the dishes when his brother Ian waltzed through the door that connected the workshop to the house.

"Mornin' little brother. How'd ya sleep last night? I heard you up rather late. Something...or someone... on your mind?"

"Shut the hell up!" Ian laughed back at his older brother. "If I want you to know what's goin' on in my life, I'll send you a memo."

Ian laughed. "I don't need a memo. I can tell that Emily has you all messed up inside. It's about time someone did. It's been too long for you to be alone. You never chose the life of a monk. Now, take Carly and me, we're so crazy in love, you'd be hard pressed to find anyone else more in love than us. And even with two little ones, the magic is still there."

Ethan threw the dish towel at his brother. "I don't need you telling me how I feel. Leave it alone. I can't and I won't let that happen again."

Ian shrugged. "OK Ethan. But, you aren't always in charge of your heart. Just sayin'."

"Don't you have something to do today with the new guys? Go and get them up to speed on our operation and then get them to work, OK? They can start on the job on the other side of the ridge until we can get the excavation crew going on Emily's place. She knows exactly what she wants for the buildings so I thought I'd bring her here to the shop to begin the design project. Probably tomorrow afternoon. How's that sound to you, Mr. Architect?"

Ian just shook his head. "Sounds good. Have a nice hike up the mountain. See you tonight for the usual gathering."

With that, Ian grabbed a cup of coffee and went back to his design office in the shop.

Ethan finished up in the kitchen, grabbed his coat and headed out to his truck. He had to stop and look around. This place was beautiful. There was a kind of magic in the air this morning with the way the sunbeams shimmered through the trees and fell onto the ground. The buds in the trees could be seen now even though they were little and the ground cover was beginning to poke up green through what was left of the snow. Probably would snow a bit more before it was all over but no more than a dusting or so. The snow drops were pushing up around the base of the house and buildings. That meant the crocuses were next. Yes, siree… spring was breaking through in the mountains. Ethan was in The Creek thirty minutes later after a quick stop at the lumberyard. Always something more to order for his various building projects. And, he wanted to make sure they would be able to handle Emily's project. It was the biggest and most complex one he had had in a long time after his own home and buildings. He had built them about five years before and had finally been finished just about the same time as the wedding that didn't take place.

Ethan parked in front of Emily's house and met Matthews and two new members of the team.

Matthews made the introductions. "Ethan, these are two of the three new members of my team. They will be working on your building crew for the duration. Lots of experience in the trades and ready to go. I thought I'd have them tag along this morning if that's ok with you."

"Sure is. Welcome aboard. I think I saw the other guy at the shop as I left. He was talking with Ian. Nice to see a girl on the crew. Might help keep these guys from being total morons all the time."

They all laughed as Emily opened the door. "Is this a private party or can anyone join?"

Matthews and Ethan both stepped forward at the same time.

Ethan stepped back laughing saying, "Matthews is in charge but only for a little while longer. I don't recall seeing any carpentry skills on your list of accomplishments."

Matthews put his hands out, "You do not want to see me with a hammer… ever! Emily, are you ready to go? I believe those two gentlemen over on the store porch that are waving their hands like lunatics may want us to join them for a minute."

The group crossed the road, laughing and joking about Michael and Ted's shenanigans as they joined them on the porch.

Ted started with, "Here's some coffee and tea for y'all and some muffins to keep you from dying of starvation up on that big ol' mountain."

Emily took the bags while Anderson accepted the drinks. "Thanks guys. This is awfully sweet of you to do this for us. I might just have to make some of my famous oatmeal chocolate chip cookies as a thanks."

Michael jumped on that. "Anytime Emily. We love homemade goodies. Just bring 'em on over nice and hot and gooey and we'll have the tea ready. Take care today and I know you'll find just the right spot for your beautiful home."

They all thanked the guys and headed to the Jeeps. Ethan jumped into Emily's driver's seat while Matthews and Anderson followed in Anderson's Jeep. It was heavily equipped with the latest telecommunication equipment. Anderson would drive while Matthews turned on and tuned in.

They drove up the same access road but turned left just before it ended. This track was not much more than a wide path. Ethan explained to Emily that he had cleared it the week before just in case they needed to use it.

Emily looked around. "This is really remote isn't it? Doesn't look like anyone's been up here in a very long time."

Emily and Ethan knew Matthews was listening to the conversation.

"Not really. The forest service clears it regularly as part of the fire prevention plan right up until the deep snow settles in. Even though this area isn't known for terrible storms, it can pile up quickly with quick snow squalls that come through without warning. Just about this time of year, they start clearing a number of paths all over the Blue Ridge just to be safe. They've been notified of the transfer of land ownership to you and have offered to keep clearing the paths and access roads all around you and even in some of the adjoining areas. I told them yes on your behalf until we could figure out where the build would be and what kind of road or roads we would need to clear for all the big equipment, and then clear the final road that leads to your house. Please, let me know if you don't like where we're planning on clearing for equipment use and we'll figure something out."

Emily was quiet for a moment, then said, "Seems you guys have figured out a lot of stuff already. Ethan, I don't want to sound like a prima donna or something, but, I do not want anything taken down, bulldozed down or ripped out that doesn't need to be. I know you have to bring the big guns in for excavation and supplies and all. I know you need lots of turnaround space. How about we go over this particular detail this weekend? I have some ideas and need to know if they will work. You would know best."

"OK. And, here we are at the end of the line. Time to get those new boots dirty."

"Very funny Sutherland. Very funny."

Ethan led the group about a mile from the track. He kept on a level heading as they were about two-thirds the way up the south-southwest facing slope. There was thick underbrush which Anderson and Ethan cleared away to make a passable path. As they came around a small curve the path opened up into a clearing. They all stood stock still and watched a herd of deer eating on the far side. One of the deer must have gotten a bit of their scent. It was a buck. Had to be ten-point. He looked their way, made a noise and then the whole herd took off into the woods.

"Wow. A National Geographic moment for sure," Emily whispered.

Matthews asked, "Do you want to take a few minutes and look around?"

Emily thought for a minute. "Let's take a look at the other site. Then I'll make up my mind."

She had been chatting with her Guides the whole time and was waiting for confirmation. Not yet was the message. Almost there, but not quite yet.

So, Ethan led then back down the path for about five minutes then branched off to the right. It took them another fifteen minutes of walking before they emerged into the clearing.

As she caught her breath Emily said, "Oh my God. This is the place. I can feel it. It has all the things I will need and want. It faces south-southwest. It has a creek nearby. I can hear it above us to the backside. I can see other mountains from here. It has a natural rise where the house can be set upon. Over there," as she pointed to the right, "is the perfect place for the barn and stables. To the right and back a ways from the house. There is even a natural copse of trees to separate the buildings. And, with a huge porch, I can just see myself sitting in the porch swing or even in one of the rocking chairs watching the sunset. Oh, this is the place. This is the absolutely perfect place for my home."

Emily stood there as if in another world. She wasn't aware of the tears streaming down her face. The others saw them and just stood there amazed at what they were seeing. Emily looked at peace, as if she had finally found her safe place.

Emily didn't know for how long she had been standing there visualizing her home. She thought it might have been a bit as she looked around and saw the others looking at her.

"Oh. I am so sorry. I guess I just got a bit overwhelmed and happy at finally finding my perfect safe place to live." She put a hand to her face and found it wet. She didn't know she'd been crying. "Sorry."

Ethan spoke softly. "Emily, I don't know your whole story, but from the little bit I do know I'm glad this place gives you some peace. Let's all take a walk and see what else is on this part of the property."

They spent the next hour exploring the clearing and the nearby forest. They found the creek that was up behind the clearing coming from the east-northeast. They followed it as it wrapped itself a bit away from the western edge of the clearing. It flowed into a pond of sorts before it went back to being a creek to the south. There were a lot of animal tracks along the banks. They found a large variety of trees, both deciduous and fir. There was even a small grove of crab-apple trees just below the pond. A lot of them. There was still some snow to be walked through though not deep by any means.

They came back to the clearing and walked to the center. Emily took the muffins out of her backpack and placed them on a flat topped boulder. There were some rather large boulders in the middle of the clearing that made for a good place to sit, eat and talk.

Matthews asked Emily in a teasing tone, "So, I guess this is the place, huh?"

"Matthews! Behave yourself." This made him laugh. He hadn't seen or heard her behave like this before. He was glad she was having a good time.

"Hey, just want to be sure before I give the go ahead to start the security surveillance. That's gonna take a few days. There will be a few more people around for this part of the project. Ethan can't even give his excavation crew a heads-up until we get the OK from the security team. All that aside, this is the first time I've seen you happy. I'm so glad you could have this moment."

Emily slowly looked up at him. "Matthews… thanks. I know all kinds of shit is goin' on and this is only a short break, but I'm not going to let that asshole and all the other demons who try to ruin my life have any control. Period. I will do as you tell me. But no one, and I mean no one, is gonna take control of me ever again."

Ethan looked at her. She was in control. Wow! She was amazing. She was not playing at being in control. She WAS in control.

Anderson looked at her, too. "Good to know Emily. We have some stuff to teach you. Martial arts stuff. That will start Monday morning with me. I don't think it's gonna pose a problem for you, is it?"

"Nope. Not at all. I'm ready when you are. Well I'm guessing this clearing is about nine or so acres all together, right Ethan?"

"Just about. More like ten. Do you want to walk out the area where you want the buildings to be? I'll take pictures of the area then you can show us where you want the house and barn."

Matthews added, "Good idea. Anderson, you take the pictures for the security team. We know they will take their own but these can get them started on the coordinates. I know we found four hot springs just in the woods. Let's take pictures of them, too. Then the geothermal engineers can get started with all their measurements and stuff."

Anderson went about her work. Matthews was on his phone with his commander. Ethan and Emily walked over to the little rise.

"Ethan, I'd like the house to face south-southwest. I would like the front center to be right about here, centered in the middle of the little rise. I don't want any of the house to be backed into the mountain. Rather, I would like to use the rise for the hot tub and outdoor shower if possible. Almost as if it were a natural part of the wraparound porch. Maybe a second level or something. Is that possible?"

Ethan walked up onto the rise and stood there thinking for a long time. Finally, he turned towards Emily saying, "Yes. I think I get what you mean. We could place the tub bowl partially into the rise and the natural slope would be a great drain for both the hot tub and the shower. It needs some work, but I think we can do it. The hot springs to the north are higher than this rise so they would be able to fill the tub with a natural down-slope flow. They are one of the largest springs I've seen on the mountain or on any of the two other mountains in the area. Good for you and for the Forest Service for not selling this place to a ski resort developer. Anyway, you and I will have to get busy with some detailed plans right away. Let's walk the outline."

By the time everyone came back together in front of what would be Emily's dream home, it was well past one o'clock. They had been outside for almost five hours.

Matthews was the first to mention the time. "It's about one o'clock. Anyone hungry?" A unanimous chorus was heard loud and clear. "Let's get going back to the Jeeps and have lunch at the store. My treat."

With a great deal of teasing all around they set off down the path and returned to the Jeeps in what seemed like no time. It took them no more than twenty minutes to get back to The Creek. Pit stops were made and they all walked into the store at the same time.

Michael looked up from taking care of a customer, greeting them with, "You look tired, famished and happy. Emily must have found her place."

"Yup on all counts Michael. It is beautiful and perfect, of course. But before anything else is talked about, we need food and Matthews is paying. So, bring it all on," Emily said.

They all laughed as Ted began to set the table. "Help yourselves to the salads and bread and tell me what y'all want and I'll get busy in the kitchen."

Orders were placed, food was gathered and everyone was quiet for a bit as they began to eat. Emily was looking around the store and noticed a man and a woman talking with Michael at the register. They seemed to know each other well and the conversation looked to be jovial and enthusiastic. As they turned to leave, they looked up at Emily.

She smiled and nodded her head. They just looked at her for a split second then turned to leave. They waived at Michael as they left the store.

Emily was a bit puzzled by their behavior but shook it off. She'd ask Michael about them later.

Ted began serving the main course and the conversation picked up.

Emily leaned into Ethan and asked, "Who were those two? I smiled at them and they didn't even blink an eye. Just turned and left."

"Those two have always kept pretty much to themselves. They've lived nearby for about ten years now. They have their own farm complete with animals and gardens. They like being alone I guess. Never had any problems with them in the past. I did go out and repair their barn roof a couple of years ago after a vicious wind storm dropped a huge old oak right through the corner. They were pleasant and respectful. Paid on time. They chat with Michael and Ted when they come in. Other than that I don't really know anything about them. Just give them time. They may come around. Their place is nowhere near yours. It's on the other side of Pine Ridge but The Creek is easier to get to for them."

Matthews heard the whole conversation even though Emily and Ethan were being discreet. He made a mental note to have those two checked out. They sounded a bit suspicious to him. Could be nothing but he wasn't going to take any chances. He'd ask Michael who they were later.

No one knew anything about Emily. No one in The Creek. The only thing anyone knew was that the feds where somehow involved and she had bought all her land to build a home on and settle down. Nothing else.

Kendra knew she was a relocation project. The feds had used Kendra's services before. Kendra did not know, as far as the feds were concerned, that Emily was in the Witness Protection Program. Kendra knew a whole lot more than the feds could ever imagine.

As lunch time ended, everyone began to gather their things to go on to their next activity. Anderson and Matthews had work to do. They needed to contact the command center and get the ball rolling for the security investigation for Emily's building site. This would take about a week before the go ahead would be issued. Matthews had his work cut out for him. Surveillance crews would descend on The Creek within the next few hours to begin the in-depth process of making sure Emily's new home was safe from all angles. He would also have the two locals that were just in the store checked out.

Ethan and Emily were deep in conversation about the plans for the house as they walked out the door. They stood on the porch as they continued an animated conversation for all to hear.

Emily was pointing out to Ethan, "Yes. The hot springs on the north side should work. What will we use for a back-up source? The springs on the west side? They're still above the house. Something to think about."

"Where do you get all this information and energy? I've never worked with a homeowner that was so knowledgeable about building and plumbing and everything. This is gonna be fun."

Emily laughed. "You haven't seen anything yet. So, your place tomorrow afternoon around one? I'll just jot down a few ideas for you."

"I'm sure you will. Have a nice afternoon. See ya tomorrow." With that Ethan jumped into his truck and drove off.

Matthews and Anderson walked with Emily across the road.

"Seems like you are well on your way to designing your place. We'll need to work with you tomorrow morning concerning security and all. How about you come over to my house around ten? That should give you enough time to wake up."

"Funny Matthews. So, your sense of humor is showing. OK. Ten o'clock it is. Thanks for today you two. And, yes, I know, if I want to drive anywhere I need to give you a few minutes warning. Thanks."

Emily walked in the front door of her little house, closed it and sighed. Alone at last. Finally time to just be in her space. She had the whole rest of the day to let go and be Emily. First things first...music. She chose one of her own rock and roll mixed CDs. The Eagles poured forth and she turned it up loud and sang along with them. She was finally happy in her own place. She could listen to her music whenever she wanted to as loud as she wanted to. This was fun. A bit of a revolution taking place in the kitchen. She decided to bake those cookies she had promised Michael and Ted.

As she began making the cookies her mind wandered back to her family farm. She saw her Mom and Dad smiling at her. She paused for a moment, acknowledging the love they were sending. She had a nice chat with them as she put cookie dough on the baking sheets and placed them in the oven. A good amount of tasting was going on as well.

"Mom. Dad. Nice to hear from you and thanks for sending the Love. It really is all about the Love isn't it? I've been so crazy this last week with trying to stay alive and safe I haven't had the time or privacy to talk with you. I love you both dearly. I need your help with this new home thing so I am asking you and everyone on the Other Side to help me. And, as if you didn't know, that Ethan guy is hot. Whew. Sizzlin'. I feel a strong connection to him. I'll go slowly if I can around him. My gut tells me he is a safe soul. So, I'll trust you guys with that and look for the confirmations as always. I loved the site you gave me. I got your message the minute I saw it. The instant vision of my home and barns is what let me know it was the perfect place. I'll keep looking for more signs as we go along. Time to take the cookies out. I'll check in with you and everyone again later. Love you. Miss you."

Emily changed the baking sheets around and slid the baked cookies onto the cooling rack. Nothing like a warm cookie all gooey from the oven.

Taste testing was an essential part of baking. She laughed. She ate two cookies and sipped her tea as she let her mind wander over the site and the plans she had for her house.

She spent the rest of the afternoon finishing the cookies and cleaning up, making a list of all the things she wanted to have in her new home. It was pages long. But, this was the only chance she would have at this so she kept thinking of every little thing she could She told herself she would make a spreadsheet later that detailed all the different areas of her home. She laid her head back against the pillows on the couch and woke up a few hours later.

As she woke up her tummy protested loudly. She looked at her phone and was surprised to see that it was almost seven o'clock. It was twilight outside. She stretched, threw off the blanket she must have grabbed while she slept and got to her feet. She caught her breath as she saw her Native American Indian warrior protector Spirit standing in the doorway to the hall. He looked so huge in this little house. She smiled, bowed and thanked him for taking care of her. She hadn't seen him for a long time although she knew he was always with her. He showed himself to her when something was about to happen around her. He always made sure she was safe. So, now, she would be well tuned in to all that was going on around her. All of a sudden she knew why he was here. She was going to be meeting with the Catawba and Cherokee chiefs on Sunday afternoon to discuss the land she was going to disrupt. OK. She would be sure to be most respectful and gracious during their time together. Ethan had set up the meeting and she was looking forward to it. Well, that explained that.

With that settled, Emily began making something for supper. She looked out across the lawn towards the south part of The Creek. She could make out a few car headlights winding their way down the mountain. That was all. It was dark and quiet. She ate her supper while watching TV. Not much on tonight as she settled with the History Channel. They were exploring the history of Bootleggers, Rumrunners and Moonshine. She smiled as she realized they were talking about her part of the world. This was her part of the world now so she had better pay attention. She liked history lessons like this. The show ended around ten and she called it a night. She was sure she dreamed as usual, but she didn't remember a one.

Saturday started out as another beautiful day on the mountain although the forecast mentioned a possibility of flurries with little to no accumulation. Emily was a little sore from hiking around the mountain. She laughed at herself as she decided she better get used to being a lot more active than she had been. She had a mountain to take care of for crying out loud. And, she would have horses and chickens and gardens. No room for sissies.

She laughed as she got her day started. She was to meet with Ethan at one o'clock at his place in the workshop. This morning she was meeting with

Matthews and his team to begin to understand the security measures they would be putting in place in and around the outside of her home, the barn, stables and the property. She didn't want to think about such horrible possibilities but they were a real part of her life for now. And, she had to take some of her cookies to the store before the meeting. Well, she was ready so why not now? Emily set out for the store and had just entered the door when she heard her name called out.

"Emily? Is that you? I have something I want to show you," shouted Michael as he came to greet her.

He gave her a little hug and looked down at the plate in her hands. "Cookies? Are those the oatmeal chocolate chip cookies you threatened us with? I'll just have to take them away from you and sample one. Hey Ted, Emily brought homemade cookies for us."

Ted appeared out of nowhere. He took one, bit into it and closed his eyes and smiled.

"This is divine. Oh my God. The chocolate is all gooey and what is that flavor I'm tasting? Just a hint of... cinnamon?

Emily was laughing at the guys. "Yes, it's cinnamon and something else. Can you figure it out?"

Michael closed his eyes as he concentrated on eating what was left of his cookie.

"Hmmm. I think it's nutmeg. Right?"

"Yes. Good for you. Not many get the nutmeg. Most get the cinnamon though. These are for you guys. Enjoy," she said as she handed the plate to Michael. But Ted grabbed it first.

"Mine," Ted exclaimed. "All mine. Fat chance you will get anymore," he said to Michael as he tried to run away.

Michael caught him by the arm and gently wrestled the cookies away. "Not so fast my friend. We share everything. Remember? Anyway, you wouldn't want Emily to think we were barbarians, would you?" He winked at Emily.

Emily was laughing so hard she could hardly breathe. Finally she begged, "Stop. Please stop. You two are hilarious. I need a minute to breathe. Since you both like the cookies so much, I guess I hold some sort of power over you just in case I want to know something and order something that you don't want to give me. *Hee Hee Hee.* I rule!"

Michael and Ted laughed along with Emily. Finally the three of them calmed down enough to chat about other things before bringing the conversation back to the cookies.

"These really are great cookies. Any time you want to make some for us to sell, just let me know. We handle some local baked goods from time to time. And, we love eating them."

"Thanks Michael. Maybe I will do just that after I get settled in a bit more. I think I'm going to have my hands full with the building thing."

Ted added, "Anytime Emily, anytime. You may want to make a gift of these to the two chiefs you are meeting with tomorrow. They love cookies, too, and the offer of a gift, especially something handmade, is a sign of respect towards them. It would make things less awkward... so to speak."

"Oh, thanks for the idea. Would you guys have a small basket I could buy? I haven't a thing yet. I'll start buying things once I'm in my home. This house is a bit small for too much more stuff."

Ted took Emily by the hand and led her to a side door just beyond the register counter. "This is where we keep our private collection. You are free to take whatever one you want."

"Oh, Ted. No. I'll need to pay for it of course."

"No. It's a gift from Michael and me. Please."

Emily displayed a small smile. "Thanks so much. You are very generous. This looks like it would do very nicely," she said as she picked up a small oblong basket with a handle. The basket was a dark brown color with a broad weave. She could place some of the decorative paper towels she had in the bottom and over the top of the cookies.

Ted and Michael both smiled as they looked at each other. They all returned to the store as Emily made her way to the door.

"Thanks again, guys. This was awfully sweet of you. Glad you like the cookies."

"I'm gonna have to hide these from Ted if I want to eat anymore. He really is a true Cookie Monster."

Ted laughed and waved as Emily closed the door behind her. She looked around as she crossed the road. No cars or trucks on the road. It was rather quiet for a Saturday morning.

Emily spent the next two hours with Matthews and one of the team going over the security systems that would be put in place. They had more equipment and technology then she had imagined and all digitally run. Indoor and outdoor motion sensors, cameras, infra-red sensors that would pick up heat signatures, recording capabilities on every piece of equipment they used, and sensors that tracked how much electricity was used and where were discussed. There would be cameras on the perimeter of the property, on the outside of every building, inside every building in every room including the bathroom. That was gonna have to be worked on. There were climate and weather reporting devices for temperature, wind speed, precipitation of all kinds, and fog sensors that would trigger other sensors to track people and animals emitting heat signatures.

Matthews explained to Emily that most of this technology was already in use in her rental house and her vehicles. He told her they would go over every piece of equipment in the next few days so she would know what to do with them if she needed help in any way. The devices would automatically set off alarms, both silent and sound, in certain circumstances. He explained that they would have some practice sessions with the equipment so she could learn how they worked, how to use them, how to reset them and how to maintain them even though the marshals would always have a technician close by to monitor and maintain the equipment for the rest of her life.

Emily sat back and was silent for a bit.

"Whew. This is really happening. I mean I know it is really happening but getting all detailed and stuff with the security thing is a bit scary and un-settling. I know you need to do this and I know I need to know all about it. Just the same, this is scary shit."

"Emily, I understand. I think. I've never been in your shoes before so I don't really know what you are feeling. I just know from my work experience how dangerous some people are and how absolutely unthinkable all the stuff that they are involved in is. It scares the shit out of me, too. That's why I'm in this line of work. I want to stop these guys and be a part of the bigger team that works to take these guys down. All my training and experience tell me that we have what it takes to not only keep these guys away from you, but to protect you as well. As far as I'm concerned, these guys are pure evil. Demons in every way. I'll be totally honest with you about something. I've seen stuff happen that there is no earthly explanation for. I am convinced that there are good forces that help us all the time. There have been times when I've seen agents take a shot that should have killed them on the spot, but, somehow, some of them have lived and recovered one hundred percent. No way they should have but they did. That has convinced me that there is a bigger some-thing in charge. A better something. Something that is stronger than the darkest enemy out there. I just don't know what it is. Just hope and pray it stays with us, with all of us as we protect you."

Emily looked up at Matthews and slowly began to move her head up and down. "Yes Matthews. I know there is a great positive energy out there. I call it the White Light. The Divine. I have felt its love. That love kept me safe when I was with Nick and got me out of there through your agencies. You don't have to agree with me. I don't need your approval. I know what I know. This is part of the greater battle between the Light and the Dark. I know it is. So glad you have decided to work with the Light. My thoughts anyway."

They were silent for a long time, lost in their own thoughts. They both looked up at each other at the same time.

"So, shall we talk about a few more security details before lunch? I do believe you have a one o'clock meeting with Ethan and it's noon already."

Emily sighed. "Yup. I'll let ya know how that goes as well. Although I'm sure Ethan will give you all the details before I do."

They finished up and Emily went home, fixed some lunch and was on the road to Sutherland Builders to meet with Ethan by twelve-thirty. Boy, was this gonna be some meeting, she thought.

She had no doubts that the two of them were attracted to each other. The air practically sizzled when they got close to each other. She smiled as she drove the winding road toward Pine Ridge to the turn off for Ethan's road. He was hot! She could almost feel his hands on her. She really liked to have her breasts touched, licked and sucked. It made her wet and more than ready to cum. She could almost imagine Ethan's mouth and tongue all over her breasts. She was so lost in thought she almost missed the turn off. Damn. She had to get herself under control fast as she was just a few minutes away from Ethan's place. She turned off the heat and rolled down the windows.

She was a bit cooler when she turned into the drive that led to the workshops and office of The Soaring Mountain Builders. She drove towards the open parking area on the right of the house and parked just outside the door to the office.

She shook herself as she got out of the Jeep. She took a deep breath as she opened the door to the office and there he was looking all masculine and hot. Damn. She could just tear off those clothes and jump his bones without a second thought.

Ethan was thinking the same thing as he looked around from the drawing table he was working at to take in the view of the goddess that had just walked through the door.

She took his breath away and made him hard. Damn. He had to get himself under control and right now. His body reacted like a teenage boy looking at a porn magazine.

As Emily closed the door behind her, Ethan stepped forward.

"Hi there. Welcome to the home of Soaring Mountain Builders. I'll take your jacket and hang it right over here," he offered. She handed him her jacket and he placed it on a hook on the wall near the door. He felt like a teen on his first date, all tongue tied.

Emily swore there was a battle between alligators going on in her belly. She felt shaky and unable to take a deep breath.

"Let's get started shall we? There's a great deal of work to do before we can even think about digging a hole for the foundation. Like deciding on the shape of the house to start."

Emily agreed. "Yup. So, where do we work? We're going to need a lot of room to spread out the drawing paper."

Ethan led Emily to a very wide drawing table. "I had this made for me as I do a lot of work that is bigger than the average house. Here, grab that stool and pull it up. Tell me what you want."

Emily almost laughed out loud. *You. Naked on a bed.* She behaved herself and began. "First of all, I would like to thank you for taking on my project. I've never designed a house before so please be patient with me. I know exactly what I want just not all the technical terms for the stuff. That's where your expertise is sorely needed, OK?"

"OK. Let's start with the basic shape of your house. Could you draw that for me? As if you were looking down at it from the trees?"

"That I can do." With that Emily took a pencil and began to draw the shape. She had to re-do a few times but eventually she had the general idea on paper.

"I want a Cape Cod style as the overall shape but want to add some more room to it. A regular Cape is way too small. What I really want is an old fashioned farm house with a few tweaks and all high tech stuff. It needs to look like a farm house from times gone by with the Cape essence. It will be three floors tall with a walk-in attic. The first floor is for business purposes and will have a huge country kitchen. All the modern stuff will be behind the scenes. The second and third floors are for my own living areas. The first floor will have a big gathering room with a fireplace in the middle of the whole structure that goes up to all three floors. It will be open on two sides on the first floor only. The central room will flow into a hallway with a large bathroom with a shower, not tub. Then the hall will continue on into the kitchen with room for at least twenty people at the table or tables. We'll have to see how that works out. Big cupboards. Two ovens, convection and regular. A big commercial fridge and dishwasher. Top brands or whatever your specialists think is the better brand. I would like a central work island with a butcher block top. The other counters will be a marble pattern. I would like a hanging pot rack above the central work island. Oh, sorry, I got ahead of myself. So, the shape is something like this." Emily pointed to the drawing.

Ethan looked at the outline for a minute then began asking questions.

"Do you have any idea about the square footage you want?

"No. Sorry. I just can't visualize the numbers as real space. How big is this room?"

"What are you thinking?"

"This room is about half the size of the big room on the first floor. If I could actually see the measurements roped off then I could get a better idea of what I need. I know this is asking a lot of you. I just want to make sure I get what I want the first time around. Could we stake the shape and rooms out on the mountain next week? That would really help me figure this out."

"Yes we can. I think that is a great idea. How about Monday morning nine o'clock? I'll pick you up. In the meantime, let's get as many details down as you can think of room by room."

"Oh thank you. I agree to everything. Ready? Let's keep going with the kitchen then."

"OK. Shoot."

"I want the kitchen to have that old country kitchen feel to it. You know. The place everyone always ends up in at the end of the day. The place where you feel loved and comforted. My mom and dad always made everyone feel welcome and loved when they sat at our kitchen table. Whether with food or conversation, you always knew you were important to them. There was always something cooking on the back of the stove or something was baking. Mom was a great baker and my dad always sampled everything she made. They were a pair, the two of them. You always went home feeling loved and welcome to come back."

"I know just the kitchen you want. My family is just like that. So how about the windows for the whole place? They are especially important in the kitchen and then the living room and your gathering room. Any ideas there?"

"Absolutely. Andersen windows and doors. The windows will have the grilles in them between the panes for easier cleaning. All the windows will have grilles."

"Great. We always suggest Andersen windows. You may want a different door as these mountains can be a bit much to handle some times. I'll show you some options. Will there be French doors anywhere?"

"Yes. On the first floor to walk out to the back porch and Jacuzzi room. I have a crazy notion to have a small porch deck thing built off my master bedroom, too. Not too sure how you would do that though. Think it can be done? With a roof?"

"You aren't asking for a lot are you?" Ethan laughed. "Yes, it can be done. It takes a great deal of early planning. We'll spend some time getting the finer details down for the architect before we can even think of building it. He really knows his stuff."

Ethan turned as he heard the door to the house opening.

"Speak of the devil, here he is. Ian, I would like you to meet Ms. Emily Henshaw. She just moved to The Creek. She is the person we are building that special project for. Emily, this is my younger brother, Ian Sutherland, architect extraordinaire."

Emily offered her hand as Ian reached for hers.

"Nice to meet you, Ian. We were just getting started on some of the details of the house here. I suspect you and I will be spending some time together."

"I suspect we will. Nice to meet you, too, Emily. Anything special you desire?"

Ethan laughed as Emily elbowed him. "She's already asking for complex stuff."

"Like what?" Ian asked.

"I would really like a porch with a little roof off my master bedroom."

"Why is that a special problem?" Ian asked as he looked from Emily to Ethan.

Ethan pointed at Emily and said, "Tell him the rest."

Emily smiled shyly as she explained, "My master bedroom is on the third floor in the back of the house and a walk-in attic above it."

Ian just laughed. "Of course it is. Why not? Anything else I need to know before I start working at making the near impossible a real thing?"

"Not yet unless you mean the wrap-around wide porch with roof all the way around and the Jacuzzi room off the back of that porch next to the hot spring. I guess you're gonna have to walk the land to see what I have in mind."

Ethan laughed out loud at this. Ian sent him a look that would curdle milk.

"My brother Ian isn't too fond of hiking in the mountains. He's more the paved walkway type and groomed trail kinda guy."

Ian not-to-gently punched Ethan on the shoulder. "Let's get something straight. Who taught you all about mountain hiking and showed you what gear to use and wear?"

"OK. OK. It was you. But it's been a long time since you strapped on the hiking boots, bro."

"Might it have something to do with the fact that we have two little ones under five years old and have been married just five years? Been a little busy designing all those projects you and Dad seem to be bringing into the business. When am I supposed to go hiking? I run around after those two little mountain muffins all the time as it is. Your niece runs one way and your nephew runs the other. They sure know how to run their dad around."

Both men laughed at this. Emily was enjoying the brotherly give-and-take going on. Seemed there was a strong family connection in the Sutherland clan.

Ian looked at Emily with his arms spread open. "Sorry, but my big brother can get a bit forgetful sometimes. Looks like we have our work cut out for us so, let's get busy."

Ethan rolled his eyes at his brother as they all returned to the drawing table. This time, Ian took charge of the sketch details.

"From this poor excuse of an outline, I guess you want something big, old country with all the amenities."

"Yes, Ian. That about sums it up. I forgot to add the dormers that look like little houses, not the Nantucket kind that are squared and look pathetic."

Ian laughed. "I guess you do have a few strong ideas about this house don't you?"

Emily just shrugged her shoulders as she said, "Yes, I guess I do. I know what I want in some respects and others I have no idea about. That's where you guys come in so we can be a team, right?"

Both guys nodded their heads in agreement.

The three of them sat hunched over the drawing table for the next few hours. It wasn't until the room began to look dim that anyone realized what time it had become.

"Well, I guess we've been busy for quite some time. The sun has set and it's getting really dark outside," Ethan said as he went around and turned on more lights to brighten up the place.

Emily sat up straight and stretched like a cat. Ethan just stood there staring at her as Ian watched. Oh, yeah, this guy was hooked.

"Don't know about you two, but I could eat a horse I'm so hungry. Jesus, it's already after six. We've been at this for more than five hours. I say it's time to call it quits. I need to get home. I'm a family man, remember?"

Ethan added, "Yup and your wife knows where you are so what's the problem?"

"It's not the wife, it's the munchkins. They want to play with their daddy."

"OK. Let's call it a day. Emily, thanks for spending the afternoon with us. I'll get busy with some calculations on supplies for the foundation. And, Monday, the three of us will walk the land and lay out the foundation stakes just to get an idea about the size of the thing. OK with everyone?"

Ian and Emily agreed.

"Thanks so much Ian for your time. I never knew a simple sketch could need so many details. I know the blueprints do but, crap, this has been hard work."

"I love designing custom homes. You keep coming up with all the details you want and I'll make them fit in. See you two at your house, Emily, Monday morning at eight o'clock."

With that, Ian left. Now Ethan and Emily were alone, unless you counted the body guards. There was one in Ethan's kitchen just on the other side of the connecting door and one in a vehicle parked just a bit behind Emily's.

The air was so quiet you could hear a flea sneeze. Emily and Ethan just stood there looking at anything except each other.

Emily finally took a step toward the connecting door.

"That way to the bathroom?"

Ethan smiled, "Yes, indeed. Through that door, down the hall, second door on the left. I'm sure you can figure it out."

"Thanks," was all she said as she set off through the door.

Ethan stood there kind of dazed. She was beyond sexy. Even after hours of being hunched over a drawing board, she still looked sexy as hell. His heart was beating so hard he thought he'd have a heart attack or something. He was sure she would be able to hear it when she came back into the room. He began walking around trying to collect his thoughts.

Emily was no better off. As she finished up in the washroom, she wondered if Ethan would be able to see her heart beat. It was thudding in her chest. She couldn't stay in here forever. As she walked back into the workroom she saw Ethan looking out the window on the opposite side of the room.

"What's out there?" she asked as she joined him.

"Nothing much although it is snowing just a little. Looks peaceful and quiet."

Emily moved right in front of Ethan to get a look through the window. Snow was falling in what seemed like slow motion, drifting down as if each flake didn't have a worry in the world.

She became aware of his scent. He smelled like fresh cut wood, the outdoors and a musky aftershave she immediately liked. He moved closer to her, touching her shoulders with his chest. Emily thought she was going to pass out. He felt great. He smelled great and she just wanted him to kiss her right then and there. She decided to take a chance.

As she turned around to face him, he put his arm across the small of her back as if to steady her. He really wanted to kiss the daylights out of her, make her breathless as he took her mouth. She looked up at him. Less than an inch from his mouth, she ran her tongue across her lips. That was more than enough for Ethan. He bent his head and softly touched his mouth to hers. She tasted hot, sweet and luscious. He pressed harder and pushed his tongue into her mouth. She opened wide for him as their tongues danced back and forth, tasting, exploring and demanding more. Their bodies seemed to move of their own accord as they pressed into each other. They were a perfect fit.

Emily could feel Ethan's hard-on immediately and that made her wet and wanting more. Ethan felt the softness of her breasts pushed against his chest as he pushed his hard rod against her. The kiss became heated and demanding. Emily sighed out lout and Ethan groaned.

Oh my God he thought. I need to stop this right now. This is no way to treat a lady. And Emily was certainly a lady that deserved respect and gentleness, not to be mauled by a sex crazed guy she had only known for a few hours. With a strength he didn't know he possessed, he ended the kiss and took a step backward.

Emily was surprised at her own response. She would have stripped naked and let him take her as much as she would have taken him. Where had that come from? Oh God, she didn't want him to think she was a cheap date. Good thing he had stopped when he did. No telling what they would have done. Wrong. They would have had crazy, helpless sex on the workroom floor in a hot minute.

"Well, I guess it's time for me to leave."

"Yeah. Ah, about, this. Sorry. I usually don't attack my clients like this. Not that there was anything wrong with that kiss. You get an A+ from me."

As Emily grabbed her jacket from the peg by the door, she turned and looked Ethan over from the top of his head to the bottom of his boots. "No worries, Ethan. You get an A+, too. I think I'm gonna like the way you say goodnight from now on."

With that, she flew out the door. The snow felt good on her face as she walked to her Jeep. She saluted the body guard as she got in and set off for home. She saw him in her review mirror and felt safe. She touched a button on the dash while saying, "Hi Matthews. On my way home. See you tomorrow."

Matthews just laughed as he answered, "Drive safely Emily. Enjoy the snow. See you in the morning for another security lesson." And with that he signed off and laughed.

Ethan was a bit dumbfounded by Emily's response. He thought she might be upset, but she had liked the kiss. And that comment about saying goodnight. Boy was he in trouble. The thought of her naked underneath him made his so hard he had to take off his jeans just to walk into his kitchen. He locked all the doors and turned off all the workroom lights from a panel set into the kitchen wall. Great idea Ian had had about this. He could control all the electrical equipment on the property from panels set around his house and the workroom and storage areas. Nice touch indeed. He took a cold shower to cool down. Damn, she was hot!

When Emily got home, she was smiling from ear to ear. She made herself some supper and turned the TV on not really paying attention. She was fantasizing about her and Ethan. After spending a couple of hours not watching TV, she decided to go to bed.

As she turned out the lights, she decided some fantasy time was needed. She was still wet from that kiss. Time to create the rest of that sex encounter.

She stripped off her jammies and lay there with nothing covering her. The soft light from the falling snow illuminated the room ever so slightly. She placed one hand on her breast and began to flick her nipple. This was pleasurable to a point but she preferred Ethan's mouth tugging and licking her nipple and breast. The other hand went down to her wet place. It found her clit and began to massage it.

She fantasized that the kiss had not ended. Ethan pulled her closer to him and she pushed herself harder into his stiff dick. Ethan then pulled back just enough to open her shirt, pull the sleeves and bra straps down around her arms so she couldn't move them then started to lick her breasts. He pulled her breast out of the bra and sucked it into his mouth.

Emily groaned as she finally freed her arms. She opened his jeans and pulled his hard dick out so she could handle him. Jesus! He was huge! She liked them big. Ethan pulled away so he wouldn't cum. He carried her to the couch, laid her down, took her boots off then her jeans and thong so she was ass bare. Her shirt and bra were next. She grabbed his jeans and yanked. He ripped his boots off then the rest of his clothes. As he lowered himself to her she grabbed his dick and began to pump him. He almost lost it.

Emily was rubbing her clit really hard as she knew she was about to cum. She just wanted to hold on just a minute more as she finished her fantasy.

He took her mouth and with his hand, moved hers away as he found her wet pussy and began to push inside. He made her cum with his finger then thrust into her as she grabbed his ass and pulled him in herself.

Emily came really hard. She jerked off the bed as she continued to rub herself until she felt the orgasm begin to subside. Oh My fucking God this was one of the best orgasms she had had in a very long time.

As she began to doze off to sleep, she promised herself that before long, the real thing was going to take place. She couldn't wait very long. She knew Ethan was the partner for her. She hoped he wouldn't wait too long before making the next move. She was more than ready.

Ethan was having a hard time trying to sleep. All he could think of was that kiss. She felt great against him. His dick was so hard it had taken a hand job in the shower to finally relieve him. He wanted more of her but he wasn't sure he was ready for that kind of commitment. Emily was not the kind of woman you took to bed a few times then said good-bye, it's been real nice.

He tossed and turned until well after three then he must have finally fallen to sleep because the next thing he knew the sun was shining in his face. Good thing it was Sunday or he would have been two hours late to work.

CHAPTER 10

Matthews had been up since sunrise on this quiet Sunday morning. He had been notified of a potential problem. Yuri was on a private jet headed west. He traveled a lot, but this time, the chatter they had been following was about Nick. Yuri was furious. He had sent some of his goons to deal with Nick but they had been denied access to the grounds. Seems Yuri had put a hit out on Nick which no one was able to carry out. The insiders at the prison had been caught and arrested on attempted murder charges. There were three of them: one guard, one night watchman and the prison warden himself. They were being held on suicide watch at another facility. Word was they had been on a suspicious activities list for a while and this capture was the result of a sting operation. Matthews and his crew knew nothing about the sting operation. As a matter of fact, only the FBI chief and the Interpol chief and two of their own operatives knew of it.

Matthews' orders changed. More security in the form of people and equipment was on its way to the area. Another headquarters was being set up in Boone. It would house the special ops crew and their equipment. A second site was being set up in Pine Ridge and an exclusive site was being set up on the mountain itself about a half mile north from where Emily was building her house. No one would know they were there except Matthews and his team. Emily was not to be told about any of this, nor anyone else. They would be put in place in the dark of night. The word stealth came to Matthew's mind. Holy shit! This was getting crazy sooner than he thought it would.

The agencies were taking this as a direct threat to Emily even if Yuri had no idea where 'Barbara' was. The agencies knew that Yuri had sent teams to find her. The only thing they had found was the smashed cell phone in the kitchen trash of Nick's house. All her personal things were still in the house. They searched, ripped open walls, dug up the back yard but still had found nothing. Yuri was thinking Nick had had her murdered and disposed of the body far away from New Hampshire. That's why he needed to get information from Nick. He needed to know if Barbara was dead. If she was dead no big deal. If she was still alive, she needed to be dead. Simple. Yuri would give the order and she would be murdered. But, no one could find her. Yuri was furious. That bitch. Who did she think she was? No one beat Yuri at his own game. No one!

That's what the agencies were up against. They had been following the global chatter since the Friday Barbara died. Hopefully, Yuri would not start thinking about the Witness Protection Program any time soon. That would add a whole other complicated level of craziness to the situation.

Kendra had a few things that needed her attention in The Creek as well. She was gone by dawn Sunday morning, headed to the farm of Kevin and Pam Johnson, the couple that had come into the country store and were rather rude to Emily. Kendra needed to do some damage control. She had appointed herself as Peace Maker for The Creek community, small as it was. No need to get the feds involved with the locals especially when they came off as questionably rude and secretive.

Kendra drove down the long dirt drive to their farm. It was a place of beauty. It blended into the landscape as if it had just grown there. She saw both of them coming out of the barn with milk pails and an egg basket in their hands.

They looked her way as she came towards them.

"Hey Kendra. What brings you out here at the crack of dawn?" Pam asked as they all headed towards the farm house.

"Hey Pam. Hey Kevin. See you're up early as usual. How's things around here?"

"Good. Things are good. It seems all the animals are about ready to give birth any day. We should have a few lambs, two cows, piglets and lots of chicks."

"Sounds great. I need to talk with you. Can you spare me a few minutes this morning?"

"Sure. Come on in and have some breakfast with us. I know you haven't eaten yet. You're up early today." Pam led the way onto the back porch and into the big kitchen.

"I accept. You two are great cooks. What can I help with?"

"How about you wipe down the fresh eggs and put them in their crates for our customers? You can even take them back with you to give to Michael and Ted," Kevin offered.

"Sure." Kendra sat down at a big maple wood table and got busy with the eggs. There were about five dozen or so here. Pam and Kevin were one of the major suppliers of organic eggs for the store.

Kevin asked, "What do ya need to talk to us about, Kendra? Must be important to bring you out here so early."

"You're right Kevin. I got wind of your last visit to the store when Emily and all the others were there. Seems you came off as rather rude and secretive. That has caused the feds to start asking questions about y'all. We don't need that. Not now. Not with everything that is about to take place. So, I am asking you two to ease up a lot. Go into the store in the next couple of days around lunch time and the next time you see Emily, please nod, smile, introduce yourselves, something agreeable, OK?"

Pam stood still for a moment. She was straining the milk. "I know we're supposed to be a bit rather stand-offish. Guess we got to playin' the role too well. Of course we'll get around to being more amenable and a bit neigh-borly the next time we go out. Can ya do that Kevin?"

Kevin agreed. "Yup. Don't want to rock the boat. Everything has come along just fine and it's just a few months before the big day. Didn't mean to be rude, either."

Kendra smiled and went over and hugged both of them.

"I know this assignment is a bit different for you both. Hell, it's a whole lot different. I appreciate your efforts and flexibility on behalf of our elders. And you know they do, too. Now, let's get started on that breakfast, if you haven't fixed everything already."

They set about finishing the cooking of their big country breakfast. Pam had already made the biscuits and gravy. Kevin fried up the thick cut bacon and eggs and Pam made the coffee, gathered the plates and put the fin-ishing touches on the table as Kevin served the hot foods. Pam was known for her homemade preserves, jams and jellies. Today's choices included peach, elderberry and strawberry to go with those biscuits and homemade bread.

They chatted about Emily's new house. They got caught up on the locals, the store and all the other things that happen in a tiny community and other stuff only they were privileged to know.

Kendra finally said her good-byes after helping to clean up. She was sent with the eggs for the store along with a few things for her own pantry. It was two hours after she arrived at the farm that she delivered the eggs to the guys.

"Hey Michael, Ted. I was over at Kevin and Pam's place. They asked me to bring these eggs to you. Five dozen. Those hens keep busy."

Ted took the eggs, agreeing with Kendra. "Don't we know it. They always have four or five dozen eggs every other day for us and we sell them as soon as they come in. Everyone loves the local, organic stuff."

Michael asked, "How are they? They seemed a bit off the other day when they were here."

"I heard about that. Seems they have a number of animals ready to give birth. Guess they're a bit preoccupied with that. I would be."

Ted nodded. "This is a critical time for farmers everywhere. The spring determines how many live births there are, how the crops will produce in the fall. It all hinges on the spring weather. So far, this year seems par for the course. Let's hope we don't have a late snowstorm. That could mess things up."

"Yes it could Ted. We'll just put it out to the Universe that we're having a great spring and all things are well and productive."

"Amen to that sister," was Michael's response.

Kendra waved as she left the store and returned to her house to take care of a few business details.

Emily woke up feeling great! That fantasy thing had been awesome. She was starving. She fixed breakfast, showered and was at her computer all before nine. She was meeting with the chiefs at one and wanted to do some research on their tribal activities and history before the meeting. She spent the rest of the morning learning about the fierce battles between the Catawba and the Cherokee up until the newcomers took the land. That was a sad day. Seems some of the Cherokee and Catawba escaped and hid when the white man's soldiers were forcing all native peoples to walk to some place in Oklahoma. This was later called the Trail of Tears. It involved all native people's across the eastern part of North America, originally called Turtle Island by the indigenous peoples. Thousands of natives died along the way. A sad time.

The Cherokee and Catawba were now federally recognized sovereign nations. They did not follow the laws of the United States when on their own land. There were other native nations, too, that had their own laws and enforcement agencies, their own courts, health care systems, businesses, some of which were casinos that raised money for the running of the nation. Education, health care, housing and more were funded by these casinos and other businesses located on the reservations. Fact is, some of these nation's laws were stronger and more detailed than the U.S. laws and the punishments were harsher as well. These nations took their sovereign status seriously.

After lunch, Emily went over to the store for the meeting.

Matthews was already there waiting for her. She noticed a couple of older looking men which she correctly guessed were the chiefs.

Matthews made the introductions as they settled around the oak table. Michael had placed a reserved sign on the table to make sure it was ready for this meeting.

"Emily I would like to introduce to you Chief Charles Running Bear Conway, Chief of the Catawba Nation."

"I am honored to meet you, Chief Running Bear," Emily said as she offered her hand to the chief.

"The pleasure is all mine, Emily."

"Emily, I would like to introduce to you Chief James Soaring Eagle Richardson, Chief of the Cherokee Nation of the Qualia Boundary reserve and peoples."

"I am honored to meet you, Chief Soaring Eagle," Emily said as she offered her hand to the chief.

"It is my honor to meet you, Emily. Shall we all get settled? We have a lot to discuss this afternoon," Chief Soaring Eagle suggested as they sat down.

"I've brought a gift for the two of you for this meeting. I made them myself," she offered as she set the basket of homemade cookies in front of the chiefs.

Both thanked her as they bit into them.

"These are exceptionally good. Thank you for the gift. Ted, we need coffee here, OK?" Chief Running Bear called out.

Ted responded with, "Charlie you know where it is. Help yourself."

All laughed at this and it lightened the mood.

"As you can see, some of the locals have little respect for the natives around here," Charlie said with a laugh. "Please Emily, call us by our names. I'm Charlie and this is Jimmie, whether he likes it or not."

Jimmie shot a look at Charlie, "Who appointed you the almighty grand chief around here, anyway? Don't we have a reputation of fierce warriors to keep up?"

All laughed and the cookies were passed around as everyone got themselves coffee and tea. Once settled, the conversation turned to Emily's land.

"I thank you for meeting with me. I want to honor your ancestors and need your help in figuring out if the site I have chosen is a sacred place for your peoples."

Charlie looked at Emily with a serious demeanor. "Thank you for thinking about our ancestors. We've been on this mountain and those nearby for thousands of years, both Catawba and Cherokee specifically. Jimmie and I take the responsibility of preserving our heritage very seriously. Let's take a look at the site map along with our special maps that show sacred burial grounds, sacred meeting places, ceremonial sites and ancient villages. I have prepared a clear overlay of the current day mountain so we can see exactly what is out there."

Matthews was impressed. "Great idea Charlie. Wherever did you get the idea?"

"My daughter's a school teacher, teaches geography. She uses these clear overlays all the time. She helped me create this thing with a program she has on her computer. We saved it and took it to the printer in Boone. He made the clear print in about fifteen minutes. Pretty cool, huh?"

Jimmie liked the idea. "Great idea Charlie. The next time we need to plan a powwow, I'll be sure to create one of my own and use your land!"

"Just try, Jimmie, just try."

Emily got the idea that these two were close friends no matter how much they harassed each other.

As the maps were spread out and the overlay was set in place, Emily began to see some very interesting things. She noticed that the country store sat on virgin land. Nothing had been here before except the land. They all quickly found her proposed site and started to analyze the area.

Matthews began. "Seems you have chosen a clear site Emily. But it looks like there are areas close by that are sacred and untouchable. Charlie, what are your thoughts on this?"

Charlie spent a few long minutes looking at the surrounding area then spoke slowly and for a long time.

"Yes, Emily, the site you have chosen is clear of ancient sacred land. Tell me, in what direction will your house face?"

"South-southwest. Why"

"That is excellent. It is the direction of open communication according to my ancestors, as well as Jimmie's, right?"

Jimmie nodded in agreement.

"For us, that means you are open to communication from all entities in the Universe. I understand you will be using the geothermal energy to heat your home and out buildings. That is OK with us as long as you give back all what you don't need. We protect our Mother Earth in every way." Emily nodded in agreement as did Matthews.

"There are several sacred places within a short walk of your land. These need to be left alone and not walked on. There is a burial ground, two ceremonial sites of which both are used by our Shaman four times a year. Only the Shaman and the Chief are allowed on this sacred ground. There is an ancient gathering place about a half mile to your west. It is on the border of your land and the national forest. Although we do not use it now, we still hold it sacred and the chiefs bring gifts throughout the year. It is called The Sacred Rock Meadow. I suggest we walk the land with you tomorrow when you, Ethan and Ian go to stake the outline of your home. I understand from Ethan this is not a formal stake setting, just one to give you an idea of the size of the house."

"Yes, Charlie, I like that idea. We're meeting at my house at eight. Jimmie, what about the Cherokee sites?"

"I don't think Charlie's done yet, right?"

"Right, Jimmie. One more site we need to talk about. Although it isn't close to your home, it still needs to be discussed. There is an archeological dig going on by Appalachian State University on the site of what is turning out to be an ancient Catawba village near the site of an old military fort. It is about ten miles east-northeast of Boone.

"It is a long way from your land, but you need to know there may be times the University may request access to areas of your land out of curiosity. I will be the final say but you have as much say as I do as far as people digging up the land you are taking care of. The decision is yours as well as mine as the chief."

"I was reading about that dig this morning. Sounds interesting. Wonder if I might be able to visit it once the weather turns warmer?"

Matthews jumped into the chatter, "I can see about that for you Emily."

"Thanks Matthews. Charlie and Jimmie, I will not let anyone disrupt the land without your approval and then only if it really adds to the story of the area." Jimmie and Charlie both nodded their agreement as Jimmie began to talk.

"Emily, the Cherokee and the Catawba were in many fierce battles fighting over land rights and usage rights. Not a pretty thing. The Cherokee were the fighters. The Catawba were a more peaceful group. They were hunters, farmers and creative artists. They wanted peace and their land. They were considered one of the most powerful Siouan-speaking tribes in the Carolina Piedmont. The Cherokee were hotheads, so to speak. They wanted more and more and would fight anyone to get their way. Glad to say the last hundred and some years we have been learning to get along together better.

Right, Charlie?"

"Exactly. We even have summer festivals together."

Jimmie continued. "The Cherokee in this area are known as the Eastern Band of Cherokee Indians with the land trust known as the Qualia Boundary in the western part of North Carolina. Our history is long and extensive as we originally migrated from the Great Lakes region to settle here and along the Appalachian regions. We have sacred sites all over the place. We are trying to work with private land owners as well as the local towns and counties to keep them sacred. As you can see from the overlay, there are a few Cherokee sites on your land, one being a burial site at the border of your land and the national forest. It is not near the Catawba burial site either. Safe to say, I don't think you'll be doing any building up there but it has been rumored that there are a couple of moonshiners not too far from the site. The two guys that live in the area know it's there and stay away out of respect. I've had a few visits from them on this issue. No problem.

"I agree with Charlie about walking around the area tomorrow. We'll need a few supplies. Ethan and Ian know what to bring. It's gonna be a long day, so be sure to pack enough food and water and other things for the outing. We'll all be carrying hiking gear so, Emily, all you'll need is a regular back-pack with your own personal stuff. How's that sound to everyone?"

Matthews added with a chuckle, "I'll be bringing a few others with me to make sure we all don't get lost."

The rest of the plans were made then everyone took their leave. Mat-thews walked Emily across the road.

"You sure you're up for this? It's gonna be very physical. Just give me a look and I'll be sure we take a break whenever you need to. The trek up to the Catawba burial site is a rough one. No real trails. My team will bring tools for clearing a path if need be. There are a few more new team members as of today. With your site being in the deep forest, the agencies decided to add more security. Never can be too careful. Just wanted you to know before you saw more people around here. Some will be setting up on the mountain for all that security work that needs to be done. You won't even know they're around."

Emily looked at Matthews. Either he was hiding something or just try-ing to be casual about the whole thing. Either way, something was up. Until he told her the whole story, she was going to leave him alone. She had her own 'security system' in place, anyway. No earthly thing could come close to the way the Divine protected their own.

"OK, Matthews. You guys know what you're doing, Thanks for the update. I think I'll spend the rest of the day doing household stuff and some cooking for the week. Then get to bed as early as I can. Gonna need a Jacuzzi after tomorrow. Think you can arrange something for Tuesday when I won't be able to breathe without being reminded about what a wimp I am?"

Emily just laughed as they went their separate ways. She was gonna have to find a massage therapist and acupuncture therapist in Pine Ridge for Tuesday. Time to search the World Wide Web. She found what she was looking for, and made appointments for Tuesday late morning. Acupuncture first then the massage. The practitioners were next door to each other.

Matthews was monitoring Emily's computer activity and had the team do a security check on the two women therapists. They were cleared by late evening. He would make sure a crew met them before Emily's appointment and did a security sweep of the building. Emily would figure this out later. She always did.

Ethan stayed behind at the store for a while, talking with the guys and getting caught up on local gossip. He eventually headed out the door with a handful of groceries. He stood on the porch looking across at Emily's house. Lights were on as it was heading into early evening. The meeting had taken all afternoon. A lot had been accomplished and tomorrow was gonna be a grueling day for everyone. He best get on his way.

As Ethan drove towards Pine Ridge, he thought about yesterday's kiss. It was awesome. He wondered if he was ready for a committed relationship. He had a lot of stuff to sort out. He didn't want to hurt Emily along the way. So, maybe the best thing to do was put the whole thing on hold until he could get his feelings in place. That sounded like a good idea. Keep his distance and be friendly, supportive and helpful, but keep his hands off her. He hoped he could do this. She was smokin' hot and knew how to kiss.

Ethan pulled into the drive and was met by the two new crew members and Ian. They had a short meeting about what would happen the next day. They would be joining Ethan on the hike. They spent the next couple of hours gathering and stowing equipment in the two Jeeps they would be using. They had been supplied by Matthews and were all rigged with the latest surveillance and security equipment. Ethan invited them in for some chow. They shared stories of growing up in the mountains and the suburbs. One last check was made before they went home.

Ethan settled in with the remote control and a beer. Just one he figured. He needed to be sharp for the next day.

Morning came way too early for everyone. Six o'clock brought the sounding of a great many alarms going off. By a quarter to eight everyone was assembled outside Emily's house loading the vehicles with last minute supplies.

Matthews took Emily aside and spoke quietly to her.

"No one, I repeat, no one knows why you are relocating here. They just think the feds helped you with a difficult land purchase. Kendra is the only one who knows it's a protection relocation. And she is not privy to the details. We've used her before. She is very discreet. If anything seems to be weird to you, just let me know. I will be at your side the whole day, including driving your Jeep. Any questions?"

Emily looked around a bit and took a big breathe. "No. I'm OK for now. This is for real today. What happens today will set the tone for the rest of my life. I'm a little cautious about today. That's all. Really."

Matthews took a moment to look at her. He saw she was a bit scared and nervous. This was to be expected. She was picking the place to hide for a very long time. He hoped they would be able to end the nightmare before too long. He patted her on the shoulder then turned to the group.

"OK. Let's get this show on the road. Ethan, you will lead with me second and the rest of you can fall in with the new crew guys bringing up the rear. See you on the mountain."

Twenty-five minutes later they were turning the Jeeps to face downhill and unloading their gear.

Ethan began with, "Let's go over to Emily's place first and take care of business. Then we'll set out for the burial site."

"Ya know, I think I like the sound of that. Emily's place. Sounds right," she said.

They set out with Ethan in the lead, followed by Emily, Matthews, the chiefs and the rest of the team.

About a half hour later they walked into the clearing that would be Emily's home.

The sight of it took her breath away. She saw angels hovering over the clearing and heard their beautiful song of welcome. She heard a gasp from behind her and turned to see the chiefs with their hats in their hands, kneeling on the ground. She knew they saw them, too. The three of them saw native warriors surrounding the edge of the clearing in ceremonial dress with a chief standing in the middle of the clearing at the stones. There was chanting along with the angelic singing. What an amazing vision to be a part of. Matthews looked at Emily and saw her tears at the same time as Ethan. They just stood there watching her staring at the clearing. They turned to see what she was looking at and only saw the air shimmering and moving like a living rainbow.

Everyone stood stock still and was silent as the chanting and singing finally finished. The Spirits bowed to Emily and the chiefs and then just disappeared.

Everyone was still for a moment more, and then Emily took a breath and the chiefs stood up. The three of them looked at each other before embracing. They had tears on their faces and smiles as big as one could be. The others began to talk all at once.

"Did you see that?"

"What was that"

"It was amazing like dancing rainbows or something."

Ethan looked at the chiefs and Emily shaking his head, "I don't know what just happened here but I'll bet it has something to do with the three of you. If I ever doubted that there was more to this being alive thing, I have no doubts now. Whatever that was, whoever they were, I do believe they were happy that Emily is building here and you two are here to take care of things. Holy shit! Sorry, no disrespect meant. Just don't know what to say."

Everyone kept talking until Matthews finally brought quiet to the place.

"Well, um, now that's what I call a special welcome. My team, this will not be a part of today's work report. Understood?"

They all agreed.

"Emily, maybe you can explain this to me. Or the chiefs. Any idea what this was all about?"

Jimmie and Charlie looked at each other before Charlie said, "It is my belief, and Jimmie's, that we are not the only ones on this blessed Mother Earth. The physical form is not the only living entity here. Jimmie and I have repeatedly observed our warrior ancestors' spirits in areas that need protection, during sacred ceremonies, during powwows. Many of us see them dancing right along with us as if they were there in the physical form. Who are we to limit what the Great Father can do? Certainly not me, and I think I speak for Jimmie as well. The appearance of these warriors and the Ancient Chief that stood at the stones in the middle of the clearing, for those of you that saw these distinct Spirits, tells us that Emily is welcome to make her home here. She will be protected by the Ancients as long as she reveres Mother Earth and Father Sky which I know she already does. Emily, welcome from our ancestors. Just one thing…"

"…The stones and boulders. Yes, I got that. I plan on moving them closer to the front of my house and making a special place for them along with adding native plants at the base."

"Exactly. I figured you had already caught on to them."

Jimmie added, "As the speaker for the Cherokee Nation, we welcome you to this place. A sacred and special place for all native ancestors."

They had all moved to just inside the clearing.

Ethan cleared his throat and suggested they get on with the day's work. Everyone grabbed their gear and followed Ethan and Emily to the place where the house would be.

"Emily needs to get a visual of the outline of the house. She, Ian and I spent a good deal of Saturday afternoon creating a shape. If my crew would get the stakes and all and follow us, we should be able to set a rough outline rather quickly."

In less than an hour, the outline was completed. One of the crew had climbed a nearby tree to get some pictures from the air and they were looking at them now.

"I think it's too short front to back. It doesn't look right. It's kinda smushed."

Matthews took a look and agreed. "Maybe if you add another twenty feet out from the front and see how that looks it might be closer to what you have in mind."

Ethan set the crew to moving the stakes. More pictures were taken and looked at.

"I think that is much closer to what I want. Could we move the west side out about ten more feet and add the outline of the west side chimney?"

It was done and pictures were again taken and looked at.

"Yes, that's almost it. Wow, you guys are good!"

"What else needs to be done Emily?" Ethan asked.

"Well, could we set stakes for the barn? We talked about building an old fashioned barn with all modern amenities. Could we outline that remembering it needs to be big enough for the horses and all? I know trees will have to be removed, but I'd like to get a better idea so I know if the place and set-up are right. Placement is everything, ya know?"

Everyone agreed. The chiefs were walking the edge of the clearing making sure no sacred sites had been left off the map. Ethan and Matthew walked with Emily to the place where the barn would be. They roped off the trees that would be kept between the house and the barn first then the crew started placing stakes according to the plans.

More pictures were taken and reviewed.

"This looks great. Just the shape and place I had in mind. I guess we'll see as far as the springs and underground streams go. I think Ethan said they run on the west side of the clearing."

"That's right. There is a small one off to the edge of this side of the clearing and we'll tap into that as a backup but excavating for the foundations should not interfere with the stream," Ethan assured Emily.

Matthews called out to the chiefs and everyone settled around the center stones for a break.

One of the crew asked if it was OK to use the stones since they seemed to be sacred.

Charlie assured them that as long as positive activities were taking place near them, it was OK to be there. "We should just remember to say a quiet 'Thank You' to the ancestors, that's all."

Everyone did just that in their own way. With the exception of Emily and the chiefs, everyone was still a bit shaken and in awe of the earlier experience.

One of the crew named the site, "I think I'll always remember this place as the 'Place of The Shimmering Lights.' Just sayin'."

They stayed at the stones for about a half hour then Ethan stood up.

"Let's pack up and move on to the burial site. It's about an hour and a half from here. There is little to no trail but no real thick forest in the way. There is a lot of undergrowth and some wet areas probably associated with the underground springs. I'll take the lead with the chiefs to make sure we don't stumble onto anything sacred. Chief Charlie says there are a lot of little places along the way. My crew will follow, then Emily and Matthews with the other team members guarding the rear. Ten minutes everyone then we'll meet on the west side of the house foundation by the chimney stakes."

Everyone went their own way then met up as directed.

Ethan took the lead and off they went. For the next two hours they cut through thick undergrowth in some places, walked in a few small open meadows and stopped a few times just to take in the view. The mountains were looking exceptionally majestic this day. The blue haze was almost palpable and the some of the tops were covered in deep snow.

It was after one o'clock when they came upon the burial ground. Chief Charlie stopped the group.

"This is as far as y'all are permitted to go. Only the chief and Shaman are allowed to enter the ancient burial grounds. I will offer gifts and prayers and ask for quiet as I do this. Jimmie, I invite you to join me as a kindred brother. Our ancestors lived and fought side-by-side for thousands of years. I would like to show them we have reached a peace and now live in harmony."

Chief Jimmie accepted with, "I am honored and humbled to accept your offer."

Both chiefs removed their outer gear and boots, donned headdresses, vests and moccasins and gathered their gifts. Chief Charlie began to chant as he and Chief Jimmie entered the site. They chanted in all the directions of the sky. They offered gifts in the center of the site. Then, they both began to sing their own songs as they circled the outer edge of the grounds. Even though the words were different, the songs were in harmony. As they completed the outer circle, they once again danced to the center. They seemed to be talking with someone but no one, except Emily, could see what was really going on.

Emily just stood there in awe and offered prayers of gratitude for being there, for being allowed to be a witness to this special ceremony. She saw thousands of ancestors in warrior dress, ceremonial dress, and little children all dancing and singing along with the Chiefs. It looked like a huge reunion was taking place. She offered positive energy and thanks to all of them and the Ancients for her gifts and for allowing her to have this land to take care of and call home.

The others were respectful and silent as the proceedings took place. Ethan thought he must be really tired because he could have sworn he was seeing native warriors walk out of the woods and surround the burial grounds. He knew he was seeing them but didn't know how that could be. He didn't have a thought one way or the other about the ghosts. But, here they were, right in front of him. He glanced at Emily and saw she was staring at the center of the grounds and saying something although it didn't sound like she was talking out loud. She was bowing a lot and her hands were in front of her, palms up as if offering something to someone. He had a mini epiphany of sorts. He was damn sure she could see things, too. Probably more than he could. What was she? Some kind of psychic something-or-other? He was on over-load. He turned back to the chiefs and saw that they were walking towards the group.

They left the grounds, changed back into their hiking gear and just stood there.

Chief Jimmie started with, "Thanks for the quiet. Our Ancestors thank you for your respect and kindness given towards those you have never known."

Chief Charlie added, "I take it some of you saw some things that you're not quite sure of. Ethan? Don't be alarmed. You must have the Gift of being able to see across the dimensions sometimes. Emily, you're a whole different story. My Ancestors tell me it is safe to talk here. Would you like to explain things yourself?"

Emily nodded then found a tree stump and sat down. She nodded to the others to do the same.

"It has been a very long time since I have been safe to tell my story. Here goes. I was given the Gift of being able to connect with energies that do not have a physical body. Some call them ghosts. Some call them spirits. I know them as a loving and beautiful Light. We are all a beautiful White Light before we agree to be born into the human physical form. We agree to this to learn to be more loving, benevolent and understanding on our journey to become closer to the Divine. Most humans, people, travel our path as it was designed. Some of us choose to walk astray for selfish reasons. Some of us choose a negative human existence to be able to understand the sorrows of others. I have chosen to be a Psychic Medium for my whole lifetime this time. Yes, I not only see Spirits, I hear them, smell them, feel them and am aware of all things connected with them. This last year I have not shared this with anyone for fear of retaliation." She looked at Matthews for approval. He nodded his head that it was OK to divulge this much, and then he shook it, as if to say no more.

Emily gave a little laugh as she continued. "I love this Gift. I see Spirits all the time. I even had to set some rules so I wouldn't be bothered when I sleep and drive. They can be real nudgey sometimes. I never get into anyone's space without their permission. And, no, I cannot predict the future. That's about it. Pretty amazing, huh?"

She waited for some kind of response. It was quiet for a long time.

Ethan looked at her. "I knew there was something special about you."

Matthews commented, "Emily and I had a talk a few days ago about this kind of thing. I believe in all of it. I've experienced some stuff that there is no other explanation for except that we are not alone. Ever."

Anderson nodded in agreement. "I'm with you on that thought, Matthews."

Agent Mello just stared off into the woods as he softly added, "Not sure about all this. It's a bit much to take in all at once. I'm open to it though. Maybe we'll talk more."

The chiefs looked around the group and saw that they were steady.

Jimmie offered, "Why don't we set up for lunch just on the lower side of the grounds. There's that little meadow we passed. It has just the right atmosphere for taking a break. Great view of the Blue Ridge, too."

All followed and soon they were set up and enjoying their lunch.

Mello asked, "Are any of those hot springs near The Creek? I'm guessing some of you out of shape types are gonna need some pampering tomorrow?"

This was met with a great deal of laughter and a barrage of verbal threats along with stuff being thrown at him.

He laughed as he added, "Hey! Just sayin'. Truth be the truth."

Charlie and Jimmie both chimed in with, "I'll be the first in the hot springs."

They both punched each other in the arm.

Charlie held up his hands in surrender. "OK, Jimmie, you win. You go in first. Yes, Mello, there are hot springs just up behind the store. You'll see the trail. It's about a five minute walk straight back. Bring a towel and be sure to wear some solid shoes. The spring is big enough to hold about twenty people and it has natural rock ledges in some places so you can sit down. It's about eight feet deep in the center where the water flows in and it's hotter there, too. Makes sense. You'll see about three places where the water leaves the spring. It flows right into Crab Apple Creek a little ways down the mountain. It's available year round. We just don't tell visitors about it. Keep it in the family, ya know?"

Matthews looked up at the tree line. "Seems to be getting on the down side of the afternoon. We've got a long hike back, but should be easier and take some less time since we cut a path along the way. Let's pack it up. Ten minutes and we'll be leaving."

They were on their way shortly after that in the same line-up as they had taken on the way up to the grounds. It took just a little more than an hour and twenty minutes to get back to Emily's site where they paused for a brief moment, looking around, wondering if more special things were going to happen. All remained quiet as they set off down the mountain for the last part of the hike back to the Jeeps.

The sun was just touching the tops of the trees before it started its way down through them. The temperature dropped quickly as everyone gathered around the Jeeps.

Matthews wrapped things up. "Good work today everyone. Rather, excellent work. Chiefs, thank you so much for everything you've done for us today. On behalf of this crew, we thank you for your patience and willingness to allow Emily to build here."

Charlie countered with, "No, Matthews, I think ya got that backwards. Emily, thank you for allowing us to take care of our own. I now understand why you get it. We will keep in touch for sure."

Emily looked at Charlie and Jimmie. "Chiefs, I am humbled to be placed in charge of taking care of this part of Mother Earth and keeping an eye on your Ancestor's homes. I'll do my best. I know we will be keeping in touch. See you all at the hot spring."

Matthews gave the signal to load up and they all left just as the sun set below the trees. The sky was beautiful. It showed deep purples, bright pinks and flashy oranges as the sun blessed them with its final rays of the day.

CHAPTER 11

Nick's arraignment had come and gone. He was to be held without bail in a maximum security federal prison for trial. The counts and charges against him included money trafficking, human trafficking, money laundering, multiple acts of terrorism against the United States punishable by death, use of false identifications, and more.

Nick was stunned. How did they know all this? He had followed Yuri's instructions to the T. What evidence did they have? He had looked at his attorney and questioned him. His attorney said they had strong evidence against him and he should consider a plea. Nick refused. He knew Yuri would get him out of this. He had to. He had done things for his boss that meant loyalty and honor. Of course Yuri would get him out of this.

Nick looked like hell. He had been beaten every night by some unknown force that would wake him up by choking him, and then throw him around the room like a rag doll. Nick was sure it was the guards even though he couldn't really see them. It was dark in his cell being all concrete walls with only a bare light bulb up in the ceiling. The switch was outside and never on when this happened.

Nick was taken back to his cell after the arraignment and told he would be transferred to a federal prison. That's all. He asked where that was and was told he would find out at a later time. He asked to see his lawyer and was told not until after the transfer. He would be transferred that day.

Meanwhile, Yuri was having troubles of his own. His contacts still could not find Barbara. He was furious. He had spent the last twenty-four hours recovering from that nightmarish thing that had happened. The message from the man in the black hat was clear: "Fix this thing NOW! Whatever it takes!"

So, Yuri had finally come up with the beginning of a plan. He had sent word to his contact in the federal court system that he needed to get a message to Nick. His contact told him it was near impossible and would take a few days at the least. He would get things going. Yuri reminded him that his life was on the line. The contact reassured Yuri that he would get the message to Nick but he had to be extremely careful with every step because the feds knew Nick was connected to Yuri. Yuri agreed with this and was now waiting to hear back from his contact.

This contact was one of the warden's security bodyguards where Nick was being held. He was known only by the name of Bob. He was on duty today, Sunday, and would be able to get into the warden's office without suspicion. He always checked the office a few times on the days the warden wasn't there. He had access to the computer system as well and had hacked into it many times. He would do the same thing this afternoon to find Nick's cell location and other information.

Around mid-afternoon, Bob approached the guard outside Nick's cell.

The guard questioned Bob, "What can I do for you?" Everyone knew you didn't mess with the warden's special guard.

Bob answered, "I need to question the prisoner. Call for another guard for backup."

The guard was hesitant. "I do not question your authority. I have been instructed not to let anyone speak with this prisoner unless his attorney is with him and there has been a pre-arranged meeting set. Not sure what I'm supposed to do at this time."

Bob instructed the guard to follow his request and he would not be in violation of any law or rules.

The guard just shook his head as he called for backup.

When the second guard arrived, they stood aside as Bob entered the cell. The door locked behind him. The guards did not look into the cell.

Nick looked up from his cot where he had been trying to sleep. He wasn't getting much rest these days and he thought this might be his transfer taking place.

Bob told Nick to stay where he was.

"I'm not here to transfer you. Just to give you a message. Yuri wants to know where Barbara is. Any ideas?"

Nick turned pale as he tried to swallow and answered, "Yuri? You know Yuri? Oh God, you're here to kill me."

Bob grinned as he said, "Not this time Nick. Not this time. I just want to know what the hell is going on and where that bitch is."

Nick was breathing fast as he answered, "I haven't the faintest idea. I was just going about my business when the feds grabbed me. I haven't seen her since she left for work. She's missing? Are you telling me she's missing?"

"No one can find her. It's as if she vanished off the face of the Earth. Did you have her killed?"

"No! Hell no. She was great cover for our business. She was just what the boss told me to get. How can she be missing? She must have her phone and car. Can't you trace her signal?"

"Her phone was found smashed in your kitchen trash. None of her stuff was missing. We can't even find her car with all the bugs we had on it. You sure you didn't have her killed?"

"No! I wouldn't do that unless I was told to. I follow the rules. No messing with Yuri. He's a mean son of a bitch. I know the rules. The feds won't tell me what's really going on. They said I'm here on terrorism charges, money laundering, human trafficking and more crazy shit. The money and drugs I do. The other shit is crazy. How the hell did I get here?"

Bob smiled. 'They must have had an informant. You sure Barbara didn't know what you were into?"

"Her? Hell no! She's too stupid to figure things out. She knew if she questioned me she'd get a beating so she stopped asking. She did what she was told. She was terrified of me just like we planned it. Maybe one of Yuri's guys took her for a few good fucks then ditched her along a remote road somewhere with a bullet to the head. Ever think of that? It's all I can come up with. Believe me I do what I'm told."

Bob kept looking at Nick for a long minute.

"You look like hell. No one is supposed to be beating you in here."

Nick just shook his head. "Every night they come. I can't see them, but they whale on me somethin' fierce. I looked like shit in court today. Where am I going?"

Bob just stood there. He'd have to replay all this to Yuri. He hadn't mentioned anyone roughing Nick up. He wondered what was going on here. No one else was connected with Yuri and Yuri hadn't instructed him to have Nick beaten.

"Well, maybe it will stop when you get to the new place. Can't tell you where it is. Gotta follow the rules. I'll tell Yuri what you said and what's been going on. You'll hear from someone else in a few days. Your attorneys have been arraigned on lots of charges just like you. They don't look so good, either. Keep your mouth shut and do as you're told. Got it?"

Nick nodded in agreement. He was scared shitless.

Bob left and soon after the transfer guards came in and put Nick in shackles and led him out to a waiting van. There were six guards surrounding him in the van and two other vans with armed guards in front of and behind his van. It took about three quarters of an hour to get to the new location. Nick had no idea where they were. He was taken in and processed, including a cavity search, and then placed in another solitary cell. Not a word was said other than what was needed for him to walk, stop, pee, dress and that kind of stuff. It must have been early evening by then. He was beyond scared. He knew Yuri had contacts everywhere but to be questioned by one was a whole other level of terror. At least he was still alive.

And that cunt, Barbara. Where the fuck was she? She wasn't smart enough to get away from him. He was so mad he hit the wall and broke his hand. His hollering brought three guards. They put him in shackles and took him to the infirmary where his hand was tended to and he was returned to his cell with a fiberglass cast on his right hand all the way up to his elbow. They had given him pain meds and once he lay down he passed out and didn't come to until the next morning when the guards brought him breakfast.

Bob returned to the warden's office after talking to Nick. He hacked into the computer to see what was going on. He noted all the important stuff then placed a call to Yuri on his disposable cell as soon as he left for home.

He informed Yuri of all he had heard from Nick. It was very clear that Yuri wanted Barbara. He figured she had turned Nick into the feds. He didn't know how she knew anything. He believed Nick when he had told Yuri she was too stupid to figure anything out and he had complete control of her through the beatings and rapes. Yuri trusted Nick with his end of the business. Nick had increased Yuri's 'revenue' by over two hundred percent. If Nick said he had her under control, then Yuri believed Nick.

Monday morning Yuri set the first part of his plan into action. He ordered all his contacts in the eastern United States to start looking for Barbara.

The FBI and Interpol intercepted the message and security was increased around Emily. Then, every known connection of Yuri's was targeted. Some were taken off the streets on outstanding warrants. Some just disappeared altogether. Others were being followed by one or the other of the agencies. And yet others were found dead, most likely having been murdered on orders from Yuri to make sure they didn't talk.

Matthews had twelve new special ops agents arriving Monday morning and they were to be kept secret. Emily was not to know about them. The agency had contacted Kendra as soon as they knew about Yuri's orders. She had secured houses in Pine Ridge and along the Pine Ridge road going towards The Creek for the new agents. She was under strict orders not to talk about these new agents. The U. S. marshals had used her for other business in the past and knew she was discreet and trustworthy.

The FBI had contacts everywhere. Information was coming in to the new command headquarters that had been set up in the Schuyler, Virginia area. It was a small town so it was a safe place for covert operations. The command center was set up on a large farm outside of the town itself. The farmhouse was being upgraded and renovated in fast order. The locals were under the assumption that a large family was in the process of taking over the farm to grow organic vegetables and raise all natural chickens for their eggs. These products would be sold to the public once the farm got going. Until then, it was just another renovation project.

It was to be one of the most high tech centers in the U.S. All wireless. Security was tight but the average person would never have known. It all looked like a farm. For the people stopping by to buy stuff, a farm stand was being built close to the road.

It all looked innocent. It would be completed within three days from start to finish. Framing and weather proofing the structures would be worked on round the clock. As soon as the word was given, the interior crews would arrive and complete everything. Multiple crews were working hand-in-hand to get this project up and running by Thursday. The locals were guessing the new owners must be really wealthy to have so many trades people working together non-stop.

There were fields available for chopper access in both Schuyler and just below The Bend in The Road Country Store. The agencies had contracted with the owners for unconditional use. The relocation project had just become a full out covert protection action. Interacting agencies across the globe were all doing the same thing: taking Yuri's thugs down and getting closer to Yuri.

Unbeknownst to Yuri, one of his top five associates, working out of Moldova, was really an imposter. He was one of the good guys, an ET, planted there by The NOVAE to keep them updated on all CON activity. He worked mostly in the area of human trafficking. He was a transporter for the business. Every time he got a truckload of girls, usually six to eight of them, to transport to their new location in the old USSR area of Transnistria, he would set them free at the closest international airport with documents and money to get them into the U.S. He would then 'deliver' what his contacts thought of as girls. They were really shape shifters. Once they were left alone in their rooms at the whorehouse they would shift back into their ET shapes and leave.

You can only imagine what a headache this was for the people Yuri had running the places. They panicked. They looked everywhere for the girls to no avail. As far as they were concerned, these girls had just vanished right in front of them. They were too afraid to report their disappearance for fear of being murdered by Yuri's thugs. So, they just grabbed whatever girls they could find off the street, drugged them and let their clients do whatever they wanted with them. As long as the money kept coming in and Yuri got his cut, they didn't really care who they had.

The NOVAE had Energies all around Emily. She knew who they were. No one else did with the exception of one other who knew who she was and that shape shifter was very close to Emily and Emily was aware of whom this was and glad of it.

CHAPTER 12

ow that Emily's site was cleared by the Native American chiefs the security phase began in earnest. The security special ops group was all set up on the mountain and already placed security equipment around the building site. The interagency board had given the go-ahead in the wee hours of Wednesday morning.

Tuesday found Emily at the acupuncturist then the massage therapist. She was hurting but not as badly as she thought she would. She was back home by early afternoon and spent the rest of the day relaxing and adding to the lists of the things she wanted in her home right down to the type of cabinet and drawer pulls she fancied.

Ethan had his hands full as he and Ian spent Tuesday contacting all the contractors they would need to get things going. They had been given a list of approved companies by the FBI and Ethan had appointments with the excavator and land clearing team for Wednesday to walk the land and stake out the access road and driveway. They would connect in a circle so it would be easier for the trucks and large equipment to get in and out of the site. First, the land would have to be cleared. Some of the larger hardwood trees would be stacked for firewood for Emily's house. She had requested that all other trees and such be placed in a number of compost areas off the roads, even if the access road was to be planted after all the building was done. She wanted to be sure to create areas for new homes for the animals and birds. Emily believed in living in harmony with Mother Earth.

Ethan estimated the road making phase would take about two weeks. Then the excavators could get onto the site and dig the foundation areas. First, the house would be dug. After the concrete was poured and set for the full basement the barn and stables area would be dug, poured and set. They, too, would have full basements. The water table was deep in this area save for the hot springs. The geologists and Ian had spent many hours going over this aspect of the building and were certain the digging would not interrupt the springs. If any artifacts were found, the chiefs would come over right away and take care of them and bless the land.

Matthews had his hands full, too. He was given an assistant as this operation had just exploded one hundred fold. He made sure Emily was kept clear of these latest details. She would have to be told about everything soon, but Matthews wanted to shield her from more stress and fear as long as possible. As soon as he could answer the questions he knew she would ask, he would bring her up to date.

Wednesday morning found both Ethan and Matthews very busy with their own projects, and Emily found herself with a free day. After breakfast, she decided to bake some of her yummy cookies and by late morning she was ready to take them across the road. As she entered the store she noticed the couple that had been rather distant and non-responsive to her a few days before. They were talking to Michael and Ted. As soon as Ted saw her, he excused himself and walked over to her.

"Hi Emily. How have you been? Did you recover from your day on the mountain yet?"

Emily laughed as she replied, "Mostly Ted. I had an acupuncture session followed by a massage yesterday then spent the day relaxing. Just a few twinges this morning. Not anything serious enough to keep me from baking you some of my yummy cookies. Here ya go."

She handed them to Ted just as Michael approached. He grabbed them away before Ted could even get a hold of them.

"Mine. All mine," Michael said with a possessive laugh.

Everyone laughed as Michael opened the basket and began to share them.

"Hey Pam and Kevin, come on over and sample some of these home-made cookies. Emily makes them and they're to die for."

They joined the group and sampled the cookies.

Pam mumbled as she ate. "These are fabulous. They melt right in your mouth. There must be a secret to your baking."

Emily thanked her. "No. No secrets. Not really. I just changed a few things from a regular recipe. That's all. And thanks."

Kevin added, "Sorry about the other day. We were a bit rude. We didn't mean to be. We just had something on our minds. Nice to meet you. Great cookies, too."

"Thanks Kevin. Nice to meet the both of you, too. I hear you have a farm around here. Organic, right?"

Pam nodded. "Yes indeed. The only way to grow things. We sell the eggs to these two and a few other things to some of the local folks. You can come by the farm anytime. Just head down the road a bit then take a right for about a mile. We are at the end of the road. We have our own vegetable garden in the summer and sell from that."

"I'd like to visit you. Maybe in a few days or so. I'm working on getting my house started and I think the builder needs me around for details. I'll get word to you through these guys, OK?"

Kevin agreed. "Sure. Come on by whenever ya can. We gotta get goin'. Its spring and our animals have started birthin' already. Need to stay close 'til they're all done."

"Michael, Ted, Emily..." Kevin tipped his hat as they left.

They all waved as Pam and Kevin took their leave then headed over to the dining area for coffee and tea. After getting comfy around the oak table the guys shared stories of the mountain with Emily and she shared stories of her recent day of hiking all over the mountain. They laughed a lot at each other's antics.

Michael inquired about Emily's house plans. "Do you have the shape of the house all figured out and all the features you want? Tell us, please. Maybe we might have a few ideas for you."

"Yes, I do. And, what a great idea. Here goes." Emily then spent the next couple of hours telling the guys her ideas about the house and stables and barn. Paper was found and she tried her hand at drawing a map of the site and where the buildings would be built. They discussed landscaping ideas in between customers all afternoon and didn't realize the time until Kendra stopped by.

"Hey y'all. What's up?"

Emily looked up. "Hi Kendra. Just talking about the house and all with Michael and Ted. They have been giving me landscaping and decorating ideas."

Kendra rolled her eyes and laughed. "They'll keep you busy for days on the subject of landscaping alone."

Ted piped up with, "Hey Kendra. We can't help it if we're the best on the mountain, can we? I'll get dinner set up. It's after six already. Anyone hungry?"

Emily looked surprised. "Really? Oh my God I can't believe we've been at it all afternoon. Yup, the sun has pretty much set hasn't it. OK then, I'm game for dinner. Too late for me to think about what I want to cook up myself. What do ya have back there Ted?"

Kendra agreed with Emily. "Good idea. I'll stay, too."

Michael was at the register with a couple of customers. Emily and Kendra gathered dinnerware, made salads and sat back down at the table.

Ted came out of the kitchen and informed them of the menu. "We have herb roasted and stuffed chicken breasts, pot roast and fixins and veggie lasagna. What is your pleasure?"

Emily chose the chicken and Kendra chose the pot roast.

"Excellent choices if I may say so myself. Mashed potatoes, Emily?"

"Of course... and gravy on everything including the veggies. Thanks, Ted. I wondered what was roasting back there. It had me drooling all afternoon."

"Crockpot pot roast, slow roasted stuffed chicken and baked veggie lasagna. I may have to sample all of them."

Michael walked by with, "Me, too. Yum!"

More customers came in for dinner and very quickly the table was filled to overflowing. People took their plates and sat around the potbellied stove and everywhere else around the store. The store looked like a major celebration was taking place when Matthews walked in with a few of the new team members. Greetings were shouted out as they walked back to the kitchen area.

"Hey Matthews, nice to see you," Emily managed between bites. "This stuff is heavenly. Better get some before it's all gone."

"What do you recommend Emily?"

"Everything!" This statement was met with more agreement from all around.

"In that case, I'll take the pot roast. Thanks. Help yourself team. No need to hurry tonight. Enjoy the feast."

More orders were placed with Ted while Michael worked the front of the store.

This was an exceptionally busy night. About the time everyone was finished with their meal, Ted took the floor and made an announcement.

"Hey y'all. Tonight is s special night. Not that anyone who's lived around here could tell. I would like to introduce the newest member of our community. Everyone, this here is Miss Emily. She's building the new place just up the mountain. Emily, this here is most everyone in Crab Apple Creek. You are most welcome here."

This was met with wild applause and sincere hello's.

Emily looked over at Matthews. He was just sitting there smiling at Emily. He knew. He had probably set the whole thing up with Michael and Ted as accomplices.

Emily stood up. "I'm, uh, surprised and, uh, glad to be here in The Creek. Thanks so much for this wonderful surprise party. I had no idea. I don't know what else to say, except, maybe, I hope to meet everyone over the next little while. And, again, thanks for making me feel welcome."

Applause and laughter was heard all around. As Emily sat down, people began to come by to say hello personally. After most of the neighbors had introduced themselves to Emily, two women approached her. They looked to be about her age or maybe a little older. She found it hard to tell with these mountain folk.

"Hi Emily, I'm known around here as Lainie, short for Elaine and this is my sister, Mo, short for Maureen. Welcome to The Creek. Nice to have someone of our generation around here." Elaine shook hands with Emily.

Mo added, "She thinks she's the boss of us. Not so. I let her think that. We live about a mile from where you're building just off the main road. Probably take about a half hour to get to us 'til you put in your own road. We have a large herb farm, right Lainie?" Mo smiled at Lainie in a 'ya know what I mean' kind of way.

Emily shook hands with Mo. "Very nice to meet you as well. Do you grow lavender and other fragrant herbs?"

"Why, yes we do. Are you familiar with herbs?" asked Lainie.

"Yes. I use a great many of them for cooking and medicinal purposes. I am in need of a ready supply until I can get my own gardens growing. May I stop by soon?"

Mo nodded her head. "Yes, of course, just pop on over whenever you feel like it. We'll brew a pot of tea and get to know one another."

"Thanks so much. I'll be sure to do just that real soon."

Mo and Lainie wandered off smiling at each other. They reminded Emily of her old best friend. They sure got into mischief a lot but never got caught. Seems that's how Mo and Lainie were with each other. She looked forward to getting to know those two.

Emily looked up as she heard a rather loud voice followed by laughter coming from the front of the store. It was that Cora woman, the one who was sure UFOs and aliens had come down onto the mountain several times. She was discussing the topic with Matthews.

"Well, Ma'am, I can't say for sure about any of this. I just got here about two weeks ago."

Cora pointed her finger in Matthews face. "Well, at least it seems you have some manners callin' me ma'am and all. But don't you sit there tryin' to tell me you didn't see those flashing lights a few nights ago. I saw you was on your front porch lookin' up at the sky same as me when I was walkin' by."

"Yes, Ma'am, I was on the porch that night. I just figured it was a private jet or something off course or maybe taking a special route to get somewhere. That's all."

"My ass it was. You just gonna stand there and tell that story like I should believe it? You must be dumber that I thought you was."

Matthews cleared his throat in an attempt not to laugh at Cora.

"We'll, ma'am, I can't say what you want to hear and have it be the truth. It was as I said. Why do you think it was a UFO? If you don't mind telling me."

"Cause I'm not stupid. No regular jet flies over this place. We're mountains here. There's no airport anywhere near here. That's why I know it had to be a UFO. I seen 'em lots of times before. You just ask the locals. They know about these things don't y'all?"

Several of the locals agreed with Cora.

"I've seen somethin' in the night sky. Didn't look like no airplane or jet. Not the right shape. The last one I saw was about a month ago. It was more triangle shaped with lights flashing at all the points. It just kinda hovered in place for maybe five minutes then took off straight up into the air. Never made a sound, either."

"I saw somethin' else 'bout six months back. Now, as most of ya know, my family's been here for about three hundred years. My kin kept journals and all. I keep one as well as do my daughters and their kin. We've been seein' lights in the night sky all these years. The one I mentioned was triangle shaped, too. But it kept comin' and goin' over the Applewood grove like it was lookin' for something or someone or maybe a place to land. That grove seems to be a favorite spot for these things 'cause my journals mention it a lot in connection to these UFO things."

Others agreed with Cora saying they, too, had seen lights over the Applewood grove many times.

Matthews chimed in with, "Now, that is very interesting to me. Wonder why the grove of all places. There are clear meadows around here for them to land in, right?"

Heads nodded in agreement.

"Anyone got any ideas about the grove? I'd love to hear them," Matthews encourage the group.

A man known as Johnson replied, "I've been wonderin' the same thing myself. Now, being an educated man and all..."

He was cut off by Cora. "Educated? Please professor, tell the truth. You're a professor at Appalachia State University down there in Boone in the archeology department. Have been for over thirty years. And you was born and raised on our mountain just like your kin before you. You graduated from Appalachia State, too. So, be tellin' the truth Johnson, or should I say Professor Johnson?!"

"Well, I guess you told me, Miss Cora. All true. No matter, makes a body wonder and all."

Conversation broke out among the group as people moved about the store and enjoyed the evening.

Emily looked around but did not see Ethan. She was just wondering about him when Ted whispered in her ear, "Don't you be worried. Ethan had some kind of late meeting with one of the contractors for your project. He asked me to tell you he'd be here as soon as he could. We even saved supper for him."

"Thanks, Ted. I guess I'm easy to read, huh?"

"Well, darlin', you just light up when he's around just like he does when you're nearby. Can't mess with fate, can ya?"

Emily was quick to respond. "Fate? Oh please don't get the wrong idea. He's my builder. That's all. Nothing more."

"Sure honey. Only thing is, your face is not convincing me of that statement." Ted smiled that all knowing smile as he went to the cash register to take care of his customers.

Emily was about to walk over to the pot-bellied stove when the bells on the door jangled. She looked over and saw Ethan just as he saw her. Their eyes locked in such a fierce gaze that fireworks would have been easily ignited if they had been between the two of them.

Ethan walked right over to Emily, gave her a peck on the cheek and said, "Welcome to The Creek. Sure hope you like this little gathering we cooked up for you. Not me, the guys and all. They really know how to put a party together. Sorry I'm late. I had meetings with the excavators and concrete form guys all afternoon. Had some details to work out. All seems good to go as soon as Matthews gives us the OK and the building inspector grants us the permit. We have a little more work to do on the design of your buildings and need to meet with you tomorrow morning if that's OK with you."

Emily eyes shined like the stars in the night sky, "Thanks for the party and all. And, no worries about being late. Yes, I can meet with you and Ian tomorrow morning. Nine sound good for you guys?"

"Yes, perfect. Now, time for me to chow down on some of the best food around."

"You go right ahead. I'm headed to the stove to chat for a while. Join us if you feel like you can move after you eat. That food is fabulous. I'm told there's quite the dessert buffet to come later on."

"Thanks for the warning. I'll try to leave some room." With that Ethan headed back to the table area and Emily joined the group around the stove. What a warm and comforting feeling this place gave. It was like a trip back in time to the eighteen hundreds or so but with all the modernisms at hand. The people really were warm and welcoming here in The Creek. She had heard that the Southerners, as a whole, where a friendly and welcoming people. She had taken a trip about five years ago to Disneyworld in Florida. Of course people were wonderful there. Disneyworld was known for its customer service training and high standards.

But this was different. These people didn't have to like a stranger coming into their hamlet to settle down. But they did, and she was grateful. Emily spent a time chatting with everyone as they came and went around the stove. Stories of fierce winters were remembered as well as the beautiful summers of the past. Stories of the old settlers were shared as well. Seems many of the locals had kin that came from Scotland and Wales with a few Irish added for variety. The history of moonshine was told with great humor and flare. Seems there were a few of the old moonshiners still on the mountain. This was all told in hushed voices of course as making shine was highly illegal. Emily was informed that those that were around were hidden so far into the Blue Ridge that no one had been or would be able to find them.

Cora added, "But don't be surprised to find a jar or jug on your doorstep. These shiners decide if you are worthy or not by leaving ya something. And, from what I hear, and I hear it all, you've decided to leave them alone seein' as they's on your property and all. Mighty decent of you."

"Thanks Miss Cora. I'm not here to change anyone's way of living. Just to find some peace for myself."

"Then you'll fit right in. Right y'all?"

"Yes, ma'am."

"Sure thing."

"You got that right."

Just then Ted got everyone's attention by calling out, "The dessert board is ready. Any takers?"

Everyone moved as one to get to the desserts. They had a long history of being the best in the Blue Ridge. Seems a number of the locals had brought their own special recipes.

Ethan found Emily and sat next to her. She had a sampler plate in front of her and was enjoying every bite.

"I don't know which one I like better. They are all so good and probably really sinful as well"

Ethan nodded and moaned as he bit into something with chocolate, nuts and what looked like cream cheese. "You said it!"

It was quiet for a few minutes as desserts were sampled throughout the store. There was a jug of shine being passed around as well, not surprisingly.

By nine o'clock the store had pretty much emptied out. Only Matthews, Emily and Ethan remained. They sat around the stove with coffee and tea and compared notes about the evening.

Emily said, "Ted. Michael. Thanks so much for the party. What a great surprise it was and the food was most excellent. I know I ate too much."

Ted patted his tummy. "Me, too, darlin'. Me, too. So glad we could do this little thing. It was way past time for the locals to get together. I think it's probably been since New Year's Day since we had a shindig like this."

Michael chimed in, "Yup. It was New Year's. We've had a few small little last minute things but ya always need a big gathering to remember what life's all about. Food and friends."

Ethan added, "I'm always ready for a food fest, especially when you two are cooking. Although I did see some of the local desserts on the board. These folks really know how to cook. Just wait for the picnics and all. And, of course, they'll be feeding us when we work on your house. I've already been told to be ready for it. They're already planning on a picnic for the day we begin digging the foundation for your home. It's a big deal around here.

Whether it's a barn raising, which will necessitate another feast day, or building a house, these folks really known how to support each other. And, just a fair warning, the ladies will be quilting while the men work so if you sew, you should be all set. You do sew, don't you Emily?"

"Yes I do. I've always wanted to be a part of a quilting. This is gonna be fun."

Matthews just shook his head. "I guess I've got my work cut out for me. Better get in shape for the building thing. No problem with the eating thing."

Ted and Michael both said, "No problem with the eating thing here, either."

"Well, I guess it's time to get home," Emily said as she stood up and stretched. She reminded Ethan of the way a cat stretches when it's all content and happy. On Emily, it was downright sexy.

Ethan went weak just watching her. He had been thinking about her all night and wondering how he could get her alone. Now was his chance.

"Emily, I'll just walk you home if that's OK. Wouldn't want you to come to any harm crossing the road and all."

Smiles were met with sarcasm and Emily and Ethan made their way out the door.

They both shivered as they stepped off the porch.

"Boy, it's gotten cold since I went in here this afternoon."

"Sure has. I noticed the temp falling as my crew and I were finishing up a project at the workshop. We had to haul long beams into the mill to be cut. They were really heavy and even though we were working our asses off we all noticed the chill comin' on."

Ethan took Emily's hand as they crossed the road. He felt a shiver go through her

"Cold? We'll get you in your house and warmed up in no time."

Emily just looked straight ahead as they walked up onto her little porch. Her heart was beating so fast and hard she was sure Ethan could hear it. She unlocked the door and the two of them walked right into the living room. Ethan shut the door with his foot and had his coat off in a second. Emily turned to hang her coat up and Ethan took it and dropped it on the floor. He pressed Emily against the wall and took possession of her mouth as if this were their last minute together. She responded by opening her mouth and taking his tongue into her own as she ran her hands up his back. Ethan groaned and shivered from her touch. He ran his hand along her side and brushed it along the swell of her breast. They melted together like well fit puzzle pieces. She could feel the bulge of his organ rocking against her. She pushed back and swayed against Ethan.

He was losing control. All he could think about was sucking her soft breast and making her cum again and again.

A flash of truck lights filled the room and brought him back to reality. Oh fuck! What was he doing? With an effort greater than he knew he possessed, he pulled away from Emily softly kissing her on the lips.

His breathing was fast and heavy. "Emily, this is not how I treat women. Please believe me. I am so sorry for all this."

He looked quite upset. Emily felt confused. She just stood there leaning against the wall. Ethan didn't know what to do. He wanted her so badly. But this wasn't the way he wanted to make love to her. He looked at her and felt like a jerk. She looked disappointed and hurt.

"Emily, please, this isn't your fault. I'm acting like a crazy animal."

Emily took a shaky breath. "Ethan, what did I do? I thought we were enjoying each other. There's nothing wrong with that if we both agree. Right?"

"That's true Emily. It's just that I... I... God, I don't know what to say. I feel like such a jerk. It's not you. You are beautiful, sexy and the way you kiss me is amazing. It's me. I just don't know if I can do this right now. Please. I'm so sorry. I guess I'd just better go before I grab you and lose all control."

Would that be so bad? Emily thought.

Ethan ran out the door and was down the road before Emily could say a word. She wasn't sure what to think. She thought they were having a great time. He sure knew how to kiss a girl. And she knew he enjoyed her kissing him. It was almost as if something had spooked him. One minute he was being hot and sexy and the next he looked like he had seen a ghost or something.

Damn! She locked the door, sat down on the couch and cried. She couldn't remember the last time she had cried. Must have been years ago. She wasn't sure how long she sat there until she woke up the next day with the sun shining bright through the windows.

Ethan cursed himself all the way home. How could he have been so insensitive? He didn't use women for sex. He wasn't like that. The scent of Emily made him crazy. He could think of nothing else when she was around except wanting to make passionate love to her. This was not the way to do that. He had acted like some sex crazed animal. He wouldn't blame her for not wanting to be around him anymore.

He didn't even remember driving home. He didn't even know how long he sat there in his truck until he realized his feet and hands were freezing cold and there was a light snow falling. He got out and went inside. He threw his jacket toward the pegs on the wall, kicked off his boots and dropped onto his bed. He awoke the next day with the sun streaming through his windows.

CHAPTER 13

It looked like any other farm. There was a farm house, a big barn, pens with animals, a chicken coop and about a half dozen greenhouses. It made sense since one of the signs read **Organic Herbs for Sale**. It was a nice looking place. Lots of gardens ready to come alive once the warming air of spring came around. Smoke rose from both the house chimneys and the barn as well. The green houses had steam rising off the roof glass. It was all frosted and made the scene look surreal. It was quiet at first until you stopped and listened. Then you heard the chickens cackling and the cows mooing along with other barnyard sounds.

There was a new looking pick-up truck parked near the barn and an SUV near the house. There were a couple of wooden trailers over by the green houses and rakes and shovels leaned against various out buildings all around the place. Not much snow left. Just a dusting from the night before. The sun shone brightly all over the place.

Lainie and Mo, were in the kitchen having another cup of coffee and homemade muffins. Breakfast had been just after sunrise. It was well on to nine o'clock now. All the animals had been taken care of for the morning and the sisters were just about ready to tend to the greenhouses. One particular greenhouse would take up most of their attention today. It was affectionately known as the medicinal herb garden. They grew a large variety of herbs for medical use: feverfew, goldenrod, sage, lavender, black cohosh, elderberry and so much more. There were flowering plants that had been seeded in January in two of the green houses. These would be sold for cash. Most of the herbal medicinals would be sold for cash as well. Cash was the only form of payment the sisters would accept as well as the occasional bartering if they needed some specific thing or work done on the place.

Lainie gathered the dishes and set them in the sink. "Well, Mo, ya ready to get down and dirty today?" she asked with a grin and a giggle.

"I sure am. Should be time to separate all those seedlings into their own pots," Mo answered with a giggle of her own.

They set out for greenhouse #6. They had taken down about two acres of trees, keeping them for firewood and other uses as needed. Some of the hardwood would be used to make furniture for the house. The pine would be used to make shelves for the greenhouses and barn. Most would be used as firewood for the many fireplaces throughout the house. The sisters had tapped into the geothermal springs on their property to heat all the buildings. They had laid electric lines underground.

The greenhouses had been set up behind the barn in two rows of three. They had left the old growth trees to shade the barn. The greenhouses faced south on their long side so they could get as much sunlight as possible. They, too, were heated with the geothermal heat.

The last greenhouse on the right side, farthest away from the road and driveway access, was greenhouse #6. It grew a special kind of medicinal herb. The Sister's Marijuana, as it was known by those who were allowed to purchase it, was grown here. No one knew it was there and if they did, it was the best kept secret of the century. The growing and selling of pot had made the sister's millionaires. They were very intelligent women. They only kept enough money in the bank to pay bills and a little extra for other expenses, like the new truck and SUV they had just purchased. The bulk of their wealth was hidden at home. They knew how to use it so no one would wonder about their finances.

The sisters had spent the past twenty years, since they were teenagers, growing, hybridizing and perfecting a number of potent strains of pot. Their parents had moved to Arizona about ten years ago and enjoyed traveling around the world. Their father had made his millions in the computer industry just as it was being created. He was a programmer and designer that had been highly sought after during the Apple and IBM PC wars. He retired early at the age of fifty and he and the girls' mother were enjoying life. They knew exactly what their daughters were doing and applauded them on their success.

The girls had taken over the family farm when their parents left for Arizona and the locals loved them all. They were genuinely nice people. They helped out in the community when someone needed help and often gave food to the needy as well. They had a small clientele that used their pot for truly medicinal uses. One client had glaucoma and another had a seizure disorder. The marijuana helped both of them live better lives. Then there were the rest of their clients who just wanted it for whatever.

Being in the marijuana business was a tricky thing as it was illegal. The farm was located on about forty acres that ran along the Blue Ridge, just north and east of where Emily's land was located. The park rangers knew the girls had the farm and pretty much left them alone. Once in a while, the rangers stopped by to chat and let them know they would be on their road a few times as they patrolled the mountains after the spring thaw but that was about it. No one else ever came by 'cause the farm was on a dead end road that ended at their place. The access road the rangers used was just before the farm to the west. The only people on their road were headed to the farm to buy stuff. Nice!

They had started out small just to see if they would have any takers. They had been growing and selling in small quantities since they were about sixteen years old. Even when they went away to college, they were able to keep growing in their rented house. Just enough for a few clients. Once they returned home they started in earnest trying to come up with a very potent strain with no bad side effects. It had taken about four years before they finally had a good strain. Once they started selling it, they couldn't keep up with demand so they decided to build the six greenhouses and grow and sell lots of plants. It was a great cover for the pot business and made them a good enough income that their purchases were never questioned. There was no curiosity since their father was a multi-millionaire himself.

The sisters had designed a number of water growing systems, known as hydro-systems, to use instead of soil systems. It was easy to keep the water warm and filtered and didn't take any extra electricity since they were using the geothermal energy to heat everything. They didn't need special grow lights either as the frosted windows on the roofs of the greenhouses, all of them, were a new kind of solar energy system that turned sunlight into electricity just like those heavy solar panels you see on rooftops and in fields alongside big warehouses. The sisters had designed a type of liquid solar panel, and after testing it on one of the flower growing greenhouses, fine-tuned the details and now all the greenhouses had this type of 'solar paint' on the roof glass. No need to be on the grid and raise suspicion.

The sisters looked like hard working farm folk but, truth be told, they held PhDs in engineering and physics. They knew how to manipulate the 'system' to their advantage.

On this day, the sisters would be potting new seedlings from a number of hybrid projects for the summer growing season with a potential harvest that would begin earlier than the usual fall harvest. They were hoping one of the hybrids they had been working with for the past five years was ready to mature in just ninety days from today. That would mean a July harvest with a possible second planting for a late October harvest. Greenhouses were wonderful because you could set your growing seasons as needed.

Mo punched in the code for the intricate lock system they'd had designed for all the greenhouses. No reason not to be careful. They were getting ready to change to a fingerprint recognition system soon. As they entered the front area and threw on the lights they were greeted with hundreds of tiny seedlings about five inches tall with at least three sets of leaves. Yup. They were ready to be set in their own growing pots. The sisters got down to business and didn't realize the time until shadows began to lie across the work benches.

Mo looked up, stretched and said, "Hey, Lainie, it must be getting really late. Didn't realize the time. Probably around four o'clock, ya think?"

Lainie looked out the windows at the west end of the greenhouse. "Yup. Probably is. We should call it a day, set the timers and take care of the chickens and all. I know we ate something around midday but I'm starvin'. How about we make some pasta, sauce and salad?"

"Agreed. Let's get done here then."

With that the sisters closed the greenhouse for the night and set out to take care of the animals on their way to the house. It took them a while to bed down the animals for the night. The night sky was beginning to take shape promising a clear night.

Lainie and Mo took a moment to look around the farm before they walked into their home.

Lainie sighed, "Maureen, we are surely blessed by all that Mama and Daddy did for us. Sure hope that bright Light is shining on them."

Mo reached over and put her hand on Lainie's shoulder. "Indeed we are, Elaine, indeed we are. This place truly is our paradise on Earth."

They stood there for a few more minutes in a shared silence of gratitude before walking onto the porch and into the house through the mudroom entrance.

Once in the kitchen it didn't take them long to get supper on the table.

As they ate they discussed the new hybrid possibilities.

Mo offered, "I'm thinking that fast growth line is going to do well this year. It sure did last summer only taking four months to mature. We'll have to keep it in its own little glass enclosure within the main room so it can be watched all along the way."

Lainie agreed. "And, we'll keep a detailed data journal with this one. It may turn out to be the main strain we keep going year round. The year round strains we have right now are great. I don't want to lose those. Maybe we can take over greenhouse #5 for the fast growth strain this fall after the harvest of the herbs in there. Makes sense."

"I like that idea. We'll have to plan way ahead as we need to make the move before the fall planting takes place. We may have to wait a month or so for everything to finish in there. We usually sell out of the small plants by mid-

May. We could move the others in with the flowering plants as they are usually gone my mid-June and the fall plants only need the first two greenhouses. We'll have a planning session as soon as we are all set with the new seedlings."

"Great idea. I'm already seeing how things could be worked around. And, we have all those new mums coming along that will need a full greenhouse to themselves. This could work. This could really work."

They threw around a few more ideas before finishing up and getting their tea and moving into the living room. It was an open room with a fireplace on the north wall. Mo set a fire and they began discussing the new law that could make them legal in the state but not with the feds.

Mo began with, "I looked into the new law that was voted into place in January. It seems that the registered growers will be heavily monitored by the state down to every single plant they grow, how much is harvested from each plant and how much is sold to the medicinal shops. They want to keep track of every ounce. I don't like that idea at all."

"Neither do I. Let's not go there then. I do want to keep researching with the oils though. Seems some are having great results especially for kids with a rather severe seizure disorder. If we can come up with a pure enough dilution that is not too strong for the kids, I know of a practitioner that would buy from us without giving our identification away. He's been a client of ours ever since we were in college. You know who I mean, right?"

"Yup I do. OK, then, keep going with your research. Have you come up with a useable dilution yet?"

"Yes. I gave him a small vial a few weeks ago. It is pure by all standards. You know how meticulous I am about my lab work. It would far surpass all public health requirements. I've tested the oil numerous times for purity. Our contact is going to offer it to three of his adult patients with seizure disorders keeping track of their response and will get back to us after three months' time. If the side effects are minimal then I will create a dilution using a weight ratio for the little ones. There is a fellow researcher in Colorado that will buy our oils once the research is finished and he approves. All done quietly, of course. I'll send all the lab research to him for his approval before I even think of sending the oil."

"That's great. Sure hope we can help those kids. Must be terrifying for the parents to watch their own suffer like that. How about our regular clients? We keeping up with their demand?"

"Yes. Just. That's why the new fast growth strain is so important. I just love growing this stuff, don't you?"

Mo smiled then got serious. "We have to discuss our new neighbor Emily. I don't think we'll have any fuss from her. I rather like her already just from the little bit we talked at the store party. It's the feds swarming all over the mountains that bothers me. Just not sure how to take all this busy stuff goin' on."

"I think that will settle down once her house is built. Then there shouldn't be so much traffic around here. The shiners are a bit concerned, too. They came by yesterday to barter and we spent a fair amount of time discussing this very thing. Emily made sure they knew that their homes were safe and that she wasn't going to take anything away from them. They were grateful about that. Seems some of the surveyors got a bit too close for their comfort the other day. About a mile away from them, but that's too close as far as they're concerned. They're thinking about suspending production until they know no one will be up on their part of the mountain. I told them I'd let them know what the latest news is and they seemed OK with that. They'll be around every few days for news until things quiet down."

Mo nodded in agreement. "We just need to be very careful about keeping the growing sheds locked at all times. No matter what. Even if we are just going to the barn for something, we need to lock the doors every single time we leave. Agreed?"

"Agreed. And Michael and Ted are great sources for the latest goings on around here. If anybody knows anything about everybody it's those two. Thank God."

Mo laughed with Lainie as they settled to watch TV for a while.

The moonshine guys were having a similar conversation. They were fifteenth generation mountain men and moonshiners known to all as Earl and Bubba whose given name was Larry. They had what was known as the best moonshine anywhere. They were carrying on the long held tradition of making whiskey similar to the way their ancestors had made it in the lowlands of Scotland for hundreds of years. The difference being the boys made it with corn mash. Sometimes they added peaches for a little flavor. But it was still whiskey.

Bubba and Earl's ancestors came from the Scotch-Irish Heritage. They along with the British had been making moonshine long before anyone else came to the Americas. They brought this tradition with them. After settling in the Appalachian mountain regions, they set up their stills and commenced making some of the best whiskey known to man using the local corn since it was so plentiful. Throughout the history of the new United States, different taxes and laws, including prohibition, tried to control the making of this moonshine but the shiners knew how to hide. Some got caught along the way. To this day, there are moonshiners in the Appalachians still making whiskey by the moonlight. Hence, the name, Moonshine.

Earl and Bubba's still was so well concealed you couldn't even see it from the air. These mountain men might seem to be simpletons at first glance. But do not doubt that they know exactly what they're doing. They know how to order supplies without raising attention and they grow their own corn on a local farmer's land in exchange for a few jugs. They keep to themselves most of the time living off the land hunting deer and turkey, growing their own vegetable garden and buying from the country store as needed. They utilized online shopping to have their orders delivered to the store.

They drove the latest pick-up trucks that they had souped-up in the traditional NASCAR way. After all, NASCAR was born from the moonshine delivery drivers' need for speed. Junior Johnson of South Carolina is one of the most famous moonshine drivers known to man. He and his buddies are the reason there is NASCAR in the first place.

Making moonshine is an easy way to make money in a very poor economy. You keep all the cash you get. You can grow the corn since corn seed is cheap. You can barter a jug for other stuff you need. And, you are your own boss. Yes, it is illegal but Bubba and Earl's family had been in the business for two hundred and fifty years and then some. Who were they to break with tradition?

The boys had built their own cabins years ago. They lived simply. Outdoor plumbing and water was obtained from the nearby creek. They had tapped into a small hot spring near their place and used that water as needed. They had run a line into the cabin for easier access. They had no electricity so they used lanterns and candles for light. They had a wood stove for cooking and heating the cabin and used coolers to keep a few things cold when necessary.

They had built a stone oven outside and used it year round. They made their own breads and cured their own meats. They were truly modern mountain men. They had the latest in shotguns and small caliber hand guns just in case they needed them. They were excellent marksmen. They used high tech bows as well. Better to be as quiet as possible - you never knew who was around these days. And that's what the guys were talking about on this early spring night.

They were sitting on the porch in their rocking chairs sipping some shine and smoking a special blend they had gotten from the sisters down the mountain just the day before when they had brought them a jug in exchange for a little herbal remedy.

Bubba mentioned the new addition to the mountain. "I guess she's alright since she told Michael and Ted she's gonna let us stay here and not change anything. That's good.

Earl nodded, "Yup. But I hope those fellas that's been all over the mountain are about done. They bother me. They haven't come too close but ya never know."

"Ted said they don't need to come by us even though we are on her land. She told them to leave us alone."

"I know. Hope that stays that way. Don't need no interference from the law."

"As long as we hold off on makin' any shine for a few more days we should be fine. We got us enough for the next bit of a while and enough to trade and sell so we should be good. Maybe we should leave a small jug on her back step just to show our appreciation for her kindness. After all, she doesn't have to do anything for us."

"Yup. Good idea. Let's leave some for her tomorrow night. Hey... this stuff from the sisters is good. Really strong. I like it," Earl said slowly.

Bubba just smiled as he inhaled again. "Yup. One hundred percent solid gold herb."

They both took a swig from their jugs, set back and let the herb send them adrift.

Ethan had been busy all day, and spent a good amount of with Ian discussing Emily's blueprints.

"I think we've finally got us a house," Ian proclaimed as he walked into the workshop. He rolled the plans out on Ethan's architect table and Ethan looked them over.

"So she's approved this look and layout?"

"Yes. We've spent the last two days going back and forth online getting the look just right for her. She likes the layout as well. She said we could go ahead and dig the foundations for the buildings as long as we consult with her as we begin decking them out. She just wants to be sure she understands everything so she doesn't make a mistake. Smart girl. So you can go ahead and contact the excavators and get them busy while I present this to the building inspector for first approval. As soon as he approves the excavation layout we can start the real work."

"The ground is soft enough now for the machines to get through. Did she say whether she wanted to keep the large rocks and boulders we find?"

"Yes she does. At some point she would like to build a stone wall along the perimeter from the stuff we dig up. I suggest we move all the rocks to the southwest end of the meadow for now. What do ya think, Ethan?"

"I agree. How about running that by Emily first though, explaining that they would be out of the way down there and we can relocate them at a later date as needed?"

OK. I'll call her right now. We should be ready to go Monday, this being Thursday. We'll have to flag the place before then and the road guys will have to clear the pathways right away."

"I'll call Karl right now and get them started this afternoon with setting the road flags. Can you leave me the blueprints for the final road and driveway and the aerial view? I'd get them but I'm in the middle of sketching the overall homestead design. I'll send that to you in a few."

"OK. You like to make the mud and stuff look pretty, don't you?" Ian teased.

"Shut up, Ian." Ethan laughed right back at him.

Ethan spent the rest of the day scheduling the excavators for a walk through of the site and a start date. He also spoke with the building inspector for the county letting him know that they would need him in the workshop the next morning for blueprint approval. Ethan set about ordering the first of the decking supplies and arranging for outhouses to be delivered late morning tomorrow as the road crew was working to clear the two access roads to the site.

He called Matthews and asked him to come over for an update meeting as soon as possible.

Matthews arrived thirty minutes later coming through the workshop door with a bag in hand.

"Hey Ethan, I bring treats from Michael and Ted. They said we should stay well-fortified so we would build Emily the best house ever," Matthews said as he set the bag on the workbench.

Ethan took one look inside and grabbed the first apple fritter he could get his hands around.

"Mmmmmm," Ethan moaned as he bit into it. "Not only are these heavenly but I haven't eaten all day and this surely is food from the gods."

Matthews grabbed one as well and took a bite. "I agree. Jesus, I'm gonna look like the Pillsbury Doughboy if I stay around very long. Gotta find some control."

Ethan looked at his wristwatch. "Damn. Didn't know it was getting so late. The lights in here keep the shadows out and I lose track of time. It's almost five o'clock."

"No problem. Let's just call these appetizers. So, ya got some info for me about the build?"

"Yes I do. Here's the scoop. We're going to start clearing the roads tomorrow. That should take the rest of the week. Ian and I are meeting with the building inspector tomorrow morning for approval of the first set of blueprints - the excavation and decking set first. The excavators are on schedule for a Monday morning start. They will take most of the week digging, setting forms and moving stuff. We are keeping all of the stuff they dig up. The rocks and boulders are being moved to the southwestern fringe of the meadow for use in a stone wall at a later date. We'll need a lot for filling in the foundations. Emily wants basements in all the buildings - a good idea. We are going to move all the trees to the northern fringe for later use, some as firewood and some for furniture. That's why this is going to take a good long week to complete. The building inspector said he is at our beck and call. I told him how appreciative we were of his attention to this project. Personally, I think he's hoping for some shine from the guys at some point. I'll let Michael and Ted know and they'll get word to them. What does my crew need to know from you?"

Matthews looked over the blueprints. "This looks great. I knew she was busy with something 'cause she hasn't left her house all day except for a quick jog to the store. I think she made more cookies for the boys. Let me take a moment to look these over."

Matthews and Ethan spent the next hour going over the plans and discussing the details.

Matthews rapped things up with, "I've already had the security checked for the crews you will be using. We had to block two men from this project. I'll get you their names and photos so you'll know who to watch out for should they show up. Just let one of the security guys know if anything seems off, even a little bit, even if you can't figure it out, just holler and we'll take over. The site will be under twenty-four hour surveillance for a good long time. If you see someone you don't know just ask to see their badge or signal to us and we'll take care of it. Monday morning I'll go with you to the site to introduce you to the members of the security team. Any questions?"

'No. I'll email Emily all this so she's kept in the loop. I'm sure she's gonna want to be there every day to watch the changes take place."

"Tell you what Ethan. You let me know when it's safe for her to be on the site and I'll take her there myself."

"Done. I think that's all for now. Thanks for coming out so quick."

"Thank you for getting this going so quickly. We'll be taking photos all the time. I'll get you a set of before, during and after pictures for your memory book."

"Wise ass!"

Matthews and Ethan laughed as they walked outside together, and Matthews drove away.

Ethan stood there for a few minutes enjoying the cold air and the quiet. This was probably the last time he could enjoy a free moment for a long time. This project was going to take anywhere from three to four months to complete even with full crews working twelve hour days. Then he would need another two months to finish the barn and clean up other little details. The house should be ready to live in by early August and the barn and stables would be ready for the horses by late October. This was going to be one hell of a busy summer as his company had three other projects in the works as well.

Matthews went to work as soon as he got back, informing his superiors of the building plans, and contacting his team to bring them up-to-date on everything. It was well past eight by the time he sat back in his chair and took a breath. He decided to wander over to the store and see what kind of leftovers they had for supper.

Emily had been going back and forth with Ian all day via email and Skype about both the outside look of the house and the floor plans for the house and the other buildings. And she had just finished another chat with Ian. He had told her they had enough to go on now for the excavation blueprints for the building inspector. He told her the inspector would be out tomorrow to inspect and approve. This meant they could begin the foundation work on Monday.

Emily was both excited and tired at the same time.

She signed off and went to the kitchen to fix something for dinner. She had some leftovers that would do just fine. She ate them standing at the front windows looking out, just staring at the road and the store. She saw something move, focused in, and saw Matthews walk up the steps to the store, probably getting something for supper, she thought, as she walked back to the kitchen to tidy up her dishes. She decided to watch a little TV and settled onto the couch.

Emily let her thoughts drift back to last night and that hotter than hot kiss thing with Ethan. She just couldn't figure out why he had pulled away. It was quite evident he wanted more. Maybe he thought she was too aggressive for him. She knew they had something going on. Why did he run away from her like that? Emily just couldn't figure out what was happening with Ethan and she didn't have a best friend or even a girlfriend to chat with. She really was alone out here. Maybe she would have to make the first move in getting to know some of the people in The Creek. She'd think about that for a while as she watched TV.

Lainie and Mo were comfy, watching a movie and Bubba and Earl were just waking up from their little trip. It was about a quarter past nine and everyone in the Creek seemed to have settled in for the night.

Matthews was just leaving the country store when a huge flash of bright white light almost blinded him. He stopped in his tracks, blinking his eyes and shielding them with his hand.

Emily jumped off the couch as that same bright white light flashed through her little house. Grabbing her coat she ran out the front door and joined Matthews in the road. Michael and Ted had come outside as well and were standing with Matthews.

Bubba and Earl came down from their high rather abruptly as that same blinding white light seemed to be hovering a little south of them. They stumbled off the porch looking up and saw a huge space ship hovering at tree top level just a short distance away.

Lainie and Mo raced out of the farm house and onto their open driveway, looked up, and saw the same huge spaceship just hanging in the sky south of them. A bright white light surrounded the ship. It was eerily quiet. That big thing did not make a sound.

Matthews and the group looked to the north as the bright light seemed to be hanging just above the trees.

Matthews was the first to speak. "Emily, it looks like it's just about over your new home site. That thing is huge and it isn't making a sound. Am I really seeing this?"

Emily nodded her head as she started taking pictures with her phone.

Matthews' radio started going nuts, screeching and blinking. He tried to turn it off but it wouldn't respond. He put it in his pocket to try to muffle the screeching.

Michael and Ted just kept looking at the light. It had started to change colors like the northern lights but it never changed locations. It just hovered above the ground.

Lainie and Mo watched as it started to change colors.

"Jesus fucking Christ Mo, what the hell is that thing?"

Mo just kept looking up. "I sure as hell don't know. It's not as if this is the first time we've seen these things around here. But it's never been so close. They were always high up in the sky, shooting around or coming and going wicked fast. Even when we've seen them in the Applewood Grove they were only there for a split second. This is different. Look at those colors. Amazing, huh?"

"Yeah… I guess it is. I mean the colors are gorgeous. I don't think I've ever seen some of them before. But, holy shit, what's it doin' here? It looks to be somewhere near where that Emily is gonna build her place, doesn't it?"

"Yeah, come to think of it. I wonder what's up there?"

Matthews' group was quickly joined by Kendra and the rest of the security team members. Everyone was talking at once.

"What the hell is that thing?"

"Look at those colors."

"It's rather big, don't ya think?"

"Matthews, shouldn't we contact the rest of the security team up there? Maybe they can give us the 411 on this thing."

"I tried but my radio's going nuts. Try yours."

The others took their radios out but they, too, were just screeching and blinking.

Matthews got a hold of himself and issued orders to the team. "You three get up to the site as soon as possible and keep trying to make radio contact. I'll contact the others and maybe we'll get some answers."

They all left with the team heading out in a hurry toward Emily's site. They took night vision goggles and hiking equipment with bright lanterns. But no sooner had they turned onto the road then their Jeeps stopped running. They were dead as a doornail in the middle of the road. They all got out and just stood there looking at the changing lights.

In no more than a nanosecond the ship was gone, vanishing into thin air without a sound. Matthews' radio came alive. One of the mountain team members was trying to contact him.

Matthews answered. "What the hell is going on up there?"

"Beats me. All of a sudden there was this blinding white light hovering right over the build site. We put our protective eye goggles on and looked up and saw this huge thing just hovering above us. It didn't make a sound the whole time it was here. I guess it was a spaceship, you know, a UFO. It started changing colors and then just vanished. It was gone. Never saw anything like it before. We took a lot of pictures. Sure hope they come out OK. Over"

"Same thing here. Document everything. Don't leave one detail out. Record the start and end times specifically. Email me the report as soon as you can. I'll contact headquarters and then check with the local air traffic controllers and the Air Force for any traffic in this area. Over."

"Yes sir. We'll get back to you ASAP. Over."

"Understood. Over."

Emily and the rest of the group just starred at Matthews. They didn't know what else to do.

Matthews asked the locals a couple of specific question. "I remember Cora saying something about seeing lights up on the mountain. Has this ever happened before? UFO sightings by any of you?"

Michael and Ted nodded their heads yes. Kendra did, too, as well as the five other folks that had joined them.

Matthews smiled at them. "Well, this is a first for me. Anything happen the other times other than you saw them then they were gone?"

"Nope. Saw them about a dozen times over the past three or four years."

"Me, too. Never saw all the colors before, though."

Kendra added, "They were never this close before, either. They were always up in the sky a ways."

Everyone seemed to agree on these things.

Michael and Ted just kept looking at the sky even though the UFO had already left.

Ted spoke out, "I've never seen anything quite like this before. Never so close."

Michael agreed. "Right Ted, never so close before. Wonder what they want with us?"

Emily just starred up at the sky. Kendra was watching her and smiling.

"Well, Emily, welcome to Crab Apple Creek!"

The others laughed and chatted for a while then started to go their separate ways.

Matthew called out to them. "Would you all mind just writing down what you saw tonight and keep those notes handy? Never know when this might happen again. Thanks."

Matthews took Emily by the arm and steered her towards his house, "We need to talk right away."

As soon as they got inside he started.

"Emily, this UFO thing is going to attract the media. You need to stay inside and keep the curtains drawn until they leave. I'll keep you safe but you have to do as I tell you. There will be two agents in your house with you at all times. Do not use your cell or the computer. If you need me, tell the agents. I'll come right over. I'll keep you up to date on all the new faces around here, sending you pictures just in case you can identify anyone. The agency had security block the road three miles each side of your site. This should die down in a couple of days. Any questions?"

"Oh my God. I never thought about the media thing. There'll probably be a bunch of UFO nuts up here won't there? And one of them could be looking for me. Oh shit! I get it. Good thing I have a bunch of movies to watch and books to read. Paperbacks, not on my tablet."

Just then there was a soft knock on the door, Matthews pushed Emily into the bathroom and drew his weapon as he approached the door.

"Agent Sanchez here. ID Project Jacuzzi"

Matthews opened the door allowing Sanchez and another agent to enter. They were in full gear. He holstered his weapon as he locked the door.

"OK Emily. Come on out and say hello to your bodyguards. They will change every twelve hours. I'll give you all the code words as they will change all the time as well. We are on full alert until further notice. Remember, this house is wired for video and sound and will be monitored 24/7."

"OK Matthews. I guess I'm in jail for a while. Better to be safe than dead."

Matthews gave Emily a pat on the shoulder. "You got that right. Lock me out Sanchez. Hope you get some sleep Emily."

Matthews left and the agents swept the house and then asked Emily what she wanted to do.

"I was going to go to bed. Guess I will. Thanks for being here. Good night."

She went into her room, closed the door part way, changed and climbed into bed. She took some herbs and fell into a deep sleep for most of the night.

Lainie and Mo decided to drive over to Emily's access road and see if anything had happened there.

Bubba and Earl started walking down the trail that led close to the site as well.

When Lainie and Mo reached the access road they were met with a blocked entrance. A sign on the post read 'PRIVATE CONSTRUCTION SITE. AUTHORIZED ENTRY ONLY." The Soaring Mountain Builders, Inc.

"Well' Mo said, "Looks like this is really gonna happen. I wonder about that UFO though. Others had to have seen it. Guess we can go on down to the store in the morning and see what's up."

"Looks like that's the only way we're gonna get any info. Let's go home. Maybe the boys will be by to chat about this."

They turned around and headed back home. Bubba and Earl were about a half mile from the site when they were met by the security team stationed on the mountain. They shined lights on the boys.

"Hi there. Can I ask what you're doing walking around the mountain at this time of night boys?"

Bubba answered first. "We live a ways up the mountain and saw that weird thing with the lights. Did you see it, too? We were just wonderin' what it was and if it damaged the mountain at all."

"Yes, we saw it, too. And it doesn't look like it did any damage. We'll take a closer look tomorrow. Just to let you know this is private property here and the owner is about to start building. Please be sure to stay a safe distance away. Wouldn't want you two to get hurt or anything. Can one of us help you home?"

Earl quickly replied, "No thanks. And thanks for talkin' to us. I reckon we know our way around these here Blue Ridge Mountains better than you all 'cause we grew up here. We'll be on our way now. Take care."

The security guy and the rest of the team that Bubba and Earl hadn't noticed watched and followed them back up the mountain about a half mile to make sure they didn't turn back. The cameras would have picked up any movement within a ten mile perimeter. The team leader just wanted to be sure. He reported to Matthews and settled back into the night watch detail. He and the team knew they had just met the infamous moonshiners and laughed and talked about them while waiting for the second team to arrive.

As soon as the second team stopped at the access road their radios came to life. They contacted the mountain team. Everyone checked in. No problems with the site. The team leader reported this to Matthews.

Matthews gave new orders after talking to the mountain team leader.

"OK Murphy. Come on back to base. Mountain team checks in all clear, no damage to the site. Over."

Murphy responded with, "Affirmative Matthews. We are at the access road entrance. Sutherland has already closed off the road for the contractors. Sending you a picture now. We'll return right away. Check in when we get there. Over"

"That's affirmative. Picture received. Over and out."

The team loaded up and set off back to base. Matthews sent an email update to his superior and waited for the team. He watched Emily's house go dark except for the bedroom and kitchen. He would talk with her in the morning to get her thoughts about the UFO incident. She didn't seem all that upset - more like surprised. The more he thought about it, the more he thought she seemed almost as if she knew they were for real. He spent some time thinking about that until Murphy knocked on his door and interrupted his thoughts.

"Hey Murphy. Good to see you're all back. The others in for the night?"

"Yes sir. Just wanted to make sure you knew all is OK. I'll key up a report and email it to you right away. Anything else?"

"No. That ought to do it. We'll all meet at seven tomorrow before the crew heads up the mountain. Thanks."

"See you then. Good night."

Matthews returned to his laptop and spent the next hour coordinating reports and sending off pictures of the UFO his team had taken along with the necessary paperwork.

Ethan was having trouble sleeping. He hadn't seen the UFO because he was in his workshop at the time engrossed in putting together the work schedule for the next few days for his four crews. He finished around ten and closed up heading into the kitchen for a bite to eat and then his bedroom. He showered and flopped onto the bed grabbing the remote and tuning in the news. That's when he heard about the strange lights on Soaring Eagle Mountain. He sat up, grabbed his phone and called Matthews.

Matthews answered right away. "Matthews here."

"Matthews, its Ethan. What the hell happened up there tonight?"

"Why?"

"I just saw the news about the UFO thing. Is the place crawling with news reporters yet? Is Emily OK?"

"Emily is fine. She was in her house like me when we saw the bright white light. And, no, there aren't any news trucks here yet. I have that under control though. They are not being let anywhere near the building site. There's extra security on the road as we speak three miles each side blocking traffic. Only locals are allowed to get through. Emily has two bodyguards in her house with her. She is in lock down until this thing clears. Please carry on as normally as possible and report any strangers to me immediately. Got it?"

"Yes. Thanks. Can I go to her house and see her? I want to be able to keep her up-to-date on the progress being made at the site."

"I'll arrange that tomorrow. Wait until I give you the all clear."

"OK. Thanks. See you tomorrow. I'll be at the site at seven to clear the road crew for access and start-up. We all secure with them?"

"Yes, Ethan. If anyone new shows up, deny them access and contact me immediately. Security will be next to you at all times. They will handle the newcomers."

"Great. Tomorrow then." Ethan hung up and watched the news for a while more before finally settling in for some sleep. He woke up around five and started his day. He wondered what else was going to happen around here. He just shook his head and got his day underway.

Ethan met with the building inspector in the workshop at six. He spent about twenty minutes going over the plans for the excavation and road access then gave his approval. He stamped and signed papers and was gone with the promise to be available whenever Ethan needed him. Ethan said he would keep him in the loop.

Ethan set out for the site around six thirty going right past the store and heading up the hill. He ran into the road block right away. He showed his ID and was let through. He arrived at the access road ten minutes ahead of the road crew.

"Hey Karl. Looks like you're ready to unload and get busy. Any questions about the path?"

"No, Ethan. The photos and prints you emailed over are great. I am going to have the guys mark the trees first. Hardwoods will have an orange tag and the pine and other softwoods will have yellow. We'll stake the roadsides as we go. Doesn't look like there's any water along the way but you never know. These underground ponds are amazing around here. We'll just build a bridge for your client if we find one."

"Sounds good. Let's get going."

The equipment was offloaded as the guys began to walk and mark everything. Ethan walked with them. As the new pathway for the permanent driveway was cleared they ran into water just under the surface. They spent about an hour planning a new strategy. It was an underground pond with connections to the creek on the other side of the site. They decided to build an old-type covered bridge to cross the pond and preserve it. For now they would build a temporary bridge that would support all the big heavy equipment that would need to use it. This was going to delay the project by about two to three days.

"Don't worry Karl. I've built in thirty days of delay for this project, it being spring and all. Ya know how it could just decide to snow a foot any time and the spring rains will probably be a problem especially with the new pond. I know you guys know how to design earth friendly run off so I'm not worried about that and the covered bridge idea is great. Emily is going to love that. Even if the bridge is small it's gonna add so much to the place. Great idea. I guess I owe ya a little something for that, huh?"

"You owe me big something for that. My bridge expert is already working on the design and should be ready to order supplies this afternoon. He'll be here in about an hour to walk the path so let's get goin' and clear some brush."

Everyone laughed and agreed and by the time the bridge designer arrived, they had the path cleared to the edge of the meadow.

They took a small break as the designer, Karl, and Ethan walked around the bridge site. When the boss returned, the crew got busy marking the access road to be widened and cleared. They started on the access road after lunch and had it cleared by late afternoon.

The second road crew arrived in the afternoon to begin moving the trees to their appointed place on the north-east side of the site and the rocks and boulders to the south-west corner of the site. By nightfall the access road had been leveled, graveled and was ready for use. Friday would find the road crew building the road over the pond. The big excavation machinery was due to arrive on Monday and the access road was ready to accommodate them. The foundation dig would begin on Monday.

Ethan's crew would be busy staking the foundations for all the buildings for the next few days including Saturday if needed. Ethan checked in with Matthews throughout the day to keep him up-to-date. Matthews informed Ethan that he had clearance to visit Emily that afternoon.

"Ethan, you're all cleared to see Emily. And, the news crews showed up a few minutes ago. Six of 'em. Please, be careful."

"Thanks Matthews. Will do. I don't plan on talking with any of them for the simple fact that I didn't see anything. Please don't tell Emily about the covered bridge. I want to surprise her and have her look at some prints of designs so she can pick out what she likes. I know not to use electronic equipment from her house. That's why I printed them out."

Matthews chuckled. "OK, Ethan. The bridge is all yours to tell. I can't wait to see it either. I think it's a great idea. How cool is that?"

Ethan laughed out loud. "No kidding, huh? OK, later." Ethan hung up and went back to work.

Thursday morning found Lainie and Mo at the country store around ten. As soon as Michael and Ted were free of customers they started in.

Mo started. "You see that UFO last night? Oh, my God, that thing was huge. And that white light near blinded us. Once it started changing colors we could really get a better look at it."

Ted jumped right in, "Shit yes! A bunch of us came together in the middle of the road and watched that thing. Matthews and Emily and their team and a few customers that were in the store all in the middle of the road. Good thing no trucks came along. Jesus Christ that thing was amazing!"

Michael added, "I've seen the things up in the sky but this was so close. It looked like it was right over where Emily is building her new home. Wonder if it did any damage over there?"

"That's why we came down," Mo asked. "Wondered if anyone had been to the site. We drove over after the UFO left but Ethan's got the road blocked off for the building crews. The military has the main road blocked but we got through 'cause our names were on the OK list."

Just as Mo finished talking Bubba and Earl walked in.

"Hey y'all," Bubba greeted everyone.

"Hey Bubba, Earl," was the mutual response from everyone.

Earl started with, "Y'all see that spaceship last night?"

Everyone nodded that they had.

"Well, we tried to walk on over to the meadow to get a look at the place but these security guys stopped us. Guess they's there for the buildin' an all. They wouldn't let us near the place. Said they wanted to make sure we didn't get hurt. And today we seen them clearing the old access road and making another one. Why do they need two roads?"

Lainie replied, "We saw all that when we drove by ourselves just a bit ago."

Ted answered Earl's question about the two roads. "Well, Earl, I guess they need two roads so they can get all the trucks and big equipment in and out without tying up the one access road. The access road's gonna be filled in with native trees and bushes when the building's done and the new road is gonna be the drive in to Emily's place. Ethan said the rangers are gonna wait to see if they need another access road. They might cut one south of Emily's place off her drive if they think they're gonna need one."

Bubba thought for a moment then said, "Well, that makes sense. Guess ya can't have those big trucks turnin' around and making a mess of the meadow. OK then. We just don't want anyone comin' up the mountain ya know?"

Heads nodded again.

"Ya think the news people will come by this time?" Lainie asked.

Michael answered. "Probably 'cause it did make the news last night on all the major networks. That thing was so close I'm surprised none of us were affected. Matthews says the security team on the mountain at the build are all OK. No burns or sickness or anything. No one lost their memory either. They got some great pictures of the thing though. Matthews has them in his house over there. But don't tell the news people, please. He wants them gone as soon as possible and so do Ted and I. Business will be great but I don't want the world to know about The Creek if ya know what I mean."

Lainie and Mo agreed as did Bubba and Earl. They all had secrets to keep. They talked some more for a while over coffee and muffins then Bubba got up from the table.

"Earl, wait here for me while I take a walk. I'll be right back."

Bubba left and was back in about five minutes. He was smiling from ear to ear. He had left a small jug of shine on Emily's back porch without being seen.

Earl looked at him asking, "All set?"

Bubba nodded. "Guess it's time to mosey on home. Nice seein' y'all."

Mo stood up as well. "Hey boys, Lainie and me'll give y'all a ride if ya want up to our place. What do ya say?"

Bubba looked over to Earl and they both accepted. The four of them settled up, said their good-byes and went on their way.

Michael and Ted spent the next couple of hours getting ready for the lunch rush. They were discussing how much they should make when the first news truck stopped outside the store. They both smiled, tripled their recipes, and had everything ready by noon when five more news trucks showed up.

Lunch time was busy in The Creek. Word got out and the locals started showing up by early afternoon. Michael and Ted recruited one of their neighbors to help with the store and they kept busy all day. Everyone who came in had to have something to eat, of course, and the talk carried on well into the evening. The news reporters were interviewing everyone on camera and said they would edit things for the six and ten o'clock broadcasts.

Everyone had a story to tell about seeing last night's UFO and the others for as long back as anyone could remember. Miss Cora, being one of the oldest in The Creek, had her say in her most colorful way. She had everyone laughing and adding their own stories to the mix.

Matthews had an agent in the store all day looking like one of the locals. He had him taking photos and Matthews sent them on to the new headquarters in Schuyler, Virginia, to be investigated. They didn't want any of Yuri's henchmen showing up in The Creek.

Matthews was concerned about all the attention The Creek was getting. He wasn't the only one.

Yuri's east coast man contacted Yuri about the UFO thing. It was in a very remote place. A good place to hide. Yuri's man, Jones, suggested he take a trip up that way and have a look around. Yuri agreed and Jones was on his way by Thursday night. He got a room in Boone at the Best Western and struck up a conversation with the registration people.

"Hi, I'm Sam Jones checking in."

"Good evening Mr. Jones. My name's Kim. I have you in one of our guest suites. It's all ready for you. When would you like me to have dinner sent up?"

"Thanks. You can have that sent up in about twenty minutes please. I only need one key card. Is the pool still open?"

"Yes sir until eleven. That gives you about an hour and a half to enjoy the pool area. Is there anything else I can do for you?"

"No. Thank you. I'm all set."

"Have a great stay with us."

Jones headed to the elevators and overheard a couple talking about the UFO sighting.

"I didn't see it but from what I hear it was right over the houses and you could see in the windows. Spooky."

"I heard the same thing. Maybe we should go check out the place tomorrow. It's only about an hour away. Should we?"

"Yes. We'll do it."

Jones wasn't sure about the windows but the news had said some of the eye witnesses said you could see it right above the tree tops about a few miles from that little place. Oh yeah, Crab Apple Creek. Just a spot in the road was how the travel guides referred to it. Great place to hide.

Jones settled in and had his dinner. Then he headed to the pool to swim a few laps. He stayed in good shape. He never knew when he would need to protect himself or take someone down.

Jones contacted Yuri to let him know he was in place.

"Good. Take pictures of all of them no matter who they are and send them back to me. I'll have my contacts run them through the face recognition program. Don't screw this up Jones."

"Yes sir. I'll keep you informed."

"You know what happens to those that do less than the perfect job,' Yuri threatened.

"Yes. I understand."

Yuri hung up and Jones headed to bed. Tomorrow he would take great pleasure in finding a whore to please him for the night after Crab Apple Creek. No, he would find two. It was always more fun with two.

Kendra had witnessed everything with the group out in the road in front of The Bend in The Road Country Store, and then some. She had always been very sensitive to the weather and had heard the wind pick up a few minutes before the bright white light was seen. This wind happened every time just before a UFO was sighted over the mountain. It wasn't a strong wind. It was similar to a stiff breeze blowing in once and again.

So, on this night, Kendra was working in her office and happened to look out the window just as that stiff breeze started to blow. She noticed the trees beginning to move then heard the sound the wind makes when it gets stronger. She stopped what she was doing, grabbed her coat and ran out the front door looking up at the night sky. She knew in her bones that a UFO was about to get close to the mountain.

What surprised her and the others was how close it actually got. In the past, you could see the lights and maybe a shape. It would stay in one place sometimes and other times it would move around a bit always staying somewhere over the mountain. It never made a sound. It was eerily silent. Then, in the blink of an eye, it would be gone.

This time, the UFO came super close. It hovered just over the tree tops. The while light was almost blinding as it pulsed. Then the white changed to a rainbow of colors shimmering and pulsing all at the same time. This went on for at least five minutes. And, again, there was no sound from the thing. Absolutely silent. Kendra just kept looking at the thing. It seemed to be about over the place where Emily was going to build her home.

Kendra would have bet anything that it was over Emily's site. They had never come this close before. Wonder what was so special about the site? There must be a reason for the UFO to hover there. She wondered if it had been there before and had come back to get something or see something again. Maybe it was leaving people behind just like they did in *Close Encounters of The Third Kind*. Yeah, it was only a movie but you never know.

Then it was gone just like all the other times. Silently gone. The sky looked awfully dark after it left. No one said a word, then everyone began to talk all at once.

They all stood around for a long time wondering if it was going to come back. Finally, the cold seemed to get to everyone at the same time. They all went off to their own homes to get warm.

Kendra fixed a cup of tea and took it to her desk. She opened her private journal where she kept notes on all the UFO sightings she had encountered in The Creek. She had seen more than a hundred sightings but tonight's was the closest. She wrote a very detailed description of the event that included her thoughts and feelings. She felt this specific UFO encounter was going to make a major difference around The Creek. She couldn't quite put her finger on it, but she knew this night had been a turning point for many.

She finished around ten and headed to bed. She meditated for a bit then fell fast asleep until her alarm softly woke her up around six the next morning.

After getting her calls and emails taken care of, she wandered over to the store around nine just in time to see Lainie and Mo and Bubba and Earl chatting with the guys.

She said 'Hey' and listened for a bit then grabbed a cheese danish and went back to her home office. There were about a dozen emails inquiring about the UFO, wondering if she had witnessed any of it. She answered them simply and quickly, denying she had seen anything. She just didn't want to become involved with the circus that was about to descend upon The Creek. Kendra knew the media folks were about to show up. She had seen the reports on TV and online. She had three big sales pending in the Pine Ridge area and didn't want anything to interfere with them. She had meetings with all the parties today at eleven, twelve-thirty and two which meant she would be away most of the day.

She was ready for two of them to sign the purchase and sale agreements and was hoping the third would be ready tomorrow. These were big properties all over ten acres each, and the owners were into conservation. They just wanted to build nice homes and barns and leave the rest as it was. It was very important to the folks around here that the forest be left as is. No clear cutting for timber and no residential developments. There was too much at risk for those kinds of things.

CHAPTER 14

O thers were watching The Creek as well. The NOVAE had sent the ship. Its purpose was to align the Earth where Emily was building to make it pure and set magnetic fields in place so that she would be able to connect with The NOVAE as easily as possible whenever she chose. The ground had been frozen so the ship sent sound waves to warm it up so the clearing would do as little damage to Mother Earth's children as possible. The trees and rocks would now move easily when the equipment pushed them away.

The sound waves created a side effect causing crystals to be formed. This usually took millions upon millions of years in regular Earth time. However, the sound waves that they used caused this to take place within a twenty mile radius of the site instantly. Not all rocks were crystallized but there were millions that were in every color of the rainbow.

There was a series of caves not too far from the site up in the national park that had been transformed and whoever found those was in for a treat.

The energy from the ship did not have any effect upon the people of the Earth nor did it leave any visible changes to the area. No one and not one thing was damaged in any way. The only problem was that a lot of people had witnessed this ship and this made them all curious. The NOVAE were going to have to keep an eye on the humans just in case any of them became too curious. They would not interfere unless the need to keep their own safe arose, and there were some of their own living right there in The Creek. They had been for centuries. They looked like humans and lived like humans but they were ETs.

The CON was furious. Yuri had not performed as they had expected. They had visited him with nightmares and night terrors. They had taken care of his mistakes with the weak humans he used. And now, one of The NOVAE's own was in hiding from him and he still did not have a lead on her. Time for some strong intervention. They would use Nick to get the message to Yuri that he was expendable.

Nick had been moved to a permanent location just outside of Baltimore in a federal prison that held only the worst of the worst. Lockdown was the norm. Nick had been placed in solitary for his own protection. The feds knew Yuri had connections in all the prisons and jails and they didn't want anything to happen to him until they got everything from him they could get. They wanted information that would convict Yuri - solid evidence that was beyond a shadow of a doubt. The agencies were looking for the death penalty for Yuri Strovonovich. They had been gathering information for the past three years and had enough for several life sentences but they wanted him and his closest partners convicted and sentenced to death.

It was after midnight when Nick woke up. He thought he heard the door to his cell unlock. He waited for the light to come on but it never did. All of a sudden all hell broke loose in his cell. He went flying across the room hitting the wall and falling to the floor. His back felt like it was on fire and he couldn't get his breathe. A small light began to brighten up the room. When he looked around he saw a horrible monster standing in front of him. It was at least eight feet tall with broad shoulders and four arms. It wasn't human. It had claws for fingers and spikes coming out of its shoulders. It was black with hair all over it and bright green eyes that glowed. There was just enough light for Nick to see that the monster was coming for him again.

The monster spoke. "You have been chosen to set an example of what happens when you disobey the CON. We are a mighty intergalactic force stronger than any human force could ever be. Your boss, Yuri, has caused a great deal of trouble for us. We are going to show him what will happen to him if he continues to disappoint the CON. You are going to be the example."

All Nick remembered was that he began to scream as the monster pierced his gut with one of its claws. It breathed fire at him and burned his face. It broke both arms and legs before Nick finally lost consciousness. The monster woke him up so he would feel his limbs being ripped from his body. Nick died. His spirit rose from his body and was taken prisoner by the CON.

The guards heard the screams and opened the cell to find Nick's body in pieces. His blood had been splattered on every surface of the room. They immediately sounded the alarm. The sight was so gruesome that the guards gagged and vomited. When more guards arrived, the same thing happened. The stench was like nothing they had ever smelled before.

As soon as the prison was secured, the crime scene unit came in with the forensic team. They all had to take a minute after they first saw the room.

"What in God's name happened in there?" the lead agent asked.

The senior guard answered. "We don't know.

I haven't got the faintest clue. This place is in permanent lockdown. No one was in the halls. All the guards are accounted for. All I can think of is that the wrath of hell came into that room and took revenge on the prisoner. Never saw anything like this in my life."

The lead agent continued, "It's going to take the techs a long time to secure this room. Please move the other inmates out of this block if you can. I don't want anything to compromise the scene. We'll move the body, as soon as the techs say we can. Until then, can you make sure no one comes down here?"

"Yes sir. Not gonna be a problem. This is beyond gruesome. I'm sure no one will want to come down here. I've never seen a living human, or a dead one for that matter, torn apart before and never want to see it again."

The block was secured. The techs took more than a week to process the cell. Nick's body was transported to the autopsy suite after the initial search. The media caught wind of this and even though they were not given any details, they knew something horrific had happened.

Yuri heard about it, too, and knew the man in the black hat had something to do with it. For the first time ever Yuri was shaken and scared. He needed to think. He needed to find that bitch Barbara and find out what she knew. Damn, this was bad. Really bad.

On the better side of things, the NOVAE were on high alert. They knew they had been seen over Soaring Eagle Mountain and this was causing a great deal of attention to be brought to The Creek. But they had the situation in control.

Anyone new that came to the area from the time of the UFO sighting on, until further notice, and got a look at Emily, wasn't going to see her as she really was. They would see an old woman of about eighty-five years old with short white hair and wrinkled skin, hunched over, leaning on a walking stick made from a local tree for support.

The NOVAE were benevolent and kind but when it came to protecting their own they spared nothing.

Matthews was informed within minutes of the body being identified as Nick's. He was given the go ahead to tell Emily, just not details about how he had died. Hell, he was told no one could figure out how he had been killed, so not telling Emily about that was the easy part.

He headed over to Emily's around four that afternoon to speak with her. Once inside, he asked the other agents to remain in the kitchen and listen from there.

"Emily, I have some disturbing news for you. Nick was found dead in his cell in the middle of the night."

Emily just starred at Matthews for a long time. "I'm not sure I know how to take this. He was my supposed husband but that was all a lie. I thought I loved him but that wasn't true. Not that I wanted him dead, but it does make my life better I guess. At least I don't have to worry about him anymore. But what about his boss? The really bad guy? What's gonna happen now? I'm sure I'm not any safer with Nick dead. I might even be in more danger. Oh God I need some time to think about this."

"Emily, you are still safe here. No one knows you're here. I'm sure you've seen the media vans. And, yes, there are a lot more people here because of the UFO but, with that being said, we have a photo of one of the bad guys and everyone is on full alert if he should show up here. He will be dealt with quickly and removed from The Creek. There are agents at the store all the time, 24/7, even when it's closed. There are agents all over the media vans at all times. They look like media tech crew members and some look like the locals. I've given the go ahead for the agents to use their laptops so you can see what's going on out there. Just ask them anytime you want to take a look. I'm going to remain in your house for the next few hours working from here and not leave you. Please, talk if you want, be quiet if you want, bake some of those cookies you like…. Do whatever you want. That therapist you asked for is supposed to arrive tomorrow but we've asked for her to be held back a few days until this circus leaves town. Tell me what you want to do."

"Well, with all that said, I guess I'll just sit here for a bit, quietly, and think about stuff. Maybe do some meditation. I need some of my herbs first though. I need to calm down."

Emily got her herbs and some water then sat down on the couch and closed her eyes. She stayed that way for the better part of an hour before she took a deep breath and got up.

Matthews got a call and walked in to tell Emily that Ethan wanted to spend some time with her catching her up on the build.

"OK. How about around six-ish. I'll fix some pasta and sauce for all of us and we can hear what's been going on together."

"OK. You sure?"

"Yes. I will need lots of time to process everything that's been happening and I want to concentrate on the good stuff most of the time. So, yes. Tell him to bring some French bread from the store on his way over."

"Yes Ma'am," Matthews said with a little grin. She was amazing, that Emily. She seemed to be in touch with her feelings and able to process the latest crazy news OK. She was a little shaky but at least she was trying.

Matthews informed headquarters of this news and set about working on his laptop while Emily prepared dinner.

Just before six there was knock on the back door. The agents checked the security camera and then let Ethan in. They searched and cleared him then told him Emily was in the kitchen. He looked at Matthews as he passed the table, both nodding a silent hello.

"Hi Emily. Smells awesome in here. What's for dinner?" Ethan asked as he came over to the stove to have a look.

"Hi Ethan. Homemade spaghetti and meatballs, salad and cookies for dessert. Did you get the bread?

"Yup. Here it is. Can I help you with anything?"

"Sure. How about making some garlic butter? The stuff is on the table just waiting for someone to get busy. Once you mix it, please slice the bread the long way and spread the butter on it. Use all the garlic butter please. Then place it on the foil and I'll close it when I'm ready to put it in the oven. Thanks," Emily smiled at Ethan before turning back to the stove.

Ethan felt like he was going to pass out. Her smile was enough to bring a man to his knees.

Matthews asked Ethan about the build, saving him from any embarrassment.

"Hey Ethan, how's the build going? Emily got you busy in here?"

"Yup and the build is going great. I'll tell y'all the latest at supper."

Emily gave some orders to Matthews. "Hey Matthews, this isn't a restaurant. How about setting the table for the five of us? You know where the stuff is."

"OK Emily. Not a problem," Matthews replied as he went about setting the table.

Just a few minutes later Emily called out, "Supper's ready. Come and get it."

Matthews told the agents on duty that the three of them would take turns and he would be the last one to eat.

"This is great. I haven't had a home cooked meal in a long time, not one this good," commented the first agent.

"Thanks so much. I do appreciate a man enjoying his food."

He finished and the second agent came to the table. She, too, complimented the food.

"You're welcome agent. Glad y'all are enjoying my efforts. It's been a long time since I cooked for a bunch of people. This is kinda fun."

All smiled as Matthews came to the table.

When he was all set Ethan told Emily about the covered bridge.

"Emily, we ran into a small problem on the place we cut through to be used for your driveway. We literally ran into a small pond just before the meadow clearing. The road guys knew these under the surface ponds were around so they weren't too surprised."

"Oh. So does that mean we have to find another path to the site?"

"Nope. Karl, our road guy, suggested we build a bridge over the pond. I agreed. So, we got to talking about it and came up with the idea of building a covered bridge. Not a big one though, only about half the size of the ones you see in pictures. The pond's a bit wide so we would need to build a ways before and after the actual edges just to make sure the drive was clear should there be any kind of flooding. What do ya think? Like the idea?"

Emily was thrilled. "I love the idea. How awesome is this to have my own covered bridge? This is great! Matthews, OK with you guys?"

"Sure. HQ approves. And so do I. I think it's really awesome myself."

"Great. So, Emily," Ethan continued, "I have a few pictures of different styles of bridges here for you to look at after supper. If there isn't one that you like we can always mix up the specifics and come up with a special one just for you."

"Really? Design one just the way I want it? This day is getting better all the time. OK. We'll start looking at the pictures after supper."

The kitchen became quite animated with talk about the bridge and the build itself. An hour later the dishes were washed, food was in the fridge and the table was covered with the bridge pictures.

"Emily, these are the six basic types of bridges found in the Appalachians. The support structure will be determined by Karl and his crew. The part everyone sees will be determined by you and Karl. Some of the exterior structures are for support and need to be kept. He highlighted those here. Anything else is for you to decide."

"OK. So, I don't really care for these two. They are rather simple and plain. This one is just too weird. So, we are down to three. Let's talk about them."

They spent the next two hours looking at the three remaining bridges with Ethan telling them about the history of their designs related to the Appalachians. Emily finally selected one of the bridges but added some exterior design work that gave the bridge its own country flavor. A sign would be placed on the top peak with the name of the farm once Emily had settled on one. She was thinking about what she would name the place with great concern. She wanted to get it just right. No hurry on this as Ethan said he would make the sign and hang it whenever she was ready.

Matthews had been on his phone a lot during the evening, always stepping into the other room. The agents kept busy with the surveillance equipment, making sure no one came near the house.

Matthews was concerned about a man who had shown up mid-morning. He talked to most of the media people and had spent a lot of time in the store asking questions and listening to every conversation he could. The security detail in the store had taken a lot of pictures of him and Matthews had just gotten word about his ID.

"This is great Emily. Can't wait to see this when it's done. I gotta get back to my place now. Work to do. See you in the morning."

The agents walked him out the back door and secured it. They came into the kitchen and looked at the bridges before walking through the house.

Ethan took his leave a few minutes later.

"Thanks for dinner Emily. It was great."

"You are very welcome Ethan. And, I love the covered bridge idea. I can't wait to see it. I feel like a little kid waiting for Christmas. I Hope all these news people leave tomorrow. I want to visit the site and watch everything. I don't want to get in the way though. Would that be OK?"

"Sure. How about we plan on Saturday around ten. I'll pick you and your crew up and we'll take a look at things - if everything here is back to normal of course."

"Great. I'll tell Matthews. Wait, I don't have to. Hey Matthews," Emily called out into the air, "Ya got all that?" she laughed. "My house is wired for sound, remember? They can hear everything."

Ethan laughed as well. "Oh yeah, that's right. So, Matthews, text us and let us know if Saturday is OK."

Both their phones dinged at the same time. The message was colorful and approving.

They laughed as Ethan got into his coat and headed for the back door. The agents were right in front of him as they moved Emily away.

"See you Saturday, Ethan."

Ethan waved as he stepped out the door and heard it being secured behind him.

Well, the night wasn't a total loss. They all seemed to enjoy themselves and Emily seemed OK with the friend kind of thing. Boy, this wasn't gonna be easy. Ethan thought about Emily all the way back to his place. She was his last waking thought as he drifted off to sleep.

Matthews was on his phone as soon as he stepped through his door.

"You're sure this is one of Yuri's men then? I had him tailed back to Boone. He's staying at the Best Western under the name of Jones. When do we take him down?"

Matthews' HQ contact answered back. "We have a team in place. The hotel has been notified and all guests on that floor have been moved to new rooms. They were told there was a ventilation problem and the hotel gave them all vouchers for free food and a free night. They seemed OK with that. We've bugged the phones although we know he has a throw away. The room's bugged so we should be able to hear his conversation and pick up the signal for who-ever he is talking to. He just requested a couple of ladies for the evening. They should arrive in about thirty minutes. We plan on taking him before that as long as he has made contact with his connection. If we have to wait until he's done with the ladies, then we will. We have agents in both rooms on either side of him and across the hall from him. From what we can gather, he didn't get any information on Emily at all today. He heard about the UFO and the place where it was seen. That is a concern for us as you might have figured out. But nothing was said about who owns the land and her name was never mentioned. Those folks in The Creek are very protective of Emily and their own for that matter. Jones, or whoever he is, couldn't get much detail from anyone."

"That's good. Emily has just picked a design for her covered bridge. Figure that. I told her about Nick. She's rather upset but has been talking about it a little. She's glad he's gone but never wished him dead. She's concerned that his boss will make things more intense in his search for her. I have doubled security around here as you know. We'll just have to wait and keep doing our job to keep her safe."

"That's right Matthews. The therapist you requested is waiting in the wings. Hopefully this media circus will be over with by tomorrow and you can get back to being just a quiet little dell nobody knows about."

"You got that right. I'll be waiting for your updates from Boone."

"I'll let you know as soon as I know. By the way, Matthews, you're doing one hell of a great job down there. And your crew, too. Please tell them for me."

"Thank you sir, I will. Good night."

Matthews checked the surveillance cameras that had been placed around The Creek and in the country store. That Jones guy was all over the place. Time to do some damage control. He ordered his undercover team to chat with the media folks and find out what they had said to Jones. He would spend some time with Michael and Ted right now. He crossed the road and entered the store just as the last people were leaving. Ted was about to lock the door when Matthews squeezed in.

"Sorry Ted, but I need to talk with you and Michael on an urgent mat-ter. Please lock the door and turn off the front store lights. We'll talk at the back table."

Ted did as he was instructed and they joined Michael in the back.

"What's up Matthews? You look very serious tonight," Michael asked as they all sat down.

"It has to do with Emily. You know the feds, us guys, are taking care of her. That's all I can say about that. The UFO thing has brought a lot of attention to The Creek. I just need to know if you or if anyone else mentioned her or her name when this guy was around today."

Matthews showed them the pictures of the Jones guy.

They both looked at each other.

Ted started with, "No. I made sure not to say her name. Michael and I have been wondering why someone like her would want to settle here. We figured she's in witness protection or something and all of us in The Creek have taken her as our own and are trying to protect her from whomever or whatever is after her."

Michael added, "Matthews, its plain to see she's really upset and scared. She tries to hide it when she's with people but we can tell. So, we all had a meeting right after y'all arrived and decided to take her on as one of our own. As far as we're all concerned, she's doesn't exist to outsiders. She's our Emily and always will be."

Matthews was amazed at these guys and he needed a few seconds before he spoke again.

"Michael. Ted. You amaze me. You simply amaze me. You and all The Creek. Your acceptance and love for Emily is indescribable."

"Matthews, Michael and I knew that guy, you call him Jones, was a bad one the minute he set foot into the store. He seemed shifty and was always looking around. He kept walking around trying to hear what people were sayin'. So, Michael and I got word out to everyone to be careful around that guy. Not a word about anything or anyone livin' in The Creek. We take care of our own. You gonna pick him up?"

"Ted, I can't tell you that stuff. But be assured, Emily will be kept safe, especially with your help today. You do amaze me. Just let me know if anything or anyone else shows up asking questions. And, guys do not tell anyone, and I mean anyone, about this conversation and the things we talked about. You may come off as simple country folk but I know better. You both hold advanced degrees in business, communication, and computer science and know just what you're doing here. We may need your security tapes so keep them on a disc of their own. Great job guys, with everything."

Ted and Michael both smiled and nodded agreement with Matthews' orders.

"Alright, I'm outta here. I'm sure you guys are gonna take a while to get this place settled for the night and ready for tomorrow morning. Emily said to tell you thanks for the muffins. They all enjoyed them thoroughly. I'll go out the back if that's OK with you two."

"Sure is Matthews. We'll see you tomorrow," Michael replied as he let Matthews out the back door and locked up. Michael and Ted spent the next hour taking care of the store and another hour making copies of the security discs for Matthews.

Matthews looked out his window before he turned in for the night. It was past two o'clock and all he would get tonight was a four hour nap. He had spent a few hours with his contacts at the Virginia HQ going over all the latest news.

Seems this Jones guy waited until he was done with his 'guests' which was about an hour. Once they left he showered and got on the phone with Yuri. The whole conversation was captured by the feds.

"Did you find the cunt? Did you kill her yet?" Yuri asked.

Jones was careful with his response. "I did not find her yet. There are a lot of media people all over the place as well as police. Seems that UFO has caused a lot more attention than we thought it did. The place is a madhouse. I spent the whole day talking to everyone about their experience with the UFO. The locals are real closemouthed about everything. They don't like strangers. The media crews were much more talkative. I got a lot of pictures which I sent to you. I didn't see anyone who looks anything like that Barbara bitch. I'm going back first thing tomorrow morning to keep watch of everyone that goes into the old country store. It's run by two fags who seem to know everything about everyone. I plan on getting them talking about the locals as soon as possible."

"I got the pictures. Good work Jones. But, I want that bitch. If she doesn't show up tomorrow then you can go back to your usual work. Nick was found dead in his cell. It looks like he was torn to pieces by something or someone. Be careful or you may find yourself in the same condition."

Yuri ended the call. Jones was shaken. He hadn't heard anything on the news about Nick. Maybe the feds were keeping it quiet. He got the shivers as he picked up the phone to call room service.

He was interrupted as agents came crashing through his door and slammed him onto the floor, breaking his nose. One of them placed his boot on Jones' neck to keep him from moving.

"Don't even try to breathe, Jones. You are under arrest for human trafficking, money laundering, conspiracy to commit murder and prostitution. Anything you say can and will be used against you in a court of law. You are entitled to an attorney. If you cannot afford one, one will be appointed to you. Do you understand your rights?"

"What did I do? I'm just a guy on vacation trying to have a good time.

The agent with his boot on Jones' neck pushed a bit harder. "Jones, or whoever you are, do you understand your rights?"

Jones took a quick breathe and answered, "Yes. Get me a lawyer. I ain't sayin' another word. And get me to a hospital. You broke my nose."

Agents got him off the floor and dragged him out of the room. The crime scene techs took over and spent the better part of a twenty-four hour day going over every little thing in that suite.

The prostitutes had been arrested as they waited for the elevator down the hall from Jones' suite. They started to holler but were told to be very quiet as the man they had just been with was known to kill for the hell of it. They both looked shocked as they were taken down to the lobby and placed into the custody of the local police. The feds had arranged with the local police to hold the women until a federal agent could question them about everything they had heard upstairs.

Jones was given first aid in the squad car and taken to the local station to be held for transport to a federal prison the next morning. His arraignment would be on Monday.

There were several federal and international agents waiting for him. He would be surrounded by agents until he was placed in solitary confinement. No other prisoners were being brought to the Boone station. They would be taken to other stations as needed.

Matthews was given all this information as well as an update on Nick's autopsy.

"Matthews, the coroner can't say what ripped him apart. It doesn't look like any kind of blade was used. It actually looks like he WAS ripped apart. Really gruesome. No doubt it's him. No one is claiming him so his remains will be held in cold storage for as long as needed. They are running every test and then some including tox screens for all known and experimental drugs. This surely is a puzzle. We knew someone would probably get to him, but not like this. It's a fuckin' mess."

"Sure sounds like it. I'll have my team be on the alert for any other strangers asking questions. Anything I need to know right now?"

"No. I'll be in touch some time later today. Get some shut-eye. Sounds like you're going to need it. This Yuri scumbag seems to be getting closer."

"Agreed. Later sir."

With that, Matthews left a light on in the kitchen, set his clock for six a.m. and was asleep before his head hit the pillow.

The rest of The Creek had quieted down by eleven. That's when the news people left for Boone. They would be back in the morning, no doubt.

Kendra was keeping a close eye on everyone. She didn't like the energy at all. It was unsettled and chaotic as could be expected with all the strangers in town. Hopefully, they would all leave tomorrow, Friday. The Appalachia State University scientists had been here late and were coming back in the morning for one last interview. She was putting the intention out to the Universe that all would be gone by noon. Things needed to quiet down around here. Emily needed to be and feel safe.

Emily had finally fallen asleep shortly after eleven herself, as she heard the last of the news vans driving off. As soon as quiet had retuned she, too, slept.

CHAPTER 15

Friday morning found The Creek busy again. The news crews were interviewing the professors from the university. There were astrologers, physicists, meteorologists and religious theorists. This took all morning. Then the news folks told everyone they had everything they needed and would be leaving shortly. A holler of joy was heard by all.

They were gone by early afternoon. Matthews had his crews do a thorough sweep of The Creek, all roads leading to and from The Creek, Emily's building site and a full sweep by air before he approved Emily's OK to leave her house.

It was well past three when Emily flew out the front door and headed for the store with her bodyguards close to her.

Ted looked up as she came through the door.

"Well, looks who's here Michael. Nice to see you Emily. What's new?"

"Hi guys. It's great to be out again. Just needed to breathe some fresh air."

"Nice to see you Emily," Michael said. "How's the build coming along?"

"Ethan tells me they're clearing and making the roads. The access road is the easiest 'cause it's already mostly cleared. My new driveway is a whole other story. Seems there's an underground pond in the way. So the road guy, Karl, suggested they build a covered bridge over it. How cool is that?"

Michael and Ted became animated.

Ted exclaimed, "Wow! That is cool. I've never heard of doing that before."

"Me, neither," added Michael. "Usually they just put in a round conduit thing and channel the water that way. This is gonna be awesome. What's it going to look like?"

"Ethan was over last night and Matthews, too. Ethan had pictures of different styles and I chose one and changed some details. They're even going to make a sign with the name of my place, as soon as I come up with one, and put it on the bridge. Ethan is supposed to have a drawing for me tomorrow. He's gonna bring it with him when we go out to the site to see how it looks. I'm so excited I feel like a little kid at Christmas."

Everyone laughed as they grabbed drinks and sat down around the woodstove.

The agents made sure they were between Emily and the two exits just in case someone new came in the door although they weren't expecting anyone. Better to be extra safe with everything going on today.

"So, y'all glad the news circus is gone? Michael and I are thankful for the business but those people are crazy - the ones that follow every UFO sighting around the world. Some are legit scientists but most of them are living in their own crazy world. Ya see those two with the whole spacesuit get-ups on as if they were ready to be beamed up? And did ya see the old guy with the foil hat? Bless his little pea pickin' heart. He kept sayin' all he wanted to do was talk with his friends from another universe."

One of the local farmers was sitting by the stove and spoke up.

"Seems the sheriff had his hands full. I hear some of them kept tryin' to get up on your land, Emily, and have a look. Your security people and the local law kept goin' after them. None of them made it though. Seems the road blocks and the choppers kept a tight lid on 'em. Do ya know if anything happened up there?"

"Not that I've been told, Hal. These security folks tell me nothing has changed and no one was hurt. Seems as if that UFO was just taking a minute to find out where it was and how to get to where it needed to go," Emily offered.

"That's what we heard, too, "Michael added. "Nothing happened. Emily, you can tell us after you visit the place tomorrow. Then we'll know it to be true."

The conversation carried on for a while as they all sat comfy around the stove.

A bit later, Ted got up saying, "Time to get dinner out of the ovens. We're having country baked chicken and biscuits, gravy, mashed taters and some veggies along with a beef stew. Anyone want some?"

"I'll take the chicken dinner but not for a bit yet. Will it be ready around six, Ted?" Emily asked.

"Yes, darlin'. I'll save some for you. Anyone else?"

164

The agents checked in with Matthews and gave Ted their orders.

"Matthews says he'll join you here around six Emily. OK with you?" asked one of the agents.

"Yup. Sounds good to me. In the meanwhile, I'll head on back home and take care of a few things. See you guys later."

"By Emily."

"Later."

Hal added, "Let me know how the land looks up there, OK? I'm just curious."

"Sure will Hal. I'll let the guys know tomorrow and they can get the info to you."

Emily went on back across the road. She made sure her hiking gear was ready along with some hand warmers. It was still cold out in the mornings although the afternoons were beginning to warm up a bit.

The agents reported to Matthews and got caught up on the day's events. Two other agents would accompany Emily and Ethan to the build site tomorrow.

Ethan was busy with his other crews all afternoon. Inspectors were at all the sites and Ethan had to be there each time. He pretty much just followed them around all afternoon.

With all the inspections done and passed, Ethan headed back to the workshop to prepare for tomorrow's hike up to the site. It would be easier because they could take the Jeep almost all the way to the meadow now. The road crew had cleared the access road beyond where it had originally ended up to about twenty yards before the meadow.

They'd finish Monday morning. The new drive was well on its way. The ground structures for the bridge had been delivered and the timbers would be delivered on Tuesday. Karl's crew had to approach the pond from its other side as well. They wouldn't be able to start on the meadow side until the access road extension was completed. All in all they had accomplished a great deal in only two days.

Ian came into the workshop while Ethan was checking his gear.

"Hey big brother, so we passed all the inspections?"

"Yes we did. Great job by the way. Those plans are so easy to read, it takes the inspectors just a few minutes to match the plans to the work. They really appreciate a gifted architect like you little brother."

"Oh, now you're making me feel all warm and fuzzy inside. Wanna hug?" Ian asked as he stepped up to Ethan.

"Get away from me you weirdo. You need to go find your wife," Ethan laughed as he moved away from Ian.

Ian laughed, too. "Awww, you just love me. I know you do."

"Get a life, dude! Get serious for a minute, will ya? Are Emily's plans all set for the foundation dig? The roads should be done by next Friday, covered bridge and all. It's being built to withstand the heaviest of the heaviest equipment vehicles but will look pretty. Karl is setting the in-ground structures in place Monday. He has already dug down and gotten everything in place today. He had four crews working on that new drive all day. That guy's amazing crazy."

"Yes, he is. But, he's the best there is and we're damn lucky to have him living around here. He only works with the best ya know. And, yes, the foundation plans are all ready and have been approved by the building inspector."

"Good. I have the lumber yard waiting for our call. They got all the materials in today. As soon as Karl gets the OK from the state guys for the bridge and road, we are ready to go full tilt. Should be by the end of next week if the weather holds out."

"Sounds good to me. Hey, it's getting late. Gotta be home by six or I may have to make peanut butter and jelly for supper. See ya later."

"OK. Give that gorgeous wife of yours a hug and kiss from me. Tickle the kids from their Uncle Ethan."

Ethan finished and decided to go to the country store for supper. When he got there around 6:30 he found Emily, Matthews, and the others all gathered around the table eating.

"Hey Ethan, what's new?" asked Matthews.

"Not much. Hey, we passed all the inspections for all the projects. That means Emily, your foundation is a go ahead as soon as the state road guys give their OK for the road."

"Why does the state have to be involved?"

"Because the National Forest access road may need to be cut through from your driveway. They get real pissy about these things. Forest fire control and all."

"Oh. Never thought of that. By the way, how many forest fires have you guys had here ever?"

Ted answered that one. "None. Not in the history of this part of the Blue Ridge. They may want access to the forest for more agricultural kinds of things."

Michael smiled at Ted as they both nodded their heads.

"You mean... oh... I thought that was all taken care of with Mo and Lainie. No one else needs to grow around here, right?"

Michael slowly agreed. "Yup. But no one knows about Lainie and Mo except a few of us. So the rangers just make it look like they're checking things out. With you livin' up there, I bet they won't be takin' time to check things out anymore. Not with your security team in place."

Emily nodded her head as she thought about what Michael was saying.

"Hey, guys, can a guy get some food around here?" Ethan asked as he headed over to the counter.

Ted jumped up and joined him.

Matthews offered the stew. "It's great Ethan, especially if you've been working hard all day."

Emily added, "I love the baked chicken and fixins, Ethan. Reminds me of Sunday dinner."

Ethan laughed as he gave his order to Ted. "How about the stew Ted? Looks great."

Ted served Ethan his dinner as Ethan gathered all the extras. The store's homemade bread was known far and wide as the best anywhere. They got the butter from the local dairy co-op. The co-op churned their own using all modern equipment but the milk was from organically fed cows. One taste of the butter and you knew you would never use anything else again. The provisions company, Foodies, Inc, delivered the all-natural locally mill-ground flour and other supplies three times a week. Everyone in The Creek knew when Foodies had been to the store 'cause a few hours later the smell of baking bread and rolls permeated the air all over the mountain. By suppertime all the fresh baked goods were gone.

You could set your clock by the bread baking routine. Every Monday, Wednesday and Friday Michael and Ted set about baking for The Creek. And every Monday, Wednesday and Friday, the locals would begin to gather at the store from late morning on to buy the baked goods and share the latest gossip with any and all that happened to come by.

That's what had happened yesterday. The usual routine was back in place after two days of craziness. Everyone had lots to talk about so by the time Emily and the others were having supper in the back room, there were still plenty of local folks hanging around. They talked about the UFO, the crazy news folks and the even crazier tourists that had happened by. And the scary ones as well.

"Hey guys, y'all remember that guy who tried to look like he was from around here? The one who was asking questions about who lived here, anyone new in The Creek? Well, I just saw the news on the TV in the kitchen and he got arrested for all kinds of bad stuff including intent to commit murder and prostitution. I knew that guy was no good."

"Yeah, Ted, I remember him," said Charlie, one of the regulars from The Creek. "He said he had a hog farm near Pine Ridge. He said his family had been on the mountain for three generations. He followed me outside yesterday and tried to get me to talk to him. I told him to fuck off," Charlie said with a laugh. "Told him we didn't like strangers here."

Smiles could be seen all around the store.

"Nice touch," Matthews commented. "Nothing like a little hostility to get a guy to leave. I saw the news report, too. Glad he's gone!" Matthews couldn't say anything more. But as he looked at Emily, he saw she knew what was going on. She looked a little pale as she stared off.

"Emily," Ethan had noticed the change as well. "Emily, you OK?"

Emily just looked at Ethan and Matthews and shook her head no.

Ted took charge. "Emily, we all here in The Creek don't know, nor do we need to know, what you're hidin' from. It must be bad with all the help you got. Know this: you are safe with us. We all had a talk the night you arrived and decided to protect you as best we could. The folks around here could tell you're a good soul. We could also tell you are scared beyond belief. As far as we're concerned, you're one of us. When that creepy guy started asking questions the alarm went out to the local folks and we refused to talk to him. Since the news people knew nothing about you, they didn't have any information for him either. So, I guess what I'm tryin' to say is this: you're safe here in The Creek as best we can make it. Can't account for the regular outsiders that come in but we'll try."

There was a moment of quiet as Emily broke down and let the tears flow. Napkins were passed her way and this brought a lighter moment around the table. The folks in the rest of the store had gathered close while Ted was talking and surrounded the table as if to show their love for Emily.

When she finally got herself together, she lifted her head, taking in all the people and smiled through new tears.

"Oh, don't worry folks, these tears are tears of thankfulness for all of you. Guess I'm gonna be baking for a long time to show my appreciation for y'all."

"Hey, she's even beginning to sound like us," someone said and everyone laughed and the mood returned to light and feisty as stories began to flow with the dessert. Before long the usual jug could be seen making its way around the store.

Things had just changed in The Creek with Ted's words. A comfortable companionship and acceptance had taken place, a sort of acceptance for Emily and the agents, among the locals. A strong and determined energy flowed freely in the Blue Ridge that night. That same fierce loyalty and determination that had built the Blue Ridge mountain folk from long before time began was apparent.

The guys had outdone themselves with the dessert buffet. Not a crumb was left when the evening began to wind down. It was close to ten o'clock when the first folks began to take their leave. They all came over to Emily to say good night. Hands were shook, hats were doffed, promises of taking care of whatever she needed were once again voiced and a few hugs were shared. Matthews had taken her agents with him stating she was in good hands for the walk home. He had decided to end the in-house detail although there were still agents outside at all times. If Jones had figured out this was a good place to hide, then the feds knew Yuri would eventually send someone else to have a closer look around. Things were going to get a whole lot worse before this was over.

CHAPTER 16

Yuri was informed by one of his east coast informants that Jones had been arrested. To say he was beyond furious was not even close to describing his anger. And fear. He knew the man in the black hat could have him killed at any time. He needed to get a handle on things immediately.

He sent word out that all the lowest of the low that worked for him were to be killed. He'd had enough of two-timing informants. With that order being given, he ordered an orgy in his suite. He demanded six young girls, no older than eighteen, and six men, be brought to him. He would dictate the sex.

He took a long hot shower and dressed in a black silk robe. He drank no alcohol and took no drugs. He wanted to be primed for this. He did take Viagra. He wanted his dick to be huge and hard for a long time. By the time the guests showed up, he was hard and ready.

After getting everyone into the room, he gave his first order.

"Remove all of your clothes and put them in a pile over there, out of the way. We are having a sex party and you are the entertainment."

The girls had been kidnapped from their homes a month earlier and had already been forced into prostitution. The men were slaves as well, used for anything they were told to do. This sex thing was new to them. All knew they had to do whatever Yuri told them to do or they would be taken away, brutally raped and beaten then killed.

Yuri made sure his robe was open so all could see his huge cock. He motioned for one of the girls to come to him. He forced her on her knees and told her to suck him. He told everyone to watch.

He told her to lick his cock. Then he grabbed her head and forced her to take him into her mouth. He told her to suck him until he came then to swallow his cum.

When he was finished with this girl, he told one of the men to lay her down and lick her cunt. He made everyone watch. He then told the guy to make her come and when she did he wanted to watch him ram his cock into her and hear her scream for more.

The men had been given Viagra as well. Yuri did not want any disappointments.

The girl began to moan as the man sucked her cunt. She used her finger to masturbate herself as well. Another girl crawled next to the man and began to jerk his dick. As soon as the girl he was sucking started to cum he thrust into her again and again. They both came at the same time, then collapsed onto the floor.

Yuri clapped his hands and said, "That was pretty good. Now for some delicious fun. You two girls will sit over on the couch and kiss each other everywhere and suck each other's tits until I tell you to stop. You two men will watch the girls and play with each other's dicks. Go."

Yuri stood and watched the sex play then decided he needed some action.

He sat between the two girls on the couch instructing them to lick his dick as he sucked their tits. And they were huge tits. He had made sure of that. He lay back and enjoyed the show until he was about to cum. Then he pushed the girls away and grabbed one of the onlookers. He threw her onto the floor and fucked her hard. She tried not to cry out but a cry did escape. This made Yuri mad so he fucked her even harder. She started saying his name and moaned out loud hoping this would please him so he wouldn't have her killed later. Yuri liked that and decided she could stay. He came hard then fell on her. He finally raised himself and sucked her tits for a while, demanding the others keep playing with each other.

When he finally got up, he told them all to pair up and lick each other's cunts and dicks and suck at each other's tits until they were ready to cum. Then they were to pair up with another partner and the men were to fuck the girls hard.

He wandered the room, touching and sucking as he went and making the men suck his dick. As they all got fucked one after the other he got hard again. As soon as they were all done, he called one of the men over and told him to suck him until he came and they were all to watch.

When Yuri was done, he had them all put robes on and called for food to be brought into the room. He wanted to make sure they were kept healthy so he feed them well. Once they were done, he dismissed them, showered again and fell onto his bed exhausted and maniacally pleased with himself.

The man in the black hat had watched the whole thing. He reported Yuri's activity to his superiors. The CON were not happy with Yuri, but his show of ruthless sex games and the killings he had ordered made them a bit less concerned. He was about to be reminded of his responsibilities to The CON. No horrible night terrors or visitations. Just the man in the black hat with a colleague. All business.

Yuri was awakened just before dawn by a soft noise near his ear. He woke up, turned on the light and saw the man in the black hat standing at the end of his bed. There was another man as well. Yuri sat up scared stiff.

"There is nothing to be afraid of Yuri. This is my colleague. He is observing, shall we say? We need to discuss a few things with you."

Yuri nodded in agreement but stayed alert. "What do you need from me? You know I am here to please all of you."

"We have been watching for the last few days. The killings tonight were a nice touch as was the sex thing. Complete control is important. We need you to gather more women for us. We need them for our own needs. Gather twenty-five of the healthiest women you can find ages eighteen to twenty-two. Bring them here and I will come get them. We want them in five days. They all must be able to reproduce so the ones you have now will not be acceptable."

"Yes, I understand. I will take care of this myself. We just had a group brought to the medical clinic tonight. I will go now and have them taken care of. How do I reach you when all is ready?"

"I will know. Just have them here. My colleague will come for them."

"I understand."

"And, now for the other matter. Nick has been eliminated. You have not found the woman yet. It is critical that she be found and eliminated as well. What do you have to say about this?"

"I am sorry for any delays. My man was arrested before he could establish a connection. However, I am certain I know where she is. I will make arrangements for her to be identified and taken as soon as possible. However, since the place has just had a lot of attention from the media, I think we should take things very slowly for a while so we do not raise suspicions. I will have the place watched for the next couple of months to learn the patterns of the place and then create a plan of attack. Does this meet with your approval?"

The man in the black hat communicated with his superiors and then answered with, "Yes. That is a good idea. They like that plan. We will be watching you all the time."

With that Yuri got out of bed and let them out the door. He did not know they were ETs. They were gone before the door finished closing behind them.

Yuri sat on the edge of the bed shaking with fear. He knew he had to get control of this Barbara thing and fast. He would spend tomorrow working on a plan to get her. For now, he called and had one of his girls sent up and played with her, or rather he had her play with him for a while until he came, then sent her away. He would deal with the Jones problem tomorrow. Now he would sleep.

He was a ruthless man. He had most of the girls he kidnapped have boob jobs right away. He sterilized every one of them, too. They didn't know they were going to have this done. He had set up a clinic with only the best medical specialists in the world. The girls were brought to this place when they were first kidnapped for a complete physical. Then they were drugged the night before the surgery and only found out what had happened when they woke up. They were told they'd had their appendix removed because they had suddenly taken sick. They believed the doctors. After six weeks of recovery they were sent to various buyers to begin their lives as prostitutes.

Yuri had people controlling these girls telling them their families no longer wanted them because they were costing them more money than they could make. The lies were endless and so horrible. The girls were kept drugged so they couldn't think straight and try to escape. Most of them were virgins as they were between twelve and sixteen years old. Yuri made big money selling them into prostitution and to private buyers.

Now he would have to spend some of his billions to set up a contract for the murder of Barbara Gordon.

CHAPTER 17

E arly Saturday morning Kendra was staring out her window thinking about all that had happened since Emily arrived. She felt strongly that the UFO visit was not a coincidence. The media thing had been crazy. She had gotten ten serious requests for property sales. Most of the requests were for the land between Pine Ridge and Boone. One of the requests had been from a man looking for about twenty acres in the immediate area. Kendra told him she would need about two weeks to research his request. He was OK with that and said he would wait for her call.

His name was Jordan Jackson. He worked for Foodie's, Inc. as a truck driver-delivery man. He delivered provisions throughout the northwestern region of North Carolina and had come to love the area. He wanted to settle down and build a modern day farm house that looked old in the Blue Ridge Mountains. He delivered to The Creek at least two times a week and had gotten to know the owners of the country store. He liked the guys. They were genuine and good business owners.

Kendra was busy working on these requests when a light bulb went off. Oh my God! She suddenly realized she needed to give Matthews the information she had on Jordan Jackson. He had said he wanted to know if anyone new was interested in The Creek. Kendra looked at her laptop and saw that it was only six o'clock. She decided to send a text requesting a meeting of utmost importance at Matthews' earliest convenience. Off it went. The phone rang within a second of the text being sent.

"Kendra, Matthews. Is now a good time?"

"Give me ten minutes then come on over."

"OK."

Kendra threw her jeans and a sweater on and answered the door as soon as Matthews knocked.

"Mornin'."

"Good morning Kendra. What's up?"

"I was just going over the requests for land purchases I got from the people that were here with the whole UFO thing. Believe it or not, there are requests for meetings from people interested in purchasing land between Pine Ridge and Boone. One client wants twenty acres right here in The Creek. As I was going over his paperwork I suddenly remembered you had asked all of us to keep an eye out for anyone interested in The Creek since the UFO thing."

"Good work Kendra. Can I have copies of the paperwork for all ten clients? This is just a bit too coincidental for my liking."

"Sure. I have Jordan Jackson's ready for you. I'll get to work on the others and bring them over to you in a little while. I didn't think they would be of interest but since you mentioned it, it does make sense to take a look at them all. Gotta be real careful here."

"That's right Kendra," Matthew said as he looked at the top sheet of the Jackson paperwork. "I'll get busy on this one right away. You can bring the others over as soon as you have them copied. Walk right in when you're ready. Thanks for being so astute about this."

"No problem Matthews," Kendra said as she walked him out.

Kendra spent the next hour copying all the paperwork she had on the other nine clients and walked them over to Matthews around seven-thirty. As she turned to walk back home she decided to grab breakfast at the store.

It may have been only seven-thirty but the store was already hoppin'.

The guys always had a big variety of breakfast breads, fruits and hot and cold beverages. This morning they had outdone themselves with bacon, egg, and cheese bagels made right in front of you. Ted was busy at the breakfast counter with the bagels.

"Hey Ted, is this a new thing today?"

"Hey Kendra. Yup. Michael and I have been talkin' about it for a few weeks so we thought we'd surprise everyone with it today. What do ya think?"

"I love the idea and I'll have a breakfast bagel with a poppy seed bagel."

"Yes Ma'am! "Ted answered with a smile.

Kendra helped herself to coffee and set her things down at the table. Emily was just finishing her bagel sandwich and looked over at Kendra with a smile.

"This is heavenly," she mumbled with her mouth full.

"I can see that," Kendra laughed as she heard Ted call her name. She picked up her sandwich and came back and sat down. One bite had her moaning with pleasure.

"I told ya so," Emily said as she took her last bite.

"Holy Jesus, these are amazing," Kendra said as she wiped her mouth, "And messy. The best part, of course."

"I know. I just came over to get a couple of muffins and stayed for breakfast. Ethan was supposed to be here at six but he called and changed the time to eight. Something about a last minute phone conference with some of the sub-contractors on one of the other jobs. He said it was no big deal. So, here I am. What about you? Busy on a Saturday morning?"

"Oh yeah, always someone wanting to look at homes or property. Mostly in the Pine Ridge and Boone areas 'cause of the schools and hospital and all. Families with kids. Keeps me busy."

"I guess it would. Keep eating. We can talk when you're finished. I'm ready to leave so if Ethan shows up early I'm sure he'll come over here looking for me."

Emily cleared her breakfast stuff while Kendra ate. Once finished they talked about a few particular UFO crazy people, laughing all the while. Ted kept busy with the bagel sandwiches and Michael was at the front register with the Saturday morning regulars.

Emily and Kendra turned to look at the front of the store at the same time when they heard the door chimes. It was Ethan and he was headed straight back to join them.

"Now, isn't this all cozy? You two ladies talking and laughing away as if there wasn't a thing to be concerned about this beautiful sunny Saturday mornin'," Ethan teased them.

"Why, Mr. Sutherland, I do declare," Kendra replied in a long drawn out Southern drawl, "what a nice addition to our breakfast table this mornin'. A gorgeous, virile hunk of a man standin' there for all to admire. And look at how polite he is taking his hat off in the presence of two beautiful ladies. You're mamma surely did raise a fine, fine respectful son, oh yes she did."

"I live to please Miss Kendra, Miss Emily," Ethan answered in the same manner.

Emily sat there laughing her ass off, as well as Ted and everyone else who happened to hear this exchange.

And Ethan just stood there laughing with them all.

Eventually he asked Emily if she was ready to go.

"Yes I am. My gear is all set at the house. Kendra, we really should do this again. I haven't had so much fun at breakfast in a very long time. Probably since college or something. Don't work too hard today. Ted, the bagel was great. You guys should have these every weekend. I bet they're a big hit by noon."

Ted waved as he continued to fill orders. "Thanks Emily. Come back and give us the latest. Be safe y'all."

With that Emily and Ethan left, going over to Emily's to grab her gear. They stowed it in Ethan's truck and set out for the build site.

"Was it good? The bagel sandwich?"

"It was great! I could get addicted to them in a hurry."

They drove on in silence. Emily kept looking out her window at the mountain. She loved this place. She was thinking about how her home would look when Ethan interrupted her thoughts.

"Hey Emily, the place is going to look a mess with the road all torn up. You will be able to make out the two roads and see where the bridge is going to be. Just don't want you to be disappointed or anything."

"Oh Ethan, I expect it to look a wreck from here on out. Probably won't look much like a home for a couple of months."

"Actually, the house should go up in about two weeks. The outside anyway, should be weather tight in about two weeks with the weather sealant wrapped around it. The roof is next and once that's in place, we'll be able to place the doors and windows. It sounds like a long time, but it actually happens kind of all at once. You can come along any day to watch if you'd like."

"I would, indeed. Just let me know when you start framing the house and I'll be here. It's only twenty minutes down the road and I'll bet my security guys would love a field trip every day." Emily sounded excited to be able to watch her house being built. She wanted to see the barn go up, too, as it was a traditional barn shape she had chosen. She had also requested it be painted a dark red, not really dark, but not the usual barn red.

"OK. I'll coordinate with Matthews and I'm sure you'll find out. The foundation should be ready to dig end of next week or the Monday after."

"I'm still looking at all the fixtures and trim and cabinet styles. God, there must be a million of them. Ian has been helping me by computer. We're gonna get together Monday to get the list down to just a few for everything. And, I found the rocking chairs for the porch and a cracker barrel."

Ethan laughed as he teased her. "You really want a country home don't you?"

"Yes I do. Always have. And, now I will have just what I want. Nothing too fancy, just solid country with all the high tech stuff, of course."

"I know. I've been working with the electrician on that. He has the electric company coming out Monday to survey the land for the underground lines and to put up a temporary power source for the build. There's going to be live access at the beginning of your drive and two more on the site. One for the house and one for the barn. Lots of stuff going on while the roads are being built. Has the landscape company been in touch yet?"

"No. I haven't heard from them. I've been doing some research on the native trees and such and have a pretty good idea, I think, of what I want to start with."

"I'll give them a jingle Monday. Well, here we are. What do you think?' Ethan asked as he pulled down the wider access road and stopped where it and the new drive forked.

Emily took a moment to look it all over then said, "Oh my God. This is really happening. This is really happening. My own home safe in the mountains."

With that she let the tears she'd been holding back all morning softly roll down her cheeks.

Ethan looked at her and pulled her close as she rested her head on his shoulder.

"So sorry. It just all of a sudden hit me. This is for real. All of it. The bad and the good," Emily said as she took the tissues Ethan offered and wiped at the tears.

"OK. I'm ready. Let's go play in the dirt and mud," she said with a strong voice as she opened the truck door.

Ethan was a mess. All he wanted to do was pick her up, hold her, tell her she was safe here and that he would always be here for her.

"Dude!" Emily hollered at him. "Get a move on."

Ethan got out and joined her and they began to walk the old access road. As they went along Emily could envision the equipment and trucks driving right up to her meadow.

Ethan explained what had been going on.

"Karl's crew, as you can see, has been widening this road. The big rocks and boulders have been moved to their temporary holding spot. That's why the meadow looks beat up. I gotta tell ya I'm surprised at how thawed the ground is. It's usually frozen until mid-May or so. But your place is all thawed. Karl mentioned that on the phone last night. He thinks that UFO might have had something to do with it. Anyway, that's why I asked about the landscape supervisor. Your designs are going to take about two years to get all planted so I wanted them to get together with you as soon as possible so they could coordinate with the local growers and all."

"I understand. And, I think the UFO may have had an effect on the ground as well. It just hung over the place for the longest time then, whoosh, gone. I don't see any snow or ice around here either. You'd think there'd be some every morning anyway. Well, good for us. Less stuff to worry about."

They walked in silence for a bit.

As they came to the end of the access road and walked onto the meadow Emily said, "Ethan, there is one thing I really want to have planted all around. Sugar maples. Red maples and silver leaf maples. Would they grow well here?"

"Yes. I'm sure they would. I'll add that question to my list of things. Why the sugar maples?"

"I want to tap the sap for syrup if we can plant a whole grove of them. I noticed when we were walking to the burial site that there was a large meadow about half way there. I do believe it is on my land and want to give back. It should hold about fifty mature trees. So, I thought sugar maples would be wicked cool. I know they take about forty years to mature enough to tap. Even so, I'd like to get them planted for the next generation to use. I'll bet there are some on the land already. Maybe I'll just contact the rangers and we can do some research on this."

"Sounds good to me. Let me know what you find. Maybe you won't have to grow a whole grove if there are a few small ones around. Maybe all you'll have to do is manage the land. That oughta' keep you busy for a while." Ethan laughed as they walked across the meadow to the entrance to the new driveway.

Emily punched him in the arm. "Wise ass!"

"That's what Ian calls me all the time."

Emily came to an abrupt stop as she looked down the driveway and saw the pond for the first time.

"Holy God. That is so wicked cool! It looks like it's bubbling up from underground. And I'm going to have a covered bridge over it all. Yippee!!!" Emily hollered as she took off to get closer to the pond.

"Take it easy. The ground is really soft like a marsh close to the water's edge."

"OK"

Emily stopped as she found herself in the softer wetter ground just a few feet from the pond's edge.

"All this was underground? How did they get it to the surface?"

"Karl said all he had to do was scoop out a few big buckets of dirt and the thing just bubbled up all of a sudden gushing all over the place. They did that Monday. He said the water needed a week to figure out where it was going before he could map the road. Turns out it's bigger than they thought. They are going to put a small conduit at the southern end to sort of guide it towards the creek. There's a natural runoff down there so they won't be altering the flow pattern as the pond flows into the creek. He said if we walk along the pond to the south we can actually see where it goes back underground."

Emily just stood there and thought about all that and stared at the pond. It was rather muddy. She commented on that.

"That's to be expected right now. It has to find its new path and settle down some. It will probably remain muddy and unclear until the bridge is completed. You can see where the pilings are going to be placed and that will definitely keep things unsettled until the underground and ground support systems are finished.

"I figure once the bridge is built, it should take about a week or so for the pond to be clear. I wonder what kind of fish will end up in it? Frogs for sure. Sure would like to see some ducks, geese and such settle here every summer. We have all kinds of migratory birds. Wonder if the sandhill crane will stop by on its way."

"I hadn't even thought of that. Oh, my God, that would be so cool. We could walk down and see them whenever we wanted to."

'I'd sure like to do that with you," Ethan said quietly.

"Oh, I'm sorry. I didn't mean that the way it sounded. I'm just so excited about this whole thing," Emily stammered as quickly as she could. She looked away from Ethan.

Ethan turned her back to him and they looked into each other's eyes for the longest time.

Emily moved closer and tilted her head up to look right into Ethan's eyes as she said, "It's OK Ethan. I want you to kiss me. Here, by my pond."

Ethan was fighting with his conscience. His conscience lost as he bent his head and took her mouth softly at first. Then he deepened the kiss as he drew her to him and held her tightly. She responded by pushing against him to fit her body with his just like two well placed puzzle pieces. She opened her mouth to the gentle probing of his tongue and that ancient dance of touch began to unfold.

Ethan made sure he kept this kiss at a slow pace. He didn't want to push her. As far as he was concerned, this was a gift from the gods.

Emily moaned as he traced her lips with the tip of his tongue. She pulled him back into her mouth and sucked his tongue gently before he deepened the kiss. The tempo picked up and Emily moved her hands so she could run them through his hair.

Ethan ran his hands along her back as they continued the dance. He broke the kiss and began placing little kisses on her cheeks and eyes then he ran his tongue along the bottom of her chin causing her to moan deeply and hold tighter to him.

He finally ended the kiss with a light caress of her lips. She just laid her head on his chest and stood there content. He held her as if he would never let her go.

A movement at the edge of the water broke their embrace. They saw a deer taking a drink from across the pond. They both held very still until the deer finally got wind of their scent and moved back into the woods.

"Now that was an awesome finish to an amazing kiss, Sutherland. You've stolen my heart with all this. Sure you didn't plan on having that deer come along when it did?"

They stepped back from each other as Ethan answered, "It was well timed, but, no, I can't take credit for that one."

As they stood there not sure what to do next, Ethan suggested they follow the pond to find the place where the water went back underground.

"Oh sure, this is gonna be cool," Emily said as they moved along the pond looking for the end of the flow.

The pond looked like it would end up being about half the size of a football field in a not- so-round configuration. More like an egg shaped thing with the point at the southern tip. The road would cross it nearer the upper half just above the widest point.

As they walked along watching the pond and the ground so they wouldn't end up knee deep in mud, Emily brought up the size of the road.

"I was wondering about the size of the driveway or road or whatever at the edge of the pond. It looks like it's going to be a lot longer than needed. Is that for possible flooding reasons?"

"Oh, so now she's a road builder," Ethan teased. "Yes, it is and for expansion when it freezes. We don't even know if it will freeze solid or just the edges since it's spring fed. That's another thing we'll have to keep an eye on over the winter. There's going to be a lot of stuff to watch for and experience the first year here. I'm sure there will be a few surprises, too."

"I wondered about the flooding. OK, then, I guess I'll have to keep a journal of all the stuff I see and hear once I'm in my house. Hey, the water's gone. Let's back up and find out where it went underground."

They passed the end of the pond while they were talking and walked a fair distance away. They turned around and looked closely at the ground for the water. They hadn't taken more than a dozen steps when they not only saw it but heard it.

"There," said Ethan as he pointed to a clump of leaves and branches about ten feet from them. "I can see it then it's gone. I don't think we should walk over there to look more closely 'cause we could end up waist deep in the muck."

"I'll take a closer look with these," Emily said as she pulled her special ops binoculars Matthews had given her from her pack.

"Jesus, where'd you get those?" Ethan exclaimed.

"Matthews," Emily explained.

She adjusted them and then began scanning the ground where the sound and the water seemed to be. It took a few minutes before she found the spot.

She handed the binoculars to Ethan instructing him with, "Go ahead and adjust them then look at that clump of leaves we first spotted. Move to the right about a foot just beyond that bit of branches. You'll see a small clear spot. The water just seems to disappear into the ground. It's the coolest thing I've ever seen. See it?"

It took Ethan a minute to find it. "This is really amazing. The water just stops flowing on the ground and disappears. It doesn't even form a puddle or anything. It's like its being sucked down underground. I'll bet the ground around there is really soggy, too. We should stay clear just to be safe."

"Neat, huh? Maybe I'll place a marker there for safety reasons. Or, maybe not. Mother Earth can take care of her own and the animals and all know just how to take care of themselves. It's us humans that need some help. Let's not mark the spot. I'll take a picture now and then as the seasons change, I'll keep taking pictures so I will know where this is and stay away from it. OK with you?"

"I wouldn't have even thought of all that stuff. Sure. Whatever you say. Makes sense to me."

They spent some time taking pictures and talking about this natural phenomenon.

"I remember hiking in a canyon in the desert near Palm Springs, California," Emily said. "We hiked down into an oasis and came upon a hot spring and spent some time there. As we left, my friend pointed to a small stream of water moving away at a good clip from the spring. All of a sudden it was gone. It just stopped and rolled into a small slit in the rock. No puddle or anything. It just moved back underground. I'll never forget that place. Right there in the middle of the desert, you walk down into an oasis of Washington palms and hot springs. The plants were beautiful and the air was cool. Great trip. So glad I had that time there."

Ethan waited a minute then asked Emily, "You ever want to go back?"

"Yes, I do. I think about it from time to time. Now that I'm free, I can go wherever I want. I WILL go back after I get settled here. Want to come along? For real? Would you consider going with me?"

"Yes, I would like to go. I've never hiked in the desert and would like to have that experience."

"OK then. Something more to plan," Emily said as she looked all around the area. "I guess we should start back, huh? You probably have stuff to do."

"I am getting hungry," Ethan offered as he looked at his watch. "And with good reason. It's almost noon. Time for lunch."

"Let's get going then. Maybe we'll see more wildlife along the way. And, ya know what I'm just thinkin', let's place a stick as a marker for now. Just because."

"OK", Emily agreed as they found a large branch and placed it next to the place where the water went back underground.

"Like I was about to say, most of the animals are well out of hibernation. We have a huge flock of wild turkeys on the mountain. Probably more than one flock. I usually see them around my place at dawn and dusk. They like to roost in the big southern pines that are all over these mountains. I'm sure once we stop making a lot of noise around here, you'll see your own bunch all the time, too."

"I'll remember to keep an eye out for 'em," Emily replied.

They set a slow pace as they walked back to Emily's meadow looking all around and chatting about the mountain. They stood looking at the site for the house and barn. It had been staked for the foundation dig. It held so much promise for Emily.

"It looks like such a big thing from here. The house and barn and all. I can just imagine what it might look like when it's finished. Hmmmmm."

They headed down the access road and when they reached the end, Ethan asked, "Would you like to walk the new drive from here to get another perspective of the layout?"

"Yes."

The headed down the drive from the highway side. It had a small bend in it before it met the pond.

"I do like this whole set up. You guys have done a great job. Thanks so much."

"You're welcome. Anytime. Let's get goin'. I do believe I would like to treat you to some lunch. How about Hank's Diner in Pine Ridge? Have you been there yet?"

"As a matter of fact I have. I like the place. Let me tell Matthews our plans so he can have everything ready. Did you see the team on the mountain? They were there. I saw them a couple of times. Feels good to have someone keeping me safe. Maybe one day soon they won't be needed."

"I did see them. No worries. The Creek takes care of their own, too."

As soon as they got on the road, Emily called Matthews and told him of her plans. He said he had a team ready and they would follow them out of The Creek.

Emily told Ethan and they slowed a bit as they went by the country store so the Jeep with the team could follow along.

A little while later Ethan and Emily sat in a booth at Hank's diner and the security guys sat a couple of booths away.

The same waitress Emily had when she first came to Hank's stopped at their table.

"Well hey there. I remember you. How y'all doin' Ethan? I see you've met one of the most available bachelors in these parts. What can I get ya to drink?

"Hi Nancy. Now you stop all that sassy talk or Emily's gonna wonder what kinda' guy's building her house. I'll have an iced tea."

"I'll have a 7-up."

"Good. Ethan, I only speak the truth. And, truth be told, you haven't been seen with anyone for a long, long time. So there. Back in a jiffy."

Emily just stared at Ethan while he turned red. Then she laughed out loud.

"So, I guess this is where y'all get all the gossip. Good to know."

Ethan just looked at her. "Nancy is a real nice gal. A big tease but a real nice gal. Don't believe everything you hear from her."

Nancy returned with the drinks and took their lunch orders. Ethan told her to add the two guys to his bill as they worked on one of the crews.

A few folks stopped by while they ate their lunch to hear all the latest news from The Creek. The UFO was discussed a bit. Emily told them all about the bagel breakfast sandwiches at the store, suggesting they come on by and try one. Call first she said because they were going fast.

With lunch over, the guys turned to Ethan and nodded their heads to say thanks for picking up the tab. They all left and Ethan returned Emily home.

He walked her to her door and they just stood there silently. They looked at each other and without saying a word Ethan leaned over and placed a soft kiss on Emily's lips. Turning he walked away, got into his truck and drove off leaving Emily looking after him.

While Ethan and Emily were on the mountain, Matthews had started the security search on Kendra's clients. This would be a long process that wouldn't be finished for a few days unless something had been flagged on one of them. Then he would be immediately notified.

Kendra was busy looking for available properties for her clients. She would email them a link and they could check them out on the computer first. A virtual tour was a great way to get started. It saved everyone from driving all over the place and wasting time.

Kendra had found a possible place for Jordan Jackson. It was just outside The Creek on the way to Pine Ridge. He had wanted twenty acres and this landowner was ready to sell twenty of his thirty acres to someone who honored the land. The area was zoned agricultural with residential options, but could not be used for housing developments. The land preservation society had seen to that over two hundred years earlier.

Kendra got started on the long process of contacting the land owner, meeting with him on the land he wanted to sell, going to the zoning board office, and checking with the building inspector along with the environmental folks to make sure this parcel was buildable. This process alone would take a good two to three weeks then she would have to contact the buyer to set up meetings and sign paperwork with him. When all this preliminary stuff was completed, the buyer would have to be investigated financially, checked for a criminal record, confirm employment history and more. It usually took a good four months to get to the point of offering to buy the land. This was a long process up here in the Blue Ridge.

Yuri was just as busy Saturday morning. He was devising a plan to kill Barbara. He was going to have to hire someone that no one knew was connected to him. He had called several of his contacts along the Mid-Atlantic coast and given them orders. They were to find someone who was in need of a lot of money, financially destitute or someone who would need a lot of money to make an expensive purchase. He told them all to take their time and make sure this person had no ties to any of Yuri's businesses. When they thought they had found someone, they were to contact Yuri and he would have them investigated by one of his paid contacts in the local town hall. Yuri needed something he could blackmail with, anything, like a gambling debt or unpaid child support. If not, then money itself would have to be the lure.

Once chosen, they would have to approach that person very carefully. The scheme would be planned once they knew how to get to the person. Yuri was taking his time with this plan. He didn't want to make any mistakes. Yuri had decided to leave Jones alone. Jones knew if he opened his mouth, Yuri would have him killed. Jones was still in solitary confinement. He would be arraigned on Monday. He was under heavy guard. The feds didn't want him being killed like Nick had been. They still couldn't figure out how that had happened. It was labeled unsolvable by the homicide unit.

Jones knew better than to say anything about anything. His court appointed attorney was meeting with him on Sunday and would explain the list of charges against him. Jones knew his life was over. He would spend the rest of his life in prison and probably be killed before long.

CHAPTER 18

T he next few weeks seemed to fly by. Karl and the road crew had the access road finished by Wednesday and the bridge road was finished by Friday. The wooden bridge structure would not be built until the need for heavy equipment and large vehicles was finished. The foundation dig began the Monday of the second week and the concrete forms were in place by that Friday. The concrete company would send six trucks in rotation starting early the next Monday morning to fill the forms for all the buildings.

Ethan was figuring that the concrete should be ready for decking a week later, weather permitting. These mountains always sent a surprise in the spring. Sometimes rain. Sometimes snow. Everyone knew they just had to wait it out. He was counting on the usual May weather: cold nights and warm days - just what concrete needed to set and dry. He was looking at the first week in June for the framing of all structures to begin with a weather tight date by the end of June. July was slated for interior work and the finishing touches should be in place by mid-August. He was planning on having Emily move into her new home by the end of summer.

But that seemed to be years away in one thought yet just as quick, it didn't seem like enough time to get everything done. Summer always brought more work so even though it was the end of April, he was already signing on summer help. He offered work to the summer crews he had employed the previous summer first. This year they all said yes. Thank God. But with Emily's project, he would need another twelve workers to get things done on time. He put the word out through his subcontractors and suppliers that he was looking for experienced carpenters and builders to work May through September. He asked that they email resumes to him for consideration. He and Ian would take their time checking all the possibilities. They had arranged with Matthews to do security checks on all the returning workers as well as the new ones. They must be very careful this year, all things considered.

Emily was very busy looking at drawings of the interior details Ian kept sending her. She was choosing things like drawer pulls, cabinet handles, and every aspect of finished plumbing you could imagine. Who knew there were so many toilets to choose from? She quickly decided she wanted the ones you waved your hand over to flush. Fun and very sanitary.

She got to choose colors as well and that brought a whole new world of planning. What colors did she want to paint her rooms? Then there were the floors. She had already chosen tongue and groove red oak for the main living areas, maple for the kitchen, and a variety of other hard woods for the rest of the house. She did not want any carpeting anywhere. Ian gave her a few sites to look at for area rugs. She wanted a large round braided one for the breakfast nook and other braided rugs for the kitchen work area. And there was so much more to think about for the rest of the house.

Then there were the barn and stable areas. Even though the two buildings were attached by a covered walkway, they had their own character and charm. The barn exterior was all set. It was the interior she needed help with so she asked Lainie and Mo if she could come spend some time with them to learn how they used their barn.

They readily agreed. She had also contacted The Kirklands. Ethan had mentioned them when they were discussing the landscaping design. The Kirkland Family Farm and Tree Nursery was going to supply all the greens she would need.

So the week when the concrete was being poured for the foundations, Emily spent a few days with the "sisters" as she called them, learning about their farm set-up and getting to know them personally.

To put it bluntly, the three of them had a blast from the very start. It was as if they had known each other all their lives. There was something special about these two sisters. Emily had great intuition and knew she could speak freely with them about her Gift. They always started their days in the kitchen with tea, coffee and homemade muffins.

"Thanks so much for having me over. I know I've messed with your routine and appreciate your efforts to educate me about farm life. This should be the last day I need to be here for a while."

Mo waved her hand as she said, "No biggie. We always like an excuse to visit with our neighbors. So, tell us a little bit about what else you're wanting to see and learn about. We're both ready for you."

Lainie laughed at her sister. "Mo, ya make it sound like a circus around here. Emily, just ask us anything you want and we'll start from there."

"OK. Let's go." They spent the morning talking about the barn - what the sisters liked and didn't like about it. They talked about the kinds of tools and machines that were needed to take care of the animals. They offered information about the local veterinarian they used. They talked about everything there was to talk about concerning the farm animals and the barns they lived in.

After lunch, they started with the greenhouses and gardens. Late afternoon found them all on the front porch sipping hot tea.

"Ladies, you have outdone yourselves. I have so much to think about. I don't know if I'll get to sleep tonight. I know it takes a great deal of work as I grew up a farm girl. But, I was never privy to all the little details that were needed to keep things going. You have been so very kind and open with me I would like to return the favor. There are only a few who know about my Gift. I'm a psychic medium and have been from birth."

Lainie and Mo just looked at each other and nodded their heads as if an unspoken fact had just been confirmed.

"We suspected as much, Emily. Mo and I have a knack for being able to know who has the Gift. This is so cool. Are you going to practice once your home is all set? Can't wait to have a gathering, a kind of psychic party with you reading us all."

Mo added, "I told Lainie the moment I first saw you that you had something special about you. I can see auras and yours was white and silver. You must be an old soul or something. I'm never wrong, am I, Lainie? Never!"

"No, never Mo," answered Lainie.

"Well, I'm so glad I was finally able to share that with someone. Matthews knows and a few of the others in his group but that's all so far. I'm getting the vibes that my secret is about to no longer be a secret. Good. Tell whomever you think should know. I haven't been able to be open about my Gift for a long time. This is kinda freeing. What a great day it has been indeed."

The three of them sat there quietly listening to the mountain and sipping their tea.

"Well, it's about time for me to get along home," Emily said softly, breaking the silence. "I'll be sure to ask questions as they come along. And, thanks, for the plants and eggs and all. You are kind and generous."

The sisters walked Emily to her Jeep setting her things on the back seat.

"It's been great for us, too, Emily. Just come on by whenever you want. Can't wait to see your place once it's all finished. Nice to have you as our neighbor," Lainie added.

"Later," Mo shouted as Emily turned the Jeep around and headed out to the road.

There were always agents following Emily. She knew they were close to the sister's place. And the sisters were OK with this intrusion on their private lives.

As soon as Emily turned onto the road, she saw her tag-a-longs drive up behind her. She saw a few of the trucks leaving the build site so she decided to take a quick look around. She activated her voice contact system and told Matthews she was making an unscheduled stop at the build. His response was immediate. Two of the workers were agents assigned to the build site. They waved as she got out of her Jeep where the access road met the meadow and started walking towards the foundations. This place was as big a mess as she expected it to be. The energy was a bit chaotic. She would send Reiki and offer thanks.

She saw Ethan before he spotted her. He was talking with someone and walking around the foundation, first the house then the barn and stable. She walked over to the house dig. It was huge. She would have never guessed she had created such a big place.

She stood for a moment realizing her new life was really in high gear. Wow. Who would have thought she would be here doing all this just three months ago? Life had seemed so horrible. And, now! She let her mind wander as she stared at the beginnings of her home. She didn't hear or see Ethan walk over until her touched her arm.

"Oh. Hi there. Just lost in thought. This is amazing. And so big! You guys have been very busy up here."

"Yes we have. Don't worry about the mess around here. A lot of the earth will be put back against the foundations once they have cured a while. And the rest will be placed in other areas as needed and some for your landscaping designs. Any questions?"

Ethan had put his arm around Emily's shoulders as he spoke and she left it there. She liked the feel of it. She leaned against him as they stood there talking quietly.

"Ethan, please don't apologize for anything. I know this is all a part of the process. I'm not worried about anything here. If I have any questions, believe you me, I'll be asking them. Can we walk over to the holes and take a look?"

Ethan laughed out loud. "Of course we can, but I think the word hole is a bit too small for these things. Take a look."

They had stopped at the house foundation.

"Jesus! This whole thing is really deep. I thought I was only building one basement here," Emily laughed as she looked around.

"You are. Ian and I talked about making the basement deeper than usual. As you are having three floors built, we looked at the specs and decided to err on the side of caution by making the foundation deeper by adding several more support structures. We don't anticipate any problems but we want to make sure this house is set on a solid foundation. The earth under the foundation is rock solid as well. There aren't any springs or underground creeks or flows that run under any of the foundations. Just being careful, Miss."

Emily smiled. They walked around the foundation talking about the current progress.

When they got to the barn, Emily told Ethan about her day at the sister's farm.

"Those women are amazing. They run the whole place themselves and have time to even sit on their porch. I feel like I've known them all my life. Ya ever meet someone like that? Someone you felt you've known forever?"

"Yup. I know what you're talking about. I do. Those two ladies are real special around here. They grew up here, went away to college then came back to take over the farm. They've added a few new plants and all to the mix and it seems they have no problem selling them and growing more. Their folks come by around the holidays each year and they open the house for a few parties. Glad you like 'em."

"I do. And I'll be stopping by on a regular basis. It's like meeting the sisters I never had. Anyway, these look just as deep if not deeper than the house. Same reasons?"

"Yes indeed. The barn has very specific support needs as you can imagine so this foundation is quite a bit different then the house. After all, you're not gonna have a herd of horses walking through the house are ya?" Ethan laughed.

Emily just shook her head and laughed along with Ethan. "Not that I plan on it. Ian showed me the interior plans for the barn including the chicken coop, if I want to fill it up. It has its own door to an outside space when they're not roaming free and it's away from the other animal stalls. Pretty smart that brother of yours."

"Damn. I should have thought of that. Only kidding. He is an amazing man when it comes to designing buildings. Listen to what he offers and be sure to ask questions if you don't get the gist of it. He takes his time explaining things so everyone can understand. Not everyone is a builder. He added some more windows to the stables as well. Did he get you the new layout of that?"

"No, not yet. I'll email him when I get home. Thanks for the update. I guess this is where the walkway will be as the foundation narrows here?"

"Yes. At first we weren't going to connect the basements then one of the guys mentioned what a hassle it would be to have to come upstairs, leave one building and to go down into the other basement. So, we did a quick redraw and here ya go."

"Smart guy. Give him a bonus for me, will ya?" Emily sassed as they continued walking around the site.

"Hey, it's your money," Ethan replied.

Emily just looked at him, rolling her eyes. "Did you come across a lot of boulders or just big rocks and where are they again?"

Ethan turned Emily around, pointing at the southern end of the meadow and left his hands on her shoulders. He bent his head to speak into her ear.

"We did dig up two very large boulders and a bunch of smaller ones. The rest were a lot of big rocks. Any idea what you want to do with them?"

Emily leaned back into Ethan as she said, "I was thinkin' if there were boulders or big rocks I could set them at the edge of the meadow where the bridge road comes into the meadow on its way up to the barn."

"I like that idea. Let's walk over and take a look although they're still covered with dirt. Once the weather warms and we are settled into the actual building phase you can come by and I'll have them cleaned off. A few good rain storms oughta take care of that. Sound good?"

"Yup, it does," Emily answered as they neared the rock pile. The boulders were off to the side.

"These are big. I think they'll do just fine. I have lots of time to work on this thing anyway so we'll just wait and see like you said. Hey, I'm getting a bit cold here with the sun behind the trees now. Time to get home and get warm."

Ethan looked at Emily imagining how he would help her get warm. His body responded with a hard-on.

"Ethan? Earth to Ethan," Emily teased.

Ethan blinked and looked around. "Oh yeah, I'm guess I'm tired and cold, too. Let's go."

Not cold enough, Ethan thought as they turned to go.

They walked the bridge road looking at the pond as they went over it.

"This is gonna look great Ethan. Thanks for the idea. I like it more and more every day and can't wait to see the covered bridge part later this summer."

"You're very welcome," he said as he took her hand in his and they walked back down the road to where the trucks were parked by the highway.

A few of the other workers were leaving as well so there was no time for a more intimate good-bye. They all waved and drove off.

Emily got home and took a long hot shower. She was a mess from the farm and her walk around the site.

Ethan headed straight home. He, too, showered, and considered a cold one before he set the dial for hot. He had a couple of meetings in the workshop tonight with just enough time to grab a bite of leftovers.

Emily's next trip was a few days later when she went over to the Kirkland's Farm for an afternoon meeting with the landscape design team. Ian had sent the layout of the property and made a few suggestions about trees, shrubs, and plants for Emily to consider.

The Kirkland Farm was extensive. Emily learned they had their own tree grove that extended into the National Forest. A partnership had been forged between the family and the forestry department to preserve the old growth forest in the area. The Kirklands had been here about as long as any of the old families and had been taking care of the forest for over two hundred years. They were the area's experts when it came to the best trees and plants to grow in any area of the Blue Ridge. They held classes for the Appalachia State University agricultural and forestry departments in their workshops and had summer camps for school programs. The forestry service sent new rangers to them for training as well.

But the best thing about the Kirkland Farm was this: they took care of family. This included theirs, and everyone else's around The Creek and Pine Ridge. They had sleigh rides in the winter and hay rides in the summer and fall. Whenever anyone had a baby or got married, they gave them a tree to plant. In memory of loved ones that passed away, they planted a tree in their honor wherever the family wanted it. Family came first. Always had and always would.

And, probably most important of all, they preserved the old growth forest. No one was allowed to cut down any of these trees in this area of the Blue Ridge. The old growth forest areas were preserved by law. There were a few groves on Emily's land as well. She was about to learn about them today.

"Welcome Emily. I'm Jason, the design team leader. Scott Kirkland gave me the information about your site and Ian sent over the plans. This here is Bev and Rickie and we are your design team dedicated to you until you are thoroughly satisfied."

"Hi Emily. Nice to meet you," said Bev.

"Hey Emily. We're going to spend so much time with you, you're gonna want to take a vacation just to get away from us," offered Rickie.

"Hi everyone and thanks for meeting with me. I know I have a ton to learn, so, shall we get the lessons started? What do we do first?"

Jason answered this. "How about a tour of the property. We all think that might help you understand a bit about our operation."

"I'm ready to go," Emily replied.

"We use these golf carts to get around this area, but when we go out into the groves we use Jeeps. Let's start with the area most of our customers use. We have two golf carts for this part of the trip."

They spent the next hour driving around the inner grounds showing Emily the sales areas as well as the workshops used for the employees and the schools.

Next they all loaded into a Jeep and set out for the groves.

Emily asked about the old growth areas.

"Are we going to see any of the old growth areas today?"

"Yes we are," Jason answered. "I thought we'd start with them and then move on to the younger groves. Bev here is our expert on old growth history and the biology of the trees themselves."

"Thanks Jason. I'm going to show you what these trees look like so you'll be able to identify them on your property. And no, none of them have been disturbed by your building projects. Ethan made sure of that before final approval was given for your buildings. There is a small grove just west of your meadow. It's about a ten minute walk along one of the animal paths. You may have walked through it when you went to the burial grounds. The chiefs know all about it as their ancestors have been protecting them forever. They are sacred - to both tribes."

"I love hearing all about the history of the forest. The chiefs and I have spent a few afternoons getting to know each other. They've been telling me the history of their people and of the newcomers to the area. That's what they call anyone who wasn't born here. I get a kick out of them. They love their people so much. They may try to come off as rough and tough guys but I know better. Especially when they ask if I'm making homemade cookies before we get together," Emily laughed as she finished talking.

Rickie chimed in with, "And I get to teach you about modern day tree husbandry. How to take care of the trees on your property. When to thin them by cutting them down or transplanting them. I will show you how disease can damage a tree and how the weather can affect the growth. You will learn how the animals use the trees for food and shelter. And, I will teach you how to plant a tree so it isn't damaged in the process. But, the best part of all is Jason's part in the plan."

"Thanks a lot guys. Emily, I get to help you learn the names of all the trees. You will learn this through leaf pattern recognition as well as the way the bark grows."

"OK. I think I'm gonna need all the help I can get. There is so much to learn."

"And you have all the time you need. We're here to take care of the forest for you," offered Bev.

"Thanks. I'm gonna rely on all of you for a very long time. Anyone want to show me how to chop wood? Guess I should learn how to do that, too - with the latest in high tech equipment, of course," Emily laughed along with the others.

"Of course we'll show you whatever you want to learn," Jason offered. "I prefer the power log splitter myself. So much easier than trying to line up the log, place the splitting tool then hit it just right with the maul. Those splitting mallets are really heavy, too."

"Oh, you poor baby," Rickie teased.

They continued on with the light chatter until Jason brought the Jeep to a stop.

They spent the afternoon walking through one of the old growth groves then on to one of the groves planted by the farm. Emily learned so much that afternoon. By the time they returned to the workshop area, the sun was setting.

"Emily, let's plan on a design session next week. That will give both of us some time to think about the kinds of trees you may want to plant. We'll work in the shrubs after that," Bev suggested.

"Sounds good, Bev. Although I do want to plant a sugar maple grove next to the old one higher up on the mountain. There is a rather large open area that I think will work. Y'all have to let me know. And red maples as well. They are beautiful."

"OK then," said Jason. " We both have some homework to do. Take care and we'll call you with a date and time for the next planning session."

With that Emily got into her Jeep and set off for home. There was so much to learn about, she thought, as she wound along the mountain road. She was home before she knew it.

While Emily was visiting the sisters and the Kirkland farm, Kendra and Matthews spent their time going over the security reports that had started coming in on Kendra's prospective clients. They were spread across Kendra's kitchen table. She had the ten files of possible new clients in front of her and Matthews had eight of the ten security reports and files in front of him.

"Kendra, let's start with these four. All of them have filed and completed bankruptcy procedures in the past two years. None of them have kept a secure job since. Two of them are still unemployed although they have a steady stream of cash showing up in their bank accounts. We're checking into that scenario. The other two have been holding two jobs each for over a year although the pay is low. One of them is making thirty thousand a year and the other thirty-two thousand a year, not what is known as a strong income base. What are your thoughts on these four clients?"

"First of all, thanks for doing all of this," Kendra said as she spread her hands out to include the whole kitchen table. "I would have done the financial checks and come up with similar results but it would have taken about three weeks compared to your ten days. I'm going to reject these four. I'll send them an email stating their financial status is not strong enough yet and so forth. Let me attach those to my files and stick a note on them."

"Two of the reports are not back yet. One on a Jordan Jackson and the other on a Shirley Hopkins. These other four look stronger. Let's take a look at them one at a time."

"OK. Let me refill our coffee cups and toast a bagel or something. What would you like Matthews?"

"A bagel sounds good. Got any sesame ones?"

"Yes I do. I'll have one as well," Kendra said as she got everything on the table while the bagels toasted.

Matthews handed a report to Kendra, giving her time to see all the details. When she was finished reading, she said, "This is really thorough Matthews. And, this client is just the type we look for. Solid financials, long work history, no criminal record and well educated. The educated part we can't look into but I can usually tell when we fill out the preliminary paperwork together. This one I'll move forward with. Next."

They spent the rest of the morning going over the other three reports. All three would be offered the possibility to buy land with Kendra as their agent.

"Thanks Matthews," Kendra offered as he put his coat on. "It's been nice doing business with the agency again. I hear the build is coming along. They should be ready to pour the foundations on Monday. Emily told me about the covered bridge idea. Love it! Nice touch wouldn't you say?"

Matthews agreed as he headed out the door, "It is and I can't wait to see it either. It's a nice finishing touch to the project."

Kendra got to work writing the rejection letters, sending them off by email. After lunch, she started the paperwork for the four clients that she had accepted. First, she sent them letters of acceptance stating she had two or three properties for them to look at. She asked for a timetable to begin setting up appointments to visit the properties with each of them. This would keep her busy for another two weeks or so. She would send the schedule to Matthews as he requested.

CHAPTER 19

The day after Emily and Ethan had enjoyed their impromptu walk around the site, Ethan set up an appointment to bring her up-to-date on the project. It was set for 7 p.m. the next day. Ethan knew he was playing with fire being alone at night with Emily, but it was the only time he had open during the next couple of weeks and he didn't want her to have to wait for updates.

Emily spent the day arguing with herself. First, she convinced herself that it was only a business meeting, the client with the contractor. Then, she would argue that he was a hot guy, they both liked the kissing that had taken place so big deal if things got hot and heavy. She liked making love and it had been forever since the last time she had been with someone who cared. Her thoughts were in turmoil all day long right up until she walked out the door and headed for the Sutherland's.

Ethan was equally distracted. He kept telling himself this was all business. Hands off. He didn't really want to get involved right now. He was too busy. He wasn't ready for a serious relationship. Truth was he was scared of being hurt again. Then, he would argue that she was a sexy hot woman and he liked the way she made him feel. Even being close made him get a hard-on. Then he would just throw his hands up in the air and scowl. Jesus Christ! Why couldn't she be ugly or something? Not that ugly women weren't beautiful. Oh, God! He would take a breath, punch something then get back to work but the vicious cycle would start all over again.

He was sure he had convinced himself he wasn't falling in love with Emily. He wasn't, damn it! He had control of his heart and emotions not the other way around. He was an intelligent and sensible guy. That was that.

Just as she was turning into the driveway at Ethan's place, she realized she had taken great care with her clothes and makeup and hair for the night. She had chosen a shirt that did not have buttons but did have a V-neck that showed the curve of her breasts. It could easily be pulled off. Her jeans showed all the right curves. Her hair had been pulled away from her face with a barrette clip on each side. Her make-up was light with just a touch of smoky coloring around her eyes and her lip gloss was a faint pink. She had even used her Oscar de La Renta perfume sprits. She was all set.

Ethan had taken a quick shower and pulled on clean jeans and an L.L. Bean button down flannel shirt. He was feeling a little bit country. He used a musky aftershave and was ready when he heard her Jeep pull up outside the door.

Here we go, he thought as he opened the door.

Here we go, she thought as she walked to the door.

If anyone else had been around when the two of them saw each other they would have sworn lightening brightened the sky and that the crackle could be heard for miles around.

"Emily, come on in. You can hang your jacket up in the usual spot. Can I get you something to drink? Soda, tea... a beer?"

"Hi Ethan. Thanks, ugh, how about a Sierra Mist? That would be great."

"OK. Take a seat at my drawing table and I'll be right back."

As Emily walked over to the table, Ethan grabbed her drink from the office fridge and thought he might need to crawl in. She looked amazing and hot! She smelled great and how in God's name was he going to get through the evening with her right next to him?

Emily watched Ethan get her soda from the fridge. He looked amazing and delicious. Her pulse had quickened at the sight of him. This was going to be a long evening.

He returned with her soda and began. "I'm glad we had the walk around yesterday. It's going to make all these plans and ideas easier to picture. We'll be using the flat screen monitor on the wall across from here. Ready?"

"I didn't know you had a monitor across from here. It's huge!"

Ethan took a deep breath before he answered, "It's kept behind the photo display when I don't need it. With the flick of this switch I can have it in place in no time."

"Don't'cha just love technology?," Emily said as she settled in her seat. "I'm ready for the show. Any popcorn?"

"Wise ass," Ethan replied with a laugh as he got things started.

"Here's the meadow before we did anything to it and here it is with everything finished."

Emily stared at the side-by-side pictures. She took a long moment before she replied, "Wow! What a change. I knew we would be making drastic changes, but this is amazing. It looks like the house and everything was always there. You can still see the original shape of the meadow. It looks as if you just set the house and barn right in place and nothing was interrupted. I need a minute to just take all this in."

Ethan just patted her shoulder leaving his arm around her as she looked between the two pictures for a few minutes.

"Ethan, this is incredible. You have managed to retain the energy of the meadow, a wild and free place and yet made the house and barn look like they were always there, like they always shared the space and energy. I don't know what to say," Emily sat back in her chair with a look of amazement on her face.

"Well," Ethan began, "I really do understand your determination to keep the land as natural as possible and only disrupt the areas that need to be. Ian is amazing when it comes to understanding the client's dreams and wishes with the type of architecture. You said country with a Cape Cod style farm house, but much bigger of course, and a Victorian farmer's porch and that's what he came up with. I know there are tons of details to work on but this is what we have come up with so far."

Emily turned and smiled at Ethan. "You guys are truly gifted. You really are. I'm so glad this is where I'm gonna be living."

Ethan could smell her and feel her body heat. His head was swimming with images of her as he ran his hand around her breast. He needed to focus here.

"Well, let's take a look at each step of the process so you'll have a better grasp of what is happening and when over the next three or so months. We hope to have you in your new home by mid to late August. Maybe a little sooner if the weather and supplies all behave."

For the next couple of hours, Ethan and Emily sat side-by-side on their tall chairs looking at and discussing the project.

Emily thought she'd die if she didn't get to wrap herself around Ethan and have her way with him.

Ethan had to concentrate on his work to keep his hands off Emily. All he wanted to do was take her right then and there on the workshop floor if need be.

They kept touching each other as they leaned over the paper plans and looked at the matching ones on the screen. They touched hands, shoulders, and arms over and over again. Each time they could feel the heat of the other. Both knew that something had to give. And soon.

"And that's all she wrote. I'm sure you'll have a million questions. Just write 'em down and send them along and Ian and I will answer them all," Ethan said as he turned off the screen and sent it back into the wall.

"Now that's really cool. Maybe I should have some fancy stuff like that in my house."

Ethan turned to her took her hands in his and looked right into her eyes. Softly, he said, "Anything you want, Emily, anything you want. Just say it and I'll make it happen."

Emily held her breath as she looked right back into Ethan's eyes.

"You would? You would do anything for me?" Emily couldn't think. There was a rushing sound in her ears and she swore Ethan could probably hear her heart. It was beating so loud she couldn't think straight. He smelled incredible and his touch was like fire.

Ethan leaned close into Emily so his mouth was just a whisper away from hers.

"Anything Emily, just to see you happy and safe."

As she tilted her head up to look at him she knew their lips would be ever so close.

Ethan couldn't wait another second. He took her mouth with his in a soft kiss. He held it for a moment before deepening it as Emily responded.

Emily pushed into the kiss and wrapped her arm around Ethan's neck as he pushed his tongue against her lips asking for entry. She opened her mouth like a blossoming flower soaking in the sun. Her hands found their way into his hair and he groaned as their tongues danced and played exploring each other.

Ethan ran his fingertips across the side of Emily's breast and her moan made him even harder than he already was. She was on fire. All she wanted to do was rip his clothes off and run her hands all over him feeling his hard organ in her bare hands.

Ethan didn't think he could hold on much longer. His pulse was racing and he couldn't seem to think straight.

"Emily," he said against her lips, "Is this what you want?"

"Ethan, it's what I've wanted ever since I first saw you."

"Are you sure?" he said as he played his tongue across her lips.

'Yes. Yes. Yes."

Ethan pulled back just a little as he continued, "Me, too. Let me take you somewhere more deserving."

Ethan helped Emily off the chair and guided her to the door that connected the workshop to his home.

"This way. Do you need your coat and stuff? I'll just grab it anyway," Ethan said as he grabbed her things and they walked through the door into the kitchen. She heard him flick a few switches and the outside went dark. The only light on was the one showing them the way to the stairs.

Ethan showed Emily to his bedroom, closed the door and turned on a soft light. He dropped her things on a chair as they made their way to the bed. He lay her down and began to undress her. As he bent to take her shirt off he began kissing her on her cheeks, her eyes, her chin, then her mouth letting his tongue explore once again. He continued trailing his tongue down her neck making her moan. He let his hand trace the outline of her breast through her shirt. First one then the other then one nipple then the other.

Emily thought she was going to melt right there. She wanted him to take her breast in his mouth. As if he could read her thoughts, he finally pulled her shirt over her head and laid his mouth on the soft flesh of her breast. He ran his tongue round one breast then the other. Then, finally, he freed her and began circling her nipple with the tip of his wet tongue. First one nipple then the other. She cried out in ecstasy. He finally took her breast into his mouth and began gently sucking it. She arched her back and put her hands on the back of his head gently pushing him onto her breast. He stroked her other breast.

She thought she would explode. She was hot and wet and ready to come. She grabbed his shirt, trying to take it off him. He resisted and continued to suck one breast then the other. Finally he pulled away long enough to remove his shirt and loosen her jeans. She raised her hips so he could take them off more easily. As he came back to her, she motioned for him to remove his as well. He did.

Ethan pulled the blankets back and as Emily lay back again, Ethan began to trace his tongue down her belly while caressing her breast with one hand and tracing her inner thigh with the other. She thought she'd go crazy if he didn't finally touch her most intimate place.

She opened her legs for him as his tongue found the tip of her mound. His fingers found her hot and wet and they began to explore her essence. His tongue began to lick her clit and she came almost instantaneously. The orgasm jerked her off the bed while Ethan continued to lick her clit and run his fingers inside her.

As she settled from this first orgasm, he came back up to her and took her breast into his mouth again sucking and flicking her nipple. She continued to moan and run her hands all over him. She wanted to grab his hard dick and feel it in her hands.

He was kneeling over her as she reached over to touch his hard and hot erection. He moaned deep in his throat as she lightly ran her fingers up and down his shaft.

He had to move away before he came. He was so close. Once again he let his tongue stroke and lick her clit as he got her ready to come again. He leaned over her, once more asking if this was ok.

"Yes. Oh, God yes, Ethan. Put your hard dick into me and make us come together."

Emily opened her legs to him as he began to enter her ever so slowly. He took his time wanting her to enjoy every second of their lovemaking.

At first he pushed gently and slowly then began to move faster and deeper as she cried out begging him to make her come. She wrapped her legs around his ass as he began to thrust harder and longer getting into a rhythm they both met. She raised her hips to his every thrust taking him deeper into her. The world had long ago disappeared and only she and Ethan existed in this space and time. She felt him getting even bigger as she neared her orgasm. Their rhythm picked up speed and just as she thought she couldn't stand another minute of this ecstasy she came bucking and writhing against him making him come. He thrust fast and hard and she kept coming. He called out her name as they both fell over the edge into the abyss.

It was a long time before Emily could breathe slowly again. Everything was silent. She lay still for a bit just trying to remember everything that had happened. She felt amazing. Ethan was a generous and careful lover. She had never been treated like this before. She hadn't opened her eyes yet as a smile played on her lips.

She took a deep breath and realized Ethan's arm was across her breast. She liked that. A lot. It felt right. And she loved to have her breasts touched and sucked, truth be told. She finally opened her eyes, turning to look at Ethan and saw him looking at her.

"Hi."

"Hi."

He began to remove his arm and she pulled it back into place making his fingers cup her breast.

"Oh, so you like this," Ethan smiled.

"Yes I do. All of it. You are amazing and generous and kind. Thank you."

"Emily, I don't know how you were treated in the past, but I don't take all this for granted. It is a special privilege to make love with you. I owe you the thanks."

"Well, then, it's mutual," Emily said as she turned on her side to kiss him. He wrapped his arms around her and pulled her close.

"I appreciate the appreciation you are showing at this exact minute," Emily teased as she felt his hard on and opened her legs to welcome him. "My turn."

She pushed him onto his back and mounted him and before he could say anything she had his dick pushing into her a little bit at a time. His hands took her breasts as she began to take him deeper into her. She rode him hard and long and knew he was about to come when he rolled her over onto her back and began sucking her breast as his hand flicked and stroked her clit making her come. She cried out as she climaxed. Ethan never stopped and she thought she was going to explode. She wanted him to stop and she wanted him to keep going. He finally thrust into her and they came hard and fast falling into a heap.

Emily fell asleep with Ethan holding her. Ethan took a bit longer, thinking how this was probably a big mistake. He wanted her but wasn't sure he could make the commitment he was sure was needed. He finally slept, holding this real life fantasy of a woman in his arms.

It was the sunshine filling the room that woke Ethan up. He rolled over to take Emily in his arms and found the bed empty. He sat up and looked around and saw a light on in the bathroom.

"Are you OK?"

"Yup. Just getting outta' here so you can get busy with your very busy day," was the response as she walked into the room fully dressed. She didn't trust herself standing next to him so she walked over and stood by the door.

"What time is it anyway?" Ethan asked.

"Around five-thirty, six o'clock."

"Really? Well, I guess I should get movin', too. Unless you have a few minutes to spare," Ethan said with a grin on his face as he moved the bed-clothes aside.

"Cute, but time for me to go. Ethan, you are an amazing man, gentle, thoughtful and sexy as hell. Last night was like a fantasy come true. I think I'm gonna need a nap today. I thoroughly enjoyed our time together. Thanks so much."

"Emily, you never need to thank me. Ever. Please."

Emily smiled at Ethan and softly closed the door behind her. Oh my God! She thought. What was she going to do now? Last night was amazing. It really was. She couldn't find all the words to describe everything. She wanted more, yes, she did.

She finally admitted to herself as she drove away from the house that she was falling in love with Ethan. Bad idea. He had no idea who she really was with her terrifying past and all the bad karma following along with it. Getting seriously involved with Ethan right now was just more craziness being thrown into the mixed up mess of things. She didn't want him to be a target for the bad guys. She had to talk to Matthews about this.

He needed to know what was going on with Ethan so he could try to keep him safe. Emily just wished the whole thing was over and the really bad guy was finally put away.

Ethan got up, showered and dressed, all the while beating himself up for everything that had happened last night. *I can't believe I did all that. I was supposed to be a gentleman, not a sex crazed lunatic. I just can't seem to help myself when I'm around her. She smells so good. When she smiles at me it's like she just grabs my heart and won't let go. I gotta get a hold of this. I do not want to be hurt again like the last time. That is not going to happen again. Never! I gotta get myself under control. Jesus! This is gonna be a damn long summer.*

Ian found Ethan slamming things around in the kitchen a little while later.

"OK, who pissed you off?"

"What? What?" Ethan said.

"I said who pissed you off?"

"Why would you think that?" Ethan asked impatiently.

"Cause you're slammin' things around like you wanna hit someone or somethin'," Ian pointed out as he walked around Ethan to get a coffee mug.

Ethan stopped what he was doing and looked at Ian. "I think I just made the biggest mistake of my life."

"And what would that be?" Ian asked.

"You know that meeting I was supposed to have with Emily last night to bring her up-to-date on everything?" Ethan asked Ian.

"I saw her drive in as I left."

"Well, little brother, that meeting lasted until about an hour ago and we didn't spend the night dong much talking about building anything."

Ian looked at his brother before he said, "No! Really? You finally got together with her? It's not like it should be a surprise. Everyone around here can see that the two of you were made for each other. What took you so long?"

"What are you talking about? I told you I didn't want a serious relationship. Not after the way things were screwed up before."

"Sometimes there's a greater power in charge and ya just gotta go with it. That's how I see things. No other way to explain it."

"I swear it's not that easy. It's not."

"She stayed all night right? She didn't run outta' here in tears right away, right? Looks to me she chose to stay. That's gotta count for something.

"Yeah, it does, I guess."

"Did she talk to you before she left or did she sneak out without you knowing it?"

"We talked. She said last night was great. She looked to mean it, too. I don't think she could lie about stuff like last night. She just doesn't have it in her."

"Then what are you so worried about? She's a grown up lady and it seems to me she knows just what she wants.

"And it's evident to me she was hurt real bad by the last guy or why would she need protection?"

"So, you've got this all figured out, have you?"

"Look, I don't want to be hurt again and I'm pretty sure Emily doesn't want anything to do with that either. So, I figure the best thing to do is put a stop to this thing right now, before anyone gets hurt."

"So, that's how you see it and you've decided to make up her mind for her without asking her what she wants. Nice plan, Ethan, great way to hurt her even more."

"What do ya mean? I'm only thinking of her right now."

Ian grabbed another cup of coffee then said, "No you're not. You're thinking only of you. You don't want to be hurt ever again so you're making sure you are the one to cut things off first. No trust here brother. As a matter of fact, and you can take it from someone who has a successful relationship and all, you're probably so head over heels in love with Emily, that all you want to do is run away before you think you might get hurt, not thinking of how a stupid move like this will hurt her - even scar her for the rest of her life. Think about that before you do something stupid big brother. You may have the brains as a builder and all but when it comes to your heart you have blinders on and can't see what the rest of us do."

With that, Ian walked out slamming the door behind him. It shook the kitchen cabinets.

Silence followed. Ethan just stood there not sure what to feel or what to think. So, for now, he decided he would keep his distance from Emily.

The rest of the day kept Ethan completely immersed in his building projects. He visited all the sites except Emily's. He got a phone update on the progress there and was satisfied with the report. Things were moving along right on schedule. The foundations had been poured and were curing as expected. The decking and framing would begin the following week.

Emily met with Matthews mid-morning. She told him about Ethan.

"Well, I wondered if something would come of this. You two looked as if fireworks were going off around you. Good for you. I'll make sure Ethan is looked after."

"Thanks Matthews. It's kinda weird talking to you about this but I don't want anything to happen to him because of me."

"I understand. And the agents will be discreet. They will be very close to you all the time but they will be discreet."

"OK. Wondered how all that worked. I'll tell Ethan the next time I see him. Guess I'll go take care of my house. See ya later."

Emily went back to her house and fell sound asleep. She woke up four hours later wondering why she was on the couch. She smiled as she remembered the night before. It had been like a fantasy come true. She had dreamed about a lover like Ethan but hadn't really expected to ever find one.

She stretched and got up to get something to eat. Jeez, all that sex really made you hungry. She felt like she hadn't eaten in days.

The rest of the afternoon and evening, Emily looked at light fixtures and other finishing touches needed for her house. She turned in and slept the night through, not even remembering her dreams.

Matthews was very busy. He had received the last two security checks on Kendra's clients. Jordan Jackson was clear. He had a solid job, a healthy bank account and no priors. The other client, Shirley Hopkins, had more money in her bank account than she earned in her current job. Matthews decided to look deeper into her lifestyle.

He called Kendra and told her about Jordan Jackson.

"Thanks Matthews. He called wondering if I had any news. I'll call him back now and arrange to meet with him to look at properties in the next few days. How about Shirley Hopkins?"

"I have some more research to do. Her financials don't match up. She has more money than she earns. I'll let you know when I know."

"Great. Thanks Matthews. Hey, have you seen Emily today? I thought I'd stop by for a visit."

"Yes. She may be napping. Seems she had a busy night last night."

"Really? Have anything to do with Ethan? Wait, don't answer that. I can figure it out for myself. I think I'll wait until tomorrow and ask her to go to the store for coffee or something."

"Good idea. Later."

Kendra just sat there and smiled after she hung up with Matthews. Things were moving along just like they were supposed to. Good. Those two needed each other. Not that Kendra was a matchmaker, but she did have a knack for knowing when two people belonged together. And those two did.

She called Jordan Jackson and told him the good news.

"Hello Mr. Jackson. This is Kendra MacDonald, the realtor in Crab Apple Creek. How are you this afternoon?"

"Hello Ms. MacDonald. I'm fine. Please call me Jordan. And yourself?" Jordan returned.

"Quite well, thank you. Jordan, I have some good news for you. Your application for a potential property purchase in the Crab Apple Creek area has been approved. I would like to meet with you to go over the details of a few properties I think might be of interest to you."

"That's great news. How about tomorrow? I'm free after supper."

"Good. Then let's meet around seven o'clock here in my office."

"OK. I'll be there. And thanks again. You've made my day."

"Glad to share the good news. See you tomorrow evening. Good Night"

After the call Kendra spent the evening gathering information on three properties she thought would fit Jordan's request. He wanted twenty acres or so, off the road. He wanted to build a house away from the road and have room for a barn. He wanted land to grow trees and shrubs, especially Christmas trees to sell when he retired from Foodies, Inc. He was planning his future. He'd been planning it for a long time and was thrilled it was all coming together.

Kendra had four other appointments the next day starting with Tim and Carol Thompson, Sandy McLevy, Carla Morganstern and then Jim Hathaway. They all wanted established homes on four to six acres of land. Kendra had appointments two hours apart beginning at nine o'clock. She had Jordan's appointment in the evening at seven.

The next day, Kendra made good on her plan to meet with Emily for coffee. She called her up and instead of the store, Emily asked Kendra to come to her place. She had made muffins and Kendra brought her own coffee.

"So, word has it you and Ethan finally got together the other night. Is it true?" Kendra asked with a smile on her face.

"Boy, not much is kept quiet around here! Yes, we spent the night together and I've been dying to tell you all about it. Well, not all, but a lot of it," Emily answered in a rush, smiling from ear to ear.

"Thought so. Spill!"

Emily sighed as she began. "Well, he is hot ya know. It's been a long time since someone has been caring and nice to me. I liked him from the first time we met, which was by mistake. Let me explain. I went out driving one day to get to know the area. I turned down the road he lives on and when I saw his place I just stopped right there, in the middle of the road. I don't remember how long I sat there but the next thing I know there's this tap on my window. I was startled and when I turned to see who it was, I was stunned. This guy was gorgeous! Drop dead gorgeous! I must have looked like an idiot 'cause he asked me if I was alright. I said yes. Then he said, "So would you please move away from my driveway so I can drive in..." or something like that. I just kind of stammered and then moved ahead and stopped again. He drove into his driveway, stopped and came back to my car. He said I would find a place to turn around up the road a ways and that would be a good idea 'cause if I wasn't there to see him then I didn't need to be on this road. I just nodded my head, closed the window, and drove off. I did find the place to turn around and when I came back by his place I stopped again. His house was fabulous. I had never seen anything so beautiful in my life. I didn't stay but for a few seconds before I drove back into Pine Ridge and had lunch at Hank's place. I just kept thinking about that sexy as hell hunk all day. Then there he was on my doorstep a few hours later. He was the builder for my home. I think we were both quite surprised and tongue tied. The rest you know."

Kendra just sat there silent for a long minute.

"Well, if that don't beat all. I didn't know you had met before the meeting at your house. So, now about last night. How did it all happen?"

"Do you want some tea or something? I see your coffee is gone."

"Oh, no, I just want to hear about last night. Hurry up with the details."

"OK. So.., Ethan had me come over to bring me up-to-date on the project. Did you know he has a TV in his wall? It comes out at the touch of a button. It's really a monitor because he can use his computer with it as well. Anyway, he showed me all the stuff the way it looks now and how it will progress week-by-week. It's gonna look amazing. Oh my God I am just beginning to really believe it's all mine."

"Get to the good stuff will ya?" Kendra asked with a laugh.

"Oh, well, after he had the monitor go back into the wall, we turned to look at each other at the same time and I tilted my head up to look at him hoping he would kiss me and get things started. I did and he did. Boy, can that guy kiss. After a few minutes he suggested we move to his bedroom and I agreed. The rest is X-rated and you can let your imagination take over. I woke up around daybreak, dressed and he was staring at me when I came out of the bathroom. We chatted and I let him know how much I enjoyed the night and was looking forward to more. He tried to convince me to stay but I knew he had meetings all day. When I left we were OK with everything. God, he really knows how to make a girl happy!"

"Holy cow girl! It's about time. Everyone in The Creek had you two together from the first time you met. Or should I say from the second time you met. It's taken you two six weeks to finally seal the deal. That's gotta be a record," Kendra teased Emily.

"Really, Kendra, give a girl a break will ya? I just got here and am trying to settle in and there is a lot going on with the house and all. But, yeah, I'm glad it took a little while. Boy, it's been worth the wait. I'm still tired but I guess that will just have to be. I have so much to do for Ian, getting all my choices together, and I'm only about two-thirds of the way finished. I need to find a few more special things today that are going to take some time. They're rather unique so I'm going to have to find the few places that carry them."

"Send me an email about what you are looking for and I'll see if I have any info for you. When are you two getting together again?"

"I don't know. Maybe Monday when I visit the site to see how the framing is coming along. That's when you can really get an idea of what it all will look like. Ethan said he has extra framers coming in so he can be finished with the rough framing of all the structures by Friday. I guess that means he will have two teams on each building. They're counting the barn and stables as two buildings even though they're connected by a hallway. Did you know they connected the basements as well? Cool idea so you don't have to go outside to get to the other one."

"No, I didn't know. That's a great idea. I'm gonna make a note of that in my specialized building file in case anyone else could use that idea. So, ya miss him yet?"

"Kinda. I'm trying to be careful and not assume anything. It was a great night but that doesn't mean we're together. I really want to keep things apart for now with all the building going on. I don't want him to feel cornered and truthfully, I don't want to be hurt. The last guy I fell for was a liar as bad as a liar could be. Everything he told me was a lie. Not that I think Ethan is a liar. Quite the opposite. But I've been damaged really badly and I just don't want to relive that again in any form. So I think I'll just keep my distance for a little while and see what he does. It's safer that way."

"And stupid if you ask me. What the fuck Emily?! You guys hit it off and now you're going to keep your distance? That's almost cruel. You don't know Ethan like we do. He's the sweetest and most caring man around here. He'd do anything to help anyone. He's got a heart as big as a mountain. Might I suggest you don't mess with him? He's ours and we don't want to see him hurt again."

"What do you mean again?"

"Well I guess someone should tell you about it. Ethan was engaged to be married. She dumped him at the altar the night of their rehearsal dinner. Word is that she secretly moved out of their apartment that afternoon while he was with Ian taking care of the last minute details. He went straight to the church from running his errands and didn't know she had left. Everyone was at the church waiting for her when she showed up, she announced she didn't want to marry Ethan anymore and she was leaving right then and there. No discussion. She announced to all that she had moved out of their place that afternoon and was heading out on her own. She left. No apology or explanation. Just left. Ethan looked like someone had beaten the life out of him. That was about three years ago. Ever since then he hasn't had a girlfriend of any kind. For a few days he just hid inside the family home all locked up. That's the place he has now. Ian tried to be there for him but Ethan didn't want to talk. After about a week he got back to building and hasn't looked back. I know he and Ian have had long talks since that day and that Ethan seems to have worked through most of that time. But he is just as vulnerable to being hurt as you seem to be. So don't mess with him. If you have a thing for him, tell him so. Otherwise stop everything right now. He can't take any more deep pain in the love department."

"Wow! What a bitch. I know this is gonna sound weird but it's a good thing she left the day before the wedding. She must be a cold bitch to do what she did. She must have had doubts long before that day. God! Thanks for sharing all that. So, I guess I'll let Ethan know how I feel as soon as I figure it out for myself. I don't play around in the love department and I don't go to bed with just anyone. So know that I've heard you, I will walk carefully as far as Ethan is concerned. I guess I'll let him make the next move then. Then I'll know what to do."

"Take some time to think about it. Speaking of time, it's time for me to meet my first clients for the day. It's gonna be a long one. Thanks for having me over this early. Send me your list and I'll get back to you in-between appointments. Your night is safe with me. See ya."

With that, Kendra left and a few minutes later, Emily could hear the clients as they pulled into the driveway. She looked out the window but stared at nothing.

She had a lot to think about. Why was it that this whole falling in love thing was not simple? There was always some kind of kink to be worked through. Oh well, she decided to get busy with her own work and think about Ethan later - oh yea, like that was going to happen.

CHAPTER 20

It was now the end of May and time for the traditional Memorial Day cookouts. The Kirkland's farm hosted the biggest party in the area. It was always held on Sunday although it really started Friday night after the store closed. The Creek gathered at the Kirkland's for a private celebration. This was a long standing tradition attended by locals only.

Emily was looking forward to this party in particular. Everyone kept saying it was something you didn't want to miss. Some of the more colorful Creek characters always stopped by and their stories of days gone by were almost magical to hear. Storytelling was a tradition in these mountains, passed down through the generations. It had to be experienced and gave you a better understanding of why these mountains were the way they were.

The Creek wasn't the only busy place in the world. Yuri's contacts had given him the names of three people they thought could be persuaded to find Barbara. They were sure she was in the mid-Atlantic region from reports they had received. The last place anyone had reported contact with her was her home in New Hampshire. Even though a car similar to hers had been found crashed off the side of a mountain and severely burned with a body being reported as dead inside it, Yuri was certain she was still alive. He had his people taking pictures of crowds all over the United States. A few promising possibilities had been identified.

One lead was in the Mid-Atlantic region near Boone. Jones had taken pictures when he visited the UFO sighting in Crab Apple Creek. One of the women in one of the pictures was signaled as a possible match to Barbara's picture. Yuri used the newest and most highly sophisticated computers just like the FBI and other agencies did. His facial recognition program was state-of-the-art. It had signaled a possible match the Thursday before Memorial Day.

Yuri had three of his people setting up in Boone to see about getting in on some of the action in the Crab Apple Creek area. The problem was that there wasn't anything going on - no public events at all. Just business as usual. So the three men were trying to come up with some way to spend some time in the area without arousing suspicion. This was going to take some time and some creative thinking.

One of them had an idea.

"Hey, what about the Fourth of July? Everyone has a parade and a cook-out, special deals at their businesses, re-enactments and other activities. I say let's look into those kinds of things around Pine Ridge and Crab Apple Creek. In the meantime, Hanson, you can apply as an instructor in the Math department at Appalachia State U for the summer term. At least you'll look legit," offered Saunders.

"I already have an interview this afternoon. Saunders, have you applied as a carpenter with Sutherland yet?" asked Hanson.

"Yes. They said they have all the crew members they need but they like my resume and will keep me in mind in case anything happens. So, at least I look legit hangin' around the area for a while. That leaves you Benson. What's your angle?"

"Well, I look a lot younger than I am so I thought I'd look for work with the Boone Parks Department as a summer helper with their programs - sports camps and beach duty. They have my application and I'm meeting with them tomorrow morning. So, it looks like we're all legit here. We each have our own small apartments so no questions there and we can fake a first time meeting at Hank's Diner Saturday morning. We should be all set at this point."

I agree," said Saunders. "The Boss will be happy with this progress. I'll send an update this evening."

Hanson asked, "What about this weekend? It's Memorial Day and I'm sure there will be lots of outdoor stuff going on."

"We'll go to all the outdoor parades, public cook-outs, and stuff like that just to get to know the area. People will see us and begin to recognize us as locals. By July fourth we should be invited to all kinds of cook-outs. Better to take it a bit slow at first," Sanders explained.

"OK with me."

"OK with me, too."

The three of them went about the business of settling into the community.

The NOVAE had been monitoring the progress locating Emily. They liked all that they saw. They knew a confrontation with the CON was coming. This had been foretold by the Ancients. This was going to be an epic battle between Good and Evil, The Light and The Dark. Magic of all kinds would be involved in this battle. The outcome would determine the future of the planet and all its inhabitants.

CHAPTER 21

Friday dawned clear and warm. The temperature was predicted to be near seventy. This was a great start to the holiday weekend. The Creek was busy preparing favorite foods, and gathering outdoor furniture and coolers for the cookout at the Kirkland's. Everyone was bringing a dish to pass and the Kirklands were supplying the hot dogs, burgers and, most importantly, the barbecued ribs. The sauce was said to be a secret - a tangy bite at first then a bit of sweet was how the locals described it. The ribs had been marinating since late Wednesday night and would be falling apart by the time they were ready to eat.

Michael and Ted had been busy with a secret salad all week. They had the recipe just right and were preparing enough for an army, according to Michael.

"Ted, just how much do you think we need? Others are bringing salads as well."

"Correct Michael, but none like ours. After all, it has a pasta base with a bit of shine in the dressing. And the veggies have been marinating in the dressing since last night."

"It is incredible for sure. OK. Just don't make anymore. I think ten pounds of cork screw pasta is enough."

"OK. I agree. The pasta's all cooked and cooling right now. I didn't cook it all the way so the dressing can soak in. I think this is one of the best recipes I've ever dreamed up."

"Could be. It does have a yummy flavor. Especially the shredded carrots. Hmmm Hmmm."

"Hey, you're not supposed to be sampling it yet. I'll give you some when I say it's ready." Ted laughed as Michael gobbled another spoonful while at the register with customers.

Emily went over to the store for breakfast to get one of the bagel sandwiches the guys had added as a regular daily item after the smash hit they had made a few weekends ago.

The store was busy and the talk was centered on the weekend's fun.

"Hey Emily," Ted and Michael said in greeting.

"Hey guys. Looks kinda busy around here. Have anything to do with tonight's festivities?" Emily asked.

"Of course. Everything to do with it. Michael and I are cooking up a storm. Are you bringing anything?" Ted asked.

"Of course. My world famous cookies, by request."

"Great!"

"And, my great grandmother's chocolate mayonnaise cake. Now don't make a face. It's really good and moist and it's topped with her butter cream frosting. Chocolate of course."

"I know just what you're talking about Em. My mom makes a great mayonnaise cake, too. It's an old family recipe. Have an open mind, Ted. You've eaten my mom's cooking a million times and you didn't even know it was made with mayo."

"Really? That cake? Wow, ya can't even taste the mayo," Ted said.

"Really Ted. Get serious. Mayo is just eggs and oil. It's all mixed in," Emily laughed along with Michael.

"Ya gotta love the guy, huh?" was Michael's response.

"OK. OK. As long as your yummy cookies will be there, too. I just love 'em."

"So guys, what time should I show up?" Emily asked as she walked to the kitchen with Ted to give him her breakfast order.

"Any time after five is good. The Kirklands are closing the business at four to set up for the night. Just park in the usual area and they will have a horse drawn wagon ready to take us to their private outdoor area behind the barns. Bring a blanket or chairs. Oh, do you have lawn chairs?" Ted asked.

"No, not yet. Do you have any here I could buy?"

"No need. We have about a half dozen. We'll save one for you."

"Great thanks. And now for breakfast. How about one of those poppy seed breakfast bagels with sausage please?"

"Sure thing. Get something to drink and I'll bring it over when it's ready."

"Thanks ,Ted."

Emily made some tea and joined the group at the table. Kendra was there along with a few of the local folks. They were all talking about the cook-out.

"Hey everyone," Emily greeted the group.

"Hi Emily."

"Mornin' Miss Emily."

"What's new?" Kendra asked. "How's the house coming along?"

"Well, Ethan tells me it's right on schedule. Even that thunderstorm the other night couldn't slow the progress. They're going to start framing Tuesday. I can't wait. I'm going to spend the day watching and taking pictures. I'm so excited about it."

"Wow. They really are keeping on schedule. Ethan is a man of his word as long as Mother Nature cooperates."

"Miss Emily, I took a look at your building site. Sure is gonna be a big place with the barn and all. I hear you're gonna keep horses at some point. Is that true?" Asked Jonah, one of the long-time residents, as he stood with his hat in his hands.

"Yes, Mr. Jonah. That is true. I hope to have a couple of my own and offer board to a few others. That will take a bit of time as I need to hire a stable master and all."

"Well, Miss Emily, you're looking at a fifth generation horseman right here. Just ask around. I'd be mighty honored to run your stables for you. You just let me know if you wanna talk about that. Ethan and Ian know me and my kin. I haven't been workin' much for the last couple of years due to the poor economy. My family's been in these parts for over a hundred years. Been taking care of horses the whole time. You just let me know."

"Thank you Mr. Jonah. I'm sure if Ethan and Ian give you a good report I'd be willing to spend some time with you. Do you have horses of your own?"

"Yes, Ma'am. We have six of our own and stable another twelve. We offer riding lessons and such. We slowed down a bit but not so much as you could tell. Once you get the fever you just can't stay away from those beautiful creatures. I've been helping my brother run our stables these past two years so I'm available if you're interested."

"I'll let you know. I'd like to come out for a visit either way if that's possible. I miss the horses I used to be around. It's been a while. How about one day next week? Maybe Wednesday?"

"Yes, Ma'am. I'll be looking for you around ten. Just ask anyone how to get to our place. It's just past Ethan's place on the left. It's called Two Moon Meadows Stables and Farm. I'll be looking for you."

"I know where that is. I took a wrong turn early on and found Ethan's place by mistake. I drove down the road a bit and turned around in one of your pasture roads. I tell ya, nothing is a coincidence."

"I agree," Kendra said.

"See you then, Ma'am. Have yourselves a great day," offered Jonah as he left.

"Ya know Kendra, nothing happens by mistake," Emily said as she sat down across from Kendra. "Just this morning I found myself thinking about the stables and horses and how I was going to have to start looking for a stable master and all. And here he is. Tell me about Jonah. Is there anything untoward I should know about?"

"He's one of the best horsemen I've ever known. He's gentle and caring and seems to be able to quiet a horse," Kendra offered. "I've known him and his family forever and there's something magical about them.

"Seems as if they know just what their animals are thinkin'. Not just the horses either. All the animals. Kindest, gentlest people around," one of the locals added.

"She's right," Ted said as he brought Emily her bagel.

"OK then. I'll get to know them and see how we all get along. I love when a problem is so quickly resolved," Emily said as she bit into her bagel. "God, this is sinful! And oh... Kendra, I meant to mention this a few days ago. I found a jug of shine on my back porch the other day. Please thank the mountain men for me. I do greatly appreciate their gift."

"Oh I will. I thought they might be leaving it soon. I'll get the word out to them today. Have you sampled any of it yet?"

Emily laughed as she replied, "No. I'm too chicken. I don't like whiskey to begin with and I think if I'm gonna sample the stuff, even a little smidgen, someone should be there with me."

"I get it. I'm sure there'll be some goin' around tonight. Maybe then, huh?"

"Maybe."

Emily spent the next few minutes devouring her bagel. As she finished she saw Ethan looking at her with a smile on his face.

Kendra saw him, too and noticed how he was looking at Emily with starry eyes and that far off look of a time past remembered.

"So Ethan how about joining us for breakfast?" Kendra asked.

"I see that look Kendra and the sooner I get outta here the safer I'm gonna be," laughed Ethan as he turned to Ted. "All set Ted?"

"Yes, Sir. Just what you asked for. I have both coolers ready. I'll bring them up front."

"See you ladies later. Behave yourselves," Ethan said as he walked to the front of the store.

"Not on your life Sutherland. You should know better than that," Kendra called out amid laughter from all around.

"If those two become partners in crime, then The Creek is gonna be in real trouble," Ted said as he set the coolers down by the register. "This here is a nice thing you're doin' for your crews. Glad to be of service."

"Thanks Ted. How much do I owe you guys?" Ethan asked as he took his wallet out.

"Here's the damage Ethan," Michael said as he gave the bill to Ethan.

"No problem. Here ya go," Ethan replied as he handed over the cash. "Keep the extra for The Creek fund."

"Will do. Ian was in earlier for the others. Must be about twenty coolers out there all together. Nice thing for your guys and gals."

"It's what my dad used to do and I remember how much it meant to the workers. So Ian and I decided a long time ago that we'd do the same on all the holidays. You gotta let your employees know how valuable they are and how much you appreciate them."

"Your dad was always like that. Just let us know about the Fourth and we'll be ready. We gonna see you tonight?" Michael asked.

"Of course. The whole family is here so we'll all be there. Mom and Dad, too. They said they wouldn't miss this for the world."

"That's awesome. Can't wait to see them. Give them our love and be careful today."

"Will do. We're quitting at two so everyone has time to get ready for the cook-out."

"Carry on until tonight," Michael said as Ethan made his way out the door.

Kendra and Emily just looked at each other for a moment.

"Have the two of you talked since the other night?" Kendra asked quietly after the table had emptied.

"No. He hasn't called and I haven't either. It's kinda weird," Emily answered.

"Really? He hasn't called and you haven't contacted him? Why not?"

"I thought about what you told me and decided to give him his space for a bit. We'll see if anything happens tonight."

"OK. Let me know if you need to talk about this. I'm here for you. Time for me to get to my chores and all. I have clients to meet with today. See you tonight," Kendra said as she took her leave.

Emily left soon after Kendra. She had some things to look at for Ian and then she got busy with her baking.

Ethan headed out to Emily's work site with the coolers. His dad had started the tradition of supplying lunch for the work crews on the day before a major holiday. They would eat around noon, taking their time, and finish up and clean up the site, leaving by two. They would be paid for a full day's work as a gift from the company. It was one of those special benefits the Sutherlands gave to their employees.

Ethan was thinking about Emily when he realized he had passed her road. Damn! That woman was occupying a lot of his time. He turned around and arrived a few minutes later driving all the way up to the house. The ground was dry today as it hadn't rained since the thunderstorm a few days back.

He got out and took the coolers to the spring around the back near the woods. They'd stay cold here in a natural small pool surrounded by rocks. It was about eight inches deep, just right for most of the cooler to sit in without covering it up. The rest of the spring was warm. He was not sure why this particular pool was cold, but he was glad that it was. He saw that a few plastic containers holding drinks had been placed here as well. Good idea. He then got started on his day. He would be working at Emily's all day today making sure the foundations were ready for decking. The timber would be delivered at six Tuesday morning and the framing would start at seven. He was going to enjoy this long weekend as much as possible because the next six weeks were going to be crazy busy with all the projects the company had underway.

A while later Emily was busy finishing the cookies and ready to put her chocolate cake in the oven. She was humming as she worked and would look out her window and see an agent looking back at her. And she smiled all the while.

She opened the door with a plate of cookies in her hand to offer them. "Hi guys. How about some homemade cookies. You deserve a break."

"Thanks Ma'am. We'll eat them as we keep working," said one of the agents. "These are really good."

"Glad you like them. I'll leave them here on the step," Emily said as she went back into the kitchen and put the cake to bake, setting the timer for twenty-five minutes. She mixed the butter cream frosting while the cake was baking.

She heard a knock on the back door and went to check it out.

"Matthews, how nice to see you. What can I do for you this fine spring day?"

"Hi Emily. For one thing, you can close your windows and stop baking all these yummy things. They smell great and it's making it hard for me to concentrate," laughed Matthews as he grabbed a cookie. "Yummy indeed. What else are you making?"

"My great grandmother's mayonnaise cake. Now, don't give me that look. It's a chocolate cake that's really moist. Instead of eggs and oil or shortening, she used mayonnaise. You'll have to try it tonight at the barbeque."

"If you say so. Speaking of tonight, there will be heightened security all weekend. I've just been notified that activity has increased in the area.

Nick's boss thinks you may be in Boone. I know. I know. It seems he has a state-of-the-art facial recognition computer and someone who was here during the UFO thing was taking pictures. Problem is, you weren't outside the whole time so I'm hoping this thing blows over."

"I've been feeling a bit uneasy for the past few days myself. I know something is building up and I'm afraid it's going to explode right here in The Creek because of me. It's just a gut feeling."

"Then your gut is correct. I won't hold anything back unless I'm told otherwise."

"I know. Thanks for the update. Speaking of updates, have you been up to my house this week?"

"No, but the team tells me things are moving right along. Something about framing starting Tuesday right?"

"Yes and I'm going to be there to drive in the first nail. That's around six-thirty just so you know where I'm going at that early hour."

"Got it. You'll have company as usual. Are you driving yourself to-night?"

"Uh-huh. Then I can leave when I feel like it. I'll be taking the Jeep full of baked goods. The guys have a chair for me and I'm bringing along a blanket, too. This shindig sounds like a lot of fun and it's been a real long time since I had this kind of fun."

"I'll be staying close to you no matter who you hang around with although Ethan tells me The Creek is on guard for you even if they don't know what's going on. They've figured out you're special and need protection. Amazing group of people around here."

Emily was quiet for a moment then said, "I know. They seem to have taken me in as a long lost relative, no questions asked. Did I tell you I found a jug of shine on my back step a couple of days ago? It was right after we started the road work. I guess my message got to the two guys that they're safe and all. I'm glad."

"The agent on duty got a hold of me right away to inform me of the present. He was laughing the whole time. None of the agents saw the guys deliver this. They really know how to lay low and not be found. I may have to talk with them to learn a few of their tricks," Matthew laughed.

"Ted says they just want to be left alone to live on their mountain. OK by me. But I was thinking, Ted also says they each have a cabin that's not too sturdy. Maybe they'll let me build them a good one with heat and plumbing but keeping it looking like the forest so no one can find them. I'm sure Ethan would do it and they would let him and his crew build it. They've known Ethan forever and trust him. What do you think?"

"Nice idea. But we'll have to approach them quietly, staying sensitive to their traditions. I'll do some groundwork without giving their identities away. You see if Ted and Michael can get a message to them and maybe you could meet with them on your site after work hours one day next week. Alright, back to my house to work. See you tonight. Just a couple more cookies for the road. Bye." And Matthews was out the door.

Emily decided to go over to the store and talk with Ted while the cake was cooling.

"Hey Ted, can I talk with you for a minute? Privately?"

"Hey Emily, sure. Come on in the kitchen while I check on lunch," Ted said as he walked in to the kitchen.

"What's up Ms. Emily?"

"Ted, I have an idea I want to get your take on. I would like to build the moonshine guys new cabins with heat and plumbing. I know this might seem like an invasion into their private world so I thought I would talk to you about it. What do you think?"

"Emily, that's a generous thing. I've know those two characters my whole life and they couldn't pull off a new place on their own. Their military pensions are good enough to get by on but nothing more. The Creek takes care of their own ya know. But, I'm not so sure that they'd appreciate others knowing where they really live."

"I thought of that. Matthews is going to do a security check on them just like he did on everyone else here. He doesn't expect to find anything so he suggested we get Ethan and some of his long time crew members to do the work. The guys know them and trust them not to give away secrets. They could build the cabins anywhere they want if they don't want anyone to really know the location of their works and all."

"Good thinkin'. I'll get word to them and let ya know their thoughts."

"Ted, I would like to sit and talk with them about this if that can be arranged. I was thinking my site after hours with only Ethan and Ian there."

"I like the way you think. I'll tell them everything and let ya know. I think it's a generous and thoughtful idea. You really are a sweetheart."

Emily blushed, "Thanks Ted. Just doin' what I think is the right thing. After all, I've been thrown into their world without their OK. Gotta make things right."

Ted smiled as they walked back into the store. The place was hopping busy and all the breakfast bagels had just been taken.

"Time to head back home and frost that cake. Later."

"Bye-bye Miss Emily."

Michael waved as Emily left the store.

Mo and Lainie were busy with their greenhouses and the new hybrid pot plant. It was growing well for them.

"Hey Lainie, I think this new hybrid is gonna be ready by July fourth just like we planned. It smells powerful strong already."

"And, it's growing fast. It's already bigger than the others. Can't wait to try it out."

"Me, too. Are we ready for the barbeque tonight? What did you make for our dish to pass?"

"I decided on fresh baked rolls and some of that garlic butter I make. It's already in the fridge. The dough is rising for the last time. It'll be ready to roll and bake soon."

"Sounds good to me. Let's finish up here then we have some plants to get ready for tomorrow's sale. They need to be moved to the front greenhouse. Should take about an hour. I'll get started while you take care of the baking."

"OK. Gosh, the dough should be ready right now. See ya."

Mo spent the better part of a half hour moving plants before Lainie came back.

"They need about thirty minutes to bake so I'm all yours for a bit."

"We should be done with these plants just in time for your buns to be done."

The sisters worked in silence moving all the new plants to the greenhouse.

"Time for lunch Mo," Lainie said as she stripped off her work gloves and headed for the house.

"Those rolls smell divine. Can we have some for lunch Lainie? Please?" Mo asked like a little kid, making Lainie laugh.

"Of course I made extra. We must sample the wares before we share them with others."

"All the best bakers do that," Lainie replied as they washed up for lunch.

"We don't really have much more to do today Lainie. What do you say we play hooky and take it easy until tonight? We deserve a break."

"I agree Mo. We are off the clock as of right now," Lainie said as she punched out on an imaginary time clock.

The sisters ate lunch and set about watching a movie that put both of them to sleep. They woke up in the late afternoon feeling ready to go.

The moonshine guys had been busy. It was tradition that they supplied a good amount of shine for this barbeque. No one asked for it. It was just done. They had been making shine for the last four weeks getting ready for tonight. Some of the jugs had already been delivered to the Kirkland's' place. The guys would bring the last set with them. They always arrived around twilight. Better to go unnoticed.

The chiefs had been invited and said they would both be there. They would be giving an ancient blessing to get things started at around six-thirty.

No one ever missed this part of the night. It was the unofficial kick-off for the summer season.

Matthews had increased security for the night at the Kirkland's, Emily's building site, and in town. He wasn't taking any chances with so many people around The Creek. He had just received an update, and The Creek as well as Pine Ridge and Boone had been put on high alert. The Command Center in Virginia had intercepted information from Yuri. He was pushing hard to find Barbara and had chosen the Mid-Atlantic region as ground zero. Headquarters and the Virginia Command Center were working hard to find Yuri's contacts before Yuri found Emily.

Ethan's family had arrived throughout the morning and everyone was finally home. His parents were in the kitchen fixing lunch and his three sisters were busy preparing their contributions for the barbeque.

"Hey Dad, did you see the latest toy in the workshop?" Mary Ellen asked.

"What toy?" Colleen and Bethany chimed in.

"You mean the hidden huge screen TV monitor? Yes, I did," their dad answered.

"I even got it to work. The picture is so real you think you're in the middle of the ocean while you're watching it," added their mom.

"Good for you, Mom. You can show us all how to use it later," Mary Ellen said while everyone laughed and teased their mom about being such a high tech wizard.

"Has anyone seen Ethan yet?" asked Bethany. She was the baby of the family and had a special bond with her big brother.

"No. But I did speak with him. He said he should be here around three or so after he makes sure the site he's on is all shut down. It's just on the other side of The Creek, about twenty minutes up the road. He's building a house and barn connected to stables for his client."

"...who just happens to be an eligible female," added their mom.

"Oh God. Really? Give us all the details," ordered Colleen.

"Well," their mom started, "seems she is new to the area and bought about two hundred acres along the national park line. She just wants to settle down here and eventually have a working stable and small farm of sorts. Maybe get some chickens or something along with large gardens. That's what Kendra says. And she's beautiful to boot. Seems your big brother has been seen with her a few times out and about, most recently at Hank's for lunch."

"Well, what do ya know about that?" Mary Ellen said.

"Well she better be real nice and good or she won't get my approval. That's for sure," Bethany added.

"Now girls, let's let your brother make up his own mind. I know we don't want to see him hurt again so let's just let him tell us about her if he wants to, OK? Give him some space," their dad suggested.

"OK."

"Uh, huh."

"Sure."

"Now girls, behave yourselves tonight. How would you feel if the three of you came after you? Now that's a terrifying thought," their mom added with a laugh and a shake of her finger at them.

"We'll behave," was the reply from all three girls as they shared a conspiratorial glance.

"Now, let's get busy with lunch and the dishes for tonight," said their mom as she took control of the kitchen.

Ethan was eating with his crew. There were only a few of them as today was the site cleaning day. The foundation guys had picked up their forms that morning. The crew was preparing for the start of framing Tuesday. The electric company had just finished installing the lines they would need. The crew had cleared all the trees and rocks that had been left close to the buildings and set them in their places on the edge of the meadow. The place finally looked good.

"Great job everyone. Let's go over to my truck for a meeting," Ethan said.

As they gathered, Ethan pulled out the coolers. He had sent one of the crew to the spring for the drinks.

"Lunch is on me today - sandwiches and sides from the store. And when we're finished you can take the rest of the day off with pay. It's kind of a way to say thanks for all your hard work. Dig in!

"Thanks!"

"Awesome!"

"Much appreciated."

They talked about everyday stuff as they devoured Ted and Michael's creations. As they finished up the talk turned to the evening's party.

"Hey, Ethan, you gonna be at the barbeque tonight?" asked Tom. "How about the rest of you?"

They all answered yes.

"Absolutely Tom. And my whole family is at the house right now cooking up a storm. What about your family?"

"Oh yeah, we'll all be there. My group's been cooking as well. The house smells so good."

Conversation about the party kept them busy as they finished lunch.

"Alright you guys, get outta' here. See you tonight," Ethan said.

It only took a few minutes for everyone to leave. Ethan found himself alone staring at Emily's house imagining how it would look when it was all finished. He could see smoke coming from the chimneys with lights on in the windows casting a soft glow onto the porch. He saw the barn and stables with a light or two on and heard the soft sounds of the horses as they settled for the night. The sky would be clear and just darkening with a star or two beginning to twinkle.

He daydreamed for a few more minutes before he turned to leave. As he did he thought he saw something move near the barn foundation. He turned back to take a second look and saw what could only be described as a ghost standing by the front entrance. He could see right through it but it still had a full human shape. It looked like a man. It was a wispy whitish-gray color and kept staring at Ethan as if he knew him.

The more Ethan looked at him the more he began to take shape. Ethan watched as he became a native man, with a feather hanging from his long braided hair. He wore clothes made of animal hide, and held a bow and a quiver full of arrows. He held a staff of some sort, not a spear, but something that looked special. It had feathers hanging from it as well. The native had his face painted with symbols. He looked at Ethan and then pointed to the west-north-west forest away from the building site. Ethan remembered this was the way they had all walked to get to the burial grounds.

As Ethan continued to watch, more native spirits showed up. As they pointed their spears to the sky an eagle flew down and landed on a rock in the middle of the meadow. It was joined by other animal spirits. The native ghosts walked and surrounded the rock. Ethan swore he could hear them chanting.

One of them motioned to Ethan to join them and before he realized it he was walking over to the big rock. When he got there they parted for him and he stood next to it. He had never been this close to an eagle before let alone a ghost. He stood there for what seemed like hours before he realized they were bowing to him and disappearing into thin air. He was alone a minute later.

Ethan stood stock still unsure about what had just happened. He cautiously looked around to see if they were there. No one was in the meadow but himself. He could have sworn he had a long and detailed conversation with the native Spirits but couldn't quite remember what they talked about. The more he stood there trying to remember the details the more he forgot. Damn! He knew he wasn't seeing imaginary things. He had seen them, spoken with them, heard them chanting. What had they said? It was something about this meadow and how special it was. He just couldn't remember more. Why not? It had just happened a minute ago. Oh God! What time was it? It must be near dark. He looked at his watch and saw that only a few minutes had passed. No way!!! He had been with the natives for hours. They had talked, chanted and given him a ton of information none of which he could remember. What was happening to him? This was just too strange.

He turned to walk to his truck and saw a feather on the ground. As he bent to pick it up, he realized it was an eagle feather. He had never seen one like this before. He knew from the chiefs that it was a special thing to find one so he would show it to them later that night at the barbeque.

Ethan got into his truck and started to drive to the end of the meadow. He took one last look in his mirror and saw the first Native Spirit watching him. He turned around to have a better look and the Spirit was gone. This thing had really happened. What did it all mean? He didn't get the feeling that they were doing something wrong building in the meadow. It was quite the opposite once he gave a minute of thought to it. It felt very right to be building Emily's home here. Maybe that's what the native ghosts were trying to tell him. That it was OK with them. He drove down to the road and headed home. He had a whole lot of questions about the last few minutes but he didn't know who to ask.

Maybe the chiefs could shed some light on all this. Maybe.

Ethan arrived home a good half hour later and braced himself as he walked through the shop door into the kitchen.

"There's my boy. Ethan," his mom said as she enveloped him in a big hug.

His dad hugged him as well then his sisters took turns kissing and hugging. He eagerly returned their love.

"Boy, y'all are a sight for these sad eyes. I've missed you very much," Ethan exclaimed as he walked over to the sink and washed up. "Now, how about a sample of all this food y'all are fixin'. It smells so good I swear I gained five pounds just walking through the door."

"Would you listen to that poor, poor man? One would think he hadn't had a decent thing to eat since the last time we were all here. When was that? New Year's I do believe," Mary Ellen said teasing him.

"What about Ian and his wife? Don't they feed you some?" His father asked with a bit of sass in his voice.

"Really, Dad? Please. They've got their hands full with their own family. Those kids can put more away than the five of us ever did."

"You know how to cook better than most so if you've been starving it's your own fault," blasted Colleen with a snap of the kitchen towel on Ethan's back side.

"Oh, so that's how this is gonna play out. No problem," Ethan shot back as he grabbed another towel and the towel war began. It carried on between the four of them until a truce was called. Ian, Sr. and Mary Elizabeth, Ethan's dad and mom, just sat there laughing at the antics. The memories of years gone by were reflected in their eyes as they looked at each other and softly nodded their heads in that unspoken acknowledgment of shared love.

"OK big brother, spill. What's with the new hottie in your life?" questioned Mary Ellen. "I am, after all, the oldest girl in this family and I have every right to know the details of my brother's love life."

"Who said so?" Ethan returned.

"It's one of the laws of nature," Bethany added siding with Mary Ellen.

"And, we just gotta know so we can protect you if she turns out to be bad," added Colleen.

"None of your business. That goes for all three of you," Ethan said with determination hoping they would stop asking questions he wasn't ready to answer. Jesus, it hadn't even been an hour since the vision thing. He was still trying to wrap his head around all that.

It didn't work. They kept it up until he finally yelled at them.

"Look. Just shut up about the whole thing. If I want you to know I'll tell ya when I'm ready," he said as he walked out into the shop and slammed the door.

"That's a healthy sign right there. Yes it is," his mom said with a grin on her face.

The sisters wanted more and started to follow him when their dad said, "Girls, leave your brother alone. He's not a little kid. He deserves our respect. He'll talk when he's ready."

"But Dad," they all started and where cut off by a wave of their mother's hand.

"Stop. Let's finish up in here then you can get settled in before we leave for the Kirkland's' around four thirty. Agreed?"

They all mumbled their agreement as they got busy in the kitchen.

Ethan walked outside so he wouldn't explode in front of his family. He spent the next half hour walking around the property trying to figure out what had happened at the build site. He knew it had something to do with Emily but he just didn't know what that was. He decided not to tell her about it until he'd had a chance to talk to the chiefs, and that would not be tonight. He decided to ask for a meeting with them in private. He didn't want to get the whole Creek involved in this thing. He would decide whether he told Matthews about it after he spoke to the chiefs as well. OK. With that all decided he headed back to the house and his sisters.

Now, if only his sisters would leave him alone about Emily. That would make this whole thing a lot more doable.

He found them all busy when he walked back into the kitchen.

"Ethan, there's food on the counter. Come join us," his dad suggested.

His sisters remained quiet.

"How was the flight from Scotland?" he asked his parents.

"Fine. No problems. We slept most of the way," his mom answered. "You're not eating?"

"I ate with my crew although that salad and cheese looks good. I'll have a little to hold me over until tonight."

"Good idea," Colleen said. "We wouldn't want you fainting from hunger or anything."

"Look Squirt, you eat your lunch and behave or I'll take you out behind the barn and spray you down with the hose just like I used to do," Ethan challenged with a laugh.

"Yeah, and you never got in trouble for it. Why was that Mom?" Mary Ellen asked.

"I don't remember anything about Ethan doing such things," their mom said with a laugh.

"Sure you don't," Bethany added. "He was always your favorite."

"That's right little sisters and I always will be," Ethan chimed in.

They kept the light banter up for the rest of the afternoon as they prepared for the evening's festivities.

Late afternoon found most of The Creek finishing up their last minute preparations and loading their trucks and cars for the Kirkland's.

CHAPTER 22

Matthews was finalizing the security plans for the night. He already had extra agents at the Kirkland's and on the road approaching the farm from both directions. The team on the mountain remained in place. The Creek group would stay in The Creek watching for suspicious activity. The agents on the building crews would look like regular party goers but would be on duty watching for new faces at the barbeque.

Matthews would be right next to Emily all night no matter what happened. He had told her about this plan and she was ready and thankful he would be so close. She had a feeling that something was building on the mountain and it wasn't going to be a good thing. A battle of sorts was the closest she could put into words.

Five o'clock arrived along with most of the people of Crab Apple Creek spilling into the Kirkland's farm in all manner of vehicles.

You could hear the greetings across the acres as family and friends saw each other and all headed around back to find the pit going strong and the mouth-watering smell of barbeque in the air. Tables made of sawhorses and planks covered in checkered cloths were set up all around. There was a separate fire circle set up away from the food area that would be lit as the evening wore on into night and the storytelling began with the passing of a few jugs.

The tables began to fill with the food everyone had made. Soon there wasn't any room for more so a couple more tables were set up and they, too, filled quickly.

Chief Running Bear and Chief Soaring Eagle were called to the tables to offer their special blessings. This had been a tradition for as long as anyone could remember.

Chief Running Bear of the Catawba Peoples began.

He called upon the Great Spirit asking for his blessing on this gathering. He thanked the Great Spirit for once again bringing life back to Mother Earth with the blessings of Father Sky. He asked for blessings on the new plants and new life that the spring had brought forth and thanked his ancestors for their protection, wisdom and guidance.

Chief Soaring Eagle of the Cherokee Peoples thanked the Great Spirit as well. He thanked the Catawba Peoples for their friendship these many years and asked blessings on them as his brothers and sisters. Then he said something rather strange.

"Great Spirit, we now enter a time of great unrest. We ask for your protection and guidance through the battles to come. I ask our ancestors to give us the wisdom and knowledge they have to see us through the coming days."

Both chiefs offered a chant of thanksgiving, then announced the barbeque ready to commence.

And it did.

The next few hours found everyone eating, drinking and visiting with those they hadn't seen much of throughout the winter. You could hear the laughter and banter all around and knew people were having a grand time.

Emily was sitting with Matthews and a few other folks when she looked up and saw Ethan and a group of people a little way off eating and laughing together. As she looked at each one of them she realized they looked a bit like Ethan. It didn't take long to figure out they were probably his family.

"Hey Matthews, is that Ethan's family with him? They look like they're really having fun."

"I do believe it is. Would you like to meet them? We could wander over after we finish eating?" Matthews asked.

"Maybe. But I don't think I'm gonna be done any time soon. This barbeque is delicious. I just may have to get more," Emily answered.

"I know what you mean," Matthews agreed.

They continued to eat and then went up to the tables for more food.

"Hey Emily," Lainie said from across the table. "Good barbeque!"

"Sure is. I've heard about Southern barbeque but this is the first time I've ever tasted it. All those stories were true. This is addictive," Emily agreed.

"The Kirklands sure know how to roast a pig. They've been doin' this for as long as anyone can remember. You could be on your death bead and you'd come alive just to have a taste of this before you met your maker. Truth," Lainie added.

"I believe you. Nothing is going to taste as good after this," Emily added more to her plate, waived at Lainie and set off for her spot on the lawn.

She found Matthews talking to Cora. Rather, she found Matthews listening to Cora.

"As I said, I haven't seen those lights since that night. Probably gonna show up again soon. They usually do come one right after the other. How's that building thing comin' along? Any problems with it? They gonna have to make the road bigger 'cause of it? They better not. I don't like that kind of change around here. No one does. You hear me?" Cora demanded an answer from Matthews. She stood right in front of him starring him in the eyes.

Matthews took a step back. "I hear you, Ma'am. And, I'm not the one to ask about the road. That would be Ethan. I haven't heard anything about changing the road permanently. Not a word. As for those lights in the sky, I haven't seen anything since myself. I'm sure you'll let us all know if they come again."

"Don't you be patronizing with me young man," Cora scolded.

"No, Ma'am. I'm not. I'm just trying to be honest with you," was Matthews's response.

"Well then, you're alright. I'm gonna get me some more of that barbeque. Those Kirklands know how to do at least one thing right," Cora mumbled as she walked away.

Emily had taken the long way around to get to Matthews and her chair.

As she sat down she was laughing. "Looks like Miss Cora set you straight about a few things, Mr. Man in Charge."

"Don't start," Matthews laughed. "She has her ways I'm sure."

"I wonder how old she is? She seems to have been here forever. When anyone brings her up in conversation they all laugh a little and shake their heads then say something about how she's always right about things. I don't think anyone knows her true age. She seems older than God sometimes with her sayings and wisdom and all."

"I know just what you mean," Matthews said as he leaned into Emily. "I won't even look her up for fear of her finding out. How I don't know how, but she would."

Emily nodded in agreement as she bit into more of the barbeque. "Hmm. This is almost better then... nope. Not going to say it. But it almost is."

Matthews just nodded as he took another bite.

Ted stopped by as he was walking along.

"Hey Emily. Hey Matthews. I see you're enjoying this heavenly barbeque," he offered.

"Yes we are," Emily said. "I ate two whole plates of food and think I'm gonna need a nap soon."

"I know what you mean. I did, too. But, no time for naps. The hayrides are about to begin. Interested?

"Sure. How about you Matthews? Up for a hayride?" Emily asked.

"Sure thing. Just point me in the right direction and off we go," was Matthews' response.

"They're gonna start in about ten minutes over by the barn. They have three teams of horses and wagons and the ride takes about a half hour. They go all over the property so you will get a good idea of how big this place is. Just wander over when you're ready."

"Thanks Ted. See you there," Emily said as Ted wandered away.

"OK to go Matthews?" Emily asked.

"Yes, I've just informed the groups and they're all over it. Anytime you're ready."

"OK. Give me a few as I throw this stuff away and wash up."

"Right behind ya."

They shared hellos as they walked over to one of the small buildings to throw away their trash and wash up. Then they found themselves with a large group waiting for the hayrides to load up and get going.

The wagons arrived a few minutes later. They loaded them one at a time and each set out about ten minutes apart.

Emily found herself sitting next to Ethan's family and the introductions began.

"Emily,' said Ethan, "I'm gonna make this easy on all of us. Emily, this is my family. Family, this is Emily. It's up to each one to you to tell Emily your name. And this here is another of my new friends. We all call him Matthews. Don't know why but it fits so we just keep doin' it. Matthews, this here is my family. Done."

With that Ethan sat down next to Emily and watched as his Mom, then Dad then three sisters all introduced themselves to Emily and Matthews.

"I think I've got it all right. Just correct me if I call you by the wrong name. I'll eventually get it right. It's nice to meet all of you," Emily said.

Agreement was heard all over the wagon. Matthews was chatting with Ian Sr. and Mary Elizabeth about their recent travels in Scotland. Ethan's sisters were pelting Emily with a million questions without giving her a chance to answer. She finally held her hands up in front of her begging them to stop.

"Stop already. I can't even get a breath in between all your questions. I think I heard some of them about my new house. Yes, your brother and his crews are building it and yes, there is a covered bridge although the canopy is not in place and won't be until the build is completed. And that's so the bigger trucks can use the bridge. As for anything else, I'm pleading the fifth."

This was met with groans and more begging. Emily didn't budge.

"She's tougher than she looks," Bethany informed her sisters. "Probably not going to get much personal stuff from her."

"That's right. You won't," Ethan commented as he took a long look at Emily.

"Boy, have you got it bad," Mary Ellen said. "No one has to ask a thing. Just look at our big brother. He's in love. No two ways about it."

The other girls agreed as they rounded a corner and Emily fell against Ethan.

"Oh sorry," Emily said as she righted herself and moved away from Ethan.

"No problem," Ethan said as he gave his sisters an "I dare you to say another word" look.

They remained silent for the first time all evening.

Ian Sr. pointed to a field and said, "Look. That field is full of new trees. Must be a couple hundred of them and all kinds, too."

Conversation turned away from Ethan and Emily as the wagon full of riders talked about the tree farm and the ponds they rode by for the rest of the ride. They retuned just as the sun was brushing the tops of the trees creating a splash of color.

Thanks were offered to the drivers as the other wagons began to arrive and all set out to gather their things.

"Folks, we've moved the party to the fire circle just beyond the barbeque pit. You'll see it as soon as you round the corner of this building. Make yourselves comfortable and we'll start the story tellin' in a bit," Mr. Kirkland explained to all.

A little while later everyone had grabbed a spot on the ground with their blankets and chairs and were settling in. A table had been set up with drinks and the makings for popcorn. The corn would be popped over the open fire in poppers made especially for this event.

Emily found herself between the Sutherlands and Kendra and a family from down the road. Kendra introduced Emily to them.

"Hey Emily, this here's the Thompsons - Gary and Helena and their three kids. They live on the road to Pine Ridge just past Ethan's place."

"Hi Emily, nice to meet you," offered Helena as she and Gary shook hands with Emily.

"Nice to meet you as well. This is my friend Matthews," Emily said as they all shook hands.

"So, you have three kids and a working farm? Must keep you beyond busy," Emily said.

"Yes it does," Helena answered. "The kids all have chores to do in the house and on the farm as well. Some say they're too young. Gary and I think a child should start learning about taking care of their own from an early age, say about two years-old. Our kids are eight, ten and twelve so they've been working for a long time. And they love it, all except maybe keeping their rooms tidy."

"I'm supposed to be all grown up and I still don't keep my room clean. Thank God for Helena," Gary said with a laugh. "It's not a real big place but we keep chickens, four cows, a bunch of pigs and two large gardens. We can and freeze throughout the fall and sell some of what we have. We barter, too. So, if you need anything, just let us know. I hear you make killer cookies so maybe we'll barter for some."

"Oh, Gary, your sweet tooth is never satisfied," Helena chided.

"Not a problem with me Gary," Emily said. "I love to barter. We'll get together soon."

They continued to talk and eat as the evening gave way to night. The fire was lit and it wasn't long before Emily saw a jug being passed around. She wondered if the shine guys were here when she looked behind her and saw someone she did not recognize.

Matthews followed her gaze and reassured her, "Emily, those are the shine guys. Well, one of them. The other is close by I'm sure. OK?"

"How did you know I was a bit scared?"

"Your body tightened up and your face paled. Take a breath. It's OK. And so are the guys. As Ted would say, they're just good ole' country boys. They'll probably stop by at some point. I asked Ted to get word to them that it would be OK with you."

"Of course. I'd love to have a private word with them. Just let me know when. I want to reassure them that their place is safe and thank them for their gift. Can I mention the cabin I want to build yet?"

"No. Let's wait for a few days then I'll arrange a meeting with them up on your site after the work crews leave, except for Ethan. They know him and are comfortable with him. They might even say no to your gift as they don't like to owe anyone anything. But if Ethan is there, they may just approve of it."

"OK then."

People wandered around visiting for a while. You could hear the music of laughter and talk as it floated through the night air accompanied by the crackles of the fire.

Then, as if a common thought had been passed around, everyone settled and quieted as one of the local mountain men stood up near the fire. He looked to be ageless, weathered by his years on the mountain. His beard was streaked with red and silver and his hair was pulled back in a pony-tail held by a piece of leather.

And then the storytelling began.

"Howdy y'all. Nice to see everyone again and welcome to our newest neighbor Emily," he began. Howdys and hellos were offered and returned in hushed tones.

"I'm known around here as Bear 'cause when I was just a young man I killed one that was goin' after my horses. Tonight, I thought I'd tell the story of how my kin came to this mountain and began the long held tradition of makin' moonshine. A tradition that carries on to this day.

"It was around 1745 when my about tenth great-grandpappy came over from Scotland with his new wife. They weren't even twenty years-old yet. They landed in the Jamestown area. They soon left because they couldn't find work and heard about the mountains and how you could just settle anywhere and own the land. So, here is where they chose. Soaring Eagle Mountain. It took them almost a year to get here 'cause this whole area was wilderness and they only had a wagon, two horses and a mule.

"Once here, they built themselves a cabin and planted a garden. My grandpappy hunted and they never went without food. They stored all they could for the winter. The Catawba and Cherokee were fighting with each other so my kin had to be careful where they traveled. The nearest post was in Boone. They only went there about four times a year for the provisions they couldn't make themselves.

"Now, one afternoon as my grandpappy was setting up his still, he saw an Indian coming along. He had no beef with them so he hoped this one would be in a good mood and not want to kill him. He noticed he didn't look like the Cherokee he had seen before so he just stood by the still with his axe in his hand waiting to see what the fella' wanted.

"As the fella' got closer, he noticed he was holding his arm close to his chest. It looked to be broken or somethin'. My grandpappy set his ax down and showed the fella' his hands in an attempt to offer help. The Indian nodded yes then passed out at my grandpappy's feet. He scooped him up hollerin' for my grandma to open the door. He set the fella' on the table and my grandma went about looking at his arm. It was broken and had a cut on it. They cleaned the arm and set it in place as my grandma knew about doctoring and all from the old country. They moved the fella to a pallet on the floor by the stove as it was still a bit chilly.

"That Indian slept that whole day and night through. When he woke up next day he didn't know where he was. It took him a few minutes to take it all in then he sat up and looked at my grandma. She smiled at him and offered him some food. He accepted and ate in silence. My grandpappy walked in as the fella was finishin' up and asked him his name.

"Seems the Indian was Catawba and his name was akin to Hunting Hawk.

"He motioned that he needed to leave and my grandma set him up with some food for his journey. He thanked them in his native words and set out on his way. My grandpappy went back to workin' the still. A few weeks later they found a beautiful deer skin that had been tanned and sewn into a shawl. They knew it was a gift from Hunting Hawk as a thank you for taking care of him. My grandpappy and grandma gave birth to seven of my kin over the years.

"Now, that Indian, "Hunting Hawk," came by a few times over the years and he and my kin grew them a long and true friendship. They met each other's kin and shared powwows and such with each other for years untold.

"I remember one story from about a hundred years back when my grandpappy went fishin' with one of Hunting Hawk's kin. Seems they both snagged the same fish at the same time but they didn't know it. They both worked hard to bring that fish in and both ended up as wet as the fish. The fish got away and the men both swore it was the other's fault. To this day that story keeps comin' around whenever both kin come together. Today, the kin to Hunting Hawk is here. Chief Running Bear, good to see you again. And you owe me a fish."

Laughter was heard along with a few colorful comments.

"So now y'all know some of the history of the mountain. That still my grandpappy set up is still in workin' order. A few modifications have been made so it makes a pure shine like none you've ever tasted before. If I was to start tellin' stories about that still we'd all be here a long, long time so I'll sit down and let someone else weave a yarn or two."

Applause and comments followed Bear to his place on the lawn.

Next to stand by the fire was a woman that seemed to be not so old and not so young. Her long flowing hair was aglow by the light of the fire. It looked like she had grabbed a piece of the night sky and wrapped it around here. Her night sky shawl had soft silvery fringe hanging from the edges. It moved with her as if it were a part of her.

She began to speak in a voice that felt like soft silk.

"I'm known as Sarah in these here parts. Always have been and reckon I always will be. My kin's been here a long time, too. Just like Bear's kin and most of y'all. I felt moved to say a piece or two tonight.

"Back in the day when time was slower and people weren't so crazy in a hurry to get to who knows where there was a special kind of light here on the mountain. A special kind of knowin' that people had about all things. We knew when to plant and when to harvest. We knew when a storm was brewin' long before it showed its strength. We knew when one of us was getting' ready to cross over to join our kin that had gone on before. I guess what I'm tryin' to tell ya is that there was a kind of magic all around. The light was different. It could change color in a breath. There seemed to be things growin' that no one remembered plantin' and things that came about of a spirit of their own.

"Now, I like modernism as well as the next one. Electricity and plumbin' and heat and I love my laptop. Make no bones about it. What I'm sayin' is that sometimes the quiet is what we need."

Heads nodded in agreement along with a few soft words of acceptance and knowing.

"I'm goin' to tell ya about a time before all these modernisms, not too long back. A time when magic ruled the mountain. Oh yes, I can see some of you remember these times, yes you do. These here mountains have always had a voice of their own and for some of us we can still hear that voice. Was a time when you always listened for that voice to tell ya how to do things. The voice of the mountains could be soft and calming and then it could be fierce and loud and powerful.

"Let me tell ya about one of those times. Many of you will remember this because it was just a few years back. In this current time we don't hear the mountain much because we aren't listening like we were taught by our kin. That's right. The Kirklands know just what I'm talkin' about. I see your heads noddin'.

"It was in the spring just about this time of the year just a few years ago. The thaw had begun and the creeks were running strong into the Pine Ridge River and that runs all the way down to the James' into the ocean. There had been a lot more snow than usual that winter and when I looked back at that time I realized the universe was giving us a heads up about the changes to come.

"There had been a lot of active weather, as the weather folks call it, with storms and tornadoes and the like all over the South. A year of vicious damage all told. The magic was very much alive here and a few of us heard our mountain talk to us. The last big storm had been in the last few days of March. That alone was not common and I knew something was about to happen. Then, all that severe weather south of here took shape. The mountain warned us time and again by holding it's leaves back from budding and keeping the critters in their homes. New births were starting late that year. Another warning from the mountain. Then, the mountain began to talk. It would send stiff breezes outta nowhere in the middle of the day. They'd last about five, six minutes then stop. I remember a number of you commenting on them time and again.

"Then our strong mountain did something that rarely happens. She moved deep within her core. It was a slight earthquake around a 2.2 and it was felt for hundreds of miles away cause it was set along an old fault line. Our mountain was talkin' to us tryin' to prepare us for what was about to happen. The quake got lots of you talking, finally, and we all began to be more aware of our place here.

"I was settin' on the porch at the country store one afternoon a few days later, with a few of y'all and we all saw the light change from its usual color to blue, then purple, then pink and it wasn't any time near sundown. It kept goin' for about a good ten minutes. Then it just stopped. The magic of the mountain was givin' us one more warning. Finally, we listened.

"The next night we all saw the lights in the Applewood grove. They stayed there for a long time, a half hour anyways. Now, whether you believe in other life forms from other universes or not makes no difference. That UFO was there and we all saw it and we all saw what it did. It made the mountain sing and it gave the best light show I've ever seen. Those lights went deep into the ground. I swear they were healing Mother Earth from the damage of the quake. You know I'm right about this. You know I am. Every time one of you tries to deny this the mountain makes you shape up. Bear, you remember when that farmer near you kept saying he didn't believe in such things even though he had been at the grove when all this happened? He was reminded by magic that all he had witnessed was true. Magic showed him how his crops would grow as if it were a movie. And, then they did grow just as it was told. He was so shocked by all this he put his farm up for sale and moved away. He didn't know how to handle the magic. I do believe there is a man coming along who will be buying his farm. He has been called by magic to this place to be with us all. He will be here soon.

"Magic is real. It happens around us all the time. The lights have returned to the Applewood grove. We know this is a sign that something is about to happen here. I have heard the mountain speak and offer you all to begin to listen with your heart. Our mountain has brought us all here for a special reason. Be aware of her voice."

There was applause and words of love and thanks as Sarah left the fire and sat down. Folks took a moment to stretch and gather more food and drink before the next storyteller took his place by the fire.

Emily took a moment to look around and saw the moonshine guys sitting on the edge of the group. She mentioned this to Matthews and he nodded.

As the next story teller took his place by the fire, there was a great deal of laughter and hootin' and hollerin' from the crowd.

"Tell us a good one, Jed."

"What's on your mind tonight, Jed?"

"Is this gonna be x-rated, Jed?"

Jed took his hat in his hand as he answered, "Now, y'all know I'm just a good ole' country boy and always try to be tellin' the truth. God's truth I do."

This was met with more laughter and colorful comments.

"Well, git to it then," Bubba hollered from the back of the group. This brought another round of laughter. More logs were thrown on the fire and Jed got started.

"First, I just want to say I apologize to the ladies for any colorful language that might slip out. No offense meant ladies.

"I'm gonna tell ya all about a bit of huntin' I took to recently. Charlie, not you Chief Running Bear, Big Ed and I set out at dawn on this particular day. We was looking for turkey. Had a hankerin' for it for a spell so thought we'd go get us some. There is a great lot of turkey in these here mountains if ya know where to look. Ain't that right Big Ed?"

Big Ed hollered back, "Sho' is Jed. Sho' is."

"That's right," Jed continued. "We set out early in my truck and went up to the ridge back of where Ms. Emily's now building her new home. Ma'am."

"Any time fellas, any time," Emily responded. Folks chuckled.

"So, it took us a while, as you know to hike up there once we left the road. We used that fire road beyond Lainie and Mo's place. It was probably about mid-mornin' when we got close to the first roostin' spot. We signaled to each other about where we was gonna stand and who was gonna take the first shot. There was turkey droppings all around. As we stood ready don't ya know a bevy of quail flew in and landed right in the middle of the roosting trees causin' the turkeys to fly off."

This brought a lot of laughter and comments from the crowd.

"Sure, Jed, blame it on the quail."

"Only you, Jed, only you."

"Now, folks, I'm tellin' ya the God's truth here ain't I, Big Ed? Charlie?"

Charlie yelled out, "Sure is. That's just what happened. For sure."

Folks just laughed harder.

"Well, we were a bit pissed, I mean upset, pardon me ladies. We talked about our next move and headed along the ridge to the next roost. Sure enough, there were droppin's all around again and we set ourselves up so we wouldn't shoot each other should we get a bead on a bird. We didn't have to wait long. A flock of about thirty came into view close by. We all signaled to each other that we had one picked out and at the same time, we set a shot. Big Ed and Charlie got themselves each big tom turkeys.

"My turkey musta known I was aimin' for him 'cause he turned and looked at me at the last minute and sat down. My shot went right over his head. Then, he stood up and looked at me again as if to say, got'cha and flew away with the others."

The crowd burst out into laughter at this and kept it up for a considerable time.

Comments were heard all around that kept the laughter going.

"Folks," Jed continued, "God's truth, just ask Charlie and Big Ed. See, they be tellin' you it was for real. Well, they had their birds so they was all ready to set out for home. And they was big ones, too. About twenty-five pounds each. Truth."

Jed took a swig from a passing jug, wiped his mouth on his sleeve and continued.

"Now, I was bent and determined to get one for me. So, I suggested maybe the boys would want to get two each as they had freezers and all. So they thought about it for a minute and they agreed it was a good idea. We set out for the next roost along the ridge. And once again, as we approached, we saw fresh droppin's. We discussed our plan and set up once again as we waited for the birds. Sure enough, about ten minutes later, another flock of about forty came our way and they were big ones, too. I set my sight on a tom close to me and signaled to the boys that I was all set. They were, too. We took aim, set our shots and the boys each got another bird. And, this time so did I. Finally.

"Only thing was I had shot two birds with the one shot. Seems the shot was so strong it went clean through the first bird, dropping it to the ground and struck the second one standing right next to him."

This was met with raucous laughter and hoots and hollers. Even Jed was laughing at this.

"I swear God's truth. Just ask my wife if I didn't bring two birds home," Jed offered.

Those close to his wife Jenny just looked at her and she was laughing as hard as everyone else. She did hold her hand up showing two fingers to confirm what Jed was saying. Folks were wiping the tears from their eyes they were laughing so hard. One comment brought another and it was a considerable while before things quieted so Jed could continue.

"Folks, it's the God's truth."

"Sure."

"Always is Jed."

"I know. I know,' Jed said as he continued once again. "We all looked at each other like we was dumb struck. How could that happen? Well, I wasn't about to hold a meetin' to try an' to figure it out. I went and got my two turkeys, bagged them and we all set off headin' for our trucks. We had to walk a long spell and as we left the ridge we ran across a flock of those birds again and I swear the one I missed was leading the group 'cause he turned to me, looked me right in the eye and gobbled so loud I swear you coulda heard him all the way back to The Creek. Sassy bastard. Pardon me ladies. And that's just how it was."

As Jed went back to his place on the lawn he was met with comments and laughter and applause.

"So, how did those turkeys taste Jed?" one of the folks asked.

"Well, the first one was right tasty. The second one's in the freezer for another day. Jenny cooks 'em up so good that ya'd just about die waitin' for them to be ready to eat."

Scott Kirkland was next to take the place by the fire.

"Folks that was a great bunch of story tellin' here tonight. Make sure you show you appreciation for your neighbors. As you can see, we're gonna be privileged to some music tonight. You all known these folks and the music they bring us is the music of the mountain folk. Sing along if ya have a mind to."

The group included men and women. Guitars, fiddles, and a mandolin could be seen.

The next couple of hours were spent listening and singing along to the old folk songs of the mountain. Ethan had joined Emily and was explaining the songs as they were sung.

They each had a story to tell about the folks who settled the mountain, about the holidays and traditions, of the wars and battles, of the magic of the mountain. Some were solemn where others were high spirited. The music was just another way the mountain folk told stories.

With the end of the music came the end of the night. It was getting close to midnight just like Ethan had told Emily it would be. Farewells were exchanged as everyone gathered their things and set out for home with promises of getting together before too much time passed by.

Ethan waved to his family as he walked Emily to her Jeep.

"Ethan, that was fantastic. I wish it could go on forever. I've learned so much about you and The Creek. It gives me a lot to think about. I'll be sure to thank the Kirklands and all," Emily said as Matthews loaded the Jeep.

"It's a heartfelt tradition around here I wouldn't miss for anything. I'm glad you were a part of it," Ethan said.

"I've heard about such traditions, Ethan, but this is the first time I've ever been a part of one. These are truly genuine folk from the heart," Matthews offered.

"Thanks Matthews, Emily. That about says it all. I'll check in with you tomorrow. Sleep well Emily." Ethan left to rejoin his family.

Matthews and Emily spent a few more minutes chatting with the folks around their Jeep before driving off.

They arrived back in the dell in short time.

"Thanks for driving Matthews. I do believe I'm tired. I'll probably sleep straight through the night. This was an amazing night. All of it. The food, the people, the storytelling, and especially the story Jed told. The music was mesmerizing and had so much history in it and emotion and all. You really

237

picked the perfect place for me to live the rest of my life. Thanks Matthews, to whomever made that decision."

"You are entirely welcome, Emily. I agree with everything you just said. And Jed is quite the character. I truly enjoyed him. I don't think I've laughed that hard in a long time. The other agents at the barbeque and the ones listening in were laughing just as hard. For what it's worth, they said this is one of the best assignments they've ever had."

"I'm glad I could accommodate them. Well, I'm going in. I hope I make it to my bed before I fall asleep."

"Emily, I have to walk you in along with these two other agents. From now on, you go nowhere without three of us. Just being careful."

"I understand. Just make sure I know their identity before they show up or I'm gonna push my panic button."

"I will. Tomorrow around ten, we'll go over each one's picture ID and info. The ones in the house you already know. These two are new. Names tomorrow. Sleep well."

Emily walked into the back door of her house, went through the kitchen, waved at the agents, was in bed ten minutes later, and asleep as soon as she put her head on the pillow.

One of the agents even turned her bedside light off for her.

She dreamed the usual dreams with the exception of a new entity. A woman Spirit that was watching over her. She felt protected and calm with this new energy.

And she slept well.

Matthews, on the other hand, had a lot of security checks to look at. It seems there were a few young people from Boone who had tried to break into the barbeque. Two agents had stopped them before they could walk more than two steps from their trucks and handed them over to the sheriff for safe keeping. Virginia HQ had finished running background checks on them and they were cleared. However, the sheriff decided to give them a warning for trespassing and called their parents in to pick them up.

Other than that the event had been quiet. All agents had been reporting in as expected all evening long.

Ethan and his family got home like everyone else and didn't take long to settle in for the night. Ethan stood at the window in his room just staring out at the night sky. It was clear and the stars looked like diamonds that you could just reach out and grab. The barbeque had been great as always. He had enjoyed sitting with Emily and telling her the stories behind the folk music. It felt so right to be there with her. He wanted more.

That's all there was to it.

Ethan sighed as he got into bed. Couldn't life just be simple and easy? He knew that was a loaded question as soon as he thought it. And what about that vision he'd had? There was so much going on all of a sudden. Maybe Sarah was right. Maybe the mountain was trying to get a message out to the people. Maybe it was talking. Something sure was. Maybe the mountain was trying to prepare them for some big thing that was coming.

Maybe so. He'd experienced a lot of stuff that couldn't be explained. He decided then and there to be more tuned in to the mountain and all the signs that were happening around him, like the magic, as Sarah had said. It was alive and well on Soaring Eagle Mountain.

Ethan fell asleep knowing Magic was real.

And The Creek slept.

CHAPTER 23

Memorial Day weekend was the unofficial start of summer across the country, and The Creek was busy just like everywhere else. People were buying plants and flowers for their yards, cleaning up from the winter storms, and painting and repairing homes and barns.

The Kirkland's opened the nursery at 6 a.m. on Saturday and Sunday for the weekend and at 8 a.m. on Monday. They closed at 8 p.m. on Saturday and Sunday and at 5 p.m. on Monday. They hosted a cookout for their customers on these days serving hot dogs, hamburgers, barbeque chicken and salads and cold drinks along with popsicles and frozen ices for dessert. It was all free to show their appreciation for their customers. They hired extra help for the long weekend as well, usually the local teenagers.

Emily was already working with their design team so she had no need to go over and visit.

Ethan was busy with his family at his own place. He had ordered plants and flowers for his home and they had been delivered Friday morning. On Saturday, his sisters were busy cleaning the gardens and planting them. His dad had a golf game with his local buddies and his mom was busy in the kitchen.

And that's the scene he found when he got home around ten o'clock after checking on Emily's build to make sure it was ready for Tuesday when they would begin decking.

The supplies had been delivered early and covered per his instructions. Matthews' security team had met with him to go over the schedule for the next week to ten days. All was ready to move forward.

But Matthews was busy with new intelligence info coming from contacts in Russia.

"Matthews, Yuri has given orders to find Barbara. He's targeting The
Creek. One of those pictures Jones took in The Creek shows a woman with a
similarity to Barbara before she became Emily. It's a random thing, but sometimes the more common a person looks, the more matches they trigger. We
have a special ops team in Boone right now looking for newcomers. I'll keep
you informed with every detail as I get it."

"It seems Yuri was beginning to get a bit scared. Our contact in Russia
hears that Nick's death wasn't his call - he knows the details and is scared.
We've found the leak at the prison and they have been taken into custody and
charged with terrorism against the U.S., a crime punishable by death. We're
pretty sure that's what they're going to get. Yuri's pissed about this as well.
Seems he's beginning to lose his control, at least that is what we're hearing
from our contacts around the world. He's obsessed with finding Barbara. He's
put out the word that he will pay anything and do anything to find her. He
thinks she knows all about his operation and he's convinced she's trying to
ruin him. I say the guy's wacked on so many levels."

"Jones isn't talking. His attorney quit when he found out Jones was
connected to the Russian crime syndicate. He's being protected as well. No
one will represent Jones and the federal prosecutor isn't making anyone take
his case. All too weird if you ask me."

"Keep your team on the alert for anyone new, especially this weekend
and into the summer. Summer help is always on the increase. Any thoughts?"

"No sir. We had a couple of teenagers try to crash the barbeque Friday
night. You know about that. No problem there. The sheriff slapped trespassing
charges on them with the caveat that the charges will go away in six months if
they keep their noses clean. I don't think we're going to have to worry about
them. Their parents were none too happy and have already informed us that
both boys will be working on building crews south of Boone for the entire
summer, six days a week. I think I like their parents way of dealing with them."

"Sounds good to me. Keep in touch. Later."

As soon as Matthews signed off he checked on all his agents in person
which took the better part of his Saturday. Sunday found him with a little down
time for a change.

The long weekend progressed with no other problems. The Creek began to show its color as flowers were planted and homes were tidied up. Kendra brought some flowers and tools for Emily to put around her temporary
home. Kendra said that since she was going to be there for the better part of
the summer there wasn't any reason it shouldn't show some color.

So Emily spent the weekend cleaning and planting right along with
everyone else. Even the agents helped out.

By late afternoon Monday, everyone was finishing up their projects and gathering at the store. Ted and Michael had been extra busy with all the customers and their own planting so Emily decided to help out earlier that day, and now they were washing up and settling around the table for cold drinks and snacks.

"Emily, you make a fine country gardener. I can just imagine your place next year with all the new trees and bushes and flowers and gardens. I do believe we'll have to get you a hat or two so you can keep your beautiful complexion flawless from the wrath of the sun," Michael teased.

"Thanks Michael. I do accept your compliment and offer of the hats," Emily said with a slight Southern drawl.

Ted and Michael laughed at Emily's teasing accent.

"Not bad. Not bad at all Ms. Emily. You keep practicing and no one will know you weren't born here," Ted suggested.

They sat around for a while chatting about whatever came to mind. A few folks wandered back to say "Hey" and talk about the barbeque.

Emily finally stood and said, "Boys, it's time I went home and cleaned up. Time to make some supper, too. See y'all later."

"Bye-bye Miss Emily," Ted said as he and Michael got busy with the store.

"Bye-bye Miss Emily. You take care now," Michael offered. "See you real soon."

Emily showered, made supper and packed her backpack for tomorrow's stay at her build site. She was going to get there before they drove the first nail. She wanted to be a part of the beginning. She had been there for the pouring of concrete into the foundation forms and now she would be there every day to watch and help build her house.

Once that was done, she checked in with Matthews to confirm Ethan would stop by for her.

She had decided to drive her Jeep following Ethan and wanted Matthews to know. He told her everything was in place.

She was all set and went to sleep that night with a smile on her face. She didn't think she'd sleep much being so excited and all. It took two hours before she finally dozed off and didn't wake until her alarm went off at 5 a.m.

Ethan and his family enjoyed a pleasant Monday. His sisters took their leave one at a time returning to their jobs and homes. His parents were staying for a couple of weeks and would leave in mid-June to visit their daughters one at a time. They would all be back together again for the July Fourth holiday and Labor Day.

Ethan and his parents had a quiet supper then took a walk around the property admiring the work everyone had done. Twilight slowly came over them as they sat on the porch.

"Ethan, I like Emily. She seems to be a very nice person," Mary said.

"I think so too, Mom," Ethan replied.

"Son, is there anything you want to tell us?" Ian Sr. asked in a soft voice.

"No, Dad."

"Ethan, I know your sisters can be a handful at times. They mean well. I just want to offer this: please don't let the past control your future. If your heart says she's the one follow her and leave your head out of the decision making," his Mom advised.

Ethan took a minute, then said, "Thanks Mom. I don't consider you interfering here at all. I love my sisters. Sometimes they need to be reminded that I do have a mind of my own, especially that Mary Ellen. Whew! I just need to sort a few things out. There's a lot going on here that you don't know about. Hell, I don't know the whole story and I'm committed to building her the best home I can. Please be patient. That's all I ask."

"We will son," Ian Sr. replied.

"How about the two of you come visit the site Friday afternoon? We should have all the buildings framed by then so you could get a good idea of how things are going to look."

"Oh, Ethan, we'd love to, wouldn't we Ian?" Mary asked.

"Sure would. It's a date. We'll finalize the plan on Thursday after my golf game," his dad said.

"OK then. Wow, look at the twilight. It's about gone. What a great color for the sky. A kind of purple. Where is it coming from? The sun's already down," Ethan asked.

"For sure. I bet it's that thing Sarah was talking about. The air being alive and sending out messages about change that's on the way," Mary said.

"Yup, Mary, you're probably right. Darndest thing I've ever seen," commented Ian Sr.

As they continued to watch, the air changed to a silvery color then back to normal. They sat there for a few more minutes then called it a night.

Most of The Creek had settled in for the night. Kendra had just set up a second site visit with Jordan Jackson for a twenty acre spread just south of The Creek on the Pine Ridge Road for ten o'clock on Wednesday morning. Jordan had said he was pretty sure this was the place he wanted. He just wanted to walk the property one more time. He had gotten a hold of Ethan for a preliminary meeting at lunch time to discuss hiring him for his build. They would be meeting at Jordan's site. Ethan had done some preliminary research and would report to Jordan that the land was good to build on and it, too, had a couple of hot springs that could be tapped into.

Jordan's financials were solid. He could afford to buy the property outright if he chose to. Kendra would be discussing the financial possibilities as soon as Jordan gave the go ahead.

Once again, a soft and quiet night had settled over The Creek.

CHAPTER 24

The NOVAE had their hands full. The time of the great battle between The Light and The Dark was fast approaching.

The NOVAE were a positive energy that walked in The Light. They offered Gifts to entities across the universes to help all connect with The Divine. The Gift of the Psychic Medium, The Gift of the Empath, The Gift of the Healer, The Gift of Premonition were just a few of the special abilities the NOVAE offered to all. Many of the people on Mother Earth chose to accept and be knowledgeable about these Gifts. Others chose not to know about them or not to believe in them. That was alright. It was one's choice when deciding to come back into the physical body to learn new lessons of benevolence and love, whether they would know about the Magic and when, or not at all.

The NOVAE had the ability to change into any physical form at will. Once these energies became physical they took on the identity known as a shape shifter. They would change back and forth between their pure energy form and their physical form as needed to accomplish their goals.

The NOVAE had been placing shape shifters on Mother Earth for millennia in preparation for this time. These shape shifters had been seen on Earth many times throughout its history. The acknowledged ascension of the profit Jesus Christ was one memorable incident. Throughout the formation and growth of Christianity there had been several sightings of angel visitations. All shape shifters. All the other religions have had similar stories told.

All these visions of saints, angels, and profits were shape shifters of The NOVAE.

Emily had chosen to have her Gifts and know about some of them from her moment of conception in this lifetime. She was aware of having knowledge and knowing things that she had not experienced in this lifetime. She knew some of her past lives and had a faint memory of some of those times but nothing more. Soon, The NOVAE would awaken her to her true identity as a High Priestess in The Light and guide her in fulfilling her destiny. She would need considerable assistance and the NOVAE was ready. A few shape shifters were already in place in Crab Apple Creek and Pine Ridge.

The recent UFO sighting was actually a dropping off of a number of shape shifters to the planet in readiness for the days to come. There had been other battles between The Light and The Dark on distant planets in other universes. Mother Earth was the place and now was the time. The outcome would determine whether this planet survived or would be destroyed.

The CON was The Dark. It was all negative energy and used promises of glory to convince it's victims that they would be better off aligning themselves with The Dark.

This time the CON had a strong hold over humankind. Greed and power played a big part in the battle. The CON had taken over several humans to gain power and strengthen the Dark's energy. So many humans wanted for power and wealth. They were willing to exchange their souls for this power. Most died early as they succumbed to their greed.

Others were taken by The CON to fulfill The CON's needs. The CON needed humans to reproduce an altered human form that would serve The CON without question - human robots.

The CON had found Yuri and was then able to secure a hold on the planet through his lust for power, wealth and control of others.

The Light and The Dark did not determine the outcome. It was the planet's inhabitants that made the final choice. That's why The CON controlled it's people on the Earth through horrific acts of violence on the human body. Intimidation was a strong persuader if you wanted to live.

Each side had Magic. Magic was a universal energy. It was not good or bad but was used by such entities as either good or bad. White Magic and Black Magic were commonly known by the Earth peoples. Ancient Magic, the magic of creation by the Divine, would be awakened and utilized in this epic battle.

The Divine had sent entities to Mother Earth to offer them a beautiful, bountiful place to live and experience the gift of life in a human body. The Divine's love was endless. The only rule was for the entities to take care of Mother Earth as she would take care of them. This symbiotic relationship went along for millennia until the human being came along and began to take more than it gave in return.

The industrial age brought great sorrow to Mother Earth because so many were greedy, wanting more and more without giving back. This is when The CON began to strengthen its hold over mankind.

The CON grew stronger and stronger on the Earth. The NOVAE continued to offer Gifts to the humans and grow the love of the Divine. It was human kind's choice to continue to grow with the CON. The witch trials were just one time of great sorrow for the NOVAE. The true Wicca were practicing quietly all across the globe. It was the greed of young girls in Salem that brought death and sorrow to so many innocents.

And, now, in the time of great technology in communication and information, the CON had a stronghold like never before. The forthcoming battle on Soaring Eagle Mountain had been foretold from the moment the Divine created Mother Earth and sent the entities to inhabit it. Those that had a need for power at any cost were causing sorrow and destruction all over the world.

The NOVAE had been planning for this battle. They had placed those with Gifts all over Appalachia from the beginning of time to share their stories with kin and friends alike so they would be ready for this great battle - the battle between Good and Evil.

Yuri was the consummate evil and Emily was the ultimate good. Their decisions would determine the outcome once and for all.

CHAPTER 25

Tuesday morning found Ethan at Emily's door shortly after six. One of the agents answered inviting Ethan in telling him Emily was in the kitchen.

"So, you have doorman service now?" Ethan asked in his greeting.

"Smart ass!" Emily shot back.

"You about ready?"

"I am. Ethan, I'm going to be driving my Jeep over so I can come and go without interrupting you. I know you're going to be wicked busy. I've even packed a bunch of food if you're interested," Emily explained as she zipped up the backpack.

"Emily, you didn't have to do the food thing, but thanks anyway. Mighty kind of you. About you driving, that's OK with me and thanks for thinking about me. I would have made arrangements for you either way."

"No problem. Ready? Let's go build my house!"

"Yes, Ma'am!" Ethan answered with a salute to the agents as they walked out the door. Once on the road it only took them about twenty minutes to get to the site. They beat one of the lumber trucks by only a few minutes. They took the pond drive and parked just inside the meadow so others could use the drive as well. Emily grabbed her backpack and followed Ethan across the meadow to the front of the house.

"I thought we'd start with the house. The crew is setting up right now and should be ready in a few minutes. They know to wait for me before they start. Shall we?" Ethan offered his arm as they walked up between the house and the barn areas. There were large stacks of lumber taking up most of the space. The tarps had been removed and Emily could see writing on the boards.

"Does that writing tell them what the boards are for?" Emily asked.

"Yes it does. More so for what part of the build. These on the left are for the decking of the house and those on the right are split for the barn and stables. The crew knows what size goes where. They have already counted the supplies twice this morning to make sure the numbers match what was counted on Friday morning when all this was delivered. I've been informed that all the numbers match. They're waiting for the signal from me to begin. Ready?"

"Yes!"

Emily watched Ethan as he gave the go ahead to begin decking the house. He took her to the exact part of the foundation where boards were being laid. He offered her a hammer to strike the first nail into place.

She accepted and holding the nail in place, she hit the nail square on the head. She had placed the first hammer hit for her house. Ethan had taken a bunch of pictures along with some of the crew. She laughed and cried as she handed the nail and hammer over to the man in charge. She knew this had been a symbolic gesture. They would be using air guns to nail the long cement fasteners through the wood into the foundation.

Ethan walked her away then waved at the crew to start. A whole lot of noise was heard as they began building in earnest.

"Emily, here are a pair of ear protectors and a hard hat for you. Please wear them whenever you are near the build for your own protection. You can see the rest of the crew have them in place. If you need to talk to me, get my attention by facing me and waving your arms or something. OK? Just stay away from the lumber piles because these guys move fast. I suspect the decking of the house will be completed by early afternoon. Then they'll start preparing the first floor walls. Any questions?"

"Nope. I'll just go get my chair and start watching," Emily responded happily

"OK. See you later," Ethan answered as he watched her walk down to her Jeep. He waited until she was headed back before he joined his crew.

Emily sat and watched, with amazement as her house began to take shape. She kept looking from one foundation to the next. As lunch time loomed, she realized she couldn't call them foundations anymore. They actually had begun to take on a shape of their own even if the walls weren't all in place yet. The barn began looking like a long building and the house had taken the expected shape just like the blueprints showed. She had taken a few walks around during the morning to watch the progress. Now she was ready for lunch. She looked at her watch and saw that it was already close to noon. It was time to eat as far as she was concerned.

And then there was silence. The air compressors had been turned off. And that silence was bliss. She guessed it was lunch time for everyone.

She saw Ethan motion to her to join him. She grabbed the food pack and walked up to the house.

"Emily, would you like to join us for lunch? We're just going to set up a quick sawhorse table," Ethan asked.

"Sure. I'll go get my chair," Emily said as she turned to walk back to her spot.

"Don't bother. I've got it," offered Tim, one of the crew.

"Thanks Tim. Much appreciated," Emily said.

"This is wicked awesome watching my house go up. I know it's no big deal to you guys, but to me it's everything."

"Just wait 'til this afternoon Ms. Emily. We're going to start the first wall after lunch. We have a few little things to finish then we should have that first wall up before day's end," offered Seth.

"That's right. And some of the crew will be building other walls as well. The barn crew will need the day to get a good portion of the decking completed. Barns require a whole different set of rules. It's almost like decking twice to be able to support the timbers for the roof," Ethan added.

"I wondered about that, Ethan. Ian had said something like that when we were going over the blueprints. It's so cool watching those blueprints come to life with my house," Emily said.

They ate lunch and chatted about whatever came to mind. Once finished they got busy with their work. Emily returned to her spot by the boulder and watched them work. It was around three o'clock when Ethan came over, removed his ear protection and motioned for Emily to do the same.

"Watch," he told her. And right before her eyes, the first wall was pulled into place. It had spaces for the windows and everything. It was the front wall on the left side of the house.

Emily just stood there and cried. This was more than she could handle. Ethan looked at her and opened his arms for her.

She moved into his embrace and cried like a baby as she watched them secure the first wall.

"Oh my God. That's my house. My safe place. I don't know what to say," Emily tried to explain to Ethan.

"Shhh. You don't have to say anything. I'm glad I get to be a part of it all," Ethan held her until she stopped crying. This felt so right. He liked comforting her. This is how things were supposed to happen. Right?

Emily moved back a step and kept looking at the house. She could hear the ring of hammers and chatter between the crew as they continued working. She could see the beginnings of three other walls on the ground. As she looked at the barn she noticed that most of the decking was done, or so it appeared.

"Ethan, are the barn and stables almost done? Looks like you built a whole foundation of wood on top of the concrete one," Emily inquired.

"Not quite. Let's go take a look and I'll explain," Ethan offered.

They spent a good twenty minutes watching the barn crew work on the decking. It was quite intricate. Ethan explained the need for all the work being done. It was mostly to support the roof tresses and second floor space. The building was long and needed extra support for the walls and roof. This would be more evident once they got some of the walls in place.

"Emily, wait until you see the roof tresses arrive. Now that's a sight to behold," Ethan said.

"When are you planning on those being delivered? Emily asked.

"In about three to four weeks. It all depends on the weather, believe it or not. If it only rains on the weekends we should be able to stay on schedule. If it rains during the day of course we have to postpone work. Night rain can be a pain as well. That usually means a day's postponement, too. Once the roof tresses are in place we should be able to get the roofs completed in about a week. Then we can enclose the buildings and place the windows and doors and be weather tight - say about six weeks from now."

"OK. Got it. I'll just have to be patient, won't I," Emily said with a laugh.

Ethan was called over to help with the barn decking and Emily walked around looking at all that had been done. She suddenly realized how tired she was and decided to go home. She waited for a break in the air gun activity then went over to Ethan to tell him she was leaving.

"I'll walk you back to your Jeep. Be back in a few, guys," Ethan told the crew.

The crew watched as they walked back down the meadow toward Emily's Jeep and smiled at each other with a knowing kind of look before returning to the work at hand.

As Emily threw her stuff in the back of the Jeep a huge yawn escaped from her lips.

"Sorry Ethan. Guess I'm a bit of a wimp when it comes to all this fresh air and physical labor," Emily said.

"Emily, you drove the first nail into your house then helped with the decking and watched them raise the first wall. You have our OK and every right to be exhausted."

"Thanks for taking time from your workday to explain things to me. I'll try to keep the questions to a minimum. I better leave before I fall asleep on my feet."

"Emily, would you like one of the agents to drive you home?" Ethan offered.

"Ya know what? That would be a good idea. Let me wave one over," Emily said as she waived her hand in the air. This was a signal she and Matthews had worked out if she needed help while at the build site.

A minute later, one of the agents that had been working surveillance from the west side of the meadow came over.

"Yes Ma'am. What can I do for you?" he asked.

"Would you please have someone drive me home? All of a sudden I'm really sleepy and don't want to risk driving myself," Emily explained.

"Yes Ma'am. Just one moment," he said as he listened to his ear piece.

"OK. That'll be me Ma'am. Ready to go?" the agent offered.

"Later Ethan. Thanks," Emily said as she got into the passenger's side of her Jeep. She caught some movement out of her left eye and when she looked she saw another Jeep approaching hers. It was another agent preparing to follow them home.

Twenty minutes later she was home and Matthews was waiting for her.

"Hey, Emily. A little too much fun for your first day?" Matthews teased.

"Must be. I fell asleep on the short ride home. Probably all that mountain air. Matthews, they already have a wall up. The front one on the left," she said as she yawned.

"Alright. Take a nap and call me when you wake up no matter the time. I want to hear all about it. Ethan sent me a picture of you driving in the first nail. Pretty cool," Matthews said as they walked into the house through the back door. Emily had her boots and jacket off in record time and was on the couch asleep a minute later.

Matthews covered her with a blanket and smiled at the agents in the house.

"I don't usually do this, but I gotta say this lady is amazing. She knows someone is out to kill her at any cost and yet she finds joy in watching her house being built. I don't know if I could do that," Matthews said.

The other agents agreed with him.

"Keep an eye on her as usual. I'll check in a bit later. Let me know when she wakes up," Matthews ordered.

"Yes Sir," they both answered as they secured the door behind him.

Kendra had been busy with her new clients all day and was ready to call it quits. She would be meeting Jordan Jackson the next morning to walk the land that he intended to buy. She had all the specs ready for him as well as a purchase and sale agreement. They would meet at eight o'clock and Ethan would join them at ten.

Jordan was busy as well. He had finished work and was just getting back to his rental house. He showered, made dinner then sat down and looked at the photos of the land he would see tomorrow. He knew this was where he was supposed to be. He could feel it in his bones. He had been looking for years all over Appalachia and had finally found his place. Funny thing was, he'd been delivering for Foodies, Inc., for over two years to The Creek. Funny how all of a sudden he 'saw' what was right in front of him all along.

No matter how it all happened, he was more than ready to buy and build his home. He had done some research about the land. It seems it was once part of a bigger spread. The original thirty acres had been a working farm until just a few years ago. The farmer seems to have had something happen with his family and decided to sell the whole thing as is. The land had been divided when someone wanted the house and buildings and ten acres with it but no more, so the owner agreed to the split. Jordan had the opportunity to buy the full twenty acres. He would walk the land tomorrow. He could well afford the whole thing as he had his savings and his veteran's benefits to add in.

Jordan sat back and took a trip down memory lane to the time when he was just out of the military. He had been in special ops for most of his two tours of duty. He had been sent all over the world and seen some good stuff, some not so good. Now, he was ready to settle down and get on with his life and The Creek was just the place he wanted to be.

Jordan had been raised in the North Carolina town of Stocksville just north of Ashville. He and his mom, dad and sister lived in an old farmhouse his parents bought before he and his sister were born. They had about five acres of land. Although his folks worked in Ashville, they still kept chickens for their own use. Though they did sell eggs to a few neighbors. Jordan's dad was a good carpenter and kept the house in great shape. He held a couple of college degrees and was a retired military man as well. He had worked in the field of computer design, mostly on architectural projects. Jordan's mom was a real country gal. She could sew, can, and freeze as needed, cook everything you could imagine and also held college degrees that gave her a good income as a civil engineer. She worked for a private firm that designed intricate steel structures for all kinds of projects from buildings to bridges and everything in between.

Jordan's folks insisted their children go to college. Jordan completed his undergraduate degree followed by a master's in geology, geothermal energy concepts and applications, all in the five years before he joined the military as an officer. His sister was just completing her PhD in Geology. She was an expert in volcanoes.

Jordan had settled in the Boone area when he retired from the military at thirty-two years old, just two years earlier. He wanted to work at a blue collar job for a while before he took the plunge into his own field of expertise. He was giving serious consideration to going after his own PhD.

He began working for Foodies just a little over two years ago when he answered an ad online. He was interviewed and hired in less than a week and the rest is history.

Jordan turned his thoughts back to The Creek. What was it that kept drawing him back there? It was almost as if an invisible force kept pulling him in. He had been raised in a small town setting. Maybe that's what it was. The folks sure were friendly and accepting in The Creek. The country store was great. It had just about everything anyone could want and need. Ted and Michael were great cooks, maybe he should call them chefs, he thought.

They created their dishes, not just followed recipes. And they always had time for everyone, even when they were busy.

He let his mind wander for a while then gave a big sigh and decided to start going through all the stuff he had accumulated over the past two years. Not much really but he knew some of it could be thrown out. He'd have to do it soon enough to pack for his move. He was hoping he would be in his new house by Thanksgiving. Ethan thought that was a reasonable time line. Jordan spent a couple of hours sorting through things before he called it a night.

Tuesday morning, he found himself at Kendra's office just before eight. He had taken the day off so he could get as much done with this land purchase as possible. He even had a blank check ready to for the down payment.

"Hey Jordan, ready to go?" Kendra asked as she gathered her stuff.

"Yes I am. Shall we?" Jordan asked as he held the door for her.

"How about you follow me to the site? Then we can get busy walking," Kendra asked.

"OK."

They got into their SUVs and set out. The land was only about ten minutes south of The Creek on the Pine Ridge road. There was a "for sale" sign marking the road where they turned. They drove only a bit down the road then parked. It was a warm sunny morning which made it easier to carry only their backpacks.

Jordan had a camera ready and Kendra took the lead. They spent the next hour and a half walking the land. Toward the back where a large rise took shape, Jordan found a cave. Kendra wondered where he had gone and was about ready to holler his name when he seemed to appear out of nowhere.

"Kendra, this is so cool. There's a cave over here. Come on, I'll show you," Jordan sounded excited.

"OK. Where is it?" Kendra said as she followed him towards the hill.

"It's kinda hidden. I would have missed it if I hadn't needed to tie my boot laces. Look, it's right here behind this bush," Jordan said as he pulled the bush aside and the cave entrance appeared.

"I didn't even know this was here. Did you go in?"

"Yeah. Follow me. It's OK. Room enough to stand in and it looks like it goes back a ways," Jordan explained as they both entered the cave.

"This is really cool. I didn't know. I don't think the farmer knew either. He would have said something if he did. I won't say anything if you won't."

"OK with me. It'll be our secret."

They continued to look around near the entrance.

"It doesn't look like anyone's been here for a long time if ever. There are some bats hanging from the higher ceiling, but don't worry. They won't hurt us. They're just fruit bats. Looks like the cave goes a long way into the hill. I'll guess I'll have to go exploring in here with a buddy before too long." Jordan sounded excited.

"I guess so. Shall we get outta here and continue walking the land? We've gone over most of it. I'll show you the pond next," Kendra explained.

They spent the next half hour walking around the pond then returned to their cars. Ethan was due to arrive any minute.

Emily showed up at her site just before nine o'clock. She set up her chair near the boulder again after she walked around the structures. A second wall had been set in her house and the barn and stables were about to get their first.

She waved at Ethan and the crew as she settled into her chair to watch. A few minutes later, Ethan stopped by.

"Hey Emily," he said.

"Hi Ethan. Looks good."

"I need to get going. I'm meeting with Kendra and one of her new clients to discuss another build. If you have any questions today, you can ask Tim."

"Great. See you later then."

Ethan left and Emily continued to watch the progress eagerly. She decided to take some pictures but would wait until lunch time as she didn't want to get in anyone's way. The whole front first floor wall structure was now in place on her house. It looked really big, bigger than she had imagined. She took a few pictures from the boulder then settled in to watch.

Ethan met up with Kendra and Jordan just after ten. He parked next to them and pulled his backpack out.

"Hey Kendra, Jordan."

"Hey Ethan. Jordan and I just finished walking the property. We finished up at the pond. That's where the hot springs are located right?"

"That's right Kendra. Jordan, let's take a look over there first then everything we discuss will make more sense," Ethan suggested.

They walked over to the eastern edge of the pond. The ground was mushy here.

"As you can see, the ground here is very wet, mucky is how some would describe it. Good for growing rhubarb and asparagus. The hot spring surfaces just a bit beyond this mucky area... over here," Ethan said as he walked east of the muck area until he reached the spring.

"Wow. I think we walked right past it earlier," Kendra exclaimed.

"If you're not looking for it, you would miss it. It's a good sized spring, it's just that some of it is covered by a leaf mat. Watch," Ethan showed them as he took a branch and removed a few large clumps of leaves. It cleared the surface of a hot spring that was about a third of the size of the pond.

"Holy shit! This thing is really big. Can you sit in it I wonder?" Jordan wondered.

"Probably after you clear it and let it settle a few days. Then you're gonna want to take a light and look into the spring to make sure it has a ledge you can stand on. Most do. I'll have one of my ground experts stop by and take a look."

"Great. I'll do a bit of water and soil sampling myself. It's what my degrees are in. It's gonna be fun getting dirty again," Jordan laughed.

"Let's walk around and talk about what you'd like to build," Kendra said.

They spent about an hour walking around the full twenty acres. They discussed where Jordan would like his house and barn to be constructed.

"I really want to build as far off the road as possible without being too antisocial. I just like the look of a long curving driveway guarded by hardwoods and flowering native shrubs. I'll have a plow on my pick-up so the snow won't be a problem. I'd like the barn a bit from the house but not too far away. I would like the house to be set at an angle to the road, nothing so cut and squared. I want a traditional barn shaped barn - dark red with a weathervane on the top. I have always wanted one of those. Sorry... I'm getting carried away with myself," Jordan apologized.

Ethan laughed and said, "No problem. I like a client that knows what he wants. I'll bring my brother Ian on as the architect if that's OK with you."

"Ian's amazing Jordan. These two work so well together you'd think they were the same person sometimes," Kendra said.

"OK. I'm done. Ian's my man," Jordan agreed.

"When do you think you'll have the go-ahead on the land Kendra?" Ethan asked.

"It will take about two weeks depending on how Jordan wants to fund the purchase," Kendra answered.

"And, I'm ready to tell you I want to sign," Jordan informed them.

"Great!" Kendra replied.

"You're going to be happy you bought this land. No one can build anywhere close to you," Ethan said.

"I know. That's one of the deciding factors. The other factor is that the original buildings are about two miles down the road. It's very important to me to have a lot of space. I just like the whole open space thing. So as I stand here, I would like my home to be built straight down this path up on the rise facing south-southwest, on an angle. Ethan, you and Ian and I will have to walk the spot and set some markers as soon as my name is on the deed. Does this sound OK with you?" Jordan asked.

"Sure does. And I'm sure you have ideas about how you want your place to look," Ethan offered.

"Of course I do. We'll discuss that later. As for the barn, I would like it set north-northeast of the house. I know this will look kinda backwards from the road, but it's gonna be so far in from the road, no one will be able to see much anyway. I'd like the driveway to go straight east for a bit then curve to the south and wrap around the house."

"Not a problem. Kendra, I think I'll use Karl for this project, too. Sound good to you?" Ethan asked Kendra.

"Yes it does. It sounds perfect. Jordan, Karl is the guy in charge of the roads and bridge at another of Ethan's projects just on the other side of The Creek. I wholeheartedly recommend him for your road. Will it be paved Jordan?"

"I don't know. That's where I need to talk to an expert. I don't want my place to look too modern but then, a dirt road requires a great deal of up-keep."

"Karl will know just what to offer. I'll talk to him this afternoon. Kendra, let me know when this is Jordan's land and I'll bring Karl over for a look. Jordan, you can meet with us and I'll have Ian here at the same time so we can set the stakes for the placement of your house. It's just preliminary work," Ethan explained.

"It's a deal," Jordan agreed.

"Now I'll let you and Kendra take care of all the details for the sale. I need to get back to the site up the road. They are placing the first walls on the barn and stables today and I'd like to see that. Nice meeting with you Jordan. You too, Kendra," Ethan tipped his hat at Kendra as he made his way back to his truck and drove off.

"Now, Jordan, let's get down to business. How would you like to finance your land?" Kendra asked.

"I'd like to pay off ninety percent of the cost and finance the rest just for credit building purposes," Jordan explained.

"Great. Let's go back to my office and get the numbers down on your purchase and sale agreement and you can have the bank send a cashier's check tomorrow."

Jordan turned and took a long look at his land. He could have sworn he saw a flash of bright light over the place where his house was to be built. He looked a moment more but nothing else happened.

"Jordan?" Kendra gently called to him.

"Oh, sorry, guess I was dreaming about my house," Jordan said as he shook his head and followed Kendra to their trucks.

Ten minutes later they were in Kendra's office where Jordan signed the purchase and sale agreement.

"I'll stop at the bank on my way home and have them transfer funds and send a check over tomorrow morning. Thanks so much. Now, I'm truly excited."

"As am I. I can't wait to see the whole thing get started. The sale and transfer of land title and deed should be completed by Monday. Then, it's time to get busy with Ethan and Ian and your plans. Congratulations Jordan. Let me be the first to welcome you to Crab Apple Creek."

"Thanks. This is so cool. I've been thinking about this for a very long time. It feels so right here. Thanks for all your help. I think I'll stop over at the store, tell the guys, and have some lunch. That place always smells so good and I never have time to eat. Today I do and I will. See you again soon."

Kendra watched as Jordan walked over to the store. He was right. This did feel right, she thought, as she went back to work completing the paperwork for this sale.

There were only a few folks in the store when Jordan arrived.

"Hey Michael," Jordan said as he walked over to him.

"Hey Jordan. What gives? Not working today?" Michael inquired.

"Nope. Is Ted around? I have some news for y'all."

"Sure. Hey Ted," Michael hollered, "Jordan's here and wants to talk to us."

"Jordan? Ya mean the delivery guy from Foodies? That Jordan?" Ted hollered as he came down from the kitchen.

"Jordan? Hey There. Not workin' huh?" was Ted's reply.

Jordan lowered his voice as he leaned into the guys. "Is there some-where we can talk more privately?"

"Sure. Follow us," Michael said.

They walked over to the big oak table and all sat down. There wasn't anyone near them.

"I just wanted you two to be the first to know, other than Kendra, that I bought those twenty acres just down the road today. I'm gonna build a house and barn and settle down. I love this place," Jordan told them.

"That's awesome Jordan. Congratulations and welcome to The Creek," Ted exclaimed as he stood to shake Jordan's hand.

"Great news, Jordan. Ya know we like you and have from the very first day you started delivering to us," Michael said as he shook hands.

'I'm so excited I don't know what to do with myself," Jordan laughed.

"Well, how about some lunch on the house as a way of celebrating?" Ted offered and Michael agreed.

"Time to get back to the front. Here comes the lunch rush," Michael said as he got up.

"I'd love some lunch. It always smells so good in here," Jordan said.

"OK. Take a look over there at the menu board with today's specials and I'll get ya whatever you choose," Ted said as he showed Jordan where everything was.

"I do believe I'll have the barbecued chicken sandwich on a bulkie roll with all the trimmings," Jordan told Ted.

"Comin' right up. And help yourself to a drink," Ted offered as he went about making Jordan his lunch.

Ted brought Jordan's lunch over a few minutes later. A few more people had placed orders and were either sitting at the table or taking their lunch away with them.

"Hey y'all, this here's Jordan Jackson. He just bought the other twenty acres of the farm just down the Pine Ridge road. Say 'hey' everyone," Ted said.

"Howdy, Jordan!"

"Welcome to The Creek."

"Haven't I seen you around here before?" Hal asked.

"Sure have. I deliver for Foodies about three times a week," Jordan replied.

"Oh Yeah. Well, welcome aboard," Hal said as he sat down across from Jordan. "Ya gonna be building over there soon?"

"Yup. I've already been in touch with Ethan Sutherland. We'll start the whole building shindig as soon as the land's in my name. Kendra thinks that title could be cleared by next Monday. She already checked with the county and there aren't any holds or anything so the transfer should be good to go. Ethan's brother Ian is going to be the architect. Seems those boys are well liked and respected around here. I feel very lucky for that."

"Those Sutherland boys are the best. You're lucky to have them build for you. I hear they're super busy this summer and had to bring on two other crews. It's good for them and us. The more people buyin' stuff from the store the better all around. What do ya have in mind for your house if I may ask?" Hal said.

"Well, I've been playing around in my mind with a real country look... a porch all around, maybe a couple of fireplaces. I'm thinkin' it might look like the small cabins from way back but bigger and all modern inside. Got any ideas Hal?" Jordan asked. "Oh, and Ted, this is incredible. I might be a regular around here instead of doin' my own cooking."

Laughter was heard all around.

"I know what ya mean," Hal said as he went about eating his lunch. "So, Jordan, I think I know what ya mean about the look for your house. There's a few pictures on the walls over by the stove you might be interested in. They're from about a hundred and fifty years ago. They might just be the design you are talkin' about."

"Thanks Hal, I'll take a look after lunch."

Jordan spent the next hour looking around the store and chatting with folks who offered advice when they found out he was moving close by.

Ethan returned to Emily's build just as the first of the barn walls was being completed. The crew decided to hold off placing it until after lunch and a thorough inspection of the decking by the building inspector had been finished. He had approved of the house foundation the afternoon it was completed.

Emily was standing around with the crew when Ethan called for a lunch break. They all gathered around the site and ate lunch.

Kendra was busy filing the paperwork for Jordan's land purchase. She sent an email to the county supervisor's office to give them a heads up about the title transfer that could take place as soon as Friday. Jordan was using a bank issued check that would clear immediately. There was no need to wait the usual seven to ten days it took for a personal check to clear. The bank Jordan used was the same bank the land owner used so the check would be more of a transfer of funds once it was sent through by Kendra. She expected the check tomorrow morning when Jordan came by to make a delivery at the store. This was the fastest real estate deal she could ever remember taking place. And she loved it.

CHAPTER 26

uri's thugs were busy in Boone. They had all taken jobs and apartments and were busy getting to know the people and the area just as they had been instructed.

Hanson had taken a summer position with Appalachia State University as a math instructor. Saunders had taken a job with a local building company as a carpenter. It was a small company that did jobs mostly in the Boone area. Benson had been hired by the state parks department as an outdoor summer program team member. He would be leading summer camp students on hikes around the area.

Their apartments were about a block apart and Hanson had wired all of them with cameras both inside and out, Wi-Fi and the latest computer programs and equipment. Yuri was now demanding daily updates. The men had been in the area for a month now, visiting the same stores, restaurants and diners so the locals would get used to them being around and get to like them. They did not have bank accounts. They cashed their paychecks every pay day at the bank that issued them. They used cash for everything. Cars had been delivered to them from a contact in Asheville. They were registered to them using their current names. It was all fake of course. Yuri thought of everything, or so he thought.

The summer parks programs would begin in about two weeks when school ended for the summer on June 11th. The first hiking event Benson would be a part of was set for just a week later and was to take place near the University's current archeological dig site northeast of The Creek. It was set for a five mile hike starting and ending at the dig. It would start out going east of the dig, then south then return to the dig going north along a somewhat wandering trail. At no time would it come anywhere near Emily's build site or The Creek itself.

The summer college classes Hanson was teaching had already started the Tuesday after Memorial Day. They would run in two six week sessions with a break around the July 4th holiday.

Saunders had been busy as a carpenter from the Tuesday after Memorial Day as well. He was part of a crew working on a remodeling job on an historic home in the Boone historical district.

The men met every day after dark to go over the details of the day and any news from Yuri.

Today, there was a great deal of news. It seems there were about four people who were about to buy land in or near The Creek. Yuri had checked their financials and targeted a man named Jordan Jackson to be his victim. He would let this Jackson guy buy the land and make the first payment then he would have his contacts in the banking industry remove all his money from his accounts and close the account. Jackson would be penniless. Yuri would have a man ready to offer Jackson help while the missing money was investigated. When it was over, Yuri would know just where Barbara was and then have her killed. Simple, Yuri kept saying to himself. Quite simple.

Yuri's contact met with the men at Hanson's apartment after nine o'clock. They wanted the neighbors to think they were watching a baseball game.

This contact was known only as Joe. Joe sat the men down and gave them their orders for the next part of the plan.

"The Boss is very happy with you three. Seems you followed his orders exactly as given. For that he asked me to give these to you. Bonuses of ten thousand dollars each. Here you go," he said as he spread the cash around.

"Please tell him thank you from all of us. We greatly appreciate the bonus although he didn't have to do it. We're glad to help him any way we can," Hanson said.

"He'll be glad to hear that. He wants you to keep the bonus anyway. Now we have a target for the information. His name is Jordan Jackson. He's about to buy twenty acres of land just south of Crab Apple Creek. He got a bank check today for the down payment. He'll give it to the realtor tomorrow and the land deal should be complete by Monday or Tuesday of next week. He'll be allowed to make the first month's mortgage payment for July then we take over. The rest you don't need to know about yet.

For now, you need to keep working just like you are. However, Saunders, you need to get to know about Sutherland's business. They're doing a lot of work all over the Boone, Pine Ridge and Crab Apple Creek areas this summer. They're probably going to do the building for the Jackson project. Get to know someone on the crew. Get introduced somehow over the next two weeks.

Get all the information you can. I think you can look up things through the building inspector's page of the town's website. They should have all the needed info the Boss wants.

"Benson, before you start your hiking trip, take a ride into the area and hike around on your own. Be sure to wear your uniform so if anyone stops you, you can tell them you're just checking the trails or something like that. You guys are good at being pretenders.

"Hanson, there's nothing for you to do except get to know the people in the area and start asking about the towns around Boone. Learn the history and stories and the like. People are always willing to talk about strange things.

"That's all for now. Keep up the good work. Hanson , I'll be in touch with you at my next visit."

With that, he took his leave as quietly as possible. The game wasn't over and he didn't want the neighbors to know he was leaving early.

Hanson, Saunders and Benson talked about the new information for quite a while coming up with a game plan of their own.

They decided Benson would be the first to go into The Creek. He would drive around getting to know the layout. He would stop into the Bend In The Road Country Store for a cold drink and something to eat. If anyone asked, he would explain to them he was a hiking instructor for the state's summer parks program and was just checking out the area. His first hike would be at the dig. He'd wing it from there.

It was after midnight when the two others left Hanson's place. Little did they know they were being watched by the feds. Anyone new to the area this summer who was working in the building trades or outdoor recreation areas was being closely monitored.

These three were now being moved to the top of the list. What did a math teacher, a carpenter and a recreation worker all have in common? This information was reported immediately to both the Virginia HQ and the local authorities. Background checks would be conducted and those reports would be gone over in minute detail.

Matthews was informed at the same time as the Virginia HQ. He immediately printed out the photos of the three men and gave all agents both a hard copy and a digital one. He set up meetings for that morning for all his agents and decided to conduct them in person. He had a bad feeling about these three. He knew they were Yuri's henchmen. Things were escalating much more quickly than he thought they would.

As soon as dawn arrived, Matthews went over to the store to bring Ted and Michael up-to-date on the three mysterious men. He called first and then was met at their back door as the store wasn't open yet.

"Mornin," Matthews said as they all walked into the kitchen. Ted was working on the day's menu items.

"What's up Matthews?" Michael asked.

Matthews handed out the photos then shared the news.

"We have a problem. These three are living in the Boone area. We have been monitoring anyone new and these three have raised a red flag. Hanson is posing as a Math instructor at ASU. Saunders has been hired as a carpenter with one of Boone's small companies. Benson has taken a job with the state parks department as a hiking guide for the summer program - he's gonna be a real problem. I would appreciate you keeping an eye out for this guy especially since they're using the trails around the university's dig site northeast of here. If he so much as sneezes anywhere outside of Boone I want to know about it. But, please, don't put yourselves in any danger by doing so. Just get to one of the agents around Emily's house or call me. You have my cell. Any questions?"

"Holy shit, Matthews. They really are coming for Emily aren't they? What is she supposed to know or have that could be so important?" Ted asked.

"Sorry fellas, I can't go into details. If I can tell you anything when this is all over, I will. Spread the word the way you do so the other folks will know who to look out for. Make copies of the photos and pass them around. Say they're the latest on the most wanted list. Whatever it takes to make everyone around here stay on high alert."

"Don't you worry, Matthews, we'll get the word out first thing this morning. No one's gonna mess with our Emily, that's for sure," Michael said.

"I've gotta go and meet with Ethan next. How about one of your famous bagel breakfast sandwiches for the road, Ted?"

"Sure, but they're really messy. Ya might wanna eat here first. Hey look... it's Ethan. Y'all can chat right here. I'll make copies for Ethan. Breakfast Ethan?"

"Hey guys, sure. How about an everything breakfast bagel Ted. Thanks!"

"Sure thing Ethan."

"Ethan," said Matthews, "how about we meet right here before anyone else comes in? Ted and Michael are up to date."

"Sure. Shoot."

Matthews explained about the three men to Ethan, and Michael gave him the copies of the photos.

"Michael, could you make about a dozen of each? I want to give them to my crew up at Emily's build. I'll make more for Ian to hand out to the others."

"Sure."

"How bad is this Matthews? Should Emily know? Is she gonna have to be kept inside her house again?"

"I'll tell her in a bit. And, no, we don't think she should stay inside for now. I'm waiting on background checks on these three to come through, then..., oh, wait a minute. I gotta take this," Matthews said as he walked away from Ethan.

When he returned he had a serious look on his face.

"These three men do not exist. Just as I thought. They are all fakes. HQ has decided to leave them alone and has placed round the clock surveillance on them. They may just tip their hands then we can pick them up."

"Fuck! Just when ya think things are goin' smooth and then all and this happens. What do you need me to do Matthews?"

"Keep your eyes on anything and everything Ethan. Security will be doubled both here and at the build. If anyone thinks they see these guys, do not approach them. Call me or the local Sheriff's office and we'll take over. Calling 911 works well, too.

"OK. Will do. Is Emily gonna be able to come up to the build today?"

"Yes, but with more security. She will not be able to drive herself though. And neither will you. She will be with security at all times. Let's hope we can wrap this thing up real soon."

"Got'cha Matthews. Thanks Michael for making the copies. I'm off to the site as soon as I finish my breakfast."

"And I'm off to Emily's right now. Later."

Matthews left by the front door as the store was now open. He walked over to Emily's and entered by the back door as usual.

"Hey Matthews. What brings you over at such an early hour?"

"Emily, we need to talk. Please take a seat."

"What's wrong Matthews?" Emily asked as she sat down.

"Emily, we've just received intelligence that Yuri has three men in Boone looking for you. Here are their pictures. Hanson is the gang leader posing as a math instructor for ASU. Saunders is a carpenter working for a small company in Boone; he's on a remodeling project for the historical society at the moment. Benson is working for the state parks department as a hiking guide. He's responsible for hikes around the archeology dig northeast of here. He's the first big problem. He could be in the area at any time. We have surveillance on all three. Their pictures are being circulated around The Creek as we speak. I gave them to Ted and Michael just now. Ethan has been told as well. He's handing out photos at your build site.

HQ has increased security. New agents and special ops members are on their way. You are no longer allowed to drive anywhere and when you set your foot even one inch outside this house you will be surrounded by five agents. No more quiet - we are on high alert. It seems Yuri is bent on finding you. He thinks you know all about his operation and where he keeps all his money. I think the guy's gone off the deep end. Paranoia is a scary thing especially in someone who's intelligent and has no morals. We're pretty sure he will stop at nothing now to find and destroy you. I'm so sorry Emily."

Emily just sat there. She had paled noticeably and it didn't look like she was breathing.

"Emily," Matthews shouted, "take a breath!"

Matthews' loud shouting brought agents into the kitchen just as Emily blinked and started to breathe.

"Get her on the floor." Matthews ordered.

The agents gently rested her on the floor with a pillow under her head. The color started to come back into Emily's face.

She looked up at Matthews and asked why she was laying there.

"Well, I guess the news was more than you could handle. You almost passed out."

"Oh. Uh huh. I remember. Could I sit up please?" she asked as she tried to raise herself.

The agents helped her sit up for a minute then they walked her to the couch. She sat there for a few minutes more before speaking.

"I knew something was up. I get these hunches and the last couple of days have been a bit off. The building thing has been great but there's been an undercurrent of unease inside me. This explains it all. What's gonna happen now?"

"Well, for the immediate few minutes, you are going to remain on that couch. Please drink the soda the agent brought in. No refusals accepted. We'll talk about everything else in a bit."

"OK. You'll get no hassle from me," Emily said as she sipped her drink.

Matthews and the agents remained in the room with Emily as they talked about the added security detail. After about ten minutes, Matthews sat next to Emily and assessed her health. She looked much better and her pulse had returned to somewhat normal.

"OK. You seem to be about back to your usual self. Let's take this a bit slower. Ready?"

"Ready. I remember you saying something about three bad guys all working in Boone. One of them is a hiking guide, right?"

"Yes. Correct. That guide goes by the name of Benson. HQ thinks he's gonna be the first to try to make contact in The Creek. I have their pictures on the kitchen table and want you to memorize them. OK so far?"

"Yes. Do they look ugly 'cause if they do I think I'm gonna throw up," Emily said.

"Funny. She's trying to be funny. You definitely feel better now."

The other agents laughed along with Matthews.

"I'm just tryin' here, OK?" Emily pleaded.

"Sure. So HQ has increased your security. They include more of our agents, special ops, and international agents as well. Any questions so far?"

"Nope. Keep going."

"I spoke with Ted and Michael and gave them copies of the photos. They are getting the word out all around The Creek. Ethan and I met as well. He has photos to hand out at your build."

"You already said that."

"Just checking to see how much you remembered before you zoned out."

"OK. Keep going."

"That's all for now. If you still want to go to your site today, that's OK. Your bodyguards will take you and stay with you."

"Yes, I still want to go. I have my panic button right here. We already ran the daily test and it's working great."

"I know. Here's a second one. Please keep it on you at all times. It's on a neck chain and will fall inside your shirt. Keep it on in the shower as well. Never take it off. Understand?"

"Yes. Thanks. Here it goes. Around my neck and under my shirt. Wanna test it?"

Yes. Push the button."

OK" As soon as she did an alarm went off on the agent's radios and badges.

"They work," Matthews said. "Emily, this panic button is different from the other one. It is set to your pulse and breathing rates. If they alter more than the preset parameters, an alarm will sound on everyone's radios, badges and earpieces. You don't even have to touch the thing."

"That's really cool. If those bad guys are as bad as you think they are, they'll probably look for a panic button anyways."

"We don't plan on them getting anywhere near you Emily. But, you're right."

"Jesus fucking Christ! This kinda stuff is only supposed to happen in the movies."

"I wish that were true. Who do you think they get their ideas from?" Matthews teased her.

Emily made a face at Matthews that made him laugh.

"Wise ass. She's a wise ass," Matthews exclaimed.

"Excuse me, Ma'am, Matthews, the others are arriving now. Kelly wants to know if she should set them up in the houses or do you want to do that?" one of the agents asked.

"Tell Kelly to go ahead. I'll join them in a bit."

"Yes, sir. Go ahead Kelly and get them settled. Matthews will meet with them later."

"Things are happening so fast. When did you first hear about these bad boys?" Emily asked.

"It's all been happening since about eleven o'clock last night. We know their names are false. We have teams at their apartments gathering formation. Their fingerprints should tell us what we need to know."

"Good. I guess I don't have any more questions for now. You know I'll be asking if I do. And, I know, Matthews, if I think anything is off, or weird, or just not right, I'll hit the panic button. You've trained me well," Emily said.

"Emily, besides all this high tech stuff, you seem to be able to tell when something is about to happen. It's probably that Gift of yours. Listen to it well and act on your gut feelings. So far, they haven't been wrong at all. I trust your gut, so to speak."

"Thanks Matthews. I'll keep you in my loop," Emily smiled at Matthews.

They both got up and walked back into the kitchen. Matthews handed the pictures to Emily.

"Get to know these faces for your own protection."

"I will. I'll make copies and carry a set with me all the time. Thanks for taking such good care of me Matthews. I'll try not to pass out again. Guess I need to eat something before we go to my house. That sounds so good - my house. Even if it's just a framework for now. It's still mine."

"Yes it is. It's all yours. I'll come by at lunch time. Should I bring some lunch with me?"

"Sure. Anything with smoked turkey, no tomatoes, but I guess you already know that about me. Thanks, Matthews"

"Got it. And, yes, I do know you that well. See you at your house for lunch," Matthews waved as he left Emily to get her breakfast.

"Agent Marks, will you be driving me today?" Emily asked.

"Yes, Ma'am... me and a few others. Just let us know when you're ready to leave and we'll get you to your house."

"Thanks Marks. I'll be ready in about a half hour or so."

Agent Marks gave a little salute as Emily went about her breakfast.

Emily arrived at her house and set up for the day. Her bodyguards set up right next to her. She could hear them talking softly into their collars every once and awhile. They all watched as the walls continued to go up.

Emily's first floor was about to be completed. She stood as they raised the last first floor wall and set it into place.

Ethan called for lunch just as Matthews was walking up the hill.

"That was impressive Ethan. Emily, here's your lunch. Will you be joining us Ethan?"

"In a few minutes. I have a call to take care of." Ethan explained.

A few minutes later he was back and some of the crew joined them. They talked about the walls and how long it would take to get the second floor in place.

"The second is a bit trickier than the first floor. All the supports are set in place in the decking for all the floors, but now, we need to add more support beams in both the horizontal and vertical directions for the second floor as well as the porch roofs. They will go around the whole structure so this is gonna take a while. That's next. I plan on starting the second floor walls by tomorrow afternoon. They should be completed by Friday. We'll start on the third floor and attic on Monday. The roof tresses for the house are being delivered Wednesday morning around ten o'clock. So, if you plan on coming by, be sure to get here before that and I'll set you up a ways out of the way. That delivery truck is huge. Ya really should be here to see it all. They'll set the tresses right up on the house one after the other and secure them into place. It should take most of the day. And then your house will really look like a house Emily."

"I can't wait!" Emily exclaimed.

After they finished eating Ethan walked her around the site explaining the progress on the barn and stable buildings.

Emily and her group settled once again by the boulder and watched and talked for most of the afternoon. Matthews had left shortly after lunch.

It was around three o'clock when Emily told the group she was ready to go home. She walked over to Ethan and waited for him to finish his conversation with one of the crew.

"Hey Emily, heading out?"

"Yes, Ethan. I just wanted to thank you for everything. You're an exceptional man." Emily reached up and kissed him softly on the lips.

Ethan automatically put his arm around her. They stayed that way for what seemed hours before Emily stepped back. She laid her hand on his cheek and he turned and kissed it before letting go.

Emily turned and walked away as Ethan watched her until she was safely in the Jeep and being driven down the meadow to the pond road.

When Ethan and Emily's story is told in years to come, everyone at the build will say they swear they saw flashes of silver light when she kissed him.

Once back in The Creek, Emily settled in for the rest of the day. Ian had sent an email telling her all the choices for fixtures, appliances and all had been placed and would arrive as soon as they were ready for them.

Kendra dropped by after supper for a chat.

"So Emily, I see there's a lot more stuff going on around here. You have bodyguards all over the place. You OK?" Kendra asked as they got comfy in the living room.

"Seems there are some bad guys determined to get to me. Matthews says they added more security people to keep me safe. It's kinda scary."

"I'll bet it is. I would like to offer you something. I don't know what your beliefs are but I practice an ancient healing energy called Reiki and would like to offer that for you."

"I'm a Reiki Master myself," Emily laughed.

They spent the next few hours talking about Emily's Gift, about Reiki, about crystals and all things metaphysical.

It was close to ten o'clock when they came up for air.

"Oh my God, Emily. Look. It's almost ten. We've been talking non-stop for hours," Kendra pointed out.

"Wow! We have. It's been so long since I had a sister to talk to about stuff. And you know what I think about all this stuff that's happening to me? I know it's something paranormal. It has to be. Nobody could be that evil. I know they haven't told me everything because they can't for national security reasons. But every time Matthews gives me an update I get this cold zing for just a second as if I'm being warned about the Dark. Sound crazy to you?"

"Not at all. I'm always wondering if things that happen are man-made or paranormal. Those UFO visits explain a lot. I, too, wonder if something is brewing."

"I'm not naïve about all the negative stuff in the world. But this guy that was in charge of Nick and his kind just sounds too evil to be a human being. Sounds like it could be more. Something to do with the Dark. I hope not. That would be beyond scary."

"I agree. I hope we don't have to face the Dark alone if it ever comes to that." Kendra said.

"I've seen the demons of the Dark and have had to do battle against them on a small scale. That's a whole other story. There are demonic energies all around. I am well protected as you probably are but they're still there. The battle between The Light and The Dark is ancient beyond time. I'm just not too keen on being a part of any bigger battles that involve me." Emily said.

"I hear ya sister. This has been an awesome evening. I'm so glad I offered the Reiki and you opened up to me. Now we have each other to chat with. I'll send Reiki as soon as I get settled. You just relax and enjoy the energy healing. Take care and thanks for the goodies. They're quite yummy."

Kendra walked the few steps home as Emily got ready for bed. She felt so much better knowing a kindred soul was right here with her. This had indeed been a great evening.

Matthews had listened to the whole thing as soon as Emily told Kendra about her Gift. Matthews knew Kendra was cleared for all levels of the operation. He was glad Emily had confided in her. Now she had someone who really understood her that she could talk to. This was a good thing. He wrote this in his daily report and sent it off to HQ. He told the agents he was turning in. They knew what to do if needed.

CHAPTER 27

The next few weeks saw Emily's house as well as the barn and stables take shape. The roof tresses being set had been an amazing thing to watch. The barn tresses were set in place the last week of June. Now both buildings looked real. The house had been roofed and the windows and doors were going in during these last days of June right up to the July 4th celebration. The barn and stables were being roofed at the same time.

Jordan Jackson's build had been staked for final inspection and his road had been cleared and staked as well. He had taken possession of the land on the Tuesday that followed his meeting with Kendra. He had owned the land for about three weeks now and was excited to see everything taking shape. He had mailed in his first mortgage payment a week early. He liked to keep ahead of things.

The men in Boone had set their plan in action. Benson was about to assist on a hike near the dig site and they decided he should stop by that country store to get a look at things. He might even spot that Barbara bitch. So, off he went on his day off to check out The Creek.

Matthews and his teams were getting updates almost hourly now about the three men in Boone. It seems there was about to be a hike at the dig site near The Creek right after the 4th of July and Matthews wanted his team to be ready for almost anything. The man known as Benson was going to be one of the guides. It was set for Monday, July 7th. HQ thought the man might try to get a feel for The Creek and had put everyone on round-the-clock surveillance.

And, just as predicted, Benson decided to visit The Creek on the Wednesday before the 4th, July 2nd. Ted noticed him first just as he walked into the store. The uniform was a dead giveaway. He motioned to Michael that he was heading into the kitchen to check on his creations. As soon as he got away from the door he called Matthews.

"Matthews, it's one of the three bad guys. The one in the forestry uniform. He just walked into the store. We have the cameras and mics on."

"Good. Act normal. One of the agents identified him as well. I'm sending someone in to keep track of him. Stay calm."

"OK. No problem. We've got the surveillance anyway."

The agents at Emily's build heard this and were told to wait for further orders. A team was sent out to the road at Emily's house to make sure no one entered or left until further notice.

Emily was informed of all that was happening.

Ted went back into the store just as an agent looking like someone from The Creek walked in.

Ted gave a look to Michael and went about his business.

Benson spent a few minutes looking around before he walked over to the coolers and grabbed a coke. He then walked over to the kitchen area and looked at the menus. Ted was getting things ready for lunch and asked if he could help him.

"Oh. Not yet. Just lookin' over the choices and all. Thanks," Benson said.

He finally placed his order and took a seat at the table. The agent ordered lunch as well and sat down across from him.

"Hey there," the agent said. "You new around here?"

"Kinda. I'm a hiking guide for the state's rec program. I'm gonna be working on a hike right after the 4th up at the dig and thought I'd take some time to get to know the area a bit. Ya never can be too careful."

"How's that, you can't be too careful? The dig is miles away," the agent stated.

"What I meant was, if we need help or anything. Just want to know all my options."

"Oh," the agent responded. "Good idea with all those kids."

"Yup. That's what I was thinkin'."

Ted interrupted them as he gave them their lunch orders.

"Enjoy y'all," Ted said.

"Thanks Ted, sure will," the agent replied.

Benson took a bite then said, "This is really good. I'm glad I stopped by."

"You're both welcome," Ted said from behind the counter.

The two of them continued to eat then Benson sat back.

"This sure is great food," Benson commented.

"Sure is," the agent agreed. "So, how long have ya lived around here?"

"Oh, I grew up in the Mid-West. Just moved here this spring looking for a change."

"Great place to live, the Blue Ridge is."

"I agree. Must be lots of new people come here to live. Anyone new here?"

Matthews had the store surrounded at this point.

"Here? Nah. Just us locals. This isn't exactly a hot spot for commerce as you can see. Just this store here. Ya have to go into Pine Ridge for more or even Boone. That's where the local Wal-Mart is. It's a college town so there's lots of stores and shops. The folk around here are mostly farmers from way back."

'No one new, huh? Why not? There seems to be land enough."

"Most of what you see is either owned by families for generations or is part of the national forest. No real land available around here."

"Oh. One of my buddies works construction in Boone and thought he heard about some new builds goin' on around here. Guess he was wrong."

"Sure is wrong. Believe me, if there was construction goin' on we'd know about it. It'd give us all something to talk about," the agent said with a laugh.

"Guess you would bein' such a small place and all. Well, I'm glad I stopped here. The food is great and I've enjoyed your company," Benson said as he got up from the table.

"No problem there," the agent returned as he got up.

"Time to hit the road. Gonna go over to the dig site for a look around," Benson said.

"I hear ya have to be invited and cleared by the archeology folks no matter who you are. They don't let most people near the dig for fear of messin' it up."

"Didn't know that. Guess I'll check in with my boss first then. Thanks for the info. Bye," Benson said as he walked out the door.

Matthews' agents were still all around the store. They looked like workin' folk. They all watched Benson as he got into his brand new truck and set off to drive up the mountain towards Emily's build. He didn't get far before he met a road block. He was instructed to turn around and go back down the Pine Ridge road through Pine Ridge, into Boone and take the highway as a detour to get to the dig site.

He turned around and was back through the Creek ten minutes later headed down the Pine Ridge Road.

Matthews had his crew stand down as he had a tail on Benson.

Ted and Michael breathed a huge sigh of relief when they heard he had left The Creek for good. Matthews walked into the store, ordered lunch and sat down at the oak table. There were a couple regulars at the table and they chatted about Emily's build, the new build for that Jackson guy, and the barbeque, among other things.

Ted brought Matthews his lunch and joined him. The others had left moments before. Michael was busy at the register.

"Matthews, that guy creeps me out," Ted said.

"Me, too. You guys did a great job staying cool. Thanks. We got the whole thing on the agent's digital recorder. I'll take those tapes from you as soon as you can get them copied."

"Sure thing. As soon as business lightens up, Michael will make a copy and get it to you. Probably an hour. Is that OK?"

"Fine. HQ wanted me to tell you thanks for all your help. You have no idea how easy you two are making this surveillance thing from your store. And thanks for letting us wire the outside. We got lots of shots of Benson and his big new truck."

"Glad to help any time. Enjoy the rest of your lunch. Oh boy, here comes Cora."

Cora walked right back to the table and sat down.

"Ted, I'd like some of your Caesar salad with chicken if you don't mind," Cora said.

"Of course, Miss Cora. And how are you today?"

"Hungry. Any damn fool could figure that out by what I just said."

"Indeed Miss Cora. I meant besides bein' hungry."

"Right fine. Right fine. Mr. Matthews, I saw you at the barbeque. What'd ya think about it?

"Miss Cora. Nice to see you again. I thoroughly enjoyed the barbeque. Great food and company. The storytelling was exceptionally fine," Matthews replied.

"That Jed," Cora laughed, "he can really weave a yarn that man can. Truth is he was tellin' the truth. Jenny swears by it."

"I wouldn't doubt it, Ma'am."

"My name's Cora. Use it."

"Miss Cora. And the singing was real special. Stories where, too."

"Yup. We got some of the best story tellin' and singin' folks around for miles. These mountains make for pretty voices and music."

"I sure hope we get to hear some more of both at the July 4th picnic."

"Oh, you will, won't he Ted?"

"Yes Miss Cora, he will. Indeed, we all will," Ted answered.

"Now, about that UFO thing. Anyone see anything since?"

"Can't say as I have," answered Ted. "Why? Have you?"

"Not sure Ted. There was some flashing lights up over the mountain a few nights back but could have been heat lightnin'. I checked with the weather folks but they didn't have any reports of heat lightnin' so I figured it was more of the UFOs."

"Can't say as I saw anything. Must a been after I turned in for the night."

"It was around midnight. I was still awake. What about you Matthews, see anything?"

"No, Miss Cora, can't say I did either. I'll ask around though. Thanks for the info," Matthews said.

"Well what good are you men if ya don't see what us womenfolk see? Can't protect us from it if'n you don't see it."

They both laughed.

"That's true."

"Yes Ma'am. That's true."

"Now Ted, that was a good salad and I thank ya. How much do I owe ya?"

"Now Miss Cora, I'd like to treat you to that lunch but I know that would be taken as an insult and I surely don't mean to insult you," explained Ted.

"So, if you will allow me, I'd like to treat you to lunch today Miss Cora," Matthews requested of Cora.

"Why, Matthews, I accept. You are a gentleman indeed. You just might fit in around here after all.

"Thanks Miss Cora."

"How's that pretty little thing, Miss Emily? She's buildin' her house up on the mountain there. I drove over to take a look this morning' and Ethan showed me around. Right nice looking house and barn she's got there. She's got a good sense for the country she does."

"Why she's just fine. She's spends her days up there watchin' her house go up," Ted answered. "I'd like to get a look, too."

"Who asked you Ted? I was talkin' to Matthews here."

"Sorry Ma'am. Just excited about the house and all."

"Miss Cora, Ted's right. Miss Emily's doing fine. I'll tell her you were askin' after her."

"Y'all know those UFOs are for her, right? She's connected to them somehow. In a good way for sure. I just know she is. It's like they was waitin' for her to git here. There'll be more and more in the comin' days. You mark my words."

The guys remained silent too long for Cora's liking.

"Y'all think I'm a bit touched, do ya? Well, you're wrong. You just wait and see. There's somethin' comin' to the mountain and it's gonna be a doosey."

"Yes, Miss Cora. I do believe you. You're always right with these premonitions," Ted said.

"Yes I am and you'd be a better man to remember that. I'm done here. Thanks for being a gentleman Matthews. See y'all later."

Cora waved at Michael as she left the store.

"She may be a character, Matthews, but she's right. Every time as far back as I can remember, her premonitions have come true. I'm kinda scared about this one though. Sounds like a battle or somethin' is comin'. She's always right," Ted said as he shook his head and continued to clear the table.

"Ted, you've got a valid point there. I've learned to listen to the folks wherever I'm located. They usually do know a whole lot more than any high tech equipment can tell us. I'll make a note of what she said today," Matthews offered. "She sure is a character - a bit of the old and mystical world around her. Should I even say the word magic?"

"Oh, Yeah. That describes our Cora. And magic is OK to say around here. These folks have seen so much that can only be explained by magic. No other way to describe it. Michael and I are relatively new here. Only been here about thirty some years. These folks have had families here for nigh on to three hundred years. They surely know more than we do. We're always learning somethin' new every day. I trust them with my life."

"I'm catching on real fast myself, Ted. I've learned to accept the unexplainable. Well, lunch was great and I'll take that copy as soon as you can get it to me."

Matthews nodded at Michael as he left.

Matthews checked in with the road block crew. He spent the next twenty minutes on the phone with Virginia HQ informing them of the Benson incident. HQ was pleased with the report and instructed Matthews to send the tape from the store ASAP.

July 4th dawned clear and sunny in all its summer glory. The Creek was ready for their usual celebrations. Breakfast was held at the store to commemorate all those that had served their country. Pancakes and the fixins were available from seven to ten. The donations were set aside for the veteran's fund. Everybody dropped by at some point during the morning. Volunteers helped Ted in the kitchen and Michael in the rest of the store.

The breakfast was just the beginning of a long day of eating and visiting around the mountain. Lainie and Mo held an open-house on their farm from ten until two offering snacks and drinks for everyone. They held their summer plant sale at this time and usually sold out before the afternoon was over. Their special pot blend was just about ready for harvest and they already had customers lined up for it. They sold pot at the same time as everything else. Their customers would notify the sisters of their intentions and when they came by, one of the sisters would take them to the barn to complete the sale. There was never a problem.

Bubba and Earl had been makin' moonshine for the past four weeks non-stop. They had an arrangement with the sisters. They'd already delivered two truckloads to the barn and the sisters would sell their shine along with the pot as requested. They had a nice operation.

The Kirkland's would be hosting the late day picnic and fireworks that started around six o'clock and was held in the same place as the Memorial Day barbeque. The difference was that anybody and everybody was welcome. Folks from Pine Ridge and even some from Boone showed up.

Matthews and the agencies were well prepared for the Kirkland's picnic. They had already placed special ops agents throughout the property. Communications had been intercepted by Interpol stating the three men would be at this event. Matthews had orders to take them alive if they got anywhere near Emily.

The afternoon at the sister's place was a great success. Emily bought some of their herbs for her small garden outside the back door. Basil, oregano, thyme, and chamomile to name a few. Everyone had a grand time and talked about the picnic to come.

The day held no problems as it came time for the picnic. Burgers, dogs, steak tips and barbeque were sizzling on a number of separate grills. Folks brought their own tables, chairs and big blankets to enjoy the festivities.

Ethan had invited Emily to sit with his family. They all arrived at the same time and parked next to each other. Greetings were exchanged and the chatter began.

"OK, then. Shall we go find a good place to set up?" Ian Sr. suggested. He and Mary Elizabeth had exchanged looks when Matthews had spoken. They suspected something secretive was involved here. They would have a quiet word right away with the girls.

As soon as their place was ready, Mary Elizabeth asked her daughters to follow her. Her tone of voice was met with quiet obedience. As soon as they were away and alone, Mary Elizabeth spoke to them.

"No comments or questions here girls. Do not ask Emily a lot of personal questions and do not ask about her friends. I suspect she is being protected from someone or something. Those friends of hers are in excellent physical shape and even wear jackets on a warm summer day. I trust your brother with all this. Got it?"

The three women looked at each other and agreed with their mom.

"Yes, Ma'am."

"OK."

"We hear you."

"Good. Now, let's get our picnic set up and give our salads to the Kirklands."

They went about their tasks and after a few minutes everyone was settled in their place on the lawn.

Rebecca and Scott Kirkland got everyone's attention by ringing a large farm triangle.

"Welcome y'all to our annual Fourth of July picnic. Everything's ready, so help yourselves and have a great time. The fireworks will begin as soon as it gets really dark, usually around nine, nine-thirty or so," Rebecca said.

Scott added, "And, we're gonna have some real country music tonight. So, if ya feel like dancin' get up and join in. We'll be doin' some of the old country dances as well, so be ready for a good time."

Applause and comments were hollered out as Scott and Rebecca stepped aside.

Then Matthews saw the first of the three men. Hanson was just arriving and settling down near the edge of the lawn close to the parking area.

"Hanson's here. Edge of lawn at parking lot," Matthews reported by wrist mic.

"Benson is just arriving and setting up near the other side of the parking lot. Blue T-shirt, jeans and new brown hiking boots," reported Agent Marks.

"Affirmative, Marks," Matthews said.

Everyone acknowledged the two reports.

"Keep alert for Saunders," Matthews ordered.

A few minutes later Saunders was spotted by one of the special ops agents in the parking lot.

"Affirmative," Matthews said.

All the other agents acknowledged this information as well.

"Carry on with the plan. Any movement towards Emily or any of Ethan's family and we take them."

"Affirmative," was heard from the team.

Ethan noticed Matthews talking into his mic and looked at him. Matthews nodded towards Ethan. Ethan became attentive as he knew Matthews expected trouble. Virginia HQ had given the order to leave these three men alone and gather as much info as possible. They had planted special operations agents posing as mountain folk in the crowd. They hoped the men would try to befriend them just like Benson did in the country store. The more information they could gather, the better.

As Emily and the gang gathered their food and settled in to eat, Mary Ellen asked Emily about her house.

"My brother keeps telling us how your house is coming along but neither he nor Ian has told us what it's going to look like. Would you please give us all the details? My brothers are so uncooperative."

"I told you it wasn't my place to tell you. It's Emily's, right Ethan?" Ian said as his wife punched him in the arm and his kids laughed at their parents.

"But, Ian, you designed the place so you know all about it," Colleen added.

"Still, it's Emily's baby. Emily, would you please tell them about your house so I can have a moment's peace?" Ian begged.

Everyone laughed as Emily nodded in agreement.

"Alright Ian and Ethan. Just remember how I'm saving you from the wrath of your sisters," Emily suggested and was met with more laughter and teasing.

"OK. My house is something like a Cape Cod style house with a lot of country charm mixed in. It has three floors and a walk-in attic storage area. It has a full wrap-around farmer's porch built in a somewhat Victorian style. The porch is ten feet out from the house with a roof all around it. It will have rockers and cracker barrels and the front part will have a porch swing hung from the ceiling."

"How awesome. I would love a porch swing," Bethany squealed.

"What's so special about a Cape Cod style house Emily?" Mary Ellen asked.

"The difference from the homes in this area is it is covered with cedar clapboard in the front. The clapboard kinda' gets squashed towards the bottom of the wall. And the other three sides are covered with cedar shingles. They look light brown or tan when they're put on then they age and become gray."

"Oh. OK, thanks."

"Anyway, there will be four dormers from the second floor and two larger ones from the third. Ian has figured out how to make them all look good. There will be several fireplaces including a big one in the middle of the house and then smaller ones in the kitchen and my master bedroom."

"Oh, God. I love fireplaces," Colleen said.

"We know,' Mary Ellen replied.

"Have you decided on a color for the front yet, Emily?" Mary Elizabeth asked.

"Yes. I've chosen blue. It's like a slate blue but not so gray. I guess I've designed my own color as well, huh Ethan?"

"Oh, Yeah, right along with a lot of other things. You've kept Ian real busy with all the stuff you want," Ethan teased.

"Ian, didn't Ethan say I could have anything I wanted?"

"Why, yes he did, Miss Emily. So he only has himself to blame for all the extra work," Ian said.

"Thanks a lot little brother. I'll remember this when things get crazy on the Jackson build."

"Bring it on, big bro, bring it on!"

"Well, it all sounds wonderful Emily. You just let me know if my boys are being difficult. I can still take them out behind the wood shed if needed," Ian Sr. offered. "I understand you are building a barn and stables as well."

"Yes sir. I've already made contact with Jonah, thanks to Ethan, about running the stables. Seems he has some good contacts for me to connect with when I'm ready to buy horses, too."

"You're right. Jonah is one of the best around. Good man and good horse sense. He'll do right by you. Good thinkin' Ethan."

"Tell us more," Bethany insisted.

Matthews was aware that Benson had set up just a few feet away. He had given the go-ahead to have him moved. But he hadn't heard anything yet.

Two men approached Benson.

"Hey there, Benson, right?" the first one asked.

"Yeah."

"I remember you from the country store the other day. You was right friendly. How's about you come and set up over by me and my pals? We wouldn't want you to think we weren't being neighborly around here."

Benson was a bit pissed as he thought he might have spotted a woman that sort of looked like their target. He looked over towards Hanson.

"Why sure. That's real friendly of y'all," Benson replied as he gathered together his things and followed the men to the opposite part of the area a long way from Emily.

"All clear. Good job," Matthews told his agents.

Emily continued. "Well, the floors are all hardwood. I've chosen a bunch of different types of wood for all over the house. The windows are Cape windows with the grilles between the panes. Much easier to clean."

"I hear ya there," Mary Elizabeth said. Everyone laughed along with her.

"The barn is going to be a darkish red like a barn should be. The neatest thing is, it is connected to the stables by a common hallway. And, Ethan suggested the basements of the two buildings be connected as well. We are going to use the hot springs to heat the house and hot water supply. I think that is wicked awesome, about having hot springs to use and all."

"It is," everyone agreed.

"The most special thing about my house isn't a building. It's the covered bridge that is being built on the driveway from the road leading up to the house."

"A covered bridge? Really?" Colleen exclaimed.

"No way," Bethany said.

"You're kidding right?" Mary Ellen posed.

"A real covered bridge. That was your brother Ethan's idea. It seems the meadows around here hide some close-to-the-surface ponds. Well, when the road crew was clearing for my new drive, they found one of them. Turns out there really is a spring fed pond just about six feet below the surface of the land. Since no one ever needed to walk on the area, and it was all wooded, it was never seen. I mean there were small puddles - kinda like a wetlands area. Ethan assures us that after the road is completed and the bridge cover is in place, the pond will settle down and decide just where its edges will be. Then we'll probably see wildlife begin to use the pond as a home and possibly, a migration stop over. It's not so small either. We walked along its banks to see where it flowed into the creek and discovered it actually flowed back underground. It's the coolest thing. Once the house is finished and all is settled I'd be happy to show you all the exact spot. It just goes back underground. Boom. It's gone!"

"Now that's incredible. I'd love to see that," Ian Sr. said.

"A pond. How cool. Can't wait to see all of it," Bethany said.

"Now, girls, you have to wait to be asked to visit. Don't just do your usual thing and show up with food offerings as a way of getting to see everything. I'll let you know when the build is finished," Ethan warned them.

"Ethan, I can take care of this myself. But thanks for trying to protect me from your sisters," Emily said. "I plan on having a big open-house once everything is in place. I'll let ya know as soon as I am ready." Emily looked at Matthews as she spoke.

Matthews gave a slight nod of agreement.

"What is your overall theme for the house?" Mary Elizabeth asked.

"Country... through and through," Emily exclaimed with a big smile.

"She knows exactly what she wants," Ethan said.

"Yes, she does, son. I do believe she does," Ian Sr. said softly so that only his wife heard him. Mary Elizabeth smiled in agreement as she looked at her husband.

"Matthews, isn't the pond thing wicked cool?" Emily asked.

"It sure is. I don't think I've ever seen anything quite like it before. And from what Ethan and Ian tell us, it will attract a great deal of wildlife. A good thing for all concerned."

"Can't wait to see it," Ian Sr. added.

They continued talking and eating for a while longer. Folks began to stop by to chat and laughter was heard all around the grounds.

Matthews had his hands full. Benson kept trying to get close to Emily until he finally gave the signal to have Benson removed from the grounds. He was apprehended near one of the out buildings by the local sheriff.

"Mr. Benson," the Sheriff said as he blocked Benson's intention to walk over towards Emily.

"Yes, Sheriff, have I done something wrong?"

"Seems some folks have complained you've been listening in on their conversations. You being a stranger and all that makes them a bit uneasy. Might I suggest you go on home now so these folks can relax and enjoy their day?"

"Why, yes, you could. But since this is an open gathering I think I'm just gonna stay."

Benson tried to walk around the sheriff but his deputy and two of Matthews' agents quickly grabbed him by his arms, lifting him off the ground and carrying him behind the building through the parking lot and over to his truck.

"Mr. Benson, you'll be leaving now. I'm not going to arrest you for trespassing. This may be an open gathering but it's on private property and the owners would like you to leave. You have a lot to learn about the folks in North Carolina. We are kind and abiding and ready to help as long as you new folks mind your manners and keep out of our business. We'll invite you in if we think you're worthy. My deputy's gonna follow you back to Boone right to your door so no one will bother you. Understand?"

Benson was pissed. He decided to hold his temper. Yuri would be real angry about this and Benson knew what Yuri did when he got pissed off.

"Sorry Sheriff. Just tryin' to meet the folks around here. No trouble from me. I'm leaving right now," Benson said as he got into his truck and started it up.

As soon as he drove away he was followed by the deputy just like the sheriff had explained. Matthews had planted GPS's on the three men's vehicles so they could be followed. Benson was being tracked by the FBI, Interpol and a few other agencies as well.

Saunders and Hanson saw the commotion and decided to lay low for the rest of the evening. They were chatting with the locals and learning a bunch of stuff but every time one of them started asking about new folks in the area, the conversation was changed. Seems these folks didn't like strangers asking about their personal lives.

It took a while for things to settle down. Folks were enjoying themselves all around. The band members were just arriving and hauling their equipment over to the area reserved for them. A floor of sorts had been fashioned and they were busy setting up their instruments and sound system. There was a good number of them.

As Emily watched the band getting set up, she thought she recognized a few of them. She wasn't sure but she thought they looked like some of the country music stars.

As she turned to ask Ethan about them, she saw him smiling at her as if he was waiting for her to say something.

"Hey Ethan, aren't some of those band people kinda familiar lookin'?"

"I was wonderin' how long it was gonna take you to ask that question."

"I'm right then? Not sure who they are, but I think I've seen their pictures or something before."

"You probably have. Three of them are current-day country music celebrities. We're in for a great evening of music."

"Why didn't anyone say something?"

"We don't advertise 'cause this place would be a hell hole if we did. We keep this kinda thing real quiet. We love our folks and want them to have a few minutes of peace when they come home."

"Oh, I understand that. And, good for y'all protecting them like this."

Ethan laughed out loud at Emily's attempt to talk like local folks.

"You make me laugh, Miss Emily. Yes you do. Thanks for understanding. It's gonna take them a bit to get everything set so how about a walk around the place? OK with you Matthews?"

"Sure, if you don't mind five guys following you. Discreetly, of course."

"Fine with me," Emily agreed.

"Me, too. It'll be no different than being followed by my three sisters," Ethan said.

There were a lot of folks walking around so Emily's body guards didn't look too out of place. Cora saw them and knew right off that there was something going on. She kept it to herself as she walked around talking to folks. She knew some kind of confrontation was coming to the mountain and she knew for certain Miss Emily was involved. No one could change her mind. She knew this deep in her soul. She decided she would just keep an eye on Emily for a while.

Twilight was about to come over the mountain as the band let them all know they were ready to play.

Folks settled real quick as the opening song gave way. This indeed was real country music just like the song said.

The group gave a standing cheer when their own came up to the microphone. Seems these Blue Ridge Mountains created great country singers and songwriters. The celebrities took turns singing their own, and favorites from years gone by and then getting the crowd on their feet to do a little country dancing.

After a well-earned break, the band got rockin' again. This time they brought out an old time caller. The caller called out the dance moves for the square dances. Seems a bunch of folks knew how to do these. Everyone else sat back and watched as four groups of four couples spent their time dancing to the moves called out by the caller.

Emily fell in love with the whole thing. The country dances from centuries past made her feel nostalgic. She couldn't quick put her finger on it as she wasn't especially fond of a lot of country music. But the old songs and dances touched her deep inside. She gave just a quick thought to the possibility that she may have been alive in those times in this place. A past life flashback, so to speak.

As the dancers and caller finished, the crowd gave them a standing ovation as was only fitting in these parts. A small break took place. Most folks took a minute to freshen up and grab a cold drink. Emily saw the moonshine guys and knew there were a few jugs makin' the rounds. One came to them and the guys took a swig, offering it to the ladies. They all passed and the jug was sent on its way.

Everyone from The Creek was here. Emily recognized a lot of the folks throughout the night and had spent a few minutes chatting with most of them. She was truly enjoying herself this night. Ethan's family was real nice and she loved the way they teased each other about anything and everything.

Matthews was busy with her security. She knew something had happened only because she knew what to watch for. It had happened very quickly and quietly and was over in a matter of a few moments.

Just then the band was back in place.

"Folks, tonight's been real special for us 'cause most of us are home for the first time in a long time. It's great to be back in The Creek, the best place in the world to be raised and live," the lead singer said.

This was met by loud hollers and applause and people getting on their feet, waving their flags.

Once they settled down, the lead singer continued.

"We're gonna finish this last session with some old favorites about our beloved country and ask that y'all join in if'n you've a mind to. Ready? Let's rock."

The next set had most people standing, dancing in place and singing along to old country favorites about how great it was to be livin' in the USA. Songs by past greats were sung, a special group of songs was offered for the country's veterans and those that had served from The Creek. Seems everyone had a flag or two to wave. There were even a few Confederate flags seen waving around.

The last songs were a medley of national favorites ending with The National Anthem, country style. As the band finished the last guitar riff, the night sky lit up with fireworks. They were all shapes and colors and carried on for about a half hour. Some of the bursts lasted a bit longer than others that just disappeared in a flash. They were always seen in the same place over the Applewood Grove. A few folks caught on real quick including Cora, Kendra and Emily.

Emily pointed this out to Matthews and he alerted all teams on the mountain as well as Virginia HQ. Emily saw six of these special lights. Cora and Kendra saw four and Ted and Michael and their group noticed three of them. There would be a lot of talk tomorrow in The Creek about this special light show.

Scott Kirkland took the mic as the fireworks came to an end.

"Just want to thank y'all for comin' out tonight. Let's hear it for the band. Our own special folks came home tonight to help us celebrate and we just want to show them our appreciation. I hear they're gonna be around for a day or two so be sure to thank them in your own special way."

Scott had to wait until all the hootin' and hollerin' died down.

"Now, folks, we know we've all had a great time tonight, so do be careful heading home. Take care and God Bless our veterans and the good ole' U. S. of A."

Folks showed their appreciation by clapping and hollering once again.

It took a while for the place to clear out. Matthews had asked the team to hold back and let most of the folks leave before them. He had Emily and Ethan's family wait with the Kirklands. No one minded because the band members came over and Emily was introduced all around. She laughed and talked with everyone and felt like a long time part of the mountain.

Matthews finally gave the signal and everyone shared good-byes with the promise from the celebrities that they would stop by the store the next day to visit with everyone.

Ethan and Emily found a quiet moment alone with only five of Emily's bodyguards close by. Ethan's folks made sure his sisters were kept away.

"Ethan, another amazing night. I thought the last barbeque was untouchable but this beats all. Thanks for including us with your family. I like them," Emily said.

Ethan just stood there looking at her. Oh damn it all to hell, he thought as he took her in his arms and kissed her long and deep like there was no tomorrow. The agents didn't flinch or look away. They did keep others from intruding, though.

Emily thought she would melt right there. She had dreamed about Ethan's kisses ever since the night they had spent together. She wondered why he had suddenly become so distant and aloof. She had tried to keep her distance but it wasn't working.

Ethan felt like he had finally come home. He knew she was the one for him. He had been doing battle with both his head and his heart. But this kiss cinched the deal. His heart won even if his head would suffer later. He gave his heart the lead and kissed her even deeper. Ethan finally ended the kiss and just held Emily close for a moment. When he stepped back he thought he heard her sigh. They just stood there looking at each other not sure what to say or do next.

Emily took a deep breath and quietly said, "Now that's the way to say goodnight."

Ethan gave her a quick hug then Emily got into her Jeep as Ethan rejoined his family. His folks were smiling and his sisters weren't saying a word.

The ride back was quiet. Emily didn't realize how tired she really was until she got home.

"Thanks Matthews for the ride and all. Tonight was great fun."

"Yes, it was. One of the best July 4th celebrations I've ever been to. Those country music celebrities were a great surprise."

"As if you didn't know they would be there."

"I did know they might show up. We didn't know if they would all make it. So glad they did. What a show. Hey, you look a little tired."

"I am. And it was a great show. Tomorrow's meet and greet at the store should be fun."

"I'm looking forward to it and so are your bodyguards."

"Speaking of being guarded, what happened back there? I know something happened so don't try to tell me otherwise," Emily said as they walked into her kitchen.

"We had to escort someone off the property. He kept trying to get close to you."

"He was one of them wasn't he? One of the bad guys?" Emily asked with a look of panic on her face.

"Yes, Emily, he was. But we don't think he was out to harm you. We have it on good authority that he and the other two are just gathering information. We are obviously following their every move. The other two were at the picnic but stayed clear after we finished with their friend. I'll let you know what we find out as soon as I do. I always do."

"Yes you do. Thanks for the update. I think I'll get some herbal tea and go to sleep. Goodnight Matthews."

"Goodnight, Emily."

Matthews gave orders that her phone was not to ring until she woke up the next day. Period.

Hanson and Saunders went straight over to Benson's apartment as soon as they got back into Boone.

After Hanson made sure all the blinds were closed and the TV was on to mute their voices he got right into it.

"Benson, that was one hell of a job you did. Looks like the sheriff had a little help from those two guys dressed in black. Any idea who they were?"

"No idea and thanks. I did exactly what we talked about. I think that Barbara person is right here in Crab Apple Creek. No matter where I went someone worked hard to keep me away from the bigger groups of people on the lawn. Not sure just exactly which one she is but real sure she's here. I tried to be a little forceful but when the Sheriff got tough I backed right down. You know they followed me home. I waited a half hour before I came over. I didn't see anyone hanging around or following me."

"I'm just thinking here," Saunders added. "If those two guys were not part of the sheriff's department then they were probably private hires. Maybe this Barbara has gotten a hold of some private guards. Or, now that I'm thinking about it, do you think they could be FBI or something? If they know she was connected with Nick, then maybe they've got her in witness protection or something like that. What do you guys think?"

"I think you may be onto something here," Saunders said. "If she is in witness protection then they know she was married to a connection to our boss. If that's the case, then she's probably already told them everything she knows. Or maybe we're just getting caught up in the whole thing. I'll bet those Kirkland people hired private security for the picnic seeing as they had all those celebrities there. Doesn't that make more sense?"

Benson and Hanson nodded their heads in agreement.

"Ya know Saunders, I think that's exactly what happened. The FBI wouldn't allow a person in witness protection to be in a large open group so soon after they went into hiding. I know that for a fact. Our boss knows that, too. OK. Let's take a look at the whole picture. I was greeted real nice at the country store the other day. Folks there were pleasant and easy to talk to," Benson said.

"And tonight, those two guys that came up to me were real friendly as well. They brought me into their group and introduced me all around. Nice folks. No problems.

"So there doesn't seem to be any proof that she's here in witness protection. I kept looking at all the women and none of them looked like her. Not really. I know those facial recognition programs are real good, but I didn't see any that matched even a little bit. That's not saying she didn't change her appearance," Hanson continued.

"So, what's our next move? Keep going along just as we are?" Saunders asked.

"Exactly," Hanson answered. "Keep collecting information. I'll get a hold of the boss in a few minutes and tell him about the picnic and how Benson was removed but not about our talk about us thinking that Barbara isn't here. It's not for us to decide. We work for the boss and he can end our lives with one word."

Everyone stayed quiet for a time then the two went back to their apartments.

Their whole conversation had been heard and recorded by the FBI. They now listened in as Hanson contacted Yuri.

"Yes."

"It's me, Boss, Hanson in Boone."

"Report."

"We all went to the picnic as ordered. We followed your plan to the letter. Benson tried to get close to the larger groups of people with anyone who looked like the photo. He was blocked several times then escorted from the property. He was met by the local Sheriff and two men dressed in black. They looked like private security. There were a bunch of country music celebrities performing that were a surprise to everyone. That's most likely where the private security guys fit in. I counted six in all and mostly around the band area after they set up. No other problems to report. I sent you a report about the locals in the area and the visit Benson made to the country store. Would you like us to keep going as planned sir?"

"Yes. For now. Good work tonight. We now know that the local sheriff is involved in the area and not just a name on a door. You're most likely correct about the private security being for the celebrities. The FBI and Interpol would not let themselves be seen if this were a detail for witness protection. They wouldn't let their client out in the open, either. Have Benson.., no.., you go to the country store tomorrow and see what's going on. Report back to me."

"Yes sir."

"And Hanson, see if anyone mentions the name Jordan Jackson when you're there."

Yuri hung up before Hanson could say anything.

He's a bastard, thought Hanson, but he did pay well. They had all received a bundle of cash through the mail yesterday. Another ten thousand dollars. The package looked like it had a book in it and the return address was the same as the mailing address. The post office stamp was from New York City. Didn't matter. It was hard, cold cash. Untraceable. That's why he worked for the guy. Cash said it all.

He called the others and told them to continue as ordered. He would be visiting the country store tomorrow and report back to them tomorrow night at Benson's apartment at nine o'clock - never the same place twice in a row.

CHAPTER 28

The Saturday after the Fourth found The Creek in full summer mode. The summer folks had returned to their cabins and homes. Summer camps were open and receiving their campers, and tourists were venturing off the main roads and getting lost. Getting lost more than anything else seemed to be a common problem.

Kendra decided to stop in and visit with Emily. She called Matthews first to get the OK which he gave readily. He called Emily to let her know.

Kendra knocked on the back door and was let in by Agent Marks.

"Mornin' Agent Marks. Nice to see you. Did you get to the picnic last night?"

"No, Ma'am. I was on duty here. I did get to listen to it all, though. That band sounded great even if it was through my ear piece."

"Glad you got to get a bit of it. Hi Emily!" Kendra hollered as she got a cup of coffee.

"Hi Kendra," Emily replied as she came into the kitchen. "I've got some muffins on the table if you're interested."

"Sure. Thanks," Kendra said as they both sat down.

"So, how did you like the picnic?"

"It was great! I've never been that close to real music celebrities in my life. I didn't even know they were from here. Not that I would. I'm not a big fan of country music. I wasn't until last night. My head's still spinning with everything that happened."

Kendra got a big smile on her face. "Can't imagine why. It might have had something to do with the big kiss Ethan planted on you in the parking area. What do you think?"

"Oh, my God! You saw that? How many people saw that?"

"Quite a few but it doesn't matter how many people saw it, it's all over The Creek. It only took about a millisecond for word to get around."

"I'm not surprised. As a matter of fact, to answer your question, it was fantastic and sweet and hot and downright incredible," Emily said as she blushed. "Sure took him a long time to kiss me after our one night together."

"I'd say it looked like a home run to me," Kendra teased.

"I'd say it was!"

"Hey, wanna join me over at the store? Seems one of our singers just arrived."

"How can you tell?"

"I just heard your agents talking about it. Ask them."

"Hey guys, is one of the celebrities over at the store?"

"Yes, Ma'am and the others are on their way. Seems there's gonna be a bit of a private 'Creek Only' visit. You going?"

"Yes I am. Come on Kendra. Let's go."

"Ma'am, could you please give us a couple of minutes to secure the place and your walk across the road? We'll let you know when we have the OK from Matthews."

"Oh sure. Sorry. I gotta wait for these guys, Kendra."

"No problem. I'll just use the little girl's room while we wait."

Agent Marks gave the OK as soon as Kendra returned and they all went over to the store. Sure enough, one of the three celebrities was already there. He was sitting around the stove talking with a few of the locals.

"Sure is nice to see you again Kenny. It's been way too long this time," Hal said.

"I know Hal. I've been tryin' to get back here since Christmas but my manager's booked me solid. I told him to give me more open time or I'd find a new manager 'cause I gotta get home on a regular basis," Kenny explained.

"You see that you do that. Your daddy and momma miss you somethin' fierce."

"I know. At least I Skype with them just about every day. That's a great invention. But I do miss the real thing. I love this old country store and sittin' around the stove we all used to do before I got busy with my music."

"Is that that no good Kenny I hear over there?"

Everyone laughed as they looked up and saw Cora comin' towards them with the other two celebrities in tow.

"Look who I found out on the porch. Miss Ashley and Mister Tate."

"Hey everyone," Ashley and Tate said at the same time.

"Hey Miss Cora," Kenny said as he stood up and took his hat off. "It's a great pleasure to see you again."

"Miss Cora? Since when did kin call each other like that? I'm you great aunt on your mama's side and don't you forget it."

"Yes, Ma'am Aunt Cora," Kenny said as he scooped her up in a big hug and twirled her around.

"Now, that's more like it," Cora exclaimed as she was placed back on the floor. "Y'all sounded real good last night. I'm right proud of all of you including the musicians. You've all grown up real good and respectful."

"Thanks Miss Cora," Ashley said.

"That's right kind of you, Ma'am. Thank you," Tate offered.

Hal got up and offered his rocking chair to Cora. It was her favorite.

"Why thank you Hal for giving me my favorite chair. Much obliged."

"Any time Miss Cora," Hal replied as he sat down close by.

"Now, why don't y'all get yourselves a seat and join us?" Cora offered just as Emily and Kendra walked through the door. "You two come on over and join us and I'll introduce you to my nephew and his friends."

"Hi Miss Cora and thanks," Emily said as she was given a chair.

"Why Miss Cora, how nice of you," Kendra said as she was given a seat next to Emily.

"Now, Kenny, this here is Miss Emily. She's new here but she belongs just the same. And you already know Kendra 'cause you grew up together."

"Nice to meet you Emily. If my Aunt Cora approves then that's all I need to know," Kenny said as he shook hands with Emily. "Hey Kendra, nice to see you again."

"It's an honor to meet you Kenny," Emily replied.

"Hey Kenny," Kendra said as they hugged each other.

"I would like y'all to meet my friends Ashley and Tate. I think you know who they might be. Ashley and Tate, these here are my kin and friends from The Creek," Kenny said.

"Hey y'all. Nice to meet you," Ashley said.

"Nice to meet y'all, too," Tate added.

"Now that all the introductions are done, can we get on with the important stuff?" Cora grumbled.

"Aunt Cora, did you take a sour pill today 'cause you're soundin' a bit sour." Kenny chided Cora.

"You mind your manners Kenny," Cora admonished him.

Kenny just laughed as he said, "I wouldn't want you any other way Aunt Cora."

"Good. Now about last night. The music and all was first rate. It was the light show during the fireworks I want to talk about."

"Hey Miss Cora, y'all," Ted said as he joined the group. "I saw something strange, too."

"Me, too," Michael added as he came to stand nearby.

"Anyone else?" Ted asked the group.

Ted and Michael had closed the store to outsiders for the day so everyone could sit a spell with their home grown musicians. Matthews had offered security and the guys had agreed. Matthews had two agents at each door decked out to look like the locals. They were standing and sitting from time to time and they switched places to keep things interesting.

Cora took hold of the group by saying, "I saw four sets of lights during the fireworks, always in the same place just over the Applewood Grove. Mostly white, but once with some blue and once with some orange."

"I saw them, too, Miss Cora," Ted said again. I saw three sets in that same area. Wonder what's goin' on?"

"I saw three lights myself right after the first fireworks went off. I thought they was part of the show until they just vanished," Hal added. "I kept a'watchin' and saw three more sets just like you did Miss Cora. One set was white with some pink color. Dangest thing I ever saw. They kept comin' back."

"I saw them as well," Kendra added. "Same thing over the Applewood Grove except I saw five of them just like y'all are describing with the changing lights."

Cora was looking at Emily waiting for her to speak up. Emily felt Cora's gaze and decided to go ahead and talk.

"Alright, I saw six sets of those lights all in the same place in the sky kinda low to the ground. I thought some fireworks had gone off early with the first set then when they kept showing up I realized I was looking at UFOs. And, yes, they just disappeared. No trail of light. No sound. Just there as if they were gathering for something or leaving or picking up something. Maybe someone should go check the status of the Applewood Grove."

"Good girl, Emily. You saw the most and I know you're connected with them somehow. There hasn't been so much activity from them since you came here. Once in a blue moon we'd see those lights but not like last night. Somethin's about to happen 'round here. Mark my words."

"Miss Cora, you've been here the longest of any of us. Please share with us how you know about these happenings," Hal asked Cora.

"Alright Hal. It's about time the whole story was told. Way back, not that too far back mind ya, when I was a little girl, my grandmother would tell the story of how she would see these lights in the Applewood Grove. She and my grandfather would talk about them for days before they went on to talk about other things. When my grandmother was getting' into her middle years, she saw the lights one summer night and decided to go over to the grove to see what was goin' on. It was the middle of the night so she took her dog and a lantern to investigate.

When she arrived she saw this thing hangin' in the air just above the tree tops all silvery and white, shimmerin' like the sun on the water. She just stood there as she watched this ship change colors from white to blue to pink and all the colors of the rainbow. It just hung there for the longest time then it started humming real soft and low.

"As it hummed it changed its tune and my grandmother said she thought it sounded like it was singin'. She kept her place as she saw the ship change shape. Then the strangest thing happened. It looked like it saw her and moved closer to her. She just stood there not sure what to do. She said she never felt scared about it. She kinda felt at ease as if this were a regular thing to happen in the grove and it was normal for her to be a part of it.

"Well, anyway, as I was tellin', the ship seemed to change shape and then it sent a beam of light to the forest floor. As my grandmother watched, she began to see forms taking shape on the forest floor as if an elevator was letting people out. The beings looked like wavy, silvery light and they danced around the grove like they were celebratin' somethin'.

"In the blink of an eye they changed shape and became just like you and me. They looked like mountain folk and they came up to my grandmother and reached out for her hand. She took theirs and they walked her into the circle of light and they all began to talk. She said she felt like she had just been reunited with long lost kin. She was happy and joyous for the longest time. Then they said they had to leave but that they would be back. This mountain was a sacred place they had been visiting for millions of years. It held the oldest magic known to exist and now my grandmother would be a part of those that would protect and keep the magic safe.

"My grandmother said good-bye as the people changed their shape back to their original wavy silvery selves. They went back into the light and the light went back into the ship. It once again seemed to change shape before it just shot up into the sky without a sound and disappeared.

"My grandmother told us she just stood there for the longest time. She felt peaceful and purely loved to the deepest part of her soul. Her dog was right by her side and her lantern was back in her hand. She took a deep breath and then headed back to the farm house. As she walked into the kitchen she looked at the clock and couldn't believe that only five minutes had gone by. She knew she was in the grove for hours. This was not possible. But there the clock was. She saw that it was still dark outside and all the creatures were quiet except for the night owls; they called out to each other like always.

"Now my grandmother had the Gift. She could see Spirits just like her mother and all before her. Some said it was a curse and abomination against God. My grandmother had a few choice words to say about that I can tell you. My mother had the Gift as well and so do I though some folks right in this room will tell ya I'm a bit touched. I am what I am.

"My grandmother didn't tell anyone about her experience until it happened again about ten years later. She was in her sixties by then and she knew she had to tell folks about it so someone would be able to keep the story goin'. I was in my twenties when she told me. I didn't doubt her. She was my grandmother. She says her grandmother had talked about the magic lights in the Applewood Grove many times but no one believed her. They said she was full of shine when she talked about them so they figured she was a bit off and all. Shine can make ya like that as you well know.

"Now, I've been seein' them since I was a young girl and I told my grandmother just that. She seemed to finally relax and we shared stories about those lights. I've never been visited by those shape changin' folks myself, but I know something real is happening out there. I feel it in my bones. They've come back and this time it's for somethin' big. I know it has to do with the magic my grandmother spoke of. I truly do."

There was a moment of complete silence then everyone started to talk at once. This kept up for quite some time before there was a pause.

"Believe what you will my friends. I know what I know," Cora said softly as if it needed to be said at all.

After a moment Michael suggested lunch for everyone. "Ted and I've been making stuff since early this morning for today. Go help yourselves. The buffet is all set."

Folks helped themselves and stories of all kinds were shared.

More folks arrived over the lunch time and the store was quite full and busy. It was like a long lost family reunion had finally come alive. News was caught up, stories were told and after everyone finished lunch. Ashley, Kenny and Tate brought out there guitars and started singin' the old songs. Some of the folks joined in and the harmonies were like a sweet sigh of angels.

Emily noticed Ethan a bit after the singing had started. She didn't know how long he had been there. He walked over to her and grabbed a chair and sat real close.

Ashley pointed to Ethan saying, "Well, look who finally showed up. Ethan Sutherland, I swear you get better lookin' every time I see you. Makes a girl go all soft inside."

Ethan blushed and the whole place laughed as Ethan replied, "Now Ashley honey, you know it don't take much from you to make a man weak in the knees just beggin' the angels for a look from you."

"Looks to me like you already got a little somethin' sweet to look at," Ashley teased.

"Well, yes I do," Ethan said as he turned to look at Emily.

Emily smiled and said, "Why, Mr. Ethan, you sure are sweet with your words. Makes a heart go pitter-patter."

This brought more laughter and a few suggestive comments.

"Ethan," Kenny suggested, "I do believe you need to get your mountain ass up here and sing a few songs with us just like we used to do when we was kids. What do ya say folks?"

Applause and words of encouragement were sent Ethan's way.

"OK. OK. I know when I'm licked," Ethan said as he joined his friends.

They sang for a while before Ethan begged for mercy and food.

"Now, that's what today is all about. Bein' with kin," Cora said when Ethan finished. "You make a heart real happy Ethan. It's been too long since we heard your sweet voice in these hills."

"Thanks Miss Cora. It has been a long time. Maybe I'm ready to get at it again."

"Yes, boy, I do believe you are," Cora said softly as Ethan gave her a hug. "Now, go get your lunch."

It was well into the afternoon when a bit of a problem arose on the store porch.

Hanson had decided to spend some time in the store to get as much information as possible about the folks in The Creek. He chose this particular afternoon.

When he arrived he saw a lot of trucks and cars parked all around the store and down the road. He figured the store was real busy being a summer holiday weekend. He saw a couple of guys just standing around on the porch by the front door as he approached the store. He nodded his head as he walked up the stairs and attempted to get to the door.

The agents recognized Hanson and sent out an alarm.

Matthews had a few more agents cover the store from the back just in case Hanson gave anyone trouble.

The agents blocked the door as Hanson walked up the steps.

"Sorry Sir. The store is closed today. Family gathering," the first agent said to Hanson.

'Oh. So I can't go in?" Hanson answered.

"No sir. Only family. There are a few more stores just down the Pine Ridge road about twenty minutes from here in Pine Ridge."

"Oh. I was hoping to get a look at the store, I heard it was a great replica of the way things used to be way back."

"Sir, if you'll just go ahead and head back to your truck, the folks here would greatly appreciate it."

"When will the store be open again?"

"Tomorrow as usual."

"OK then. Thanks," Hanson walked back down the steps. He decided to take a look from the side of the store and as he walked around the corner he was stopped by more agents.

"Sir, please return to your truck and leave The Creek."

"I just wanted to get a look inside, that's all."

"Sir, please allow us to escort you back to your truck," the agents said as they took him by the arms and moved him forcefully toward his truck.

"Hey. You don't have to manhandle me. I'm goin'," Hanson complained as he tried to free himself.

"Sir, you were told numerous times to leave and you refused."

By this time they had arrived at Hanson's truck. One of the agents opened the door and all but threw him in.

"Sir, please leave immediately or we'll be forced to contact the local Sheriff."

"Alright. I'm leavin'," Hanson yelled.

He started the truck and left. Matthews had a vehicle follow him all the way to Boone. Matthews was thinking that he was number two of the three. He wondered when the third one would make his move.

Hanson reported to Yuri as soon as he got home. Yuri was delighted with the outcome.

"Keep them looking at the three of you so we can get close to the real target. You will report to Johanson from now on. He will be in touch." Yuri hung up.

Hanson didn't have to wait long. The call came just a few minutes later.

"Hanson, this is Johanson. You will all leave The Creek alone until further notice. I want Saunders to check on building permits for Boone and Crab Apple Creek. These are public records so they shouldn't be hard to find. They should even be on the Internet. Make it happen. The three of you need to keep going to work and gathering all the information you can on everything you hear. Report back to me every night at midnight using this number. Any questions?"

"No sir."

Johanson hung up without another word.

Hanson sat there for a few minutes and wondered what was going on. Had the boss changed his mind or was this the plan all along? Maybe he and the others were just a diversion while the boss did something else? Who knew? He would do as he was told, which wasn't much.

Hanson told Saunders and Benson about the new development. They all agreed that the plan had changed and they would do as they were told.

Jordan Jackson had attended the picnic as Kendra's guest. She and Ethan introduced him around as the newest addition to The Creek. He was immediately accepted by all and made to feel at home.

He spent Saturday with Ian designing his house and barn. The barn was the easier of the two. It was a barn, or so Jordan thought. By the end of the day, Jordan learned barns could be just as detailed as houses. And his was. The shape and color were the quickest things to choose. Having a basement was new to Jordan and he readily agreed to Ian's ideas about that. Selecting the interior of the barn took the better part of the day. When they called it quits, it was ready to be drawn onto a blue print and sent for approval to the building inspector. Among other things, it would be wired for Wi-Fi. Now that was cool.

Jordan planned to meet with Ian after work for the next week to solidify the shape of the house. All other details like the final floor plan would take more time. No matter, this was an amazing experience for Jordan. Ian had informed him that the road plan and the rough stake outline for the house had been approved by all the agencies that needed to. That meant the road was going to be built starting Monday with a completion date of just a few days later. It would be a paved drive so all the equipment could get in and out without any problems and it would be easier to clear it in the winter. Jordan really had wanted a stone drive so Ian had suggested they line the sides with a blue stone he liked. It would be great for runoff, too.

CHAPTER 29

Yuri was watching Jordan very closely. He had targeted him as a way to get all the information he needed on Barbara. Yuri was just waiting for a few more weeks to pass before he put this part of his plan into action. He was so pleased with himself he called for another sex party. This time he took part with all his guests. He only wanted sixteen year old girls and twenty-five year old men.

He especially liked to watch the men play with each other's dicks. After all who knew what a man liked better than a man?

He ordered the girls to suck each other's breasts as he watched the men suck each other's dicks. He was getting so aroused that he grabbed one of the girls and threw her to the floor. He pushed his dick in her mouth for a minute before he rammed it into her pussy. He kept ramming into her until he came, then he fell on top of her and stayed that way for a few minutes before he got up and continued watching the sex play.

He ordered men to lick the girl's pussies and the girl's to masturbate other girls. He was drinking forty year old scotch and thoroughly enjoying himself. He got aroused again and this time he chose a man to suck his dick until he came. Then he ordered everyone out. He showered and collapsed onto his bed and slept with an evil smile on his face.

The CON were watching. They liked seeing Yuri control others. But they had a job for him that he wouldn't like. No matter. Either he did the job or they kill him. There were always others to use. He would be visited by the man in the black hat soon so let him have is fun for now. His time was about up.

The CON sent a message to Yuri while he slept. He would remember it when he woke up and be terrified. The dream showed Yuri being tortured bit by bit and killed. He would do as he was told or the dream would come true.

Yuri woke up in the middle of the night and was not sure why. He had a headache and just wanted to go back to sleep. As he tried to settle down he began remembering the dream the CON had given him and started to pace around the room.

The man in the black hat suddenly appeared in front of him while he was standing at a window. He began asking him what he wanted when he realized he couldn't speak. It was as if his voice had stopped working. He tried again but still no sound came out of his mouth. He began to panic as he was dragged to the bed by an unseen force. He tried to free himself but couldn't.

He was thrown onto the bed on his back, and his wrists and ankles were tied to the posts so that he was spread eagle. He saw forms come out of the air. They were hideous. They had three red eyes and double rows of sharp teeth. They stunk so bad he thought he'd puke.

They moved their hands close to his body. They had long claws on each hand. With one silent movement they had ripped his clothes off leaving him naked.

Yuri began to tremble. The man in the black hat nodded to the monsters and they began to torture Yuri. The dragged their claws from his chin to his penis cutting into him. He screamed but no one heard him. It was a silent scream. He began to bleed. Then they began to probe all the openings in his body. His ears and mouth. His anus and penis.

The monsters went deep into his body while the man in the black hat began to speak.

"You agreed to do whatever we ordered in exchange for power and wealth. You've disappointed us numerous times. We gave you many chances to appease us yet you disobeyed. Now you will pay the price. You are weak and must be punished before you die."

Yuri was terrified. The monsters kept pushing their claws up his penis and anus and the pain became too much to handle. He lost consciousness. They stopped and made him wake up. They weren't done with him yet.

The man in the black hat spoke again. "You remember how they found your man Nick? We did that and we'll continue to do worse for those that don't obey."

Yuri tried to scream and this time he had a voice. He screamed as they began to dislocate his joints. He finally died as they ripped his body apart.

Yuri was trembling so badly that he fell to the floor. He was beyond scared. He grabbed a waste basket and threw up. He didn't know what to do. He hollered for the man in the black hat to come to him. He waited for hours sitting on the floor trembling before the man materialized before him.

"What haven't I done to please you?" Yuri asked.

"So, you remember the dream. Good. Now, we need one hundred more young girls right away. My contacts will be waiting for your call and information to pick them up. You have two weeks to get them."

"Yes. OK. I will do this. Anything else?"

"Not at this time. There are circumstances beyond your control now that I will have to make happen."

"I am here to serve you. Just let me know and I will do it."

"Good. We like obedient servants." The man in the black hat evaporated right before Yuri's eyes.

He started to calm down and the trembling finally stopped a while later. The sun was just starting to show itself. Yuri got into the shower and started making phone calls to all his contacts around the globe telling them he needed young girls fifteen to seventeen years of age right away. They all acknowledged his orders.

Yuri called his man Johanson in Virginia and ordered him to escalate his search. He needed her dead now. No more waiting.

Hanson got the call and new orders early in the morning. He called Benson and Saunders before they went to work to give them the new orders and to tell them to meet him at his house right after work that day. It was July 7th and by midnight Barbara would be dead if Hanson had anything to say about it.

The three of them were at Hanson's house by six.

"We have orders to kill Barbara right away. We know who she is so tonight she dies. We will go to her place after midnight, kidnap her and take her out into the woods. There we will restrain her, rape her then kill her. We'll all have a turn with her just as I promised. Make sure you clear everything out of your place now. Wipe it all down with bleach and use the dumpsters in Pine Ridge just like we planned. We shouldn't have anything to throw away besides some food. Pack your equipment and load your trucks after dark. Be careful. We'll meet on the Pine Ridge Road just where it leaves town and head to Crab Apple Creek. We'll take my truck and leave yours in the used car lot as planned. When we're done, I'll drop you back at the lot and we'll all go our separate ways. Keep the throw-away phone ready for further instructions as you travel. Any questions?"

"Nope," both answered.

"Let's get busy then."

Virginia HQ and all the other agencies heard this conversation and went into full attack mode.

The Boone special operations unit went live. They would follow the three guys and apprehend them as soon as they took the woman they thought was Barbara.

Matthews was moving Emily out of The Creek to a safe house in Asheville for the duration.

"When did all this happen Matthews?" she asked as she was packing a bag and being rushed out into a black SUV with her agents.

"Just now. Don't worry. Agent Marks is in charge and will get you and your guards to Asheville without incident. I'm staying here to manage everything."

"OK I guess. I'm just a little terrified to say the least."

"I know. You'll be OK. I promise."

Matthews gave the signal and they left. Emily was trembling in the back seat with two agents beside her.

"Emily, can I offer you something to help calm you? It won't knock you out," Agent Marks said.

"Ah no. I have my own herbs here. I didn't know I was shaking."

Emily dug through her backpack and took out some capsules and a bottle of water.

"Don't worry Agent. This is a combination I call my calming herbs. They work well for me although I've never used them when I was running to save my life."

Emily swallowed them then sat back with her eyes closed. She opened them a few minutes later realizing she was hungry.

"Hey guys, I'm kinda hungry here. I was just getting ready to fix supper when all this happened. When can we stop for food? Not that I want to mess with the plan or anything."

"I'm sorry, Emily," Agent Marks replied. "We need to get a good hour away from Boone before we can stop. We're taking all back roads to avoid being seen. It should take us about three and a half to four hours give or take. We can stop as soon as we get close to Spruce Pine. There are a number of country stores in the area that serve food. I have some munchies if you'd like something. Take a look."

Emily chose the Fritos and a Sierra Mist.

"Thanks Agent Marks. You do know my weakness for munchies," Emily said with a little smile.

"You're welcome. I like those myself."

Emily ate her snack as they drove through Pine Ridge and turned right away from the road to Boone. They were heading west into the heart of the Blue Ridge towards Tennessee. Emily watched as they drove along. The views were breathtakingly beautiful. They passed through the small towns of Heaton and Elk Park before they got onto state road Route 19-E heading towards Spruce Pine. This town was far enough away from Boone to allow them a few minutes to grab some supper and eat on the road.

It was about eight o'clock when they came through Spruce Pine. The team had found a family diner that was open until ten and they stopped for take-out and a rest break for Emily. They had parked close to the door and all the agents were dressed like the locals so no one gave them more than a quick look as they headed towards the restrooms. She was back five minutes later waiting for their order.

They were back on the road by eight-twenty with food in hand. Emily chowed down as the agents took turns eating, too.

"This is really good," Emily said between bites. "These local places really know how to cook. If I never eat at a fast food place again it will be too soon."

Eleven o'clock found Emily being settled in the safe house just outside of Asheville.

Matthews kept getting updates of their progress. He was relieved to hear they had made it without incident.

Matthews gave an update on his current situation.

"The three men have left their apartments. They loaded their trucks so we're pretty sure they're gonna run after they try to kill Barbara. We have GPS's on the trucks so we won't use a physical tail until they leave Pine Ridge. We have The Creek on alert as we have an idea of who they think Barbara is. That's gonna be tricky and a bit interesting. I'll keep you posted."

"Yes sir," Agent Marks replied. "Emily is settling into her room. She's tired but a bit restless about the whole thing. I'll keep her updated as you ordered."

"OK. Over and out as they used to say," Matthews said as he hung up.

"Emily, you decent?" Agent Marks asked.

"Sure. Come on in. This place isn't half bad."

"Matthews wants you to know the three men have emptied their apartments and are on the move toward Pine Ridge. We'll pick up their vehicle as they leave Pine Ridge. Your place has been secured although we're not sure who they think you, or Barbara, is. We'll keep you posted as this thing plays out."

"Thanks, I think. This is really weird thinking that someone is about to kidnap me and kill me. It's kinda surreal."

"You're safe with us. But I get your drift. You can join us in the living room or stay here. Your choice."

"I think I'll join you. I'm not about to fall asleep anytime soon."

They returned to the living room to find the TV on although the sound was low as the agents listened to their earpieces and talked.

Meanwhile, the three men were dropping two of the trucks off in the used car lot and getting into Hanson's truck. It was just after midnight. They headed for The Creek a few minutes later and they were followed all the way by a number of vehicles including three different trucks. They didn't think anything of the extra traffic as it was summer in the mountains and the place was busy with tourists and summer people.

They drove through The Creek and turned down a little two track dirt path. They had backed in for a fast getaway. They grabbed their things and headed further down the road toward the sisters' farm. They had targeted a small cabin set a ways off the road. There was a single woman by the name of Brittany who lived there.

She did resemble the photo Yuri had sent out and she was about the same age as Barbara.

The men had been watching her at the picnic and decided this must be the new Barbara.

They cut the power to her house right before they burst through the door.

Brittany had been replaced by an agent. She acted surprised at the intrusion and feigned fear.

Hanson grabbed her saying, "So, you never thought we'd find you Barbara? You don't know who you're dealing with." He slapped her hard across the face which momentarily stunned her. They bound her hands behind her back and pulled her out the door. They headed down a path behind the cabin into the woods. Just as they got to where they were going to kill her they began asking her questions.

She said she didn't know what they were talking about again and again. She was thrown onto the ground her hands were untied and held by Benson and Saunders as Hanson started to rip her clothes off.

All hell broke loose as agents and sheriff's deputies came out of hiding. The three men were subdued quickly and the agent posing as Brittany was given first aid.

"You OK Agent?" Matthews asked as her cuts and bruises were taken care of.

"Yes sir. Nothing more than a bump or two."

"You're still going to the medical center in Boone for a thorough check-up. Protocol."

"Yes sir. Glad to help in any way I can. She OK?"

"Yes Agent. She's OK. Good job."

The three men had been taken to the road and put into separate vehicles before Matthews spoke with the agent. They were hollering something fierce about their rights and wanting a lawyer and all. They didn't receive a response from anyone. This made them even madder until one of the deputies had to get physical with Benson. He was kicking the vehicle he was in. He was subdued with force and was now quiet as his face was swollen and he couldn't talk.

Matthews was on his phone as soon as the scene was secured for the crime scene crew.

"Agent Marks, we have them in custody. They're not going to hurt anyone ever again. It was the cabin owned by Brittany they targeted. She's safe as well. She'll be staying with family while the agency repairs her place. You can return tonight or tomorrow whatever Emily prefers. Just let me know. Good work all of you."

"Thanks Sir. I'll give her the news and get back to you soon."

"Emily," Agent Marks said, "They've captured the three men and you're cleared to return home tonight or tomorrow morning, whatever your choice. I know it's late. It's about one in the morning so you decide."

"I think I'd like to sleep for a bit then we can go back home OK?"

"Yes Ma'am. I'll tell Matthews. You get some shut eye."

As Emily fell asleep Agent Marks informed Matthews of their plan.

The rest of the night saw Matthews and the sheriff interrogating the three men.

They were in separate rooms at the sheriff's department and would be held in the jail until the FBI came for them.

Matthews started with the man named Saunders. The sheriff sat in.

"I am Special Agent Matthews with the U. S. Marshals Service. What is your real name, It's not Saunders."

Saunders didn't say a thing.

"You don't have to speak. You've been read your rights. Let me explain a few things to you. Your apartment and truck were bugged as soon as you came into Boone. We wired your place with cameras and sound equipment. We have every conversation and phone call the three of you've ever made. So I guess there's no need for you to talk."

"Fuck off!" Saunders replied.

"We know who you work for and what your mission was. That was very obvious when you attacked our agent at the cabin tonight. By the way, that wasn't the woman you call Barbara. And don't worry about your boss. I'm sure he'll have you taken care of once we get you into the federal prison system just like Jones and the guy named Nick. That was an especially gruesome murder. He was ripped to pieces while he was still alive. The CSU folks are still trying to figure that one out. If I didn't know better I'd say some kind of demonic power was involved. Wouldn't you sheriff?"

"Yes I would. I couldn't even look at the pictures without getting sick. What do you think?" the sheriff asked as he threw a few pictures of the crime scene that had been Nick's body on the table.

Saunders took one look, paled and almost threw up.

"Get those out of my sight," he hollered as he looked away. He was in shackles so he couldn't use his hands.

"Makes ya sick, doesn't it Saunders or maybe you'll tell us your name. Oh wait, we don't need that 'cause your prints came back with your real name. It doesn't matter what you call yourself, you're going away for the rest of your life however long that may be."

Saunders didn't say a word. He was pale and he had bruises and cuts all over his body from the beating he received trying to escape earlier.

"Sheriff, the charges so far are attempted kidnapping, attempted rape, attempted murder, carrying a concealed weapon without a license, and money laundering across state lines. That's a good start. I'm sure there will be more added as we go along."

"Now Agent Matthews, you were telling me about his boss. That Yuri fella'. Seems he's into some pretty nasty stuff - human trafficking of young girls being the worst. He sells them to prostitution rings around the world. He runs those prostitution rings so he controls those girls as well. Seems a good number of them disappear as soon as he has them kidnapped. No trace of them. Can't seem to find them anywhere. Word has it he keeps the best ones for his own use. Young boys, too. Sick bastard!"

"That does seem to be the general consensus. And then there's global drug trafficking, global money laundering and thousands of murders he's had committed not to mention the moles he has in all levels of the government. We know all about him Saunders so we really don't need you to tell us anything. He'll have you murdered within a few days of being locked away. No way to hide from him."

"Shut the fuck up! Just shut the fuck up! I want a lawyer," Saunders said.

"OK. Sheriff those are the magic words. No more talking to this prisoner without his lawyer. Of course it's going to take a few days to get you a court appointed lawyer if any of them are willing to represent you. Seems your boss has a bad reputation for killing those court appointed lawyers as well. That Jones guy still doesn't have one."

"Agent Matthews, why don't we have this fella taken to the lock up until the feds get here. I'm sure the locals would love to have a chance to get to know him."

"Like hell you will. Put me in solitary!" Saunders yelled as Matthews and the sheriff left the room, leaving the two agents to stand guard.

Sheriff Donohue had the ol' country sheriff thing down to a T. He was just as tech savvy and intelligent as Agent Matthews. They played off each other well.

Matthews and the Sheriff moved on to Hanson. He wasn't talking much either so they had him put in a cell as well.

Benson was a different story. He was a mean bastard. "You're goin' down for beating a prisoner. I have my rights."

"Which would be?" Agent Matthews asked.

"The right to be treated decent," Benson answered. "You can't just beat someone up for the hell of it."

"Now Agent Matthews I do recall this here Benson fella kickin' the hell out of the back of one of my cruisers. He was politely asked to stop and when he didn't and began yellin' profanities we did have to subdue him so he wouldn't hurt himself."

"I do recall you explaining that to me and being corroborated by my agents and your deputies that were on the scene."

"You fuckin' bastards. My boss is gonna rip you to pieces. He's an angry cuss all the way around," Benson hollered. He was trying to stand up but he, too, was in shackles and couldn't move much.

"Settle down sir," the sheriff ordered, "before you hurt yourself even more. We already had the paramedics here to take care of your wounds. They're still on the premises should they be needed."

"Fuck you and your mother to hell!" Benson yelled.

Matthews and the sheriff just stood there waiting for him to stop yelling and settle down.

Once he stopped Matthews got in his face and explained how Yuri did things with those of his crew that got arrested.

"Your boss, Yuri Strovonovich is a sick bastard. The worst kind. Sheriff Donohue, you have those pictures we showed the others? Please show them to Benson, or whatever his name is. As I explained to your pals, we have your ID in hand. It's not going to matter once you get into the federal prison system because your boss is going to have you murdered real quick. Seems he doesn't like his crew to say anything against him to cut a deal. You're going to get the death penalty anyway so if your boss kills you first it saves the tax payers quite a bit of money. Your boss had this guy torn to pieces while still alive. Could be you and your pals are next and this guy was in a maximum security solitary cell at the time in lockdown. Now, you try and figure out how they got to him 'cause that's what's gonna happen to you."

Benson took one look and threw up all over himself. Matthews ordered him cleaned up and put in another room. Once that was done the interrogation continued.

"What the hell were those pictures? You had them made up just to intimidate me," Benson said.

"No we didn't. They're real. I do believe the prisoner's name was Nick Gordon. Oh, so you do know who he was. I do believe it was his wife you thought you had taken at the cabin. Yup, thought so," Matthews said as he looked at Benson and saw him pale even more. He began to tremble.

"You're just trying to get me to talk. Not gonna happen. I want a lawyer now!" Benson demanded.

"Yes sir. We'll try to get you a lawyer but as I explained to your pals, seems no one wants to represent your kind as your boss keeps having them killed. The federal judges are not assigning anyone to these cases at this time. You'll just have to wait in prison like your pals," Matthews explained.

"Bullshit. I don't have to wait. The law gives me the right to a speedy trial and I want that now," Benson demanded.

"No, it doesn't when it comes to human trafficking involving young girls and young boys. You no longer have any rights at all," Matthews said in a quiet strong voice.

Benson just stared at him.

"We'll have him taken to a cell for the remainder of his time here," Sheriff Donohue said as he and Matthews left the room.

It took four deputies and agents to move Benson to his cell. He was a mean bastard and fought them all the way.

Matthews and Sheriff Donohue spent the next hour on a telecom call with most of the agencies involved around the globe. The three men were known throughout the world as Yuri's main killers for hire. They had been on the FBI and Interpol's most wanted list for the past few years. It was great to finally have them in custody. They had long lists of charges against them but these latest ones would land them on death row real fast with short dates for execution.

It was well past dawn when Matthews and Sheriff Donohue could finally take a break and sit down for a minute. It seems The Creek had heard what had happened in the night and Ted and Michael had sent breakfast to the entire sheriff's department as thanks.

Matthews and Donohue finally had a moment to eat.

"Those three are pure evil Matthews. I've seen some evil in my time but these are the worst. Just pure evil through and through. Glad they're off the streets."

"I agree. They're eyes are dead. Did you see that?" Matthews said as Donohue nodded in agreement. "Pure evil is right. The FBI is sending a secure transportation team to move them to the prison outside of D.C. They should be here later this afternoon. Our meeting went well. Anything else you can think of to add to the report?"

"Not right now. I'll get started and send a preliminary to you and the Virginia HQ guys as well as our state police. I'll finalize it in a day or two after I have time to think about it. The whole operation was recorded, sight and sound, so I'll send copies of the tapes to you later today. I have our tech guys working on them right now. No editing, just putting them on a single source file. They'll be sent to my boss and you and the state as soon as they're finished. We'll be going over them for a long while picking them apart for details. This should be an air tight case against these three demons."

"Agreed. Hey, not to change the subject, but Ted and Michael have outdone themselves. This is great," Matthews said as he continued to eat.

"It sure is. First rate. My Granddaddy would have said, 'Pure solid gold one hundred percent'. You woulda liked my granddaddy Matthews. He was a hard working, common sense kinda guy who knew how to have fun. He lived to be one hundred and two and drank a bit of the shine every day. I swear I can hear his voice from time to time; sometimes gentle, other times a bit loud and firm. I do miss him."

"Sounds like a great guy and I do believe I would have liked him. I can sense a bit of him in you Donohue. That no nonsense part. Well, I'm gonna take my team back to The Creek and get busy with our own paperwork. I'll be in touch." Matthews said as they finished their breakfast.

"Alrighty, Matthews. Give our thanks and regards to Ted and Michael for the food. Always a nice distraction when we don't have to deal with the scum of the Earth."

Matthews and his team left Boone and were back in The Creek by eight o'clock, just a few minutes after Emily and her group returned home. Matthews walked over to Emily's house wanting to meet with her and make sure she was OK.

As he walked into the kitchen Emily walked in from the living room.

"Hey Matthews. You look a little messed up. You OK?"

"Sure am, Emily. It's been a long night. Just wanted you to know those three men are in custody, in shackles, and in separate cells at the Sheriff's Department waiting for transport by the feds. They didn't say anything but we were able to ID them through their fingerprints. Seems they're the bad guy's three main murderers. We've been looking for them for the past two years. So, thanks for being the situation that brought them to our attention and their arrest."

"No problem. What else can I do for the feds?" Emily said in a wise ass kind of way.

"How about taking a few days to relax and rest? Maybe a massage and acupuncture with your favorite people?"

"Matthews, that's a great idea. How about tomorrow? And can they come here? I would feel safer if I didn't have to leave The Creek for a while except to go to my new house. I'd like to go over there this afternoon for a quick look around. OK?"

"Yes, I think that's a good idea. The whole Creek knows about last night so I'm sure they'd like to see that you're OK."

"Oh, I'm sure they already know. Ted brought breakfast over for all of us to make sure I was OK. He even said so. He's a sweetie, that Ted is. I assured them I was just the same only a bit tired. He believed me only after I ate breakfast," Emily explained as she laughed along with Matthews.

"I knew he was here checking up on you. It seems The Creek has taken you on as one of their own and I know for a fact they protect their own."

"I'm beginning to understand. And I'm sure you know Ethan called checking up on me as well. I'll let him know I'll be at the house later."

"OK. You know the team up there will be notified before that."

"I know. And thanks. Now, if you don't mind, I'd like to get a nap. The last few hours have been crazy."

"Sleep well. I'll check in with you later."

Emily waved as she left the kitchen. She was sound asleep just a few minutes later.

Matthews spent the next few hours gathering info on the night's activities and writing a report. A messenger delivered the downloaded tapes from that night and he started reviewing them. Those three were ruthless and so very stupid at the same time, he thought. The CSU was still going over their apartments and trucks. That would be a whole other part of the investigation that would add evidence, not only against them, but against Yuri as well. The whole case was finally falling into place, piece by piece.

Matthews wasn't convinced that they had seen the last of Yuri. Once Yuri found out that Barbara was still alive he would go ape shit trying to get to her. The agencies were ready for him, or so Matthews hoped. He thought about the conversation he had heard with Cora and the folks at the country store the day after the Fourth. Seems she was certain some other worldly forces were about to do battle on the mountain. Matthews wasn't sure anyone would ever be ready for something like that. He hoped the good guys would be watching out for The Creek should something like that ever take place.

He spent a few minutes thinking about good and evil then shook himself and got back to the work at hand.

CHAPTER 30

The talk at the store was all about the night's activities. Heck, the talk all over The Creek was about the night's activities. Everyone gathered at the store to hear and share news.

"Our Emily is alright. I went over this morning with breakfast and saw her for myself. She's gonna take a rest then go over to her house for a bit," Ted told the group that had gathered mid-morning.

"Good. She's a sweet thing, she is, and I wouldn't want anything to happen to her," Hal offered. "There's just something about her that makes ya wanna take care of her."

Heads nodded in agreement.

"Those guys that caused all the trouble last night are in jail in Boone. It was on the news this mornin'," someone added.

"They're gone and good riddance. I sure didn't like that Benson guy, or whoever he was, hangin' around here askin' all kinds of questions. I knew he was trouble from the start," Michael said.

"Hey Kendra," Hal said as she walked in the door.

"Hey Hal, y'all. Everyone OK this mornin'?" she asked.

"Yup."

"Sure"

Doin' mighty fine."

"Good. I hear Emily is, too," Kendra said as she got herself something cold to drink and joined the group at the oak table.

"Yes she is. I was just tellin' everyone I saw her a bit ago. She's napping right now," Ted added.

"What the hell is goin' on around here that these horrible people think she's some kinda threat?" Kendra asked no one in particular.

"Beats me. I can't figure it out either," Hal replied.

"For God's sake, this is The Creek. We don't do bad around here. We're just a bunch of mountain folk livin' our lives and takin' care of each other," one of the folks said. "Why would anyone think we were a part of some big espionage or drug-king world?"

"Beats me like I said. I don't get it either," Ted answered. He looked over at Michael and they passed a look between them. Kendra saw it and remained quiet about it.

"Hey y'all," Helena greeted everyone as she walked over to the table.

"Hey Helena. Where's Gary today?" Michael asked.

"Oh, he's home with the kids. He promised to put up that big ol' tent we have and let the kids play in it all summer. They've been at it for about an hour now so I thought I'd slip away for a few minutes of peace and quiet. Glad to see everyone's doin' well."

"We sure are. Hear about last night?" Kendra asked.

"Why, yes I did. Did ya ever? Right here in our little dell. Glad it's all over. We don't want to worry about the kids runnin' through the woods and the tourists and all. Whew. Sounds like it was crazy for a while."

"It must have been with the three of them in jail now and having to have those special agents and the sheriff's men to take them down," said George, one of their neighbors. "I bet it's all over the newspapers and that Internet tomorrow."

"It's already all over the Internet, George. The web doesn't need time to edit the writing. Most stuff shows up as its happening. There aren't any pictures of last night but there are pictures of a few of the guys they arrested. They look real mean if I do say so myself."

"Really? That fast, huh? Well, maybe I oughta get me one of those computers then. Don't want to be left behind the times. Michael, could you help me with that?"

"Sure George. You just let me know when you have time to sit for about an hour and I'm all yours," Michael said.

"OK. How much does one of those things cost anyway?"

"Well, George, anywhere from three hundred dollars up to thousands. You won't need the real expensive ones. I think a laptop would work well for you. We'll say from about four hundred to eight hundred. Will that be OK?"

"Sure. Sure. I got that in an old tin can in the barn," George teased back. "But really, that's OK. I can come up with that no problem. How about tomorrow afternoon around four or so. I gotta pick some supplies up in Pine Ridge and then I can meet with you here."

"Sure thing George. And welcome to the Twenty-first Century," Michael teased right back.

"I may be a simple country boy but I'm still willing to learn the latest in technology. Yes I am."

Everyone applauded George's decision to get a computer.

"It's about time George. I've been on the net for years myself," Hal said.

"Wonder if Cora would ever get one?" George asked.

"Probably not, knowing our Cora," Kendra offered. "I've been trying to get her to come over and take a look at mine. No way. She's happy with her TV and doesn't want to be bothered with anything else. She doesn't even have a cell phone. Gotta love her."

"So, what do ya think's gonna happen next? Any more bad things?" George put out there.

"Sure hope not,' Ted said.

People came and went all afternoon and into the evening talking about the crazy night. Emily woke up around mid-afternoon and took a long hot shower then fixed something to eat.

She settled with her laptop and played games and looked at landscaping plans to get more ideas.

There was a knock on her backdoor around eight o'clock and Ethan walked right into the living room, pulled her up into his arms and held her close for the longest time. She melted right into him and they stood with their arms wrapped around each other for a long while.

With a sigh he let her go and they sat down on the couch.

"Jesus Fucking Christ! What the hell went on around here last night?" Ethan asked.

"I don't really know. I wasn't here. I was taken to a safe place before all the craziness happened."

"I know. I know. I was just sayin'."

"Sure sounds like a whole lot of craziness happened in the woods. The agent pretending to be that Barbara person got roughed up. I guess she was slapped or punched in the face and she got beat up a bit. Matthews says she's really OK. She sent a note around telling the agents and me that she was OK."

"Those men were stupid to think they could get away with anything around here. Guess they didn't do their homework very well."

"Guess not."

"Just glad you're alright. God, I don't know what I'd do if anything happened to you."

"Really?"

"Oh, yes. Really."

He pulled Emily close and they sat there for a minute before he turned to her and kissed her gently.

"Yes. Really," Ethan said quietly. "So, what are you doing?"

"I was just looking at more landscape designs. I want to see as many as I can so when it comes time to decide on what I want I have some ideas to think about.

"Oh. Want some company?"

"Sure. Look at this one. It's on a hill and I like some of the rock garden ideas. I'm thinking about something like this for the southwest edge where the meadow meets the woods. There are going to be so many rocks around that I'm thinking of a having a stone wall made for that part of the property. Probably from near the pond around the south end then west up to the hot springs in the back northwest area. How does that sound? Do you think I have enough rocks to build one that long?"

"Well, I do think you have enough for that idea. Probably about three feet high. You should have enough. I'll get the Kirkland's design guy out and we'll work on it. There are going to be more rocks as we settle the driveway and re-plant the old access road."

"Oh Great! Let's look at some more."

They spent a couple of hours looking at designs for gardens and stone walls and even fixed popcorn along the way. Emily started to yawn so Ethan called it a night.

"Emily, it's time for you to get some sleep."

"I guess so. I can't seem to stop yawning. I think the last twenty four hours have caught up with me," she said as she yawned again.

"Come on, I'll tuck you in," Ethan said with a grin.

"Oh sure you will and I suppose you'll be joining me?"

"Is that an invitation?"

"Yes."

"I accept."

They got into bed and Ethan gathered Emily in his arms. "Sleep for you tonight. Other things will have to wait."

She turned and kissed him so long and hard he thought he had died and gone to heaven. She put her head on his chest and fell sound asleep. He held her all night long and they woke up with the sun the next morning.

As Matthews settled in for the night he had a smile on his face. Good for her he thought. It's about time the two of them stopped fighting the inevitable.

Ethan and Emily got up early the next day and Ethan left to go home and get ready for work. Emily would go out to her build site later. Matthews continued with the follow-up from the arrests of Yuri's men. Kendra was busy completing paperwork for three more clients who were buying homes in the Pine Ridge area.

Cora was busy writing down her thoughts about the UFOs and what they meant. She soon saw a pattern emerge. It seems that every time there was a battle of sorts that involved the mountain these UFOs and lights showed up closer and closer together. She was looking at her grandmother's notes when she saw the pattern. Seems there was a time in her young childhood when such a battle took place. That would put it around the 1940's. There was a group of moonshiners scattered throughout the mountains that did very well back then. They had escaped the revenuers for decades and kept on making and selling their shine. They were wealthy even by today's economy. They kept their money at home. They didn't trust the banks. They had all been through the Depression.

In the summer of 1945 the world saw the end of WW II in Europe, and in August of that summer the moonshine boys were in a heated battle to stay ahead of the revenuers. The government had targeted the mountain folk and wanted to put an end, once and for all, to the illegal making and selling of moonshine. One by one the old stills were found and destroyed, and the owners were arrested. Most of them only spent thirty days in jail. A few of them were never found.

These folks and their ancestors had been guarding the magic of the mountain for hundreds of years and to have their only source of income taken from them for the greed and power of the government caused great sorrow and chaos. The mountain wept as these harsh changes took place.

One thing about these mountain men: if they didn't want to be found they wouldn't be. One of the most epic confrontations occurred with the great-granddaddies of Bubba and Earl, known to all as Samuel and Archie. These two old mountain men were known for their superior shine. The revenuers thought they only had one still, and that's exactly what Samuel and Archie wanted them to believe. It was a small one that only produced a gallon or two of shine at a time. The big one was so well hidden that not even the most experienced mountain man could find it. The mountain kept their secret.

The revenuers found the small still and smashed it to pieces. They knew it belonged to Samuel and Archie but didn't have any hard evidence. This last battle to find evidence took place on a bright summer's day in August. The mountain folk knew the revenuers were coming that morning. They had seen lights in the night sky over a place where a grove of Applewood trees stood. The mountain folks knew this was a sign from the stories that had been handed down throughout the generations. The lights had started about a year before and they appeared more and more frequently as the summer wore on. By July, they were seen almost every other night by one or two of the folks.

So, on this August morning after the lights had been seen in the old Applewood grove every day for seven days, they all knew the battle was about to begin. And so it did. Just at dawn the revenuers burst into the cabin they thought belonged to Samuel and Archie. Unfortunately for them, it was empty except for a family of bears that lived there. The revenuers were so surprised they stood stock still for a moment until the mama bear began to growl and move towards them. The revenuers turned tail and took off through the woods as fast as they could. The mama bear only chased them for a minute then she returned to the cabin and her two cubs.

The revenuers finally stopped running to catch their breath and realized they were back at their trucks empty handed. They were mad as could be. They took their time and came up with a new plan. They decided to search every cabin in a five mile radius no matter how long it took. This meant they would be bothering folks that had absolutely nothing to do with moonshine. The first few homes they attacked were heavily damaged as they broke down the doors and broke all the windows trying to surprise the men and keep them from escaping. These were simple country folk with their families. Samuel and Archie were nowhere to be found. The owners of the homes and cabins raised their shotguns at the revenuers, threatening to kill them if they didn't leave.

Word got around faster than the revenuers could move and when they approached the next few cabins they were met with raised shotguns and buckshot. They were getting angrier as the day went on and so was the mountain. Seems this mountain, known to the locals as Moonshine Mountain, had a bit of magic in her. She decided to take control of the battle to protect her guardians, the mountain folk. To this day folks will tell you that the mountain began to speak. The wind began to whisper and the sky began to darken. The revenuers wanted revenge against the mountain folk. They were sure these folks were hiding Samuel and Archie and making the revenuers look like fools.

But the mountain had other plans. The mountain folk knew she was about to fight back against the invaders so they gathered their livestock and belongings and headed inside. They knew some fierce weather was about to come down the mountain. The revenuers were not paying attention to the weather. They wanted Samuel and Archie. Just as they were about to break down the door of a small cabin set way back in a hollow, the mountain spoke. She rumbled and shook something fierce. The revenuers were thrown to the ground. They got up and looked all around as they thought someone had set off an explosion. They looked around and couldn't see any smoke or fire.

They shook their heads and decided to keep going. Just as they were ready, again, to break down the door, the mountain spoke again. This time she shook so hard a few old dead trees near the cabin came crashing down throwing the revenuers to the ground again. This time some of the men started saying how maybe this wasn't the right place to be and they should all head home. The man in charge told them to do as they were ordered.

So, they attempted to break the door down a third time. This time Father Sky let loose. He sent a bolt of lightning to the ground and it surrounded the revenuer's group.

They were knocked unconscious and a couple of them were killed. The leader of the group lost his hearing and was terrified. He yelled at the others to get out of there, leaving the dead men there. He would send someone for them later. As they were all running back to their trucks a great wind and driving rain was let loose upon the mountain, but only where the revenuers were. When they got to their trucks they had to sit there and wait for the rain to let up. It finally did but it sent a torrent of water along a small creek that ran over the road. Their trucks were swept into the creek and were found about two miles down the mountain in the creek bed. Only thing was, the creek bed was just a little trickle of a thing and the land around them was dry. Legend has it that the mountain and Father Sky created the storm just to get the revenuers away from the folks.

It seems the revenuers got the message loud and clear. They never came back to arrest Samuel and Archie. The official report states these two men must have perished in the sudden storm that came over the mountain that day. No one in the revenuer's office questioned the report even though they knew it hadn't rained a drop that day on the mountain. The two men who died were recovered and their deaths were labeled as accidental.

Samuel and Archie kept right on making their shine in their big still hidden on the mountain and to this day Bubba and Earl use the same still that's in the same location as it always has been: hidden deep in the protective love of the mountain.

Cora sat back and let out a sigh. She knew deep in her soul another battle was due. The lights had been seen by a lot of folks on July 4th and wasn't it smart of those ETs to play in the fireworks like that. She laughed out loud. Gotta give 'em credit for their craftiness. She knew the battle would take place in August and that the ancient Magic of the mountain would be used once again. Only thing was she didn't know what the battle was for and who was involved. She had a strong hunch it had something to do with Emily and why Emily had chosen to live here or why this place had been chosen for her. She knew the ancient Magic was involved. She felt restless and apprehensive and knew these feelings wouldn't go away until the battle was finished.

Ah, well... she thought as she put her journal and the old papers away. Time would tell as it always had.

CHAPTER 31

The next three weeks saw a lot of tourists come to the mountain. The country store was busy from the minute it opened until long after it closed as Ted and Michael wrapped things up for the day and prepared for the next. They had hired six of the local teenagers to help and this made a big difference.

Emily's house, barn and stables were now weather tight and the interior work had begun. She had finalized the color for the house and it was being painted during these last few days of July. The other buildings would be painted when the house was finished. Jordan had decided on the design for his house and barn and the excavation had taken place with the forms in place and ready for the concrete to be poured during the last couple of days of the month.

Jordan was about to send in his mortgage payment when he got a phone call from his bank. Seems his account was empty. The balance was zero. The bank had no idea how this had happened. Jordan had transferred more than fifty thousand dollars two days earlier from his special savings account to his checking account. He asked them to check on the transfer and his savings account. They did and told him both accounts were at a zero balance without any evidence of him withdrawing the money. They had no idea what had happened to his funds and they would begin an investigation right away.

Jordan was pissed and scared. How was he supposed to pay his mortgage and bills without any money? The bank had better find his money and fast. He still had eight days to make the mortgage payment. He decided to wait to hear from the bank before he would decide what to do next.

Emily was at her house watching them paint. It was wicked cool she thought, to be able to watch your house take on its own character right in front of your eyes. She had asked if she could help and the painters let her paint most of the front clapboard. The floor boards were southern yellow pine set like tongue and groove flooring, all mismatched. The rails system was being attached while the painting was going on. The rockers and swings she had ordered had arrived the day before and were being stored in a shed the crew had built. It was portable and they told her they could have it moved wherever she wanted when the build was over. It was good sized and being used to store supplies and equipment during the build.

She painted all morning without knowing how much time had passed. She was a bit surprised to see Ethan on the porch next to her. She had painted the whole right side and was ready to take on the left side.

"Hey there, Miss painter lady. It's lunch time. Your agents are getting a kick out of watching you work. I think they may even be placing bets on how much you get done," Ethan teased.

"Wise ass!"

"Yup, that's me. Come on. Let's join the others for lunch. Your group's already on their way over here with your stuff. Let's sit under the canopy. The sun's really hot today even here on the mountain. Looks like we might be brewing some thunderstorms for tomorrow."

"OK. Thanks guys," Emily said as her bodyguards joined them all under the canopy. "So, now you're a meteorologist. Great. I guess I don't need the weather channel anymore. Fellas, just ask Ethan here about the weather before you make your outdoor plans."

Ethan threw a rolled up paint towel at her. She blocked it saying, "Way too quick for you Sutherland. Now eat."

They spent a nice lunch time chatting and eating and teasing all around. As Emily looked at the house she felt happy and proud to have had a hand in creating it. She spent the afternoon painting the front left side of the first floor.

When the painters left around four, she was still painting. They left her the supplies she would need. She finally finished around five-thirty. She took a few steps back and looked at her work.

"Not bad if I may say so myself," she told no one in particular.

Emily took a moment to realize it was quiet in the meadow. She looked around and realized she was the only one working. Her bodyguards, with Ethan, were standing in front of the house watching her.

They applauded as she came down the front steps. She took several bows.

She noticed the railing system was in place along the front of the porch so she stepped onto the ground and turned to look at it.

"Wow! This is really looking good. It already has so much character and charm even if the rest of the house isn't painted yet. Can't wait for the doors and shutters to be painted blue and the white trim to be in place. And the railings are going to be so cool!"

They all laughed with her and spent quite some time talking about the details that would make the house look even better. They finally gathered their things together and headed for their trucks. It was well past six and everyone was hungry.

"I have an idea guys. How about we all descend on the country store for pizza and beer. I'll call Ted and he can get things started," Ethan suggested to the group.

"Sounds good to me."

"I'm in."

"Me, too," Emily said. "Everybody in?"

All said yes. Pizza varieties were discussed and Ethan placed the call. They would all meet at the store after getting cleaned up.

Thirty minutes later they burst through the door laughing and teasing each other and headed for the oak table. Ted had just set four pizzas on the table. They all grabbed a drink and supper was underway.

They talked about the house and the meadow. The rock pile was getting bigger due to the digging for the well. It was going to be a back up to the county water line that had been laid from the main road and hooked up already. It was capped and would be opened as soon as the finish plumbing was completed. That would be in about three to five days. The building inspector had begun to stop by every morning just because, as he said, it was easier for everyone. This way they wouldn't have to be making phone calls trying to find him. He said the Sutherland boys were keeping him quite busy this summer. Someone asked about the covered bridge.

Ethan told them they were ready to order the lumber and hardware for the cover. The cover would be built on site in the meadow and a crane would place it on the support frame. He said Karl was thinking it might be ready in about four weeks. By then they didn't think they'd need any more heavy equipment on site. They'd decided to keep the old access road in place but would place a bar fence across it so no one would be able to use it unless Emily gave the OK.

Ethan mentioned that he had noticed the pond had cleared and every morning he saw ducks and birds on it. He had stayed late one night and was getting ready to leave around eight-thirty, just about twilight, when he saw a family of raccoons drinking from the edge.

This made Emily happy that the disruption of the Earth for her sake had given the creatures a new place to drink from and live.

The group broke up a while later and Emily and Ethan walked over to Emily's house.

"Ethan, that was one of the best ideas you've ever had," Emily said.

"Really? Well, then I agree. Ah, Emily, how about coming over to my place later. We could watch a movie and just relax. You've had a busy day."

"Ethan, I like that idea. OK. Let me get cleaned up and I'll be over in a while. I'll clear it with Matthews so he can make arrangements for my group."

"OK. Later," Ethan said as he bent his head and kissed her lightly on those luscious lips of hers. He went off and Emily walked into her house talking to Matthews.

"Hey, Matthews. No need to call since you can hear every little thing that goes on in here. I'm headed over to Ethan's as soon as I get cleaned up. Some of us had a busy, physical kinda day."

Matthews walked in the back door and said, "Well, good for you!" He started laughing at the sight of her. "I guess you did. But I gotta say you really don't have much paint on you at all. Not bad for a novice."

"Listen Mr. Special Agent smart ass, I'll have you know I've been painting houses since I was a kid."

"OK. OK. I give. I'll have the arrangements set by the time you're ready to go for as long as you need them."

"Thanks, Matthews. Much appreciated. Do the agents have to be in the house?"

"Yes, but they'll stay away from wherever you are. Out of sight only. And Emily, I'm glad things are working out for you two. You look real good together."

"Thanks. I think so, too."

Matthews left and an hour later Emily was on the road to Ethan's. Agent Marks was off duty so one of the others was driving her with two more agents in the Jeep. They were being followed by a second vehicle with another three agents armed and ready.

Ethan heard them drive up and was outside waiting for Emily. He waved at the agents then ushered Emily into the kitchen where he gently pushed her against the counter and kissed her as if he hadn't seen her for years. She kissed him right back running her hands under his shirt and through his hair.

"Now that's what I call a warm welcome," Emily said pressed against Ethan's mouth.

"Is there any other kind?" Ethan replied as he took a step back. "How about a movie? What are ya in the mood for?"

"Got the Blues Brothers?"

"Yes I do. Let's take this popcorn up to the movie theatre. I have your favorite drinks waiting for you there."

"And that would be?"

"Sierra Mist and IBC root beer."

"Correct on both counts," Emily said as they walked into the home theatre room.

"Ready?" Ethan asked as Emily settled into her soft leather seat.

"Let 'er rip."

They spent the next couple of hours singing with the Blue Brothers and laughing at their antics. When the movie was over Ethan turned to Emily.

"Anything else you want to see," he said with a grin on his face.

"Yes. You," Emily answered softly.

"Follow me," Ethan said.

Emily followed Ethan into his bedroom and came to a sudden stop. There were flowers everywhere and candles were glowing all around the room. The bed was turned down and a beautiful purple rose lay on the pillow.

"Oh my. This is beautiful," was all Emily could whisper.

"All for you Emily. You've had a rough few weeks and I thought a little pampering was more than due."

Emily walked around the room looking at the flowers and candles and Ethan.

She came back to where Ethan was standing and just looked at him. She pointed to the bath and was gone for a few minutes. When she came back she was wearing his bath robe which was way too big for her.

"You look real cute there Miss Emily. I think you could use that as a blanket."

"It's quite cozy Mr. Ethan."

Ethan led her to the bed saying, "Shall we see if it'll cover both of us?"

Emily dropped the robe. She was wearing a short silky nightshirt in the most sultry shade of dark blue that just barely covered her assets.

"Whew!" Was all Ethan could say.

He took her in his arms and began kissing her. First her lips, then her eyes, moving all around her face. He then let his tongue trail along her neck to the place where her night shirt revealed the soft and full curve of her breast. Emily sighed and began trailing her hands along Ethan's chest down to his belly. He shuddered and decided to move them onto the bed.

He removed most of his clothes as he lay Emily across the soft satin sheets. He resumed his discovery of her breast. He unbuttoned her nightshirt and spread it open so he could look at her and make love to her breasts. He began by kissing first one then the other. Then he began trailing his tongue across them before he let his tongue begin the soft play across her nipples, first one then the other. They were tight and beautifully pink.

Emily felt like she was melting. Her body was responding to Ethan's touch in ways she never knew it could. She felt like liquid heat was coming from deep within spreading along her body to her most sensitive place. She felt hot and wet there and she could feel a pulsing sensation that she wanted to keep going forever. She thought she was going to explode if Ethan didn't take her. He kept his love making slow. He wanted her to feel things she had never felt before. Just when she thought she couldn't stand one more minute he began licking her nipples again. First one then the other. She grabbed his head and pushed him onto her breast. He took her breast into his mouth and began to suck. Emily lost all contact with reality. She was floating on a wave of heat and sensations she had only ever fantasized about. Ethan began to suck more strongly as his hand started to travel along her belly to her mound. He spread her legs and touched her and found her wet and hot. She moaned and began to push against his fingers.

He brought her to her first climax while sucking her breast and barely touching her sensitive spot. She rose up off the bed as her climax possessed her. He kept sucking her breast until she fell back and the climax left her. She opened her eyes and found him watching her. She smiled and closed them again as he began trailing his tongue down her belly to her soft mound then he opened her and began to kiss and lick her.

Emily wasn't sure how much more of this she could take. She wanted to feel his hard cock inside of her. She began stroking his hair until she couldn't hold back. Once again he brought her to climax and this time he didn't stop licking her until she called out his name.

"Ethan! On my God. I need you inside me. Don't make me wait another second."

"Anything you say."

He pulled away and moved over her. She looked at him and took hold of his hard cock and began to play with it. Ethan moaned out loud. He let her keep touching him until he knew he would lose it. He moved her hand and lowered himself between her legs. She opened them and raised them to allow him in. She held onto his cock as she guided him to her place and then pulled him down into her. He began to enter her slowly at first. He didn't want to hurt her and he wanted both of them to enjoy each other as long as they could. He felt like he had come home. She was hot and wet and soft. He picked up the pace a bit moving from side to side as he pushed in and slowly pulled back just a bit. With each thrust he went deeper. Emily began to push up to meet his thrusts and they moved in harmony. She felt her climax beginning and wrapped her legs around Ethan pushing against him harder and stronger. He felt her climax a second before she did and he began to thrust hard and fast as he moved deeper into her. She began to buck and writhe as he thrust faster and deeper until he couldn't hold off any longer.

They climaxed together falling over the edge into that sweet abyss of pure sensations. As their climax began to soften they lay entwined in each other's arms for a long time. As Emily began to return to reality, she opened her eyes and found Ethan looking at her.

"Hmm. Delicious. Holy God, Ethan you're amazing. I don't know if I'll ever be able to move again."

"You are so beautiful Emily. I can honestly say I've never felt anything like this before."

He began to move away but she kept her grip on him. He was instantly hard and she made sure he didn't move away.

She began to move on him so he closed his eyes and simply enjoyed her. She began to get excited again and he felt the change. He moved onto his back and she rolled with him keeping them together. She began to ride him hard as she was close to climaxing again. He put his finger on her clit and massaged her to her climax as she pushed hard into him. He pushed up into her and they reached their climax together again. He held her close so she could be free to move as she wanted to. As she came down from her climax she fell to the side of Ethan.

"I think I'm gonna need to work out at the gym if we're gonna keep up this pace. I can't seem to get enough of you."

"I'm singing the same tune Emily."

He rolled over to her and held her close for a few minutes as they calmed down.

"I know this is going to sound crazy but I'm really hungry. Can we raid the fridge? If I can even walk. Man what have you done to me, Sutherland? You truly are amazing. It's like you're connected with me on a soul level."

"Glad to accommodate you. Anytime. Really, I think you must be right on with the soul thing. I can't even begin to describe what just happened. You truly do have complete possession of my heart and soul. And I don't mind telling you that scares me to death… in a good way."

"Same here. I don't even know how to think about this so I'm just gonna let it be. If we can begin to untangle ourselves, I'll head for the bath then we can go raid that fridge."

"Deal," Ethan agreed as they got themselves out of bed. They headed down to the kitchen a few minutes later. The agents were nowhere to be seen but they both knew they were in the house. For tonight Emily tuned out the whole crazy out-to-kill-her thing and tuned in one hundred percent to her and Ethan and the magic they were sharing.

They spent some time in the kitchen eating, kissing and touching each other. When they were finished with their snack, they headed back to the bedroom and made long slow love again until they fell asleep in each other's arms.

They slept until the morning sun woke them. They made love again, showered, and then dressed for the day.

Breakfast was made and the agents were invited to join them. Emily had called Matthews to tell him about the breakfast thing so the agents wouldn't feel awkward.

They all sat down at the table and enjoined a big country breakfast.

Ethan and Emily parted ways as he went off to her build site and she headed home with her agents.

Kendra was just leaving her house when she saw Emily arrive home. She came over with a look on her face that begged the question about where Emily had been.

"Come on in Kendra," Emily said as they walked into the kitchen.

"Oh God I can't wait another second. Were you with Ethan all night? Are you two finally together for good? Spill!"

Emily laughed at Kendra as she answered her. "Yes to everything."

Kendra hugged Emily as she said, "It's about time. The whole Creek's been wondering when this would finally happen. I'm so happy for you two. WOW! This is great."

"Thanks for being my own personal cheerleader."

"Well, I just had to know and now I have to get going. I'm meeting one of my clients at their bank to take possession of their down payment for their new home near Pine Ridge. Actually, they're paying for the whole thing then they're going to hire Ethan to remodel and add on. This has already been a great day and it's only seven o'clock in the morning. Woo Hoo!"

Emily laughed with Kendra. "Glad to help out. See ya later."

Matthews was at his desk smiling about all this but not for long. He was about to call in to a teleconference to learn about the latest developments.

He knew that the thing with Yuri's men was only the beginning. Intercepted telecommunications throughout the world showed things were escalating. The Directors of the FBI, Interpol, the U. S. Marshals Service and other agencies were working to build a strategy to stop Yuri once and for all.

"This is FBI Chief Wallace here. Let's bring everyone up to date. The three men arrested and detained in North Carolina were transported, arraigned and are being held in the federal maximum security prison outside of Baltimore. They have not been assigned attorneys because the federal judge is holding them on terrorist charges and has great concern for anyone connected with them as others have been murdered and gone missing. We have been intercepting communications both electronic and written from Yuri Strovonovich and his allies directing them to find and kill Barbara Gordon. They have targeted Crab Apple Creek from a somewhat questionable photo match Yuri received from Jones during the UFO incident. When our technicians looked at the photo and compared it to that of Barbara from the first time Nick Gordon met her, they concluded that there was a vague match. That is what Strovonovich is going on. Now, put the current picture of Barbara next to the photo match and they do not have much in common. Only the eyes could be thought to be somewhat similar. Our client looks healthier and all the other matching points do not fit."

"That being said, Strovonovich is still bent on finding our client in Crab Apple Creek. Matthews, I agree with you that those three men were just the beginning of Strovonovich's crusade. His communications are now targeting the financial status of anyone in the greater Boone area, within a fifty mile radius. We're looking at land and home purchases that have taken place in the last forty-five days. There seems to be about twenty of them with three in the immediate area. So far everything looks stable. We're also looking at new employees in the trades. All the employees of Sutherland builders are being checked for connections for the past ten years and any new friends in the last sixty days. So far everything checks out. This bastard has his hands in everything. I swear if I didn't know better I'd say he sold his soul to the devil. We've shut down a number of his prostitution houses around the world in the last five days. Forty-three to be exact. We're continuing with that operation. I'm sure we are pissing this guy off so he'll probably make his move in Crab Apple Creek soon. We've set up a tactical command post just north of Barbara's new home site. It's on the same road about three miles north in an old farm house just like the one in Virginia. They're already there. Matthews, you already have all the specs on this."

"Yes, Sir, I do and we've already met and are fully operational."

"Thank, Matthews. They moved in late last night. The folks in this area are a bit protective of their own and they've included Barbara in this group. We witnessed this during the holiday festivities. I've never seen anything quite like this group of people before."

"You've all been briefed on the plan when this goes down. Your unit commanders will keep you all informed of any changes. Good job all around. Sam, why don't you say a few words on what you've found."

"Thanks Chief. I've received reliable intel that Strovonovich is restless and acting paranoid, among other things. He seems to have been scared by something. One of our inside contacts says he looks like hell most of the time. We know he doesn't use the drugs he handles but he does like his aged scotch. He has reportedly given the order to abduct about a hundred young girls between the ages of fifteen and seventeen for his prostitution rings. Since we have and are continuing to shut those down we think he is also trafficking for private sales. We have him being watched around the clock as well as watching his top twenty contacts world-wide. No other info is available right now."

"Thanks Sam. I'll keep everyone posted as new intel comes in."

Matthews ended the call and sat back thinking about this new information. He had his own hunches about this whole thing. He felt there must be something otherworldly involved to bring about a global coordination of trouble. He spent the next few hours coordinating the security details around The Creek and the plans for a counter attack when it became necessary.

Emily took a nap after her busy night with Ethan.

Ethan was busy on her site when it happened.

CHAPTER 32

A
t exactly twelve-noon the mountain began to fight back against the evil it knew was heading its way. The mountain began to speak.

An earthquake shook the area for about one minute knocking things off shelves, breaking windows and setting off alarms. The water in the ponds and lakes grew waves that washed over their edges about six feet and the creeks flowed backwards for just a few seconds then surged downhill at twice their speed and with three times the volume they usually carried. People driving along the mountain roads were pushed to the sides of the roads without warning. Dead trees crashed down.

Emily's site seemed to be near the center of the quake. The buildings swayed but sustained no damage. The supplies on the meadow fell over and one of the crew happened to be by the pond when it suddenly grew white caps and spilled over its southeastern edge. Vehicles rocked a bit but no damage was visible.

Ethan and some of the interior crew were in the house when the quake hit. They got off ladders and just stood on the floor holding onto the walls for support. They all ran outside as the quake subsided to check on each other.

"What in the name of God was that?" One of the painters asked.

"It was an earthquake," Ethan answered. "I was in a couple when I was in California a few years back. I never thought I'd feel one hit this mountain. Is everyone OK?"

The crew had all gathered by the boulder. They reported no injuries and no damage to the building's interior.

"Jesus! Let's just stay here for a spell 'cause there's usually aftershocks and some can be as strong as the original quake," Ethan told them.

They decided to take lunch and spent the next hour eating and waiting in case another trembler came along.

"OK. Looks like we'll be good for a while. Let's go as a group to inspect the house and the barn and stables from outside to inside."

The crew spent the next hour checking the foundations and structures and found no damage anywhere. They walked to the pond and found it without damage as well. It hadn't changed shape and the water level looked the same.

"I'm gonna take a walk down to the pond. Charlie, you come with me. The rest of you can get back to whatever you were doing before the quake."

Ethan's phone rang as he and Charlie started their walk around the pond.

"Hey Matthews, no damage here. How about with you guys?"

"Everyone's OK. A few things smashed at the store when they fell off the shelves but everything else is good. The gas pump and holding tank are intact. No fires have been reported. The U.S. Geological Society contacted me. They're sending a full crew our way. They say the center was just a few steps northwest of Emily's place so expect company any minute. They've been cleared by the FBI. Call me if anything weird happens at the site with anyone or anything."

"Yes, Sir, Matthews. This is the weirdest thing. And, we haven't had any aftershocks. That's the strangest thing of all."

"I'm thinkin' the same thing Ethan. I wonder if all the stuff Cora was talking about is for real and about to happen. Can't keep it off my mind."

"I'm thinkin' the same thing, Matthews. I'll bet a lot of us are. I'll go see Cora this afternoon."

"OK. Later."

Ethan and Charlie continued their walk around the pond. Ethan was headed to the place where the pond went back into the earth. He had an inkling that this had been changed by the earthquake, and that the earthquake was created by the Magic of the mountain. He believed all the stories Cora had told them since he was a small kid. The only other time the mountain had quaked was back in the Forties when the revenuers were in town.

Ethan walked very carefully once they reached the southern end of the pond.

"Charlie, it gets real soft and mucky here so stay behind me. I got a hunch the quake changed something down this way."

"I get ya Ethan. That was no real earthquake. The mountain's talking again. Just like Miss Cora's been telling us since we were kids."

"Here. The flow's changed. It used to go back into the earth over there by that marker Emily and I made when we first found it. Now it goes underground right here. It's a good ten feet to the west of the original spot. I'll mark it."

"Now that's something I've never seen before. Just like that it just goes underground. Awesome!"

Ethan took the stake and flag he had brought with him and placed it next to where the stream went underground.

"That's a huge change Ethan. Ya don't have to be a geologist to figure that out."

"I agree Charlie. When the USGS folks get here, I'll bring them down here and explain the pond. They should be here real soon. Let's get back to the house."

They got back to the house at about the same time an official USGS truck towing a trailer pulled in followed by another truck.

Ethan waved them over to a safe place to park.

"Hi y'all," Ethan said as the USGS crew got out of their trucks.

"I'm Ethan Sutherland in charge of this project. I've lived on the mountain my whole life. So ask me anything you want. We'll all help you with whatever you may need."

"Nice to meet you Ethan. I'm Rich Parker, senior geologist for this investigation. And, may I just say that house is absolutely gorgeous. I've never seen anything like it before. Beautiful, strong and full of charm all at once. The color scheme is something I recognize from the East Coast, just like Cape Cod. Love it."

Everyone made similar comments.

"Thanks everyone. I'll be sure to tell the owner. It was her idea all the way with a little help from my brother Ian, our architect and engineer. But about the quake... it felt strong right here but nothing was damaged. You can take a look at the foundations and buildings just like we did. We haven't noticed any changes or little cracks anywhere."

"Thanks, Ethan. It'll take a while to set up our equipment. Can we set a tent over by the rock piles?"

"How about closer to the boulder? Wouldn't want anything to happen to anyone near the rocks."

"Good idea. The center is just a few steps to the northwest of the property line and about a mile down. That's what our preliminary findings are. We'll fine tune the details now that we're on the site."

"Wow. Really close. Let me know if you need anything else. Feel free to use the portable facilities. We have electricity here and the water's being connected tomorrow morning. If wet weather comes in please feel free to set up in the barn. Just stay clear of any plumbing fixtures. When you get a minute Rich, I'd like to take you for a walk near the pond. There is something I think you should see."

"OK. I'll come find you and thanks for the use of the barn. I'll tell the crew."

Ethan returned to the house and the USGS crew spent the rest of the afternoon setting up. They took a few readings late in the afternoon just as the first aftershock rumbled through. It was not as strong as the initial quake but was felt by everyone.

The folks in The Creek were all charged up. They began to gather at the country store shortly after the quake and it wasn't soon before most everyone was there.

"Here it comes just like Miss Cora said it would."

"The mountain's startin' to talk again," Hal said.

"Anyone get hurt? No one up my way," one of the local farmers asked.

"I don't think so. Hey, anyone get hurt?" Michael asked the crowd.

The general responses were no, all around.

"Had some stuff fall outta my cabinets. Broke a few dishes when they hit the floor," someone offered.

"Me, too. Just a few things fell off the shelves and broke."

"A plant hit the floor and the pot shattered. I was able to save the plant though."

"Well, OK then. We can always replace things," Ted replied.

"Why don't we all help Ted and Michael clean things up. We'll keep a list of the stuff that's broken," Hal suggested.

Everyone agreed and the cleanup started while they all continued to talk about the earthquake.

"Ya know, there are usually tremors or aftershocks so be prepared folks," Michael warned.

Heads nodded in response.

Emily wasn't sure about what had just happened. She got up from the floor where she landed during the quake. The agents were helping her up before she knew they were even there.

"What the fuck was that?" she said.

"If I get my guess right it was an earthquake," Agent Marks answered.

"An earthquake up here? Are you kidding?"

"No. I've been through a few recently and this is just what they feel like. I'd say this was somewhere around a 4.0 with stuff falling off shelves. You OK, Emily? Anything broken?"

"No Agent Marks I think I'm OK. Just a bit surprised. I guess I'll have a bruise or two from the fall but nothing more. Is everyone else OK?"

"Yes, Ma'am. Matthews is on his way over."

Emily looked up as the back door flew open.

"Emily, you OK?" Matthews walked over to her to make sure she wasn't hurt.

"Yes Matthews. See, everything moves just fine," she said with a laugh as she danced around in a circle moving her arms and legs.

"Funny Emily. Agents, I guess that was an earthquake. About a four wouldn't you say?"

"That's my guess," Agent Marks agreed.

"I agree."

"Felt like a four to me, too."

"First quake for me. I'll go along with you experienced folks."

"Strange to have one here, ya think?"

"I'm about to get a call from the USGS. The Chief says they're gonna send a team here. They're all being cleared now. Oh..., that's probably the chief now," Matthews said as his cell phone chirped.

Matthews walked into one of the bedrooms and was back just a few minutes later.

"We should expect a USGS crew of five here in about thirty minutes. I need to call Ethan. Seems the epicenter was just a few yards from your place Emily. Get packed and we'll head up there in about ten minutes. I'm calling Ethan now."

"You read my mind Matthews," Emily said as she began to pack her backpack.

A few minutes later Matthews came back into the kitchen.

"Ethan says not one little thing was damaged at your build. Not even tiny cracks in the foundations. Nothing. Rather odd. A 4.0 or higher usually leaves a tiny crack or two somewhere in a foundation. Hmm. This whole thing is adding up to not your usual earthquake. It's been fifteen minutes and there hasn't been one aftershock. Odd. Ready Emily? Team? Let's go."

They arrived at the site twenty minutes later. They saw a few trees down along the road and a few boulders that had rolled down the mountain stopping at the road side. Nothing else.

They arrived a few minutes before the USGS crew. Ethan was no-where to be seen. Emily asked one of the crew where he was and was told he and Charlie were taking a walk around the pond to see if anything had been changed by the quake. Emily knew immediately what he was looking for: the place where the water went back underground. She'd bet her new house on it. Just as she saw Ethan and Charlie coming around the pond a truck pulling a trailer came into the meadow followed by another truck that had the USGS seal on their doors. They were from the United States Geological Society. Ethan was directing them where to park.

"Emily, let's allow Ethan to take care of them and we'll take a look at the house and barns," Matthews suggested.

"Good idea. Let's go to the house first," Emily replied.

Ethan saw Emily across the meadow and waved. She waved back as she went up onto her porch.

She and the team spent quite a bit of time looking at the walls and floors on all levels of the house. They had all been painted and looked OK to her. No cracks. The floors were still just the rough flooring but they looked OK, too. They walked all around the basement with flashlights and could not find one little crack in the foundation anywhere.

When they came out of the house Ethan was just walking up onto the porch.

Emily, her group, and Ethan's crew all reported the same thing. No damage of any kind.

One of Ethan's men came over from the barn and reported the same thing.

"Well, then, it's too late to start any new stuff so let's call it a day. Take care of your own families and let me know if you need anything. See y'all at the usual time tomorrow."

The crew left Emily, Ethan, and the agents standing on the porch.

"I was told you went down to the southern end of the pond. Want to take me over there?" Emily asked Ethan.

"You bet, but let me get Rich from the USGS team. He's in charge and I think he should know about this. Although I'm here to tell ya it was the mountain that made the quake. She's startin' to talk again just like Miss Cora said she would."

Ethan met up with the USGS team under their tent and asked Rich if he could join him.

"Sure Ethan. What's up?"

"I'll explain as we walk. Emily and some others are going to join us," Ethan answered.

They started the walk over to the pond and Ethan explained about the stream that just went underground south of the end of the pond.

"Emily and I discovered it just after the pond was discovered. The road crew was clearing for the driveway and they happened upon the pond. It tends to happen around here every once and again. I guess it's something to do with how the glaciers retreated way back in the day. Once the pond was cleared and began to settle, Emily and I decided to take a walk around the edge out of curiosity. We found a little stream that emerged at the southernmost edge and followed it. All of a sudden it was gone. It just disappeared.

"Emily said she had seen that very thing in a palm canyon in the desert around Palm Springs, California. Her friend showed her how the water just went underground. It didn't even look like there was an opening.

"We walked back to where we could see the stream and Emily cleared a bunch of leaves and we found the spot where the water disappeared. It was really cool. We set a marker near it so no one would walk into the wet marshy ground by mistake. It looks solid but it really isn't.

"Today, with the quake, I had a hunch that the spot where the water went underground might have moved. So I took Charlie and one of my crew with me and we found just that. It's moved about ten feet due west. Here it is, the new marker and, as you can see, the water just stops flowing and disappears right there."

Everyone took a long look at the water going back into the earth. It looked rather surreal.

"Ethan, this is great. Good thinking on your part. You must be part geologist," Rich said.

"Not me. It's Emily. She's the one who found the first spot."

"And where is that?"

"See that marker over there? That's it although I haven't gone over there yet. Not sure what to expect," Ethan explained.

"Well, how about walking with me? I suspect it's gonna become part of the pond in a few days so it's probably real muddy."

That's just what they found. The water had changed direction and the pond was doing the same. Rich took a lot of pictures and made notes as he looked at the stream.

"This is a great find Emily. So, is anyone in your family a geologist?"

"Nope. But I think if I have the chance I may go back to college to become one. I love the whole earthquake and volcano thing, all those things that can't be controlled or predicted by man. You just gotta love Mother Nature."

"Well, in that case, you're welcome to join my team anytime you want while we're here. Not sure how long that may be. Could be two weeks anyway. Lots of things to measure and take pictures of and sensors to set up on the mountain. I'm meeting with the local Native American chiefs tomorrow. Maybe you should be here for that, too. I'm gonna need permission to walk the mountain and set up sensors and I don't want to interfere with sacred places and private property."

"That's a good idea Rich. Just let me know what time and I'll be here."

"The meeting is set for ten tomorrow morning."

"OK. Matthews?"

"OK here. We'll get you here on time. This whole stream thing is incredible. Glad I'm around to learn about it."

"Well, I'm all finished here for now," Rich said as he rejoined the group. "You can see where the pond is already moving to keep aligned with the new recapture site. That's what we call the place where the water goes back underground. And it is wicked cool. If you come back here please bring someone with you and be very careful. The surface of the land will be the last thing to change as the water builds up underneath it. It will just fall into the pond as the water overtakes the soft ground underneath. My team will be documenting the changes every thirty minutes from here on out. We'll set up high resolution cameras in two different places to capture the changes."

"Now this is awesome. Never know what's gonna happen around here," Ethan said as they walked back to the boulder.

"My team is going to take a look at the epicenter area just beyond your property line now. We'll let you know what we find. Ethan, I have your phone number and yours as well Agent Matthews. I'll be in touch," Rich said with a salute as he rejoined his team to discuss the pond.

"Well, Emily, it's been quite an afternoon around here. What's say we get you home?" Matthews said.

"OK. Ethan, call me later OK?"

"Sure. But it's gonna be a long while. I have to check as many of my build sites as possible before dark. That gives me about four hours. I should be able to get to all of them. Ian is at one of them right now. His family is OK. No damage other than a few dishes and stuff. Just like the rest of The Creek."

"Be careful," Emily said as she got into her Jeep.

"I'm just gonna lock up here and then I'll be leaving as well."

Matthews returned Emily to The Creek. They all decided to join the group at the store to compare stories and grab some supper.

"Hey everyone," Ted said as they all walked into the store.

"We're here for supper and conversation," Emily said.

"Well, you've come to the right place," Michael replied. "Miss Cora is on her way over so things should get real interesting."

"Great!' Emily replied.

Greetings were heard all around as Emily got her supper order placed and was given a spot at the table. The agents stayed close and they all waited for their orders. Just as they started to eat Cora walked in and the night took on a flavor of its own.

"Hey Miss Cora," Ted called out. "Come join us at the table. What can I get you for dinner. On the house of course."

"Oh, you sweet talker you, Ted. How about some of that barbecue chicken without a bun and some slaw and beans," Cora replied.

"Yes, Ma'am. Comin' right up."

Cora took a chair next to Emily and it wasn't too long before she started talking about the quake.

"It's happening just as I said it would. The mountain's startin' to talk. Twice now. One real loud then just a bit ago rather softly. I warned y'all about this, didn't I?"

"Yes, Ma'am you did," was the general response heard all around the store from near the stove to the table out back. People had congregated on the steps to the kitchen area and there wasn't much breathing room left anywhere in the place.

"I've been feelin' it ever since Miss Emily came to The Creek. Now that's not a bad thing, and you don't have any control over it so just be aware and listen. The battle between good and evil is ageless and has been taking place right here since the mountains were created millions of years ago. For some reason the powers that be decided that our mountain would hold the ancient Magic and sent our ancestors here to protect it. The duty to protect this mountain has been passed down from kin to kin and now all of us are to take part in this ancient ritual.

"This time I'm thinkin' things are gonna be different. I don't think this is gonna be a simple thing, not that any battle is. What I mean is I'm getting flashes of a big battle, maybe the biggest of all battles. Seems the powers that be have been preparing for this for a long time. I'm hopin' The Light wins. Otherwise, our lives as we know them will end. The fight for humanity to accept The Light over The Dark has been going on since creation. We've had many chances to choose and now the time has come for the final confrontation."

Lots of agreement was heard around the store.

"That's all for now."

The evening was a good time with the people and the food. More stories were told and news was shared. The group broke up around nine and Ted and Michael enjoyed the help everyone gave to settle the store for the night. The Creek was mostly quiet by ten.

Matthews was busy trying to process all that Cora had said along with the information he was constantly receiving about Strovonovich. He would be up for a while.

He wondered if the things Cora was saying were real. Strovonovich was pure evil as far as he was concerned. He agreed with the thought that each person made their own choice to be good or evil. He didn't believe in a specific religion but that there was a benevolent being that was all about love and positive things. So what was so far off about a battle between good and evil? Why couldn't there be energies or whatever you wanted to call them that were bigger than a human being? Cora called them The Light and The Dark. Who was to say they didn't exist out in the universe somewhere? And who was so small minded to believe that humans were the only living beings in the universe?

Maybe there was more than one universe. Matthews firmly believed in other beings and that they had visited the Earth many times. He just kept those thoughts to himself. He liked working with the U. S. marshals and knew thoughts like this would get him unemployed real fast.

Mathews took a moment to collect his thoughts and focus on current problems at hand. But, really, weren't they the same problem?

Emily settled in as soon as she returned home. She was planning on checking in with her Guys on The Other Side. Ethan had called as they were cleaning up the store and said he would check in with her at her house in the morning before the meeting.

She lit a white candle and some incense and began to channel her energy for a chat with her Guys on The Other Side. It didn't take but a few seconds before they began connecting with her. The information they gave her was truly indescribable.

"Thanks for my Gifts and especially for my new home. The people here are just what I need. I so appreciate you taking care of me in this way."

Emily sat for a long time as she received her new Gifts and instructions on how to use them.

The first new Gift was that of instant premonitions. She had experienced a few throughout her life but not like this. Her Guides started teaching about this Gift by showing her what would happen within the next five minutes. First, they showed her that Agent Marks would get a snack from the kitchen cupboard. She opened her bedroom a little bit and listened as he did just that. The cabinet squeaked a little when you closed the door. Next, they showed her what would happen at the store. She walked into the living room and looked out the window. Sure enough, an old blue Ford pickup truck with a big container in the back pulled up. Just as it came to a stop, the container fell sideways and rolled around in the back. No harm done. It was empty. Emily tuned in to this Gift to get used to how it worked.

The second new Gift she received was that of telepathy, being able to connect her thoughts with others. She knew there was a specific use for this Gift and would have to wait to see when to use it.

The third new Gift she received was that of kinetic empowerment. This meant that she could move physical objects with her thoughts and/or her body. She practiced moving the pillows in the bedroom with her mind for a while then she opened her eyes and tried moving them with the wave of her hand. Her first attempt made her laugh out loud. She tried to move her slipper across the floor and it hopped about a foot away like a bunny rabbit. She tried again concentrating harder and this time the slipper moved from her bedside to her closet door right where she had intended it to. This was a wicked cool Gift. She practiced for a long time, working at fine tuning this new power.

As she began to grow tired, she sat back down and tuned in to her Guides, Angels, Fairies and everyone else that watched over her and blessed her. She thanked the Divine for her new powers and confirmed the sacred promise she had made long ago when she became aware of her Psychic Medium Gift to do no harm and to use these new powers for the good of all creation. She also affirmed that she would not use them for self-gain for herself nor at the request of others.

She closed her session with Reiki, sending healing energy through herself out to all in need in the universe, human, ET and all things in existence.

She ended her connection around midnight tired and happy. She fell asleep and did not remember her dreams.

Emily met up with Ethan at her house just before the meeting the USGS had with the chiefs. They had decided to meet in the USGS tent so the crew would not be bothered.

The chiefs arrived a few minutes later, introductions were made, and they got settled under the tent. The sides of the tent had been opened for better air flow. After all, it was a gorgeous summer day on the mountain.

"Thanks so much everyone for coming together today," Rich started. "We've been monitoring the mountain and have recorded the initial quake with about ten smaller aftershocks. I know some of you have felt them but the majority of them were less than a 1.5 magnitude. They were too small to be felt by humans but definitely known by all the creatures around here. Just before the last one, about an hour ago, my team noticed hundreds of birds taking to the air close by. About thirty seconds later the aftershock was recorded on our instruments. We didn't even feel it and it was centered at the epicenter just a few yards from here.

"That's why I asked you all here. Chiefs, I would like you to walk with the team as we place sensors around the mountain today. We already have Emily's permission to place a few on her property as long as we don't interfere with the wildlife. I am very sensitive to the heritage of these Appalachian Mountains."

Both chiefs agreed with Rich and said they were ready to set out.

"OK then. Let's divide into two teams and get busy. One thing though: we've been studying the fault lines and the closest one around here is the Linville Falls Fault line. Its close enough to cause a quake but it's not responsible for this one. We have our work cut out for us to try and find out what set your quake into motion."

"Thanks Rich. We know whatever you find will be interesting," Emily said.

"Yes it will. Ready folks? Let's get going," Rich said.

The two teams left and Emily decided to walk through her house and see if there was anything she could do to help. Ethan was on the third floor measuring things as she came up the stairs.

"Hey builder guy, what'cha measuring?"

"Hey homeowner lady. I'm measuring your floors for a final time before we start laying the hardwood."

Emily walked right into Ethan's arms. He planted a big fat kiss on her and she gave him one right back.

"Now, that's what I call perfect," Ethan said.

"Me, too."

She kissed him again deep and long and he gave back the same. They finally parted.

"Emily, if we keep going I might have to lock that door and have my way with you right here and now."

"Sounds good to me," Emily replied as she ran her hands under his shirt and up his back.

"Oh God, Emily. I can't right now. The building inspector is due any time to give the OK for your interior plumbing to be turned on. You have noticed all the caps on the water lines right?"

"Yup."

"As soon as he gives the OK we can start bringing in the cabinets, laying the floors, and placing all the toilets, showers, and tubs. By the end of the week all the water fixtures along with the cabinets, will be in place as well as some of the flooring. We're getting close."

"Yahoo!!!!" Emily shouted. She went over to the window and hollered again then waved as the crew outside looked up and laughed. They probably thought she'd just scored with Ethan.

"This is so beyond amazing. I'll finally get to see all those things Ian had me choose and how they really look in my house. Well, what are you waiting for? Chop chop, dude!"

Ethan laughed at Emily as he finished his measuring detail.

"The chiefs and the USGS guys are out of sight. Guess they're gonna be busy all day. I already know no fault line caused the quake. It was like Cora said. Something's about to happen here. Don't know what but I do believe her. You?"

"Yes, Emily, I do. I trust Cora. She's never been wrong about these things. Don't worry. I'll be with you all the time."

"I know. Maybe I should say that to you. I'll keep you safe. A sharing kinda thing."

"OK. Back to work."

"The painters don't need me here so I'm going into the barn and see if they could use some help over there. Later."

Emily spent the rest of the morning in the barn and stables complex doing odd jobs, serving like a builder's helper. The barn area that needed painting was being sprayed on and the rest was being left natural or being hand stained. The tack room was being worked on by craftsman who were building a special work bench and desk combo with mahogany and teak wood.

Ethan found her hauling scraps in a wheelbarrow when he came to get her for lunch. He took the barrow from her and told her to get cleaned up.

They joined the crew on the porch.

"I gotta tell y'all this is wicked cool sitting here on my front porch having lunch with you."

Just as they finished lunch the USGS teams and the chiefs returned. They hurried over and shared their discoveries with them.

"Folks, I'm here to tell ya I've seen things today I've never seen before. The chiefs showed me pictures of the way things were before the quake. Have a look here," Rich said as he passed his camera around.

"What Rich's talking about is the meadow just past the small woods northwest of you Emily. You remember the place? It's called Sacred Rock Meadow," Chief Jim asked.

Yes I do Chief."

"Well, you remember how all those boulders were just thrown around helter skelter, no real pattern or anything?"

"Yes"

"Sure Jimmie," Ethan said as well.

"Well, now, they're in two circles with openings to the four directions. All exactly the same distance apart in the circle with a flat boulder, kinda like the one here, in the dead center. No damage to the ground. It's like someone just picked them up and reset them."

"It's like he said," Chief Charlie agreed. "Dangest thing I've ever seen. We've both heard the legends from our grandparents and shaman but have never seen anything like it in our time. For what it's worth, Miss Cora is right. Something is about to come together around here and I, we, think that meadow is gonna be the center of it all."

"I don't know what to say. We know where the epicenter is but there's no fault line mapped to support it. I'm as puzzled as everyone else," Rich added.

"Why don't y'all grab your lunch and join us. Plenty of room here thanks to Miss Emily's plans and all," Chief Jimmie suggested.

They all gathered around the porch and talked about the quake and Cora's warning. Chief Jimmie shared a few of the stories he had learned as a young boy.

"The Cherokee believe that Beaver's grandchild, the little Water Beetle came from the sky realm, and through his curiosity of what lay beyond the water he was blessed with bringing the first mud to the surface of the water planet, creating the Earth. The Earth was then populated by all animals and humans.

"The legend says the Great Spirit made the Earth to provide for her children. My ancestors and family have always known that the signs, visions, dreams and powers we have are all gifts of the Spirits and that both our worlds are intertwined and presided over by the spirit world.

"We know that all things have a life or energy of their own including the things most people think of as not alive like our mountain. My ancestors have handed down the stories of this mountain talking just before a great battle between good and evil. From what I've seen and heard over the past few months, I'd say the mountain has begun to speak and we should all listen. I believe the wisdom of my ancestors."

Chief Charlie agreed. "I believe the same thing Jimmie. The time has come for a confrontation between the Light and the Dark. Your ancestors and mine have lived side by side for thousands of years and the stories and legends tell about such battles. We all believe this mountain holds ancient Magic and needs our protection. The USGS can look all it wants but it's not going to find a fault line that connects with yesterday's quake. That was indeed the mountain speaking. And we'd all be the wiser to stop and listen. The spirits will show us the way. They always have."

"I've heard many legends from many of the North American natives and they all have a common thread; that of ancient Magic being a big part of daily life. I'm not going to say magic doesn't exist. I am going to do the required research and report my findings. I'm so glad the chiefs have shared their legends here. It's gonna make me less crazy when I can't link a fault line with your quake," Rich said.

"Glad to help," Chief Jimmie replied. "Now, if you don't need me anymore today, I've got to get going. There is work to be done."

"What kinda work you got waitin' for you?" Chief Charlie teased Jimmie.

"More than you've seen in a good long while you old coot," Chief Jimmie replied with a punch to Charlie's arm.

"Oh, so you wanna start a battle right here? I'd win, hands down."

"No, not today," Chief Jimmie said. "I feel mighty forgivin' today."

"Yeah, right!" Charlie said as they all laughed at the antics of these two old friends.

'Ya know what Chief Soaring Eagle, maybe our folks would like to get together for a blessing ceremony soon. It's been a while since we did that," Chief Running Bear offered.

"Great idea Chief Running Bear. Let's get it planned in the next few days. Maybe we can have it about the time Emily's place is finished and include her."

"Now that sounds like a great idea. We'll do it."

Everyone thought the idea was a good one and wanted to be included. The chiefs said they would email everyone as the plans came together. They left a few minutes later.

The USGS team went back to their research and just as Emily and Ethan were about to go back to their own projects the ground gave a good shake.

As the shaking subsided, Ethan said, "I guess the mountain approves of our talk today. Seems she's getting us to see things her way."

"I guess so," Emily replied.

"I'll go check in with everyone. How about you go set up on the porch until I'm done?"

"OK."

Emily sat on the porch steps as Ethan checked on the crew and buildings.

Emily saw Rich and one of his research people approaching her.

"Now, that's what I call cause and effect. We talked about Magic and the mountain spoke back," Rich said. "We're going over to check on the upper meadow. Want to join us?"

"Sure," Emily replied as she looked at Agent Marks. He held his hand up in the wait a minute sign, "just as soon as my group gives me the OK."

"Alright, we'll wait with you," Rich said.

A few minutes later they set out for Sacred Rock Meadow with the newly formed rock circles.

As soon as Emily stepped into the meadow the ground began to shake but it was more like a soft vibration than a shaking one. The agents felt it as well as the rest of the group and reported it to Matthews and HQ. The USGS team checked their sensors and shook their heads.

"Nothing's showing on the sensors. They're not picking up the vibrations at all. And we checked with base camp and the sensors there aren't picking up anything. This is really strange. You can all feel it, right?" Rich asked.

Heads nodded in agreement.

Emily began to walk over to the rock formations and the vibrations grew stronger. She took a few steps backwards and they lessened.

"I guess my being here has something to do with all this. I don't know what though," she said as she walked forward again.

As soon as she entered the rock circles the vibrations increased and a humming sound could be heard.

"Can anyone else hear this? It sounds like the rocks are humming," Emily said in awe.

"We all can. What is that?" Agent Marks asked as he tried to get close to Emily. He was blocked as he tried to enter the rock circles.

"Hey, I can't get in there. It's like a force field is holding me back. Are you OK Emily?"

"Yes, Agent Marks. I am perfectly alright. No harm will come to me in here." Emily didn't know where those words came from but she knew them to be true.

Matthews was listening to the whole thing. He was about ready to drive up there when Emily told him not to.

"Matthews, I'm alright. No harm will come to anyone in the meadow. You can stay there."

How'd she know what I was thinking? Matthews thought. Emily wondered the same thing then remembered one of her new powers was telepathy. So, I guess that's how it works, she thought to herself with a smile. Good to know.

She sent her thoughts out to the Universe. Anything else you need me to know right now? She waited for the response. It came right back to her. Not right now but you must be prepared. That's what she 'heard' within her own spirit.

OK then she thought. Time to leave the circles.

As soon as she stepped out of the rock circles, the humming sound stopped but the ground vibrations stayed the same.

Rich and his assistant were busy trying to get readings from their sensors. Not one thing was recording. Rich finally told his assistant to stop.

"I really don't know what's going on here but if I had to say anything I'd say that ancient Magic the chiefs were talking about is alive and well on this mountain in this exact spot. It's the only thing I can think of to explain all this. It's like nothing I've ever experienced before."

Rich and his assistant joined the rest of the group.

"All I know is it all feels right. It's as if we're all being prepared for something, that's for sure," Emily offered.

They headed back to Emily's meadow and went about their separate business.

Emily found Ethan and told him what had happened in Sacred Rock Meadow.

"That's amazing Emily. I wish I'd been there."

"I'm sure if we go back a little later the same thing will happen again. I know it will."

"Then something is about to happen. This is all so surreal."

"I know what you mean and for me to be the one making the rocks hum is beyond comprehension."

"You OK with all this? It seems you're connected to the Magic."

"I guess so."

"It's a lot to take in all at once."

"No kidding!"

They just stood there looking toward the upper meadow.

"Well, everything here is OK. I'm gonna go back to my stuff. How about you?" Ethan stated.

"I think I'll go back to The Creek and see if I can't find Cora. I've got a whole bunch of questions for her."

"OK. I'll check in with you later," Ethan said as he gave her a quick kiss.

"Now, that does help make better sense of this whole thing,' Emily said as he walked over towards the barn.

"We're ready when you are Emily," Agent Marks said.

"OK then, let's pack up and head home," Emily's responded.

On the ride home, Emily called Ted and asked if he knew where Cora might be. He told her Cora was in the store and Emily asked him to ask her if she'd stay so Emily could talk with her. Ted said Cora said she knew Emily was coming. She was in the store waiting for her. Emily thanked Ted and hung up. Of course Cora was waiting for her. That woman had a lot of explaining to do.

CHAPTER 33

Things in Yuri's world began to crash. His prostitution ring had been smashed. Most of his brothels had been raided by the authorities and the managers were being arrested and held. The girls had been taken to safe houses and were being returned to their families. He was losing millions of dollars every minute.

He was angry as hell and scared shitless at the same time. He wanted his money. He knew the man in the black hat was watching him. Yuri had to get the hundred young girls to him right away. He didn't want to think what would happen to him if he didn't do as the man in the black hat ordered. He sent word out to grab as many young girls as his men could get and bring them to an abandoned warehouse in a small village just north of Moscow. No one would be around to see anything. These warehouses were derelict reminders of the old USSR and the village where they were located had been empty for years. He told his men that if they did not produce the girls they would all die a painful and slow death.

Matthews heard about the first kidnappings six hours later. Word came across the net that young girls, teenagers, were being reported missing all over the globe.

Interpol had intelligence that showed Strovonovich was the one directing the operation. The interglobal agencies were looking at remote areas of Russia for possible hiding places. This was going to take some time but they hoped to have it narrowed down to just a few villages within the next twenty-four hours.

Matthews sat back and shook his head. This Strovonovich guy was mad, insane, and beyond crazy. He was the worst evil Matthews had ever been involved with. He was sure he knew what was driving him. The fact that Emily had gone off the radar and he couldn't find her. No. He couldn't control her. That's what was eating away at this crazy man. A woman had bested him. That's what it all came down to.

Matthews knew in an instant that Strovonovich was going to come to The Creek to find Barbara and kill her. He got on a secured line with his chief at the Virginia HQ and told him what he knew.

"Chief, I do not have physical evidence but I'm telling you Strovonovich is coming to Crab Apple Creek. He wants Emily dead for one reason and one reason only."

"What's that, Matthews?" the Chief asked.

"She got away from him and he can't control her. It's consuming him that a woman got away from him. He's more than insane chief. I do believe he's possessed by evil, his own evil need to dominate everyone and everything."

"You have a valid point Matthews. Keep talking."

"Sir, since all the men he's sent to kill her have failed, he thinks he's the only one that can do the job. He's obsessed with her beyond reason. He's consumed. Look at what he's doing right now, having all those young girls kidnapped for his prostitution business. You'd think he'd lay low for a while then start back a little at a time. But no. He's beyond all reasonable thought about controlling women and Emily's his prize catch. He's blinded to any kind of common sense if he ever used it to begin with. He's coming here, sir. I know he is."

"I believe you have a valid profile of this crazy man. I have the profiler on this case listening in. Stand by Matthews."

"Yes, Sir."

"Matthews, the profiler agrees with your description and evaluation of Strovonovich. We've escalated your mission to a code black. Agents will be arriving by midnight and you'll meet them at Emily's new house site. They'll be fully briefed and armed. I've already ordered more surveillance equipment as well as drone flyovers from the east coast, over the Appalachia area, and from Virginia to South Carolina. Your computers have been upgraded with new software so you can connect with the surveillance drones. They'll be briefings every thirty minutes until we have confirmation that Strovonovich has left Russia. Then we will be on 24/7."

"Understood, sir. Let's hope he doesn't leave any time soon. I think he's in some kind of trouble with the prostitution ring being seized. He'll probably do whatever it takes to get some of it back into operation before he heads our way."

"You're thinking is the same as the profiler's, Matthews. Let's hope we have a week or two before this all goes down. We may need to move Emily soon to keep her safe."

"I don't think she's going to agree with a move, sir. She's going to want to stay here and get this over with. One thing I know for sure is she's a fighter."

"OK. We'll assess things as they begin to happen. Keeping her alive is our top priority."

"Yes sir. I'll have a talk with her in the morning."

"Alright Matthews. Let us know if anything else comes to mind or happens around there. I hear the USGS isn't able to confirm that the quake activity was connected with a specific fault line."

"That's right, sir. Do you want them to leave in the morning?"

"No. Let's let them work for another day then I'll decide when they should leave."

"Yes, sir. Thank you, sir."

The chief ended the call and Matthews got busy with all the new info coming through his printer and laptop.

He met with the agents located in The Creek before he set out for Emily's build around eleven-thirty. Just after he got there the new agents arrived. There were thirty of them. They set up a temporary headquarters in the barn for this meeting. Matthews gave them the latest news then directed them to the established site the first security team had set up. It was far enough north not to be seen by the building crew, and they used camouflage mesh to cover their tents. Emily had been able to find them from her attic but only after looking for more than half an hour.

Once they were gone, Matthews set out to meet with his agents that were members of Ethan's crews. They chose a place in the national park area south of Boone. He gave them the new intel, instructions and their new equipment. When he finished with them, he headed back to The Creek. It was three in the morning when he parked his Jeep in his driveway. He sat there for a few quiet minutes wondering if these were the last quiet minutes he'd get before it was all over.

As he walked over to his back door he heard his name being called.

"Hey Matthews, it's Michael."

"Let him pass agent. Hey Michael, what can I do for you at this lovely hour of the night?"

"Matthews, we need to talk."

"OK. Come on in," Matthews said as he held the door for Michael.

"Somethin's about to go down here. I can feel it. And, you being all over the mountain in the middle of the night just tells me it's so."

"Oh Michael. I can't tell you anything more than you already know. But do know this we are doing everything we can to keep Emily alive and safe. You all just keep doing what you're doing and that will be a huge help."

"Alright. Ted said you wouldn't be able to say much. We'll get the word out to make sure Emily stays safe."

"Michael, you'll probably notice a lot of new agents in the area. Please don't ask them questions. Just take care of them the way you've been taking care of all of us from the minute we got here - and that would be most excellently, by the way. I've already increased your food order delivery for this morning. My team has rations but once they hear about your bagels and other fare it's gonna be hard to not take them some food," Matthews added with a laugh.

"Thanks, Matthews, and I suppose the feds are paying that bill?" Michael laughed.

"Why, yes we are Michael. Wouldn't have it any other way."

"No problem Matthews. Just giving you a hard time. Thanks for the heads-up. Get some sleep. I sure as hell need some," Michael said as he left.

Matthews crashed on the couch and was up by six later that morning. He had to tell Emily what was going on to prepare her for what was about to happen. He had already called her counselor and asked her to be at Emily's by nine and the acupuncturist was set to arrive by eleven. He was keeping everyone except Ethan away from Emily today. She was going to need some space to process everything he had to say to her. The fight for her life was about to take an ugly turn.

Emily was just about to leave for her build site when Matthews called. He told her he was on his way over with news.

She had a bad feeling about this. She unpacked her backpack and was standing in the kitchen when he arrived a few minutes after nine.

"Emily, there's no easy way to say what I have to say so I'm just going to say it. Strovonovich is coming here himself to try to kill you."

"I knew this was bad news. What now?"

"We've increased the detail by thirty agents who moved in last night. They're with the surveillance team north of your build site. Some of them will be sent here to increase the detail in The Creek. They've brought some heavy equipment with them."

"It sounds like you're expecting a war of some kind."

"We are. This Strovonovich is pure evil, Emily. My chief suggested we move you to a secure location far away from here until we can eliminate this guy. I told him I highly doubted you'd agree to that."

"You're right Matthews. I'm not leaving my home. This bad guy can't make me leave. He has no power over me. The sooner he sees that the better."

"Emily, this guy has no connection to reality. We truly believe he is pure evil and will do whatever he wants to get to you no matter how many people suffer along the way."

"What'd I ever do to him? I don't even know this guy."

"You're right. But in his messed up brain you have showed the world that you're smarter, stronger and have control over him by getting away and staying alive. As far as he's concerned, you're telling the world all about his sick business and he's got to stop you at any cost."

"Sick doesn't even begin to describe him. God, I hope you guys get to him before he gets to me. And The Creek."

"That's our plan Emily. Don't go to your build site for a few days until we know exactly where this guy is. We think he's going to stay in Russia for a few days to take care of some of his sick business. If that pans out, we'll let you return to your house. But the minute we hear he's left Russia, you're staying here. Got it?"

"Yes, Matthews. Jesus fucking Christ. Just when all the really cool stuff is about to happen at the house. I know. I know. But I gotta stay focused on the positive and good for as long as I can. I am acutely aware of the danger that's taking place. This is not good. Not good at all."

Matthews was signaled from outside.

"Emily, I took the privilege of asking your counselor to come over. She's here if you want someone to talk to. I'll brief Ethan next. I see his truck just pulling into the store now. He can come over after you're done with your counselor."

"OK. Yes. Send her in. I'm not sure just what to do at this moment. So, yes, send her in. Maybe she can help me sort things out for the time being."

Matthews walked over to Emily and placed his hand on her shoulder.

"I know you can get through this. Look at how you got away from Nick. You survived a long time in his hatred and got away. You'll get through this now because you have a man that loves you and will protect you with everything he possesses and the best special ops team on the planet taking care of you."

"You're right Matthews. Thanks for pointing that out."

"And, your acupuncturist will be here at eleven for a session. I knew you'd need her. Ethan can hang out with you after that. OK?"

"Yes. Please tell him all this so he won't worry. Thanks Matthews."

Matthews left as Emily's counselor walked in. They spent about an hour together and Emily felt a little more calmed after she left. The next hour and a half was spent with her acupuncturist. It was a great session. Emily felt more relaxed and centered by the time Ethan walked in the door. She was on the couch in her shorts and a big t-shirt, just hanging out.

Ethan brought lunch for the two of them and set it up on the coffee table.

He stood there looking at her for a long moment.

"What can I do to help you with all this?" he asked Emily in a soft voice.

She patted the couch next to her and he sat down and took her into his arms.

She didn't even know she was crying until she felt the tears on her hand.

After a while she took a deep breath and sat up.

"I'm starved. Let's eat," she said with conviction. "That bastard's got no hold on me."

"Yes Ma'am," Ethan said as they got busy with lunch.

While Emily was with her counselor, Jordan had arrived with the Foodies delivery for the day.

"Hey Ted, looks like you're going to feed an army or somethin'," Jordan commented as he unloaded all the extra supplies.

"Jordan, looks like the tourists have been talkin' about this place. Business has really picked up in the last few days."

"Not surprised. I love your food, Ted. As a matter of fact, I'd like to order an everything bagel breakfast thing to go please."

"You got it Jordan."

"How's the house comin' along?" Michael asked as Jordan brought the last load into the store.

"It's moving faster than I expected. The blueprints have been approved. The road was approved and I do believe Karl and his gang are out there right now making it happen. This is so cool. I'm gonna go over on my way back to Boone."

"That sounds great. Ethan is really busy this summer. I hear Emily's build is almost finished. Some interior stuff to complete that should take about two more weeks she told us. She's gonna have a big shindig for everyone when she moves in. Of course you're invited 'cause you're a resident of The Creek."

"Wow. That's sounds so good, a resident of The Creek. I'm getting used to that real fast. Thanks for the bagel, Ted. What do I owe you Michael?"

"Nothin'. Think of it as a welcome gift."

"This day just keeps getting better. See ya in a couple of days."

"Keep us posted on your building project," Michael hollered out as Jordan left.

Jordan set out for his build site where he would eat his breakfast.

He parked his truck along the road as his driveway was under construction. He grabbed his bagel and coffee and started down the drive looking for Karl. They had cleared a little more of the brush at the sides and were grading the rough dirt. There were mounds of gravel and sand in the meadow next to the driveway. He found Karl a few yards down the drive.

"Hey Karl, looks like you're makin' great progress here," Jordan said in greeting.

"We sure are. The rain from the other night actually helped loosen some of this stuff. We're about ready to lay the gravel, then the sand, and then smooth everything out. I'm planning on paving tomorrow. With a three day curing time we should be ready for the bluestone perimeter by Monday.

"That sounds great. How's the house coming along?"

"Getting ready to frame. That's why there are tire tracks all over the place - lumber deliveries. We'll put everything back to normal before we're finished."

"No worries Karl. I know we have to mess things up a bunch before we're done. No worries."

"Ya got some time to walk over to the site?"

"Sure. I'm on a break anyway and the guys at the store helped unload so I'm really about thirty minutes ahead of schedule. Let's go."

They walked over to the house and watched as the crew sorted lumber. A small backhoe was working near the barn site.

Jordan watched as a bucket of earth was dumped on the meadow and saw something big and shiny.

"Hey Karl, can you ask the operator to stop for a minute? I just saw something shiny in the last bucket of earth he dumped. I'd like to take a look."

"Sure." Karl told the operator to stop and Jordan walked over to the pile of earth. Sitting on top as if it belonged there was a huge crystal the size of a coconut. It was clear quartz with purple and blue spikes.

"Holy cow. This is beautiful," Jordan said as he came off the dirt pile. "I've seen some crystals before but nothing as big and spectacular as this. What d'ya think Karl?"

"I've been diggin' in the dirt my whole life around these mountains and I've never seen anything like this before. Bet it'll be even more spectacular after you get it cleaned up. You gonna try to sell it?"

Jordan was just staring at the crystal without sayin' a word. All of a sudden he saw this place in a different light. It was as if he'd been taken back in time. The land looked somewhat familiar but there were more trees and a circle of them with a flat boulder in the middle. There were men in robes circled around the boulder chanting and placing crystals like the one he had in his hand on the flat surface. He was mesmerized.

"Ah, hey, Jordan, Earth to Jordan," Karl said as he nudged his shoulder.

Jordan came back with a start.

"Sorry Karl, just kinda got lost looking at this. It sure is spectacular like you said. And, no, I'm not gonna sell it. I think I'll place it on the fireplace mantle. Others should see the surprises the Earth holds and sometimes shares."

"I like that idea. I'll keep a watch for others and put them in my truck for you."

"Thanks Karl. This foundation is really huge. It looks bigger than the house."

"That's because it is. We have to open things up a lot bigger to be able to place the forms. Once the foundation is complete and the forms are re-moved, we'll let the concrete cure for about a week. We'll fill in after all the rough plumbing and utility work is finished, then it won't look so huge. You do have a big house being built here. Don't forget that."

"I know. And I like the way things are starting up. Fantastic!"

They walked back to Jordan's truck.

"Thanks for the time Karl. I'll take a look in a couple of days. I sup-pose you'll have the driveway blocked but I can always follow the other tracks."

"That's right. Take care now and bring that crystal back when you get it all cleaned up. I'd love to see it."

"I will. So long."

Jordan set off down the Pine Ridge Road thinking about the crystal sitting next to him. It was surely an amazing gift from the Earth. He couldn't quite put his finger on it but he felt like he'd seen it before. All of a sudden he knew everything about this crystal such as its origin, its energy, and its ability to heal. Something was happening to him and he wasn't sure what was going on. It felt good so he wasn't worried about anything demonic or evil. Now, where had that come from? Those thoughts about good and evil? He wasn't a religious man. He felt like he was flying at super speed with the thoughts that suddenly filled his head. He knew stuff he'd never learned before. It was like some switch had been turned on in his brain and couldn't be turned off.

All of a sudden his phone rang and the new thoughts stopped. It was the bank.

"Hey Jordan, it's Sandy at the bank. Just wanted to give you an update on your account."

"Hey Sandy. Find the problem yet? I've got to get that mortgage pay-ment transferred as soon as possible. And, thanks for setting that up. I like the ability to transfer from my account to the bank's mortgage department without having to write and mail a check."

"No problem. Unfortunately, we have not been able to follow the ac-tion back to whomever is responsible. We have our best technical people work-ing on it. We do know you were not the one who moved the money. You've been hacked as they say. You do have until the fifteenth of every month to make the payment and still be on time. We are hoping to resolve this problem by then. We've asked the federal folks to put a hold on your payments. We're waiting for their response. We're thinking they will because we have evidence that you've been hacked. Your account is insured by the FDIC up to a quarter million dollars. But since you have more than that in your combined accounts we are looking at other ways to insure the rest. I'll keep you informed of any new info as soon as I get it. I'm really sorry for this mess, Jordan."

"Me, too. Thanks, Sandy. I'll keep watching the account. What about my paycheck that's on direct deposit?"

"Good question. We've left the original account open to watch for any traffic. However, we've opened a new account for you under a false name. Stop by as soon as you can and we'll give you an ATM card and the passwords. We're going to deposit the same amount of money as your paycheck into your fake account from the bank's funds per the feds. We want your account to stay active to monitor any more hacking."

"Great idea. I'm almost in Pine Ridge, then I'll be in Boone this afternoon around two. I'll see you then."

"Thanks Jordan. See you around two. And, again, we're really sorry for this mess. And we're frustrated just like you."

"Bye Sandy."

Jordan spent the rest of his morning and early afternoon delivering his goods. He stopped at the bank and signed the papers for the new 'fake' account. He was worried that they would never find his money and he would lose everything. He was at a stop sign thinking about this and happened to glance at the crystal. He could swear that thing just started to glow really bright. He blinked his eyes and it was back to the way he had found it - muddy and beautiful.

Something was definitely happening to him. Maybe he needed some time off or maybe he needed his eyes checked. He planned to make an appointment as soon as he got home.

CHAPTER 34

Yuri's men were reporting in. They had, collectively, kidnapped seventy-eight girls and all were headed to the warehouse. He had two other men working in Russia and they had grabbed thirty young girls that were already there. Yuri made sure they were warm and well fed as he had been instructed by the man in the black hat.

The CON was watching the collection of human girls. They liked what they saw. They were ready to take them as soon as all of them were together. They sent their liaison to Yuri with a message.

Yuri was at the warehouse when the man in the black hat showed up. One minute he wasn't there and as soon as Yuri turned to look out the window again, he appeared next to him.

"You have done well. We will be collecting the girls soon. This place is big enough to hide our transportation vehicle from the outside. You need not be here."

"I understand. I want to make sure all of them are in place before I leave them with you. They should be arriving by tomorrow morning, then they're all yours."

"Agreed." The man in the black hat walked away.

Yuri was smiling. He had made those bastards happy. Good. As soon as they took delivery of the girls he would be free to travel to North Carolina and kill that bitch Barbara. He was feeling good. He returned to his apartment in Moscow for the evening.

The CON liked what they saw. They were in a hurry to get the human girls. They were ready to impregnate them with their own hybrid seed. They needed to build their forces as quickly as possible. After all, they would win the upcoming battle and gain power over all the universes. They would then be able to use all the human girls to make more of their own.

The NOVAE had placed more shape shifters in Crab Apple Creek the night before. These were in the shape of eagles and other animals. They had cloaked their ship so no one had seen them. They were coming back tonight to give special powers to Mother Earth.

This time they would most likely be seen. They had been to the Earth five times in the last ten days. They needed to visit every day now until the battle took place.

Cora and Kendra were leaving the store at the same time that evening. It was late almost ten o'clock and the sun had already gone down. They both happened to look in the same direction at the same time and saw the lights descend from the sky over Emily's new house.

"I knew it. It's comin'. They're here again. Wonder what they're leavin' this time?" Cora asked.

"I see it, too. You think it's another UFO don't you?" Kendra asked.

"No. I know it is. Come on and drive me over to Emily's place. I gotta see this for myself."

"OK. Get in," Kendra agreed as they got into her car. The lights were still there when they got to the driveway. It was blocked by security.

"Evenin' ladies. Sorry. Can't let you in. Not sure what's going on up there," the agent said as he pointed to the lights in the sky overhead.

"Well, I do know what's goin' on. They're here again and getting ready to do battle. It's nothing you can help with young man so don't even try to explain yourself."

The agent just stared at Cora then Kendra.

"She knows what she's talkin' about," Kendra offered.

"Yes Ma'am. Either way I can't let you in."

"We understand. Thanks."

They got out of the car and stood there watching the craft as it began to change colors. They continued watching for about half an hour and were joined by a few other folks from The Creek. All of a sudden, the craft shot back into the sky and was gone quicker than you could take a breath.

"Whoa!"

"Holy shit!"

"Where'd it go?"

"It's gone back and will be here again tomorrow night and for two more nights after that. It's the full moon. That's gonna be the tenth. Mark my words," Cora said to all gathered there.

"Ya think so, Miss Cora? You'd know about these things," Hal said.

"Yes, Hal, I do."

Kendra dropped Cora off at her place and was home a few minutes later.

CHAPTER 35

All one hundred and eight girls were collected together in the warehouse. Yuri was watching them from his office on the second floor. They were all gathered around tables and chairs looking scared and angry. He didn't know what the man in the black wanted them for and he didn't ask. He just wanted them gone so he could get underway and take care of the last bit of business before he was free and be the most powerful man on earth.

The man in the black hat appeared at noon. Yuri watched him walk in the door, or at least he thought he saw him walk in the door. If he didn't know better he'd have swore that man just walked through a wall. He must be more tired than he thought. So many strange things were happening lately. He just shook his head and headed down to the main floor. The man in the black hat met him in the middle.

"I see you have what we asked for. Good. Now, stand back away by the walls as we take them."

"What? You need to pay for them first."

"Oh yes." He handed a briefcase over to Yuri.

Yuri nodded and walked away. All of a sudden he heard a loud noise behind him. As he turned to look he saw a spaceship coming through the roof. It was as big as the warehouse. The girls were screaming and trying to run. They were taken into a bright beam of light and one after the other they disappeared into the ship. The whole thing took only about a minute, then the ship just vanished back into the sky. All fell silent. The warehouse was empty.

Yuri just stood there terrified. He couldn't think. What the fuck had just happened? He was trembling and mumbling to himself. He was the only one around. He finally got control of himself and ran from the building.

His car was still outside right where he had left it. He jumped inside and dropped the keys trying to start it. It took him several attempts but he finally got the thing running and sped away from the place. He didn't even remember the long drive home. He was in his apartment standing in the kitchen when he finally realized where he was.

What had happened back there? Who were those people anyway? Were they even human? He just didn't know what to think. He poured a couple of shots of scotch and threw them back one after the other until he could finally breathe. All he knew was he was tired and scared out of his mind and he wanted to get to the United States to kill Barbara. He fell asleep on his couch and woke up in the middle of the night. Thank God he didn't have another one of those night terrors. That would have been too much for him to handle.

He woke up with a clear plan of action. He showered, packed, bought an airline ticket online and set out for the airport. He would be in North Carolina by Friday. He would need a day to get his bearings then he would set his plan in action. By Sunday that bitch would be dead. He smiled.

Thursday was another beautiful summer day just like most of them had been this summer. People were gathered at the store and kept coming and going all day long. Talk was about the lights the night before. Most folks didn't see them but the ones that had gathered on the roadside at Emily's new house were trying to figure things out.

Emily had been cleared to leave her house and was walking into the store. She saw Hal talking with Michael and heard him say something about a spaceship over her new house.

"Hey guys. What's that you're sayin', Hal? There was a UFO over my new house last night?" Emily asked.

"Yes, Ma'am. I saw it with my own eyes. Miss Cora and Kendra were there, too. It was just hangin' in the sky over your place. It stayed there for the longest time. It changed colors a few times then it just flew up into the sky and was gone in a second. No sound. Just gone."

"Well, can ya beat that?" Emily said.

"Miss Cora says it's gonna happen every night right up until Sunday. That's when the full moon comes again and Miss Cora says somethin' big's gonna happen," Hal added.

"Really?" Michael asked.

"Yes. And she's always been right about these kinda things." Hal finished.

Emily had a strange feeling in her gut that what Hal was talking about was true. She'd been having strange thoughts ever since the other night when she received her new Gifts.

Matthews was just settling down to work when his phone gave off the alert signal he had set when Yuri was traveling anywhere. His earpiece came alive at the same time. It was his chief in Washington, D.C.

"Matthews."

"Yes, sir. I hear you loud and clear," Matthews replied.

"Yuri's on the move. He just left Moscow via Russian airlines and is headed to D.C. He should arrive by tomorrow morning, Friday. He's reserved a Jeep. We know he's headed your way. He should be in Boone by nightfall."

"Yes, sir."

"We are now on for everything. Try to keep Emily surrounded at all times from here on out. No matter where she is, she has at least five agents attached at the hip."

"Understood."

"I'll keep you posted. You can track him using the Code Black security pass."

"Yes, Sir. I got it. Thank you."

"I'll be in touch regularly from here forward. Keep your earpiece on at all times."

"Yes, Sir. I'll inform the team now."

"Thanks, Matthews. Let's hope we get him before he gets anywhere close to you."

"Agreed, sir. We're ready for him if he gets this far."

"Alright. Later, Matthews."

Matthews sent the Code Black signal out to all team members. Five minutes later he was updating them on the information he had just received. He set up a schedule for security on Emily that went into effect immediately.

Kendra and Emily were surprised when five agents walked into Kendra's house and stood next to Emily. Matthews was right behind them.

"Emily, I need you at your house right now."

"Sure, Matthews," Emily said as she followed him to her house.

"The bad guy is on his way here. He's leaving Moscow in about thirty minutes and is scheduled to arrive in D.C. tomorrow morning around ten. You'll have five agents next to you, if not bodily attached, until this is over. Understood?"

"Oh, my God. This is really happening? Now? Right now?"

"Yes, Emily. Right now."

"OK then. Matthews, I'd like to go to my new house for a little while right now please."

"OK, Emily. No problem. Agents, it's a go. See you in a few minutes at your new house."

Emily arrived twenty minutes later and went looking for Ethan. She knew he was staying late to make sure everything was turned off and locked. She found him in her new kitchen.

"Hey, Ethan," Emily said as she stood and looked at the place in awe. "This is amazing and beautiful and amazing and wonderful and amazing."

Everyone laughed quietly at her response to seeing her kitchen completed for the first time.

"I take it you like it then," Ethan said with a grin.

"It's more than I could have ever dreamed myself. I have to remember to thank Ian, too, for all his ideas. I do thank you for yours. I think it's gonna take me a long time to get used to all these things. Wow!"

Everyone walked around and took a look at the details and agreed with Emily that the place was truly incredible.

"Hey, Ethan, can I borrow you for a minute?" Matthews asked.

"Sure. Let's take a walk on the porch. I think the rockers came today. And the porch swings were being hung when I was last out there."

"Ethan, the bad guy is on his way here to kill Emily. We're keeping her surrounded by agents until he's in custody or dead. She's going to be kept at her house until Sunday morning then we're going to bring her up here. Only the locals know about this place and it'll keep the folks in The Creek from being harmed if we need to use fire power."

"Holy shit! It's really happening. How's she taking it? Can she spend the night with me?"

"If you don't mind five agents in the same room with you."

"That serious, huh? No problem, then. I think I'll set us up in the living room at my place. Big enough for all of us and we'll save the intimacy for another time."

"That sounds good. I approve. Why don't you go ask her and make some plans. Her mic is on her shirt and active at all times so I'll know the outcome."

"OK."

They walked back into the kitchen and Emily was looking in all the cabinets and appliances. The agents were offering kitchen advice as well.

"Hey Emily, how about spending the night with me? Matthews says it's OK if you say it's OK. We can camp out in the living room and watch movies or whatever. There's room for your whole entourage."

"I like that idea. But I want to take a look on the porch before we leave. I heard you say the swings were hung. I think I'll have to try them out," Emily said as she went out the back door and walked the whole porch around the house.

"These are just perfect," she said as she sat on one of her swings. "They're just what I envisioned. Things couldn't be more perfect."

She swung for a few minutes as they all talked about the house.

"Ethan, this place looks ready to live in. Is it?" Matthews asked.

"Almost. Just a few small details that should be completed by early next week. Then the building inspector will come for the last inspection and should give us the occupancy permit right then and there. As soon as he does, I will need Emily to be here when the furniture arrives. Hey Em, you'll need to direct the movers as they bring your stuff into the house. You up for that?"

"Really? So soon? For real? Oh, my God. This is just too much for a body to take in all at once. You mean I could be living here by this time next week?"

"Yup. For real," Ethan answered her.

Emily became very quiet as her swing came to a stop.

"I can finally start my new life in my new home with my new friends. Yes, I am ready."

They talked and followed Ethan around as he checked everything, locked the doors, then made sure the barn and stables were secure as well.

As they walked back to their trucks, Emily turned to look at her house. It looked just as she had dreamed it would. She saw a flash of light above the house and knew her guardians were there for her. She took a deep breath and nodded her head ever so slightly towards her house to acknowledge them.

They all piled into their trucks and set off for home. Emily would go to her place first so she could grab a few things then her agents would drive her over to Ethan's. He offered to fire up the grill to everyone's delight. The agents and Matthews would bring food from the store with them to add to the feast. Emily would bring her cookies.

The evening at Ethan's was a great success, all things considered. They all pitched in with dinner and clean-up then sat on the back porch for a while watching the night fall over the mountain. They spoke softly sharing words and silence.

As the evening finally gave way to the mysteries of the night, Matthews stood to leave.

"Time to get back," he said. "These agents are staying here. They will be outside as well as in the living room with you."

"Understood, Matthews." Ethan quietly said as he held Emily's hand a little more tightly.

"See you in the morning, Matthews," Emily said as he walked down the steps to the yard.

A short while after he left, Emily, Ethan, and her team went inside. They settled on a comedy for their movie choice and spent the next two hours laughing, eating popcorn and enjoying themselves.

As the movie ended, Ethan suggested they all get settled for the night.

Once everyone was in their place, Ethan and Emily curled up together on the big comfy couch and talked quietly for a while before Emily fell asleep. Ethan kept his arms around her the whole night and they slept peacefully.

Matthews was up most of the night getting updates on Yuri's progress across Europe. He would be landing in D.C. as scheduled at ten o'clock Friday morning. That was today.

Here we go, Matthews thought as he saw the first soft glow of the sun sneaking up into the dark sky.

CHAPTER 36

The UFOs were arriving every night just as Cora said they would. The NOVAE had everything in place. One more trip on Saturday night to communicate with their own and all would be ready for the Great Confrontation.

The CON had impregnated the girls they had taken. A few were killed because they failed to conceive. No problem. The CON would just get more.

The CON were ready for the Great Confrontation. They knew their human, Yuri, would do what he was told to do. The man in the black hat would join him once he got to the meadow.

Jordan was checking in with his bank. He hadn't heard anything and was worried.

He stopped in and spoke with the manager.

"Has anyone figured out what's happened yet?" he asked.

"Mr. Jackson, I'm so sorry. No, we have not. The feds are taking over the case and said they will not have an answer for thirty to forty-five days."

"Oh no. That can't be. I need to make my mortgage payment. It's already inside the grace period and will be late in a few days. What am I supposed to do?"

"I wish I had better news for you. There isn't anything the bank can do to replace the funds until the feds finish their investigation. I'm so sorry."

"This is really bad. It's only my second payment. Could you loan me enough money to pay bills until the feds finish? I have my paycheck from this past week but that's not enough."

"I'm sorry Mr. Jackson. I have been told to tell you there isn't a thing we can do for you at this time," the manager apologized. He watched Jackson leave then evaporated into thin air.

"FUCK!" Jordan stormed out of the bank and sat in his truck trying to think of something, anything he could do to make his payment on time. He remembered those commercials on TV about overnight loans. They probably had high interest rates but it would only be for a few weeks. He'd look into one of those. Jesus! Just when you thought your life was going along fine something fucked it up.

He grabbed his mail on the way into his house and threw it on the table. There was an envelope with just his name on it. It looked strange. All of a sudden he knew something was very wrong. He put on gloves before he opened it. There was a message inside that made his skin crawl:

> *We have your money. If you want it back you will tell us what we want to know. Leave a note like this one on the top vegetable shelf above where the peas are in the Wal-Mart in Boone between eleven forty-five and midnight tonight or you'll never see your money again and your credit will be ruined for the rest of your life no matter what you do to fix it. We will ruin you. We know about your new house and will destroy it as well. Do not tell anyone about this note or you and they will die. We want to know the following: Is there a woman living in Crab Apple Creek that looks like this picture? She just moved there in April of this year. Leave the answer as instructed and if we find her your money will be returned. If not you're a dead man and so are the people in Crab Apple Creek.*

Holy Shit? What was this? Who were these people? How did they know about him? This was really bad. What was he supposed to do? He needed time to think. He spent a few hours trying to make sense of the whole thing. Then he had an idea. He keyed up a letter, printed it out and addressed one to Ted and Michael and the other to Kendra and instructed them to get the note to Matthews. He would put them in the mail slots in their doors after he delivered the note to the Wal-Mart. That way if anything happened to him, someone would know what was going on. He included copies of the note he had received and his response. He then placed the original threat in a plastic bag in his safe.

This was surreal. He set out for Wal-Mart and set his envelope where he had been instructed to. He waited until well after one in the morning but never saw anyone take the envelope. He next went to The Creek and delivered his notes as planned. He didn't see anyone following him. He returned home and wondered what he should do next. It was well into Saturday morning before he finally fell into an uneasy sleep.

Yuri waited for Jordan to leave Wal-Mart from his truck near the entrance. It was after one in the morning when he finally saw Jordan exit the store and leave in his truck. Yuri waited a few more minutes then went after the note. He found it right where he had told Jordan to leave it. He had what he wanted. The note said yes. Yuri was deliriously happy. He went back to his hotel room and slept until late in the afternoon that Saturday.

He had found his contact earlier in the day and gathered the guns and ammunition he had requested. He killed the man while he was sitting in his truck at a local liquor store later that night. No one was around to witness the murder.

When Yuri woke up he set the rest of his plan into action. He went to the local diner for supper and watched the people there. He was pleasant and charming to his waitress. He left the diner and decided to drive through Crab Apple Creek. He tried but the road was blocked so he turned back. He didn't want to be seen by anyone.

Matthews knew exactly where Yuri was every second since he had arrived in Boone. He knew he had contacted a man and met him earlier. Although the guns were in sports equipment bags, Matthews knew what they were. Three agents were assigned to follow Yuri. They had watched the gun transaction and watched Yuri murder his contact. They couldn't stop him. He was so fast and thorough.

They watched as Yuri placed the envelope in Jordan's mailbox. And Matthews was awake when Jordan put his envelopes in the door slots in The Creek. Everything was being recorded.

Matthews took a crew over to the store and was met by Michael. He told Michael to move away and picked up the envelope Jordan had left. Matthews returned to his house and opened the envelope. He read the contents and got on a secured telecast with his Chief in D. C.

"Sir, I have a note from Jordan Jackson. I've already sent a digital copy to you. How are we to proceed?"

"Get Barbara away from The Creek now. Take her to her new house. I've already alerted all teams. Take that bastard down."

"Yes, sir."

It was two in the morning.

Matthews called Sheriff Donohue and requested he pick up Jordan to keep him safe. Matthews had a hunch that Yuri would kill him before coming to The Creek.

Matthews ordered Emily's move. She was startled as Agent Mark's woke her up.

"Emily, it's time to move you to your new house. Get dressed. We leave in five minutes."

"Fuck! That bastard's here?"

"Close by. Matthews will be here in a minute."

Agent Mark's left Emily to dress as Matthews walked in the back door.

"How is she?"

"She's scared sir."

"Scared shitless, Matthews," Emily said.

"Let's move."

Emily was hustled out to a black SUV and was taken to her new house. They parked in the barn and secured the doors.

"Emily, we've set up a safe room in the basement of the stables. We're moving you there now. Follow along."

"Jesus! You planned this a long time ago, didn't you?"

"Yes. Ethan has known about the safe room from the start. He still doesn't know the details. That's for you to tell him if you wish once we take that bastard down."

"OK. I guess I don't need to tell you I'm beyond terrified."

"I know. I will keep you safe at any cost. We all will."

"That's a sobering thought, Matthews. Let's pray it doesn't come to a fire fight. I'd feel horrible if anyone lost their life to protect me."

"Emily, we took an oath to keep our clients safe. It's what we're trained for. We don't want to lose our lives either."

Emily remained quiet as they walked through the basement into the safe room underneath the stables.

"Holy shit! This looks like a fort. I don't think anyone could get in here if they tried."

"That's the whole idea," Agent Marks replied as he set Emily's things on a bench and proceeded to speak with Matthews on his radio.

"Emily, we're ready to seal the door. We'll open it once this whole thing is over. You OK with that?" Agent Marks asked.

"I guess so. Let's hope it's a short while."

"OK Matthews. I'm sealing us in until I get the all clear from you."

Agent Marks closed and sealed the door.

Emily looked around. It was actually three rooms. A common room, a bathroom and a kitchen of sorts. Well stocked, too. The common room had all kinds of digital equipment. There were four monitors on one wall that showed the two roads to the property, a surround view of the house and the barn and stables complex and a perimeter camera that showed the entire meadow where it met the forest, including the pond. The pond camera images were set into the meadow monitor.

There was a radio-communication set-up on the bench below the monitors. There was even a small monitor on the wall with weather information for her meadow. These guys were serious about taking care of her.

"Agent Marks, this is incredible, all these monitors. What a great view of my place. I hope we get to keep some of these so I can watch everything change throughout the year. And I'll get a better idea of the whole landscaping project."

"Only you, Emily, would think of something like that at a time like this," Agent Marks replied shaking his head and laughing a bit.

Emily heard the name Jordan come across the radio.

"Is that Jordan Jackson? Is he involved in this? Is he OK?"

"All I can tell you at this time is to please be patient."

"I met him at the store just last week. He's building on the other side of The Creek. He seems like a great guy. He's all excited about his new house and barn just like me. I hope he's gonna be OK. God, I'd hate to have anyone else involved with that maniac."

Matthews had just gotten word that the sheriff had picked up Jordan and had him at the sheriff's department in safe custody. The Sheriff reported that a black Jeep was observed a few houses away from Jordan's when they arrived. As deputies approached it, it drove away from Jordan's place. It was being tailed and currently, it was reported heading west out of Boone. Matthews told the sheriff he knew it was Strovonovich and to remain a distance back and to replace the department car with an old pickup truck if possible. The sheriff agreed and ten minutes later, the deputies' car turned away and an old pickup truck came onto the road a few blocks later.

Matthews had an open mic with all HQs involved. He reported that the Jeep seemed to be headed to The Creek. The Creek teams were given the go ahead to take Strovonovich down as soon as he cleared the other side of The Creek. There weren't any houses between The Creek and Emily's place so no one would be in danger in a fire fight.

The NOVAE were ready. There were entities surrounding Emily's meadow and the Sacred Rock Meadow.

The CON was ready, too. It had demonic entities near Emily's meadow and the Sacred Rock Meadow but couldn't get past the force field the NOVAE had set up. The CON was planning on having Yuri kill Barbara before the NOVAE could get a hold of her. Once that was done they would be able to take over the Universes without interference. Emily was the key to the whole confrontation and didn't even know it. Yet. That would change in a matter of minutes.

As soon as Yuri passed The Bend in The Road Country Store, the mountain started to speak. A low rumble was heard before it was felt. The ground began to shake.

"Did you feel that?" Agent Marks asked.

"Yes," Emily said.

Agent Mark's received numerous affirmatives over his radio.

"I'm just outside the barn. I felt it but haven't seen any damage," Matthews reported.

The teams on the mountain reported the same.

Yuri felt his Jeep shake a little bit but ignored it.

Ethan felt it as well and started for Emily's build site.

Kendra felt it and set aside the work she was doing. She stood in the middle of her kitchen and waited.

Lainie and Mo were awakened by the rumble. They quickly dressed and stepped out onto their porch.

Bubba and Earl were still awake and felt the mountain move. They headed out toward Emily's build site, too.

Cora was awake. She was expecting the rumble. She set out for Emily's place.

Yuri was about half a mile from Emily's build site when the mountain spoke for a second time. This time is was strong. Anyone standing was thrown to the ground. Trees crashed and boulders rolled down the mountainside.

Yuri's Jeep was sent sideways and crashed on the side of the road against a group of young trees. He was momentarily stunned. He tried to get out of the driver's door but it was pinned tight against the trees. He tried the passenger door and found it could open. He crawled into the back to get his gun bag then left his vehicle. He decided to walk the last half mile to Emily's meadow.

Everyone reported in to Matthews and said that they were all OK.

Ethan held on tight to the steering wheel as he passed through The Creek as the bigger quake hit. He stopped until it was over then started up again. As he got close to Emily's he saw the black Jeep on the side of the road. He called Matthews.

"Hey Matthews, I'm less than a half mile away and I found an abandon black Jeep on the side of the road. Looks like someone left in a hurry. The door is still open."

"Ethan, hold on. Attention all teams, Ethan has just spotted the black Jeep abandoned about a half mile from here. The target is approaching on foot. Let me know the minute you spot him."

"Affirmative," was heard from all teams.

"Ethan, have you seen anyone on the road and where are you now?"

"I'm here at the pond drive blockade. I did not see anyone on the road."

"Alright. Stay where you are. Follow the orders of the team leader. Do not approach the house."

"Yes, sir."

Yuri was just approaching the southern end of the pond. The pond cam was recording his progress.

"We have him on the pond cam. Take him out."

The mountain shook hard and the sky sent bolts of lightning toward the pond. The wind started to blow and no one could see Strovonovich on any camera.

Just as the mountain shook for the third time, the door to the safe room opened and as Agent Marks watched, Emily was lifted off the floor by an unseen force and disappeared from sight in an instant.

"Emily's gone. The safe room door just opened and she disappeared. Like in an instant. Just gone. I'm leaving the safe room and don't see her anywhere."

"Barn team, assist Marks!"

Matthews ran to the barn doors but they were still closed. No one could find her.

"Where is she? Give me a location on Strovonovich."

"No one is able to find him. It's as if he disappeared, too."

As the lightning struck, Yuri found himself lifted off the ground. When he looked again he was in a field with a bunch of boulders set in a circle.

Emily saw herself rising from the floor and the next thing she knew she was in the Sacred Rock Meadow standing next to the altar stone.

"Matthews, I know where they are. They're at Sacred Rock Meadow. I just know it. This thing is bigger than any of us," Ethan said as he started to run across Emily's meadow toward Sacred Rock Meadow. "Look at all the lights over there."

Matthews was near the house when Ethan called. He turned to the northwest and saw an amazing light display. Lightning was shooting in all directions and it looked like there were UFOs just above the tree tops over Sacred Rock Meadow. He joined Ethan as they ran for Sacred Rock Meadow. Matthew's teams were following as well.

Cora was just approaching the meadow from the pond drive when she saw the lightning and the UFOs.

"Ma'am, you can't be here," one of the agents said.

"Son, this is bigger than any of us. I was called here. I'm walking on over to the Sacred Rock Meadow and you can't stop me. They won't let ya."

The agent tried to move and he found he couldn't. Not one inch. It was like he was frozen in place.

Cora patted him on the shoulder as she walked by. "Nice young man."

Cora kept a steady pace as she walked across Emily's place and around the west side of her house.

The wind had picked up in intensity and was now roaring around Sacred Rock Meadow.

As Ethan, Matthews, and the teams approached the edge of the meadow, they saw Yuri standing outside the circle of boulders with a sniper rifle in place. Emily wasn't quite sure how she'd gotten to the meadow. She looked around and found herself standing in the inner circle of stones next to the altar stone. As she continued to watch, her clothes changed into flowing purple and silver robes that looked like they were made from gossamer. You could see her body right through them. Her hair began to blow away from her as well and had ribbons of gold in it.

Ethan and Matthews looked at Emily and couldn't believe their eyes. Matthews motioned for some of the team to get Yuri and the others to protect Emily.

No one could move. No one. It was as if a force field had been placed around the circle of stones.

Yuri saw this and smiled. He figured this gave him a clear shot at Emily.

Cora arrived and walked past everyone into the outer circle of stones and stood in front of Emily. Before she could say anything a pure white light beamed into the inner circle of stones and a figure appeared as the light moved away.

Kendra was standing next to Emily. She looked like Kendra put she didn't. She had on silvery and purple robes as well. The same kind as Emily but she had a staff made of wood, feathers and crystals in her left hand. She tapped the staff on the ground and thunder like no one had ever heard before burst through the meadow. It was deafening. As the sound calmed, animals and birds of all kinds began to walk into the meadow. As they got close to the circle of stones they shape shifted into translucent beings.

The man in the black hat appeared next to Yuri. He removed his hat and turned to Yuri. He looked horrible. His skin looked like it had been burned and he had three red eyes just like the monsters in Yuri's dreams. Yuri tried to scream but found he couldn't. Just like before.

"It is time for you to kill that human over there. She is a High Priestess of the NOVAE and must be killed so we, The CON, can rule the universes. It is what you were chosen to do."

Yuri found his voice had returned.

"Who are you? You're hideous."

Yuri turned the rifle on the man in the black hat and squeezed the trigger. Nothing happened.

"You can't kill us with a mere rifle. Now, kill that human and we will leave you alone for the rest of your human life. You can have all you want. No limits. Just kill her. Now!"

As Yuri raised the rifle once again and looked at where Emily was standing he was dumbstruck. She had changed. What was she? And who were all those things with her? He took aim and the ground shook so hard that he was thrown down and lost hold of his rifle.

As he got up he noticed no one else had fallen. All the creatures around Emily were watching him. He headed over to her and was stopped by her voice.

"You are a soldier for The CON. You walk in The Dark. You cannot be allowed to complete your mission."

"Who the fuck are you? I can do whatever I want. Watch me."

As he started to walk into the outer circle, Emily raised her arms and pushed the air towards him and he was thrown back into the meadow to where he had been standing.

"Bitch. I don't know how you did that, but no one pushes me around."

"Why do you think you can do whatever you wish?" Emily asked.

"Because I am the most powerful person in the world," Yuri yelled.

Kendra and Emily and all the shape shifters laughed at Yuri.

"Who told you that lie?" Emily asked.

"You will stop laughing. I am the most powerful person here and can have you killed in an instant. This creature here has given me the power to control all the Earth," Yuri yelled as he pointed to the man in the black hat.

"What creature?" Emily asked.

Yuri turned to look at the creature that had been the man in the black hat and he was gone. He was nowhere to be seen.

"He was just standing right here. He must have gone to get help to kill all of you."

"That is not going to happen. Never." Emily looked across the meadow to where the voice had come from. She saw Cora approaching the outer circle.

As all watched, Cora's clothes changed into robes of gold and pure white and many creatures of the earth came to her as she stepped into the inner circle of stones and stood next to Emily and Kendra. An eagle softly landed on the stone altar and bowed before the three of them.

As Yuri watched all this, the man in the black hat returned with creatures of his own , just as hideous as he was, and surrounded Yuri.

Yuri began to yell at them to move back.

The man in the black hat waved his hand at the creatures and they separated to allow Yuri to be seen by all.

The creatures began to raise their arms, pointing at the altar stones and Emily.

With one swift wave of her arms all the creatures were thrown into the air and then fell back to the earth impaling themselves on broken trees and sharp rocks. They were all dead and their bodies became fireballs as they disintegrated into thin air.

Emily lowered her arms and stood there quietly as Yuri screamed.

"How did you do that, you bitch? But your tricks cannot touch me. You are just a weak woman and need to be reminded of the power I hold over you."

"You hold no power over me."

"Yes I do. Who do you think made Nick marry you? Me! I control all!" Yuri said with a maniacal laugh.

"Really? Who do you think killed Nick? It was your friends and their like that did that to teach you a lesson."

"No it wasn't."

"Why not ask them? Your pal is right there beside you again."

Yuri turned and saw the man in the black hat once again. He was momentarily terrorized.

"She speaks the truth. My kind killed Nick as a warning to you."

Yuri just kept staring at the man in the black hat for the longest time.

The mountain had endured enough of this delay. She spoke so loudly that all within twenty miles of her were thrown to the ground. Trees and boulders moved and fell as before but this time even small buildings came crashing down the mountain. No human was hurt as the mountain took care of her own. Yuri's sniper rifle was smashed to bits. Those in the inner circle were protected as were the agents and residents of The Creek that were watching the confrontation. The man in the black hat was finally destroyed when a large tree fell on him. He exploded in a ball of fire, too.

Yuri got up and tried to get his balance. He couldn't figure out what had just happened. He was furious and scared. He was no longer in control.

"There's no way you made that earthquake happen. And why aren't you on the ground like the rest of us?" Yuri said as he looked around. He realized he was the only one that had been thrown to the ground.

"Why aren't any of you on the ground? What kind of evil is in this place?"

Cora answered him. "You are the evil in this place. It has been foretold that this day would come and a great battle between good and evil would ensue. You are the human form of evil and Emily is the human form of good. The two of you will determine the outcome of Mother Earth and of all humankind."

"You're nuts, old lady. I don't know what kind of craziness you have going on here but it's time for Barbara to die. She knows all about my business and needs to be shut up once and for all."

"I know nothing about your horrible business. You just think I do."

"No. I know you do. You need to die now," Yuri yelled as he started to run over to where Emily stood.

He was stopped so suddenly he fell to the ground. As he got up he looked around and couldn't figure out what had stopped him.

"What the hell was that?" He demanded to know as he stood upright and tried to run at Emily again. He was stopped as before. This time he was momentarily stunned.

The mountain spoke again and the stone circle closed in and became tighter around the women.

Yuri found himself back at the edge of the meadow for the second time. He was furious.

As he stood there he found a rifle in his hands. It had just materialized out of thin air. He didn't care. He was beyond reason. He raised the rifle and aimed at Emily.

Agent Marks raised his weapon but Matthews signaled him to stand down. Agent Marks was closest to Emily, only a few feet away on the edge of the inner circle.

Yuri once again started to enter the outer circle with the raised rifle.

"Now you die cunt!" Yuri hollered as he pulled the trigger. Nothing happened.

"I suggest you leave if you do not wish to perish."

Yuri laughed an evil laugh and replied, "And you think you can do that?

"Yes. You think if you talk long enough I'll get sidetracked and you'll get close enough to me to break my neck on the stones. I'm only a stupid bitch anyway, right?"

"How the hell do you know what I'm thinking? What kind of demonic stuff is going on here?"

"You are the demonic entity. The CON has manipulated you all these years to do their bidding on Mother Earth. It is time for you to perish and The CON to be sent back to its own hell."

"You're really crazy, Barbara. I'm going to kill you and live free and happy."

"Just try."

"OK. Whatever you say."

"Matthews, your team cannot interfere. They have to stay away. Yuri and I will determine the outcome of the fate of Mother Earth and humankind. Take your men and leave the Sacred Rock Meadow.

"No, Emily. I can't leave you here."

"Please. Ethan you must take Matthews away from here."

"I can't leave either Emily. You mean the world to me and I'm not leaving you alone to fight this mad man.

Cora exclaimed, "This is a battle between The Light and The Dark. Only their kind can fight this fight. Only one will win. It has been foretold."

When folks would tell the story about this night no one would even think of believing them. It was a fantastic legend to tell. The only reason anyone would believe it was because of the people that would live to tell the tale.

The NOVAE had encircled Emily with protective energy. The CON began to send fire bolts to the earth. A wall of fire grew around the circle of stones. No one could see through it. Emily faced Yuri while Kendra and the shape shifters worked at protecting her. Father Sky let down a wall of water that drowned the fire. As soon as it disappeared, The CON sent thousands upon thousands of giant hornets into the circle.

Emily raised her hands and in a sweeping motion she threw them back into the sky where they exploded like millions of fireworks. The sky was full of light and sound that could be heard throughout the Blue Ridge. The CON physically moved Yuri so that he was standing closer to Emily.

"It is time for you to die bitch," Yuri proclaimed as he once again raised the rifle to his shoulder.

"You have that wrong. It is time for you to perish" Emily replied.

As she once again raised her arms, Agent Marks shot at Yuri. Before the bullet could reach him, The CON retaliated and hurled a sword of dark energy at Agent Marks. He was killed instantly.

Emily cried out at such violence. She sent Love and Light to Agent Marks' spirit.

The mountain began to shake again and did not stop this time. Father Sky sent wind and rain and lightning to Mother Earth to protect her from The CON.

Yuri took aim at Emily. He never got the chance to shoot.

Emily had raised her arms and with all her might she threw an energy ball at Yuri. It was pure white with silver shimmering all through it.

It hit Yuri square in the chest. He was vaporized in an instant.

Next, Emily, Kendra and Cora began to chant, asking all the shape shifters to join them. The sound grew and grew and the team could feel the vibrations of their combined voices.

As everyone watched, a wall of vibrating color rose from the ground surrounding all in the meadow. The rocks began to vibrate and move. They combined to form one large circle with Emily and the altar rock in the middle and Kendra and Cora standing near the edge.

Emily began to levitate ever so slowly. Kendra and Cora began to rise up as well. The sound continued to grow and Matthews and Ethan looked at each other as they felt the vibrations move through their bodies. Cora was awash in the colors of the sound. She was smiling and crying while watching the unbelievable.

The man in the black hat had come back, again, and turned to look at Emily. She looked at him and with a slight nod from her head he was vaporized as well.

There was a great growling heard for miles around as The CON tried one more time to kill Emily. This last time they threw spears of electrical energy at her from all directions.

Emily was lifted into the air by the sound vibrations as the spears merged and were sent back into the sky, exploding the ships of The CON into millions of tiny pieces that burned up before they could fall back onto Mother Earth.

The CON had been defeated.

Emily was placed back on the earth where she had been standing. The chanting had stopped and not a sound could be heard. All was silent.

Emily looked down at herself and was shocked at how she looked. The last thing she remembered was when the ground had shook in the safe room. How had she gotten here and what was she wearing?

She heard a soft voice say to her, "You are a High Priestess of The NOVAE. You chose this path before you came into the body this time. You have fulfilled your most important mission. You have saved Mother Earth and the human race from the demonic energies known as The CON. They were bent on taking over Mother Earth, destroying her, and using humankind for procreation of more of their evil entities. They have been trying to control all of the universes for a millennia. Tonight was the final battle between The Light and The Dark for this control. You will remember everything now. We love you my child. We rejoice in your accomplishments this night. Blessed Be."

As Matthews, Ethan, Cora, and everyone else watched, Emily began to smile. She turned to Kendra and they hugged each other. They walked over to Cora and hugged her as well. All three women were crying and smiling as they left the circle of stones and joined the others.

Ethan just looked at Emily. He didn't know what else to do. Matthews' radio was going a mile a minute demanding someone respond. Agent Marks lay on the meadow, silent in death.

Emily walked over to his body and knelt down beside it. Matthews was right behind her.

"He protected you with his life. That's what he wanted to do."

Emily was crying. "I know and I understand. But my heart is sad that he had to leave so young. I know it was his destiny but still I am saddened."

"We will take care of him and treat him with the honor and dignity he so richly deserves."

"Thank you Matthews. Could someone please cover him now. Let him rest knowing he was loved."

One of the agents took off his jacket and covered Agent Marks with it. He made the sign of the cross over him and said a short prayer.

"I guess I had better talk to the radio for a few minutes. No one is going to believe what I tell them but here goes anyway," Matthews said as he began to answer the millions of questions being asked by HQ. He told them first about Agent Marks and the radios went silent for a moment.

As Matthews was talking to his people, Emily looked above Agent Mark's body and saw his Spirit. He was a pure white light as she knew he would be. He smiled at her and touched her shoulder. She smiled back at him and bowed her head in response. She sent the message that she would always remember him and he was always welcome to visit her. He smiled as he crossed over the rainbow bridge and joined the others in The White Light once again.

As Matthews continued talking, Ethan walked over to Emily where she stood next to Agent Marks.

"Emily?"

"Yes, Ethan? Oh, you want to know what all this was don't you?" she said with a smile.

"How do you know what I'm thinking? That's exactly what I was going to say."

"Ethan, you've got a lot to learn," Kendra said with a wink at Emily.

"And you? Who the hell are you anyway? You one of those ET things? I don't know what to think any more. And Miss Cora, what about you?"

"Now Ethan, you take a few deep breaths there and try to settle down. I knew something otherworldly was on its way but I didn't have any of these details. Gotta say though, these young women are the most beautiful creatures I've ever seen."

"Are you one of them?"

"Why Ethan, not like you think. Just a regular person I'm just like you except I have some pretty special Gifts. Emily, too. It's Kendra that's the best kept secret around here. Has been since she came to us."

"Miss Cora's right Ethan, Matthews. I'm an Extraterrestrial. An ET. My kind are known as shape shifters. We can change form as we need to. We are here to bring the Light and Love to all creatures and creation. Mother Earth and you humans have been our biggest challenge for a millennia. Although I gotta say I like the way things worked out tonight."

Matthews heard the whole thing and was just staring at Kendra and smiling.

"I knew it. Yes I did. Boy, is this report gonna take a long time to write up. Not really sure what to put in it."

"Matthews everyone here will remember everything tonight. You all will not report the truth. As far as those that live away from The Creek, they think one hell of a thunderstorm has hit the place the likes of which haven't been seen here before. Only those of us right here know the truth. You were very wise Matthews, in your conversation with your people. You told them there was a huge storm and Yuri had been hit by lightning and died instantly, burning up in the process. You may have heard yourself saying other things but this is what they all heard. You're all safe. You can talk about this with each other and folks in The Creek.

"They know what really happened. Some of them watched the whole thing. Bubba and Earl and Lainie and Mo to name a few along with the guys from the store and Hal. I'm sure you recognize Pam and Kevin. Pam and Kevin are right here. They are in their original form right now. They, too, are shape shifters like me."

A moment of silence was quickly replaced by everyone talking at once.

It took quite some time before the chatter died down.

"Well, I don't really know what to say. Thank you to everyone that made sure I was safe. And I'm happy beyond words that the evil bad guy is gone. Really gone. I think I'd like to walk back to my house for a few minutes," Emily said in a soft quiet voice.

"I'm not sure what to say, either," Ethan agreed.

Everyone else said the same thing.

"Let's go back to Emily's place. It's really dark out here so please be careful," Matthews suggested as they all left Sacred Rock Meadow.

"I'd like to come back here in the daylight soon just to see how things look after tonight," Emily said.

"Me, too," Cora replied. "Me, too. This has been a long time coming and I wanna see in the sunlight what happened to this place."

As the group left the meadow and walked over to Emily's, Ethan and Emily turned to take a last look at Sacred Rock Meadow. It looked like a million fireflies were dancing over the rocks.

"Alright everyone, let's head home and get some sleep if that's possible. The teams have their orders. We'll get together tomorrow morning to go over everything that happened here."

"Matthews, since the bad guy's dead can Emily ride with me without her entourage?" Ethan asked.

"Yes, Ethan, I do believe that is alright."

"Thanks Matthews," Emily said as she followed Ethan to his truck.

"Hey Emily, see ya tomorrow. Take care of your robes. Ya never know when you'll need them again," Kendra added.

The meadow was empty and silent. You would have never known that a battle of epic proportions had taken place just a few minutes earlier.

As Emily settled down in her own house she realized she no longer felt the terror she had lived with for so long. It was gone.

CHAPTER 37

E mily slept until late Sunday evening. She woke up long enough to
eat something and then fell back to sleep until Monday morning
when the sun shined through her house and woke her up.

The first thing she realized was that her house was abso-
lutely quiet. Then she remembered she was alone, really alone for the first time
since she'd left New Hampshire in April.

She stretched herself and got out of bed and into the shower. A long
hot shower was just what she needed. She dressed and ate breakfast and for
the first time she set foot outside her little house a free woman. It felt great!
She did a little happy dance and headed for Matthews' house.

As she knocked on his front door, she hollered out, "Hey Matthews,
this here is Emily Gail Henshaw. I am free and victorious and full of piss and
vinegar."

Matthews walked outside replying, "Why, yes you are and looking
mighty fine."

A few of the agents working inside came out and joined the celebration.

"I gotta say this whole thing has made me do some deep thinking.
Amazing stuff," Agent Anderson said. "And, if I hadn't seen it with my own
eyes I would have thought the whole thing was some kind of dream or something. You look especially happy this morning Emily."

"I am Agent Anderson," Emily replied.

"When you get some time, we're going to need to look at my notes
Emily," Matthews said.

"OK. Let me know when and I'm all yours," Emily replied as they turned to watch Ethan stop on the road near them.

"Mornin' all. Looks like we've all recovered from the other night," Ethan offered as he joined the group.

"Hey Ethan."

"Miss Emily, I have here in my hand a very important piece of paper. Seems the building inspector will be arriving at your home around noon and is ready for the final inspection. Would you care to join me?"

"Really? Does that mean that I could be living in my house in a few days?"

"No, Miss Emily. It means you could be living there a few minutes, any time after noon today. Once the building inspector signs this paper. Oh, did I mention it was the occupancy permit?" Ethan said with a sly look on his face.

"Oh you big tease. You're gonna have to pay for this," Emily said as she punched Ethan in the arm as hard as she could.

"Hey, this little lady sure has a strong fist there," Ethan said as he feigned injury to his shoulder. "Yes, it is the occupancy permit. The inspector and I met yesterday and the punch list is being completed as we speak. The crew is already there workin' hard."

"I will be there! Just try to stop me and see what happens," Emily said.

"I think we all know what you are capable of after yesterday," Matthews said with a laugh.

They talked for a few more minutes before Ethan left for Emily's meadow.

Emily went across to the store for a chat and Matthews went back inside to work on his report for HQ.

Matthews was receiving the itinerary for Agent Marks' wake and funeral. It was going to be held in Washington, D.C. on Wednesday and Thursday. He knew Emily wanted to be a part of the proceedings and decided to tell her about it on Tuesday. After all, she deserved a day of celebration with her new house and Ethan and her freedom.

Sheriff Donohue reported that Jordan Jackson had been picked up by his deputies before Strovonovich could get to him. He was safe and back in his home.

As Emily walked into the store Michael and Ted rushed over and gave her big hugs.

"Oh my, oh my, Emily, that was some amazing something in the night. I don't even know what to call it and where to begin with it all," Ted said as he kept an arm around Emily's shoulders.

"Me either, Ted."

"Emily, I will never forget this. It really explains a lot of things that have happened in The Creek over my lifetime," Michael commented as he held onto her arm and they moved into the kitchen.

Ted kept crying and laughing along with Michael. Emily didn't know what to say. She took a seat and just sat there looking from one to the other and just shaking her head.

"For a bunch of college graduates we sure look pathetic not knowing what to say," Michael said. They all laughed and began to talk.

A few minutes later, Kendra and Cora walked in and joined them. Ted got everyone drinks and food and they began to share their thoughts on the whole thing that had happened in Sacred Rock Meadow.

"Well now, I knew something was comin'. I did, but that something out there in the meadow was beyond belief. I've been writing it all down since yesterday afternoon. I keep remembering things and have to go back and add them in. It's beyond all comprehension," Cora said.

"Yes, Miss Cora, it surely is. That's what Ted and I've been sayin' all day," Michael replied.

"Good to see no one was harmed and The Creek is all OK," Kendra said.

"And, you, Miss Shape Shifter," Ted started with, "What have you got to say for yourself? Pretending to be one of us for your whole life and then, WHAM! You're something totally different. Well, say something." Ted demanded of Kendra.

"Now Ted, I have never been anything more than what you've loved for your whole life. The outer wrapping has changed but the inside, the soul of me, is still the same loving spirit it always has been."

"So you say. It's just gonna take some time to get used to you like that."

"I get it. Did you want to see the other me? I can change right here and now if you want me to," Kendra said with teasing in her voice.

"No, no. That won't be necessary. I don't think I could handle that right now. Maybe in a few thousand years. OK?"

"OK, Ted. No problem."

Michael looked at everyone for the longest time then asked, "So, how did all this come about? When did all this start? Is it over? What will happen next?"

Kendra looked at Cora. Cora looked at Emily. Emily looked at Kendra. Then Kendra began to talk.

"There has always been The Light and The Dark since the beginning of the Universes. And, before we go any further I need for y'all to try to wrap your head around this: time does not exist."

Hal looked at Kendra as if she had lost her head. "What do ya mean time doesn't exist?"

"Now this I gotta hear," replied George.

"OK. Let me try to explain. The Divine, God, The Great Spirit, gave us the concept of time while our Spirit is in the body on the Earth plane. Time is a way for us to measure our accomplishments and goals we set for ourselves while in the physical body. When we are in our energy form time does not exist. All things happen at the same time, so to speak."

There was silence for a bit.

"So, let me get this right," George replied. "Since time doesn't exist all things are happening at the same time. Right?"

Kendra smiled, "Yes George. Exactly. Our time here on Mother Earth is a learning time for our souls. We decide what we want to experience so we can have a better understanding of the human experience. Most of us come to the Earth plane many times as we work at experiencing the complex existence that is the human condition."

"Why do we do that?" Hal asked.

"It's so we can be a more benevolent and understanding entity as we work at walking close with the Divine," Kendra explained.

"I get it, I really do," Hal said with a smile on his face. "Makes sense to me."

"I'm gonna need some time to think about this," George said.

"OK Kendra, I get that. But when did all this on the mountain start and why?"

"Michael, the best I can do is to start with the mountains themselves. When Pangea separated millions of years ago and the Appalachians were formed they became the oldest mountains on this northern continent. I don't have a specific answer as to why since this mystery is a well-guarded secret. All I can think is that The Light decided to hide Magic in these mountains for a very special reason. I don't know the reason but I think I can come up with a good explanation. How about you Miss Cora?"

"Well, yes I do believe I can give it a try. I know I've been in these mountains before. As soon as I could reason beyond the thoughts of a young girl, I became aware that this place felt real familiar to me like I'd been here before. I was drawn to Sacred Rock Meadow time and time again. I saw fairies and angels there and we became good friends. Even though the veil between dimensions should have blocked their world from mine, I kept right on seein' them. After I talked to my grandmother about the lights over the Applewood Grove she began to teach me about the Magic here. It felt real good, like I had known about it before. When I told her about that she smiled and said I had been here before in another life or two. I was about twelve years-old at the time and just smiled at her. It sounded like a good fit. Whenever the mountain spoke, I knew it was Magic happening. As I grew up into my adult years I began to see and talk to Spirits just like Miss Emily and Kendra do. Kendra's kinda special anyways. Miss Emily's human like the rest of us so she knows what I'm talking about."

"Yes I do Miss Cora. Yes I do," Emily offered.

"And now you can go about sharing your Gift with anyone that asks for it without worryin' about anything."

"Yes I can."

"Good. Now, back to the Magic. I do believe that The Light sent the Magic here to be protected by those of us that have these Gifts. And, The Light chose our little dell and the folks here because we have always had a special connection to Mother Earth with our growin' things and all. You know what I mean. Yup. This is a remote place that most folks stay away from so The Light knew their secret would be well protected. They also knew that the battle that just happened would have to be in a remote place so all of mankind wouldn't be destroyed. Just imagine if that battle had taken place in New York City. What a mess that would have been.

"The Light and The Dark have forces throughout the universes. This battle has finally settled which one of them will be here with us on Mother Earth. It is The Light. Now we have a big job ahead of us to help restore Mother Earth. She is in desperate need of healing energy and we are the ones to give it to her. As each one of us crosses over there will be more to take our place. We are here to heal and to teach others how to walk in The Light. That's what I know."

"I believe it to be so, too," Ted whispered.

"So, there aren't going to be any more battles like this one here on our mountain? Is that what y'all think?"

"I don't believe there will be any more like this one. There may be little ones that involve a person or two, or a Spirit or two, but they will be seen as tiny compared to this one. That's what I'm thinkin'," Kendra offered.

Emily smiled as she said, "I have no idea myself. I need some time to process all this stuff. The more we talk about it the more I'm gonna begin to understand it."

"I gotta say that light show was amazing. No fireworks are ever going to compare to that," George said.

"I agree. I've never seen so much lightning all at one time in my life and the colors were like nothin' I've ever seen," Ted offered.

"It was the wind that had me speechless. It was all over the place and the sound it made I can't even begin to describe. Sometimes like crying and sometimes it sounded like a pack of wolves howlin' at the moon," Michael added.

"I know and I was in the middle of it all and I can't even begin to process all I saw and heard and felt. Maybe I'll just have to write it all down like Miss Cora does, in a journal," Emily said.

"Ya know, that's a good idea Emily. We should all write down everything we experienced up there. It might just help us figure it all out. And, it's be good to have for the future in case something like this happens again. Then folks will have something to compare it to," Kendra said.

"Well, I'm glad some of you have been listenin' to me all this time. I keep tellin' y'all to write it down," Miss Cora said with a laugh.

"Yes, Ma'am," was heard all around.

"Now, how about we all get together here for supper. I've got some things to take care of and then we could all talk some more," Hal said.

All agreed and went their separate ways.

Emily glanced at the wall on the sideboard and saw it was almost noon.

"Folks, sorry to say, but it's time for me to be on my way. I've got a date with the building inspector at my house. Ethan tells me the occupancy permit is going to be signed today. I gotta be there for that great moment. Then the party plans will begin."

"Oh, my God! Does that mean you'll me moving in soon?" Ted asked all excited.

"Yes, Ted. It means I'll be moving in less than one hour," Emily replied all excited as well.

"Well, then, I guess we'll just have to cook something special for the party," Ted offered.

"Thanks Ted. Sounds great!"

"We will start planning your house warming, or should I say barn raisin'?"

"Sounds like a plan. See y'all later," Emily said as she left.

"Now Ted, the barn's already up so she won't need no barn raisin'," Cora said.

"Miss Cora, there's always more work to be done. Some planting, or tidying up. The Creek will be there for her."

"Well said. And we will. It's time for me to mosey on as well. Take care and thanks for the take-out Ted, Michael. You boys make your mamas proud."

"I'll walk with you Miss Cora. Bye y'all and thanks for the mornin'," Kendra said as she joined Cora.

Kendra and Cora left and the store got back to its usual Monday ritual. A few minutes later the Foodies, Inc. truck arrived. No one knew about Jordan's role in the big event. Matthews had wanted to keep him out of the public eye for now.

"Hey y'all," Jordan said as he came through the door with the first of the deliveries.

"Hey Jordan," Michael replied.

"Heard about that big storm that hit The Creek Saturday night. Everyone OK? Any problems?"

"That's right. Not one thing damaged. It sure was a noisy thing."

"I'll say. I heard some of that thunder my way and that's a considerable distance. I checked on my build and nothing was moved or damaged. Even the ground has already dried mostly. There was one big puddle behind the barn area. It almost looked like a small pond, and that's good to know so I won't plant anything there. I wouldn't want it to be drowned or damaged should we get another storm like this one. Ya never know."

"No, you certainly don't," Michael said slowly.

Jordan finished his deliveries with the cooler load. He was just about to enter the kitchen work area when Ted came through the door.

"Oh, Jordan. Let me hold the door for you," Ted offered as Jordan passed him and placed the boxes in front of the coolers. "How is the house coming along?"

"Great. Thanks for asking," Jordan replied. "They're gonna be decking in about a week, I think is what Ethan said. Really cool. Ethan said I could be in by Thanksgiving if all goes well."

"That's awesome. Let's hope so. We do up a real big community Thanksgiving Day dinner and all right here for The Creek. Michael and I roast a bunch of turkeys and hams and everyone brings the rest of the meal. We spend the day here from morning 'til night together. Please plan to join us this year. We already see you as one of us."

"Wow! That's so generous of you. I accept. Let me know what to bring. I can cook but not at the level you guys do."

"Great. Now, how about some lunch for the road. What can I get ya?"

Jordan placed his order and was back on the road twenty minutes later. He stopped at his build site and ate his lunch sitting in his truck. The work crews were busy getting everything sorted out for the decking, and trenches were being dug from the road for water and utility lines. Jordan decided to just stay in his truck and watch. He left a while later, content with the progress.

He had received a call from the bank that morning and was told his funds had been returned. He immediately transferred his mortgage payment monies and paid his other bills - all on time. Today was a good day on all counts for Jordan Jackson.

Emily arrived at her house just before noon. She drove the pond driveway and parked her Jeep in the space by the barn. All the paving and stone drive was in place. The whole thing looked completely finished.

She walked over to her house and was stepping up onto the porch when Ethan came out the front door.

"Hey Emily," Ethan said as he gave her an unexpected sweet kiss.

"Hey Ethan," Emily replied as she returned the kiss with a squeeze of his ass. "I do like the way I'm greeted at my house."

"I'll say you do. Maybe we could make that a regularly occurring thing?"

"Could be. So, where's the building inspector? Is he here yet?"

Ethan looked out over the meadow as he replied, "Yup. He's arriving now. Let's go meet him."

They walked over to where the inspector had parked next to Emily's Jeep.

"Hey Ethan," Derrick said as he got out of his truck.

"Hey Derrick. I'd like to introduce the home owner and designer Emily Henshaw."

"Hi Emily. Nice to meet you. This house is beautiful. You're design just shouts comfort and hominess," Derrick said as they shook hands.

"Thanks Derrick. Nice to meet you as well. So, what do we do now?"

Everyone laughed at Emily's enthusiasm.

"Ethan has a list of things I told him needed to be completed by today. Is that list completed?"

"Yes, sir. Shall we start in the barn and stables complex first?" Ethan said as he led the group into the barn. They spent the next hour going over every detail of the punch list.

As they returned to the kitchen after checking all the things on the list for the house, Derrick said, "Emily, the punch list is complete. Congratulations! Let me sign your occupancy permit and the house is yours, ready to live in this minute."

Derrick signed the permit with a flourish and handed it to Emily. "You keep this one and I'll file this second one with the county. How's it feel?"

"Indescribable. Wow! All mine. I'm here. The house is ready to be furnished. I'm home." Emily just stood there smiling and laughing.

"Thanks Derrick. This is a big moment for Emily and for all of us who have been working on her build. Thanks for being here every day. It's made things go much faster. I'm sure you'll be invited back for the celebration in a few days."

"I'll be here. And you're very welcome. Let's do the same thing on the Jackson build on the other side of The Creek. When are you planning on decking?"

"In about a week from today. You can check things out whenever you have time. The basement foundations were poured and are curing. How about Thursday or Friday? Let me know."

"Will do. Enjoy your new home Emily and I'll see you at the celebration. I never miss a party in The Creek."

"Bye. Thanks," Emily replied as she stood in the kitchen watching Derrick leave.

"Emily, what's going on in that head of yours?" Ethan asked.

"I'm just trying to take this all in. My house. My freedom. The mountains. Everything. It's gonna take a long while to get used to everything and then it's only gonna take a minute. Know what I mean Ethan? Well, I guess you don't. Doesn't matter. You've made a lot of this possible - you, your building crews and your amazing brother. That Ian is a frickin' genius when it comes to the little details. I really wouldn't have considered a lot of those details without him. I do believe I'm gonna have to give your little brother a kiss for all his efforts."

Ethan laughed and hugged Emily all at once.

"I do believe I like an appreciative client. Just how appreciative are you?"

"Oh, well, you just get yourself out here after work and I'll be very happy to show you."

"No preview?"

Emily just smiled as she pulled Ethan to her and kissed him deep and long running her hands across his crotch feeling his hard on growing. She massaged him through his jeans until he had to pull away for fear of exploding.

"Now that's what I call a great preview. I'll be here."

They kissed again and then walked outside. Emily stayed on the porch watching Ethan get into his truck and drive away. She soon returned to her rental house and began packing her things. She packed all her clothes and personal things along with her computer. Matthews had told her he would have everything else packed and delivered to her so she wouldn't have to worry about anything.

She next went to the store and told the guys that the house was hers and she was moving in right then and there.

"Oh Emily, how wonderful," Ted said.

Michael agreed.

"So, will you be staying there alone the first night?" Ted asked in his most endearing way.

"Ted, I don't plan on it," Emily said as she walked away.

Michael just laughed and waved as she left the store.

The rest of the afternoon found Emily settling in. She kept finding new things to look at and try out and it took her hours to unpack her clothes and set up her computer.

She noticed shadows starting to come through the house and looked at her phone. It was well past six.

She was in the kitchen working on supper when Ethan came through the kitchen door. He was carrying flowers and champagne. He put the champagne in the fridge and found a vase for the flowers.

"Why, Mr. Ethan, these are beautiful. Thanks so much. And that champagne is my favorite. How thoughtful of you," Emily said as she gave him a little smooch.

"Smells good in here. Garlic? Yum. Pasta as well? Even better."

"Of course. Great food for our private celebration. Garlic sautéed chicken over pasta with pesto, salad and garlic bread."

"Sounds heavenly. I'll go get cleaned up and be right back."

Ethan showered and was back in the kitchen just as Emily was placing the garlic bread under the broiler.

She had set the small table next to the windows that overlooked the barn.

Ethan took the bread out of the oven as Emily brought dinner to the table.

"Emily, this smells wonderful and everything looks beautiful. Having fun in your kitchen?"

"Yes I am. This place is amazing. How about getting the champagne and pouring?"

"Yes, Ma'am. Anything your little heart desires. And I do mean anything." Ethan said as he took care of the champagne.

He handed a glass to Emily and said, "To you and your new life. Only the best for you."

They drank while gazing into each other's eyes.

"That was a sweet toast. Let's eat."

They spent the evening eating and talking about their day, the battle, The Creek and whatever else came to mind. The night began to come on and they moved out to the porch settling on the love seat.

"I love this time of the day when the sun is just at the horizon and the night begins to take over. My folks called it the gloaming. I can feel the magic of the mountain at this exact minute."

"I know what you mean. Me, too," Ethan said as he pulled Emily close to him and they watched as the last bit of twilight gave way to the night.

They sat there quietly for a spell then Ethan began to touch Emily. He traced her face with his hand then let his finger follow her neck to her shoulder then to her breast. He caressed her breast ever so softly through her thin shirt and felt her shiver in response. He continued tracing the lines of her body. Next he let his finger trail down her middle over her belly to her mound. There he began to draw circles across her mound adding pressure as he drew. His other hand began to trace her inner thigh from her knee to her mound. Then he went back to where her shorts ended and ran his fingers inside along her skin until he reached her most intimate spot.

Emily lay back, opening her legs and letting her arms rest at her sides. She closed her eyes as Ethan's touch began to make her hot and wet. She reached up and unbuttoned her shirt so her lacy demi bra showed her breasts to make them easier to touch.

Ethan caught his breath as he looked at her breasts. He bent over and began kissing them lightly at first then with more pressure before he freed them so he could begin sucking them, first one then the other.

Emily moaned out loud and reached for Ethan's cock. She liked to touch him as he sucked her breasts. She found him hard and bulging against the fabric of his shorts.

Ethan opened Emily's shorts and pushed them off. He touched her and began stroking her clit as he continued to suck her breasts. She was delirious with all the sensations that possessed her.

Ethan brought her to her first climax this way. As she calmed from it she tugged at Ethan's shorts. He stood and stripped naked in front of her. He pulled her to her feet and freed her of the rest of her clothes.

They were naked on the front porch in the dark of the night. The only light was a soft glow coming from the far side of the kitchen.

Emily moved to lean on the railing facing Ethan. He stood in front of her and she touched his hard pulsing cock while he watched. She first ran her finger ever so lightly along his shaft feeling the soft hot skin that covered his hard pulsing rod. She next let the tip of her finger touch the tip of his cock ever so softly causing Ethan to moan and grab the post for support.

Emily wrapped his cock in her hand and began to pump ever so lightly. Ethan was ready to lose it. He took her hand away and placed his fingers in her hot wet pussy. He found her opening and began to push in. Emily opened her legs for him as he pushed in further. He bent and licked her breasts as he began to thrust with his hand. He felt her getting ready to cum. He took his hand away and masturbated her to her second climax. She grabbed him to hold onto so she wouldn't fall while she climaxed. He carried her to the love seat lay her down and took her into his mouth licking her and sucking at her mound while she climaxed again.

Emily was jerking all over the place. These feelings were nothing she had experienced before, even with Ethan. She wanted him to stop but she wanted him to never stop.

As her climax finally exhausted itself she felt as if she had no hold on reality. She didn't know how long she lay there but when she opened her eyes Ethan was kneeling next to her. She stroked his face then reached for his cock which she found hot and huge.

He helped her to her feet and she pulled him over to the railing where she raised her leg and wrapped it around him so his cock was pushing into her. Ethan began to push into her and kept at it for a time. Then he turned her around and she bent over holding onto the railing as he started to rub against her pussy pushing into her again. He kept the pace even and each thrust was a little harder. She could feel another climax beginning and rocked back against him. He reached for her clit and rubbed it hard and fast. She climaxed, pushing hard against him and he thrust even harder to make her climax longer.

He let go as she screamed out his name. They both reached the pinnacle of that magical place at the same time then began the slow motion fall into oblivion. They collapsed onto the floor and fell asleep tangled in each other's arms. When they woke up they dressed and grabbed the champagne. Ethan fell asleep in one of the chairs and Emily sipped her champagne and looked out over the meadow.

The porch sex had been amazing. They eventually found their way up to the master bedroom and fell asleep in each other's arms

Tuesday afternoon found Emily and the guys at the store creating her housewarming party.

"We'll bring all the main food items. Everyone else will bring their own donation. We'll have the grills set up Saturday morning before anyone gets there. Ethan has that all taken care of. Now, for the quilting. We've spoken to the ladies and they like your main room. They'll bring the quilt frame and everyone else will bring their own chairs and quilting supplies. The ladies have been making their quilt squares for you since the minute you arrived. Surprise!" Ted said.

"Really? Oh, my God, how cool is this? I can't wait to be a part of this. I can work on it, can't I?"

"No worries, Emily. The ladies want you to know you are most welcome to help out. They can't wait to show you how to make their special stitches," Michael reassured her.

"Oh great!!! I suspect I'm responsible for my cookies. Thought so. I guess I'll need extra ingredients to take home with me today so I can bake them on Friday. Anything else we need?"

"Let's see. We have the food covered. The quilt is all set. The shine will be left on your back doorstep sometime late this week. Just store it in the kitchen out of the sun. The guys will be bringing their tools to help with the planting and barn stuff. Jonah will be here to look over the stables and make a list of the stuff you will need. He will be able to get some of it from other horse farms and the rest you will need to buy new. The entertainment is a surprise! Don't even think you can read my mind, Ms. Emily."

"Don't worry. I won't even try. I'll only use that in real emergencies to keep you safe."

"Whew! Only kidding. I think we've got it all covered, right Michael?"

"I do believe we do."

"Emily, Michael and I just want you to know our thoughts are with you this week as you say good-by to Agent Marks. The Creek has set up a fund for his family to use as they see fit. Matthews is taking care of giving them the information. It's the least we could do for all he did for one of our own."

Emily began to cry as she tried to say thank you. She gave up and just hugged them both for the longest time. When they finally sat back down they all had tears on their cheeks.

"Thank everyone for me please and let them know about the party. It's the least I can do for you all."

"Got it," Michael replied.

"Now, before we lose it altogether, I need those cookie supplies and a sandwich to go. How about barbecued chicken with the works, except tomatoes, please?"

Ted jumped up heading to the sandwich board. "You got it, Miss Emily."

Emily spent the rest of the day sorting through some of the things that Matthews had had delivered from her New Hampshire storage unit. Just as she was ready to open another box, her furniture delivery vans showed up - five of them.

It took the delivery guys about two hours to put everything in the house just where Emily wanted it. They mentioned how beautiful her place was and how lucky she was to have Sutherland Builders create her home for her. She thanked them with cold sodas and cookies.

Wednesday found Emily continuing to unpack. Matthews was still writing reports and finalizing plans for Agent Marks' funeral service the next day. Ethan was wrapping up a few bits and pieces on Emily's build.

Agent Marks' services were set for Thursday. Emily, Ethan and Matthews were taken to D.C. by special helicopter. It landed at the special chopper pad just south of The Creek Thursday morning before sunrise. Emily had requested she be able to meet with Agent Marks' parents before the service. She wanted to thank them for their son's service in giving his life for her. The meeting was emotional and heartfelt. His parents were glad they had met Emily. It made their son's passing a bit easier to understand they said.

The service was beautiful and solemn but with a bit of laughter as well. The gathering afterwards was well attended. Emily met with some of the agents that had taken care of her throughout her escape. They got caught up in Emily's new life and seemed genuinely happy for her. The day finally ended around sunset.

They returned to The Creek late that night and went their separate ways. It was a sad day for all.

Friday found The Creek getting ready for Emily's party. True to their word, Emily found six earthenware jugs of shine on her back porch when she got home Thursday night. She and Ethan shared a good laugh before they retired thanks to Bubba and Earl.

Mo and Lainie came by with flats of herbs for Emily's various herb gardens. These needed to be planted in the late summer or early fall to be ready for the next year. They also left a small container on her back porch as well. When she finally opened it, she was pleased and surprised to find a note telling her it was their best blend ever. It sure smelled potent as any pot she had ever been around.

They also left about six flats of various colored mums for her gardens around her porch.

The Kirklands showed up in the late afternoon with trailers full of trees, shrubs, plants and all kinds of mulch and soil. Emily directed them to unload near the barn. They unhitched the trailers with a smile and said they'd be back with more.

And they did come back. All total, they left six trailers full of stuff. This was gonna be an amazing party.

When Ethan got home that night he took a look around the place and just stood there shaking his head. Emily was laughing her ass off.

"Holy landscaping, Batman. This is gonna be a day to remember," Emily finally said.

"Yes it is. And it's about time we had something like this. Especially for you. You've been through so much I just don't know how you can find laughter after all the horrible things you've been through. You amaze me."

"I don't know either really. I just know I'm supposed to be here after all that chaos and you're one of the big reasons I can smile. Thanks for accepting me just as I am and loving me. You do make me smile."

"You are very welcome but I think you've got that backwards. It's you I want to thank for giving me the chance to love again. So, thank you for allowing me into your life."

"You are very welcome."

"As are you," Ethan said as he gently kissed her under the rising moon.

"Let's call it a night and get an early start tomorrow. I'm sure a lot of folks will be here early to start the planting. I'm guessing they will be arriving by seven or eight."

"My thoughts exactly. That's why the big coffee pot Ted brought over is all ready to go. The thing is on a timer set for six-thirty. I don't even have to get up to start the coffee."

"Yup. We can stay in bed a little while longer," Ethan said as they headed up to the master bedroom.

"You have something in mind Mr. Builder Guy?" Emily asked as she slowly peeled off her clothes.

"Something we're gonna have to work on all night long," Ethan said as he pulled her into the bed.

"I like the way you think," Emily sighed as Ethan began to trail his hand across her breast.

The rest of the night was magical for them both.

Saturday morning found the coffee ready, Emily setting fresh muffins in baskets across the butcher block counter and Ethan sampling the baked goods.

"These are yummy especially the blueberry chocolate chip ones. Make more of these often, will ya?"

"For a price."

Ethan laughed as he kissed Emily with blueberry on his mouth.

"They are good," Emily said as she kissed him back.

Ted and Michael found them kissing as they came in through the kitchen door.

"Now isn't that a sweet way to get your day going," Michael said as he set baskets full of food on the marble top counters next to the fridge.

"Sure is Michael. The only way," Ethan said as he bit into his muffin. "Ya gotta try these muffins. Blueberry chocolate chip. Hmmm."

Ted came around the counter and grabbed one. "Don't mind if I do."

"Me, too," Michael chimed in as they both took a bite.

"God, Emily, is there anything you bake that isn't sinful?" Ted asked as he got himself a cup of coffee.

"I highly doubt it, Ted," Ethan answered.

"Thanks boys. Love you, too. Enjoy this little bit of heaven 'cause I hear the sound of trucks coming across the bridge. We are about to be invaded," Emily laughed as she walked through the living room and out onto the front porch.

Sure enough there was a line of trucks coming up the drive and parking around the barn and stables. It wasn't long before the place was full of trucks and cars and everyone who lived in The Creek. They had all come to help celebrate Emily's new home.

The ladies set up in the kitchen and dining areas. The quilt frame was being assembled in the main living area by a few of the men and chairs were being placed around the frame. A few minutes later the bottom layer of the quilt was placed on the frame then the filling, the quilt batting, then the top was laid in place.

Emily stood there in awe. It truly was an amazing thing to behold. There were so many squares she didn't think she'd have enough time to look at them all. But she tried anyway. She saw the one from Mo and Lainie and laughed right out loud. It was a marijuana plant and was created in great detail as a fully mature plant with buds and all. The detail was amazing and their initials were sewn to look like leaves.

Emily found one for Bubba and Earl. It was an earthen crock - fitting for the shine boys. She saw so many squares that meant something to her since she moved to the Creek, it made soft tears roll down her cheeks.

Cora placed an arm around her shoulders. "Miss Emily, these folks love you. It shows in their fine needle work. We'll talk about this quilt a bit later on as we begin to sew it together. You dry those tears and let's help get some of this food out under the tent. They already set up the big coffee urns and juice kettles out there. You are a smart girl to have electricity set up all around the porch and yard. Makes it real nice for this kinda stuff."

"Thanks Miss Cora. This is truly a work of art. I am honored to be a part of it."

They joined the rest of the community outside around the food tent while everyone was saying their good mornings and sharing a bite to eat.

The Kirkland crew got the day started when they suggested anyone wanting to help with the planting join them over at the trailers, and the work began in earnest.

Ethan had a crew working on the barn and stables. They were finishing the details in the tack room and each stall. Jonah was making a list of all the supplies that Emily would need.

Matthews was working with the landscaping group digging holes and planting shrubs around the house.

As Emily looked around her farm she felt a great deal of love for these people. This was what a community did for each other. One minute they were in your way and the next they were right there helping you out, no questions asked.

It was just past noon when one of the women rang the farm triangle calling everyone in for the mid-day meal. Sawhorse tables had been set up between the barn and house and there was enough food to feed an army.

As everyone settled down to eat, Ted and Michael asked for a moment.

"Folks, this here barn raisin' and planting day is Emily's first. The farm is lookin' real good. Lots of work's getting done. This feast is greatly appreciated, ladies and gentlemen. I hear there's some quilting to take place soon. Now, Emily, that's somethin' you've been lookin' forward to. Enjoy. This here is what neighbors do for each other. Welcome home, Emily. Welcome home," Michael said as he raised his drink to salute Emily.

Everyone did likewise and the feasting began.

As the meal came to an end, Pam hooked arms with Emily and said, "Time to start the quilting. Let's go."

They walked into the main room and Emily smiled. "This is gonna be great. Where do I sit?"

Pam motioned to a seat next to Sarah saying, "Sarah here is a right fine seamstress and will show you some of the patterns we use. Ladies, let's get started."

The afternoon found the quilt coming together and the ladies telling stories of past quiltings.

"I'll tell ya the story of my own quilting party," Clara began. Clara's family had lived in The Creek for as long a time as most others.

"Now, I'm no spring chicken, but I'm not so old as I need help to breathe either."

This brought smiles and laughter all around.

"It was about a month before my sixteenth birthday. That's when we young girls had our quilting parties, when we turned sixteen. It has been a rite of passage for centuries handed down from one generation to the next. The quilt squares are worked on for a long time before the quilting day comes on. The squares are from family and close friends in the community. They show some special thing that has been a part of the girl's life growing up. Some have a memory from the person making the square that the girl knows about. Some squares show a place or season that has special meaning for the girl. The quilting party takes place in the girl's family home and all the women kin and friends are invited for the day. When the quilt is finished, it is presented to the girl as a symbol of her entering womanhood. A fine party follows with food, song and dancing long into the night. It's a community gift for the girl.

Now my quilting party took place in the late fall as my birthday is just before Halloween. My mother and grandmother and aunts had been working hard on their squares as had all of The Creek. It was set for a Saturday and everyone had been cooking and sewing to get ready. The men were gonna have a gathering of their own over at the store."

This brought a round of hooting and laughter from the ladies.

"They were gonna eat, drink some shine, and play some pool is what they were gonna be doin'." Pam offered.

"Yes indeed," Clara agreed. "So, with the men folk gone, the women began to arrive and the quilting got under way. As the day grew on into the late afternoon the sky sort of darkened early and as one of the women looked up she was surprised to see snowflakes falling quietly against the windows. We all ran to the windows to have a look and, sure enough, it was snowing. The first snowfall of the season right on my quilting party.

"We didn't think too much about it as it had been known to snow in late October many times through the years. It usually didn't snow more than a couple of inches, though. So, we all got back to the quilting and then set about getting the meal ready as the men were due to arrive any time.

"They came in and we had a great time eating and telling more stories. Everyone looked at the quilt and commented on the different squares. The music started up and the singing and dancing kept right on until someone took a look outside. Seems this was gonna be a bit more than a couple of inches of snow. There was about four inches on the ground already and it didn't look like it was gonna stop any time soon.

"Folks decided to end the evening and get on their way so they could make it home before any more snow fell.

"Well, those that did set out were back a short time later. Seems there was about a foot of snow on the roads just south of our farm and no one could get anywhere. My quilting party turned into an overnight party with folks sleeping all over the farm house. One good thing was someone was awake throughout the night and kept the fires going in the cook stove and the fireplaces. For the first time that I could remember, I wasn't cold throughout the night. And there were plenty of quilts to go around as we had a lot for our family and folks had brought their favorites to show to everyone.

"The next day the snow finally stopped and most folks were able to get going by noon time. There was no church that day so my Mother suggested we sing a few hymns and have a prayer time right there in the living room. Most of the men folk didn't cotton to the idea but one look from their wives made them change their minds. It was a special quilting party for me all the way around."

"Sure was. I remember it well," Cora said.

"My mother tells the story often," Sarah added. "That year the snow started on that quilting party and never stopped until May of the next year. We had record snowfall that winter, all on account of Clara."

The ladies laughed and told a few short stories of their own.

"Pam, tell us about your quilting party. It wasn't that long ago by some of us. Only maybe twenty or so years ago."

"OK Miss Cora. Now my sixteenth birthday is in the summer. Late June. And that summer it was already hot and beautiful. The women in my family had planned on the last Saturday in June for my party and the invitations were sent out. Everyone planned on comin'.

"A tent was set up outside, it bein' too hot inside. A good breeze was blowin' and that made the day better. We set up around eight and everyone showed up shortly after that. The kids were playing around the farm and some of them took off to the pond with a few of the older boys. The men were gathered in the barn and the passin' of the jug started around noon.

"We all gathered for lunch and then got back to the quilting. It was getting hotter and that breeze felt like a piece of heaven. It was nigh on to mid-afternoon when I noticed the first bee flyin' around the quilt. We all left it alone knowing it would leave soon. It didn't. More bees began to buzz around and then I swear the whole hive descended on our quilt. We all ran away as fast as we could hollering and screamin'. A few women got stung so they headed down to the pond for some mud and herbs to put on the stings.

"The men came a runnin' when they heard us and couldn't believe their eyes. The quilt was completely covered with bees. Never saw anything like it before. There weren't any hives on the tent frame and the chairs. We couldn't figure out why all the bees were on the quilt.

"Well, that ended the quilting. We had to leave everything just like it was. The men were gonna keep an eye on the quilt as night came on 'cause the bees should have flown back to their hive. They didn't. They settled in for the night.

"So, before sunrise the next morning, a couple of the men set up an ice bath right next to the quilt. They carefully took the quilt off the frame before the bees woke up and placed it in the ice bath. A few bees flew around but most of them were killed. That's when one of the men saw it. It seemed the queen had set up house on the underside of the quilt and all her drones had followed her as they are supposed to do. They thought the quilt was a new home. The quilt was set up on the clothes line to dry and the quilting was finished the next Saturday - without the bees."

Once again chatter and laughter were heard all around.

Sarah had been teaching Emily how to make some of the stitches and Emily was hard at work sewing along.

It was close to supper time when Ethan and Matthew came in.

"Hey Emily, ladies. This is lookin' real good," Ethan said as he walked around the frame.

"This is incredible. I've heard about these quilting parties but to see one in progress is truly a gift," Matthews said as he watched the progress.

"Emily, the folks are beginning to set up for supper so I thought you should know," Ethan said.

"Great. Ladies are we ready to stop?" Emily asked.

"Sure.

"For now"

"Time to get supper goin'."

"OK ladies, let's leave this just as it is. No reason to take it apart. We can finish it tomorrow it that's OK with you, Emily," Pam offered.

"Yes. It's just fine. Let's get on with the food. I'm starvin'," Emily said with a laugh.

Everyone headed outside to gather for the evening meal.

What Emily saw was that a stage of sorts had been set up near the front of the house. Seems there was gonna be some musical entertaining going on.

"Ethan, what do you know about this?" Emily asked with a smile on her face.

Before Ethan could say a word, Tate walked over, shook hands with Ethan and gave Emily a big hug.

"Hey Emily, my friends and I thought we'd do a little singin' here to-night. OK with you?"

Emily just smiled and shook her head yes. "Who am I to say no to y'all?"

With that, the celebration kicked into high gear. The grills were being mastered by some of the men while everyone else got the tables all set up with food and drink. The impromptu stage was ready for the band and they took a break to eat with everyone else.

Emily took a minute to walk around the place after dinner. It looked amazing. The gardens were all set for the winter. The mums, in a riot of colors, had been planted all around the porch along with sage and a few other things. The winter veggie garden was in place in the southwest corner of the meadow along with a variety of trees and bushes. The stone wall was wrapped around most of the meadow looking just like she had dreamed it would. There were a few openings along the wall with one that led toward the Sacred Rock Meadow.

Just as she came back to the front of the house Ethan joined her.

"Well, what do ya think?"

"I have no words to describe what I'm feeling. None."

Ethan put his arm around her shoulders and they stood there looking out over everything for a few minutes.

"The guys are ready to get the music started. Let's go join the gang," Ethan suggested.

Emily fell in step with Ethan as they joined everyone in front of the little stage.

The music that night started with an old folk song called "Aunt Dinah's Quilting Party." Everyone sang along and the harmonies were beautiful. The music went on into the deep dark of the night. Ethan even got up with Tate and the gang to sing a few of the old songs.

It was nigh on to midnight when things finally wound down. Good-byes were offered with promises of returning the next day to finish the quilt but not until noon time anyway. Hugs and handshakes were exchanged and Ethan and Emily watched as the last truck headed over the covered bridge. The top of the bridge had been put in place earlier that week and it looked perfect.

"This has been such a great day. How do I thank everyone?" Emily asked through a yawn as they headed up the stairs.

"You don't have to. This is what friends and family do for each other. It just is. You offered your farm for the gathering. Enough said."

As they looked out the bedroom windows they saw millions of sparkling lights dancing across the meadow. It seems the Ancients approved of the day as well.

Emily and Ethan fell sound asleep as the music of the mountain softly floated through the windows.

Excerpt:

Return
to
Crab Apple Creek

CHAPTER 1

Finn was headed home. It had been a long time. A little over a year ago Finn had lived through the greatest sorrow of his life. He had left The Creek to try to get some breathing space. He was so confused, sad and angry. He couldn't stay in The Creek with that horrible day replaying in his head 24/7. He decided to leave hoping he would get some peace the farther away from The Creek he traveled.

That day started to replay in his head once again as he saw the first signs for North Carolina on the highway.

He and his twin brother Jason, known as Jay to all, had just graduated from grad school together. They had returned home to The Creek at the beginning of the summer and planned on working locally before looking for jobs in their fields of specialty.

They had been scooped up by Ethan Sutherland, the owner of The Soaring Mountain builders, before anyone else could get to them. The boys had worked for Ethan all through high school, college and grad school and were excellent carpenters. Ethan was thrilled to have them back one more time before they went out into the big wide world on their own.

It was late August just about a week before the Labor Day holiday and the crew was finishing up. Five o'clock found everything settled and the crew heading for their trucks and a well earned weekend. The brothers were heading out towards Tennessee to a cookout with friends from their childhood days that now lived just over the state line.

The evening was a great success and the brothers finally set out for home. It was around eleven o'clock when it happened. Just as they got into North Carolina on US 321, a semi veered into their lane and hit the boys head-on. Their truck went airborne and set down on its side in the middle of the road. The semi jack-knifed and rolled off the road down a small ravine.

A passerby called for help. Finn came to as he was being pulled from the truck. He was badly injured and kept fading in and out of consciousness. As he was being loaded into the rescue rig he came to and saw his brother Jay standing next to him, smiling. Finn smiled back as he faded out again.

The next time Finn came to was after his emergency surgery to remove his spleen and set his leg. His right wrist was broken as well. He didn't know where he was but he was glad to see his brother standing next to him. He heard a lot of voices as he fell into a fitfull sleep. Hours later he finally woke up and began to understand where he was.

He saw his parents next to his bed and tried to smile. He groaned instead and raised his hand to let them know he was OK.

"Finn, its Mom and Dad. We're right here with you. You're in the ICU at the medical center in Boone. You're going to be OK."

"Hey, son, it's Dad. Open your eyes again."

Finn opened his eyes and looked at his Dad and Mom. Jay was standing right behind them.

"Hey," Finn tried to speak but his voice was all messed up. He tried again. "Hey, I'm awake. Really. What the fuck happened?"

Finn's Dad cleared his throat and answered him. "You boys were hit by a semi-truck just inside the state line. Good thing there were a few other trucks around. They called for help right away. You got some broken bones and your spleen's gone. Sure gonna be a mess a hurt for awhile. We'll be here with you all the time."

Finn looked from his Mom to his Dad and saw that they were crying.

"Hey, why all the tears. We're gonna be OK. Looks like Jay didn't get hurt all that bad. He's lookin' real good standin' there."

Finn's mom nearly passed out. His dad set her down in the chair next to the bed. She was sobbing hysterically.

"Mom, why are you crying so much? We're OK. Really. I'll be up and around in a week or two. You just watch me."

Finn started to look around the room and realized there were some medical people and someone else standing there. They all looked real sad.

"Hey, what's goin' on anyways? Why are y'all looking like someone died?"

There was a deep silence all around.

Finn's dad took ahold of Finn's hand as he tried to speak. "Son, we have some bad news. I gotta tell ya," Finn's dad had to stop as he was crying real hard.

Finally he took a deep breath and tried again.

"Finn, Jay died in the accident. He died instantly. He's not in this room. You don't see him like you think you do."

"The hell I don't. He's standing right there between you and Mom. He's patting Mom's shoulder and holding her real close. He's gotta hold of your arm, too. I know what I'm seein'. Don't try to tell me he's dead. He's standing right here," Finn yelled and pointed to his brother. "He's right here. It must be someone else who died. He's right here!"

Finn was yelling real loud and getting pissed off. "Why y'all standing around like this? I'm not crazy. I know what I'm seein' and it's Jay."

One of the nurses walked over to Finn's bedside and took ahold of the IV line. She was about to put something in his IV.

"Hey, don't give me those knockout drugs. I don't want them. I'm as sane as the next guy. That's Jay right there. Do not give me more drugs," Finn yelled.

"OK son, calm down. Why don't y'all leave so my wife and I can talk with our son?"

Finn's dad shooed them all out of the room. When everyone had left he looked at Finn.

"OK son, tell me what you see. I wanna hear about this."

"Dad, I swear it's Jay. He's got the same clothes on we wore to the cookout. He's standing right here next to me. Hey, bro, why haven't you said anything yet? You never shut-up," Finn teased him.

There was no response. Finn began to become scared.

"Dude! Say something. This is kinda scary."

Silence.

"Dad? Mom? Why isn't Jay talking? What's going on here?" You can see him, right?"

Finn's mom replied through her tears, "No, Finn, We can't see him. He died instantly when y'all were hit by the semi. He didn't suffer. That's what they tell us. I wish I could see him one more time. Just one more time. This is a nightmare. God help us."

"Son, I wish I could see him just one more time, too. I'm lost here."

"Dad? Mom? You really can't see him? He's as plain as day. He has his arms around both of you holding you tight. Jay. God, it can't be true. Jay? Are you really dead?"

Jay's spirit nodded yes with a sad look on his face. "Tell Mom and Dad I love them to the moon and back just like they used to say to us when we were little kids. You can see and always will. You have the Gift just like Grandma Jenny did. Don't be scared big bro. It's gonna be OK. So much has happened in just a few minutes. Take all the time you need to figure this out. Just don't take too long. You gotta lot of work to do with those of us on the Other Side. Finn, you've been the best brother anyone could ever wish for. Don't ever forget how much I love you. Take care of Mom and Dad."

"Jay. Really? You're a ghost? It must be the drugs. If you can make me see you, show yourself to Mom and Dad. They really need to see you're OK ya know. Not hurting and all. Can ya do that? What am I saying? This is all so surreal."

Finn's mom and dad looked at each other and became aware of a shape taking form between them. They stepped back and suddenly saw their son Jay standing right in front of them. He was smiling at them.

"Mom, Dad. This is a very special moment. I'm OK. This is my Spirit here. Finn asked for me to show myself to you one more time. I'm really OK here in what you call heaven. It's beautiful. A pure white light shines all around. I will love you always and always be with you until it's time for you to come home."

They looked at him and hugged him one more time. Jay smiled at Finn, passed his hand over him and then he was gone. Finn's mom and dad grabbed ahold of his hand and they all just stared at each other for the longest time. The quiet was peaceful and sad.

"I don't know what just happened but I liked it," his dad said.

"Now Hank, don't you fret about this. I've always known about the Other Side from Grandma Jennie. Just never saw anything like this before. I need some time to think about this."

"I hear ya' Diane. Just hard to take in all at once."

"I don't know what Jay did when he passed his hand over me, but I'm not in any pain right now. I am really tired. I think I'm gonna take a long nap if that's OK with you two? How about you go home and get some rest. Come back, hey, what time is it anyways?"

"It's about noon, the next day for you. OK Diane? Let's get some rest and come back this evening."

"OK you two. I know Finn's gonna be OK and I guess we better start the whole process for Jay. He never wanted a funeral, he wanted to be cremated. So, we'll talk with the sheriff and see what we need to do next."

"OK Mom, Dad. Love you to the moon and back." Finn said as his eyes closed and he fell asleep.

His parents talked with his nurse before they left reassuring her that Finn had accepted the death of his twin brother and he was gonna be OK. He didn't need the chaplin they had standing by.

Finn spent about a week in the hospital recovering from all his injuries. His family and friends spent a great deal of time with him. As his bruises began to change color they teased him about how beautiful he looked. Lots of love and kindness was all around him and his parents.

About the Author

Born and raised in the Mid-West, Karmle L. Conrad moved to New England in 1985 and built her home on Cape Cod in 1988. She completed her Doctorate in Public Health from Capella University in July 2022. Karmle has been Gifted as a Psychic Medium from birth.

The ***Crab Apple Creek*** set of ***The Crab Apple Creek Anthology*** is now complete with ***Return to Crab Apple Creek*** and ***The Other Crab Apple Creek.*** Karmle has created a series for middle-aged kids called ***The TreeHouse Gang Mysteries.*** The first 3 books are available on her website: **www.thecapecodpsychic.com.**